Spooks, Spies, and Private Eyes

Spooks, Spies,
and Private Eyes

Black Mystery, Crime,
and Suspense Fiction

Edited by Paula L. Woods

DOUBLEDAY

New York London Toronto Sydney Auckland

PUBLISHED BY DOUBLEDAY
a division of Bantam Doubleday Dell Publishing Group, Inc.
1540 Broadway, New York, New York 10036

DOUBLEDAY and the portrayal of an anchor with a dolphin are
trademarks of Doubleday, a division of Bantam Doubleday Dell
Publishing Group, Inc.

Library of Congress Cataloging-in-Publication Data

Spooks, spies, and private eyes : Black mystery, crime, and suspense fiction/edited by
Paula L. Woods.—1st ed.
    p.   cm.
Includes bibliographical references.
1. Detective and mystery stories, American—Afro-American authors. 2. Detective and
mystery stories, English—Black authors. 3. Afro-Americans—Fiction. 4. Blacks—
Fiction. I. Woods, Paula L.
PS648.D4S64   1995
813′.087208896073—dc20   95-17052
CIP

PERMISSIONS TO BE FOUND STARTING ON PAGE 338.
ISBN 0-385-47827-5
Copyright © 1995 by Paula L. Woods
All Rights Reserved
Printed in the United States of America
November 1995
First Edition

10 9 8 7 6 5 4 3 2 1

The workings of the human heart are the profoundest mystery of the universe. One moment they make us despair of our kind, and in the next, we see in them the reflection of the divine image.

—Charles W. Chesnutt, *The Marrow of Tradition,* 1901

To my father, Ike Woods,
who's probably telling a big one
in Heaven right now

Acknowledgments

NO MATTER whose name appears as editor of an anthology, there are many people whose contributions, ideas, suggestions, and helpful criticism make them valued allies and coconspirators. Thanks go to the following for "aiding and abetting": Frankie Y. Bailey, author of *Out of the Woodpile: Black Characters in Crime and Detective Fiction* (Greenwood Press, 1991), for the depth of her scholarship and her listening ear; John McCluskey, Jr., Professor of Afro-American Studies at Indiana University, for his insightful analysis and editorial thoroughness in *City of Refuge: The Collected Stories of Rudolph Fisher* (University of Missouri Press, 1987) and his advice in locating mystery stories predating the Harlem Renaissance; Charles L. Blockson, curator of the eponymous Afro-American Collection at Temple University, for likewise suggesting other valuable sources for early twentieth-century mystery fiction; Connie Scarborough of *Ellery Queen's Mystery Magazine* for her assistance with the Hughes Allison story; Gary Phillips, fellow mystery writer and enthusiast, for his support and introduction to Njami Simon; Raquel V. Cogell and Michael Rudette of Schomburg Center for Research in Black Culture and Avril Madison of Moorland-Spingarn Research Center, for their unflagging ability to identify hard-to-locate and out-of-print material essential to the search.

To all of the authors who contributed stories despite impossibly busy schedules, simultaneously working on other novels, and personal hardships—your contributions are not only deeply appreciated but provide testimony to the vitality of the African American contribution to the mystery genre.

To Faith Childs, who encouraged the detective mission I chose to undertake, my eternal gratitude. To the Doubleday team (Judy Kern, Brandon Saltz, Steve Rubin, Martha Levin, and many more), thanks for giving me the chance to bring to light another aspect of the African American literary contribution that has been ignored for too long. And, last but in no way least, thanks to my permanent "in-house" counsel, Felix Liddell, who despite an avowed disinterest in mysteries, has offered useful criticism and unbridled, passionate support.

Contents

Introduction

WHILE I AM a voracious reader of African American literature, I also harbor a secret obsession that not all of my friends or colleagues understand. My obsession is usually played out on long plane trips or vacations, where a random search of my luggage would probably reveal an Agatha Christie, Sarah Paretsky, or P. D. James novel as often as one by Toni Morrison, Alice Walker, or Ernest Gaines. These are admittedly flings, guilty pleasures that seemed for years to rarely intersect with my first love, African American fiction.

All that changed however, in 1991, while I was doing research for my first book, *I, Too, Sing America: The African American Book of Days*. I came across a citation for the 1934 premiere of a mystery play by Rudolph Fisher. The source document indicated the play was adapted from Fisher's novel *The Conjure-Man Dies* and claimed it was the first mystery novel written by an African American. A lightbulb went off in my head. *Rudolph Fisher?* How had I missed him? My 1960s and 1970s classes in black literature had included Fisher's non-mystery short stories, but Chester Himes was always considered the first African American mystery novelist, an error reinforced in many minds by the successful screen adaptation of two Himes novels during the Blaxploitative '70s. Discovering Fisher started me on a quest to locate a copy of *The Conjure-Man Dies,* one that ended at UCLA, where I was introduced to his pioneering sleuths, Dr. John Archer and detective Perry Dart.

Now I was curious. Fisher could not have sprung up without a single colleague or predecessor in the mystery genre. And it couldn't be true that there were no black mystery writers between Fisher, Himes, and Walter Mosley, then just gaining recognition for his second novel, *A Red Death*. Surely my love and my obsession had to have crossed paths more frequently than this!

Indeed they had, and much of the result of my search for those meeting points is contained in the pages of this book. Not only did I find *The Conjure-Man Dies,* and a later mystery short story by Fisher, but I even found mysteries, crime stories, and political thrillers written by George S. Schuyler that were serialized in the *Pittsburgh Courier* and short stories by Alice Dunbar-Nelson, both contemporaries of Fisher during the Harlem Renaissance. Furthermore, through the scholarship contained in Frankie Bailey's landmark *Out of the Woodpile: Black Characters in Crime and Detective Fiction* (Greenwood Press, 1991), I learned that Rudolph Fisher was preceded by W. Adolphe Roberts, a Jamaican-born author of several mysteries, including the 1926 novel *The Haunting Hand,* who went unrecognized for almost three quarters of a century, perhaps because his characters were not black. My own research uncovered even earlier black mystery writers, Pauline E. Hopkins in 1900 and J. E. Bruce in 1907. All of these stories had languished in African American magazines, were seldom reprinted, and were certainly not considered within the context of other mystery fiction. It was this contextual framework that I was seeking, one that firmly fixed these and other black writers I identified in the two worlds they rightfully inhabited—the realms of mystery fiction *and* African American literature.

The extent of the black presence in mystery fiction has yet to be "discovered" by many mystery enthusiasts, regardless of race, or by many mystery scholars. To see Pauline Hopkins's use of the locked-room mystery device pioneered by Edgar Allan Poe in "The Murders in the Rue Morgue" raises tantalizing questions about that mystery master's influence on early black experimenters in the genre. Understanding that Roberts, Fisher, Schuyler, and Dunbar-Nelson wrote mysteries during a period that coincided with the Golden Age of detective fiction places their characters' patterns of speech and habits, and even the authors' plots, in another context, one that gives a more complete picture of the era's cast of players than heretofore imagined. Reading the early fiction of Chester Himes, written while he was incarcerated for armed robbery in the 1930s, adds an additional dimension to the hard-boiled detective fiction written by Dashiell Hammett, Raymond Chandler, and others during the period. Knowing that while readers were devouring the latest Robert Ludlum thriller, John A. Williams and Sam Greenlee were also writing of CIA "spooks" and government conspiracies with blacks as central characters gives additional insight into the concerns of all writers of this mystery subgenre. Knowing that Sarah Paretsky's V. I. Warshawski has contemporaries in Eleanor Taylor Bland's suburban Chicago detective Marti MacAlister and

Valerie Wilson Wesley's Newark detective Tamara Hayle lets readers know that African Americans are not just the victims or perpetrators of crimes, but are also those who try to correct the balance that murder upsets.[1] But as important as it may be for readers to understand that black writers have been active, albeit largely unheralded, participants in the major eras of mystery fiction and its subgenres, it is equally, if not more important to place these writers and their fiction within the context of African American literature and to trace their origins within, and influences on, black literary and cultural trends.

Building upon the substantial literary legacy of Frederick Douglass, Harriet E. Wilson, William Wells Brown, Frances E. W. Harper, Paul Laurence Dunbar, and other nineteenth and early twentieth century writers,[2] the first widely recognized cultural movement involving African American novelists was the Harlem Renaissance. Some of the most influential American writers, artists, and intellectuals, including W. E. B. Du Bois, Aaron Douglas, Alain Locke, Langston Hughes, Countee Cullen, James Weldon Johnson, and Zora Neale Hurston, rose to prominence in this decade and a half. Rudolph Fisher, a handsome young physician, was one of the more popular figures of the period, known for his essays, award-winning short stories, and a nongenre novel. However, an equally important contribution was his 1932 novel *The Conjure-Man Dies: A Mystery Tale of Dark Harlem,* the first mystery novel to feature African American characters. While Bailey has shown that Fisher was not the first black to write a mystery novel, he was the first to set his story in the black community and to address issues important to American Negroes, including their relationship to their African ancestry, color prejudice, and superstition. George S. Schuyler, a journalist and author most noted for his satirical novel *Black No More,* also addressed some of the same issues as Fisher in his serialized stories. Schuyler is also distinguished for his inclusion of plot elements dealing with African politics, intrigue, and the struggle for black equality in the U.S. and Africa in the serialized stories "The Black Internationale" and "Black Empire," making him arguably the first black author of an international political thriller. Conversely, Alice Dunbar-Nelson,

[1] See the Appendix for a chronology of mystery fiction including some of the more significant black writers.

[2] Her experiments with elements of the mystery genre in the 1900 short stories "The Mystery Within Us" and "Talma Gordon" and her 1901 novel *Hagar's Daughter* distinguish magazine editor, novelist, and short story writer Pauline E. Hopkins as the earliest African American writer of mystery fiction. Because she predates the Harlem Renaissance (1917–35), Hopkins can rightfully be considered "the foremother of African American mystery fiction."

whose short story "Summer Session" was written around the same time as Fisher's novel, did not address such concerns; her work, like Roberts's, did not include black characters.

For some historians, the end of the Harlem Renaissance is marked by the 1935 riots in New York City. For African American writers from the mid-thirties through the 1950s, the years of riots, lynchings, Jim Crow laws, the Depression, the shabby treatment of African American soldiers during and after World War II, all contributed to a worldview that resulted in the emergence of literary realism. Chester Himes was perhaps the earliest writer so influenced; in fact, his incarceration for armed robbery occurred a few years before the end of the Harlem Renaissance. And while he did not develop the hard-boiled, crime-fighting detectives of his "Harlem domestic series" for another twenty years, the hard-bitten worldview in such early Himes stories as "His Last Day" not only links him to Hammett and Chandler but gives a hint of what was in store for Coffin Ed and Grave Digger Jones on Harlem's mean streets during the 1950s and 1960s. Hughes Allison's groundbreaking 1948 police procedural "Corollary," the first mystery story by an African American to be published in *Ellery Queen's Mystery Magazine,* also reflects a harsher reality and highlights the role of the detective, Joe Hill, as an intermediary between black and white cultures.

While later black mystery writers owe much to pioneers like Himes and Allison, an equal debt is owed to nongenre writers Richard Wright and Ann Petry, whose powerful depiction of the impact of racism and hard times on African Americans in their respective stories "The Man Who Killed a Shadow" and "On Saturday the Siren Sounds at Noon" foreshadowed themes they would revisit in their influential best-selling novels *Native Son* and *The Street.* All these writers, whether working in the mystery genre or firmly outside it, have had their influence on black writers' views on crime, its consequences, and detection.

The social upheaval that began with the Civil Rights era of the 1950s and continued through the 1970s gave birth to a second black cultural renaissance, popularly called the Black Arts Movement. The movement was reflected in the writings of Imamu Amiri Baraka, James Baldwin, Ed Bullins, and Larry Neal, the mystery-influenced fiction of Ishmael Reed and others, and a subgenre not previously explored by black writers in novel form—the political thriller. Chester Himes, whose last novels in the Harlem domestic series, *Blind Man With a Pistol* (1969) and a novel he had worked on for over a dozen years, the posthumously published *Plan B* (English edition, 1993), reflected his increasingly pessimistic view of the inevitability of urban violence, whether in the form of a riot or organized revolutionary action,[3] existed at one end of the spectrum. On the other end are Himes's literary offspring, John A. Williams and Sam Greenlee, among others, whose work, excerpted and reprinted here, created a fictional landscape where organized black violence and the inevitable societal and governmental response were seen as the sad but logical result of long years of social and economic inequity.

By the 1980s and 1990s, African American mystery writers were participating in what is becoming known as a Third Renaissance of black thought and writing.[4] These writers, led by such critically acclaimed authors as Toni Morrison, Alice Walker, Charles Johnson, Gloria Naylor, John Edgar Wideman, Maya Angelou, and Ernest Gaines, among others, are presenting a more diverse range of black experience than ever before. Perhaps as an outgrowth of the hunger Americans of all colors have developed for black writing, African American mystery writers have also begun to claim the spotlight. Most notable among them is Walter Mosley, whose Easy Rawlins series of novels is a unique revisioning of the hard-boiled detective, recast not as the loner Sam Spade or Philip Marlowe, but as a black single father, a racial outsider but cultural insider, whose knowledge of and connections to the black community are essential in the police's ability to solve crimes. Mosley's new protagonist, Paris Minton, of the short story "Fearless" included here, also brings this ability to get on the inside to a *noir* story set in post–World War II Los Angeles.

In many ways Easy Rawlins, a man of the 1940s to 1960s, is the fictional godfather of two detectives whose beats are the streets of modern-day Los Angeles, Gar Anthony Haywood's Aaron Gunner and Gary Phillips's Ivan Monk. Their exploits, in novels as well as their new short stories "And Pray Nobody Sees You" and "Dead Man's Shadow," expand the territory of the black mystery, which also includes the unnamed stand-in for Chicago in veteran mystery writer

---

[3] As early as 1944 in *The Crisis,* Himes wrote of the futility of unorganized riots. By 1970, in an interview with Michel Fabre in *Le Monde,* the expatriate Himes said, "I realized that . . . was the point I had been trying to make in *[Blind Man with a Pistol].* . . . I do not believe that anything else is ever going to improve the situation of the black man in America except violence. . . . If the blacks were organized and if they could resist and fight injustice in an organized fashion in America, I think that might be enough."

[4] B. Preston Rohan, "Renaissance of Words," *Chicago Tribune,* February 3, 1995, and Sam Fulwood III, "Intellectuals in the Promised Land," *Los Angeles Times,* April 9, 1995.

Percy Spurlark Parker's "Death and the Point Spread" and a chilling projection of that same city in Hugh Holton's law-and-order nightmare "The Thirtieth Amendment." The Third Renaissance among black mystery writers also reaches into the diaspora, with France's Njami Simon giving us a skillful send-up of Himes's classic detectives Coffin Ed Johnson and Grave Digger Jones in "Coffin & Co." and Silver Dagger winner Mike Phillips explores the black immigrant experience in England in "Personal Woman."

The literary inheritors of Pauline Hopkins are equally compelling as they use the mystery form to explore issues of black identity, racism, crimes against women, infidelity, color consciousness, and sexuality. Leading the "Sistuhs in Crime" is Eleanor Taylor Bland's "The Man Who Cried I'm Not," its title a literary twist on the John A. Williams novel also excerpted in this collection. BarbaraNeely, whose Blanche White series of mystery novels debunks the stereotype of the stupid black maid while simultaneously addressing issues of race, color, and class consciousness, treats us in "Spilled Salt" to an unusual and powerful account of the impact of crime on not only the victim but also the family of the criminal. Her sense of outrage is shared by Charlotte Watson Sherman, whose protagonist in the nongenre short story "Killing Color" exacts a mysterious revenge on the perpetrators of violence on Southern blacks. This section of the book concludes with mysteries by two newer voices—Aya de León, whose "Tell Me Moore" sets up a funny, suspenseful tension as neophyte detective Madeline Moore tries to relate the story of her first solo case to her card-playing girlfriends; and Penny Mickelbury, whose excerpted novel *Night Songs* features interracial partners, police lieutenant Gianna Maglione of the Washington, D.C., Hate Crime Unit and investigative reporter Mimi Patterson, as they try to solve a series of murders of black prostitutes, murders often ignored by law enforcement in fact as well as fiction.

Once upon a time, the only black detective I ever saw was the bumbling, eye-rolling Birmingham Brown, the Negro sidekick in Charlie Chan movies. But knowing the wealth of talented black mystery writers, both past and present, including those represented in *Spooks, Spies, and Private Eyes,* lovers of mystery fiction *and* black literature can now confidently proclaim, "Birmingham Brown is dead! Long live the renaissance of black mystery fiction!"

Part I

Black Mystery

Forefathers and Foremothers

Pauline E. Hopkins

Talma Gordon

PAULINE E. HOPKINS (1856–1930), one of the vastly underappreciated writers of the early twentieth century, enjoyed a three-decade-long career as a playwright, musician, editor, short story writer, novelist, nonfiction author, publisher, and journalist. Most notably, she was the author of the 1900 novel *Contending Forces,* as well as editor of and frequent contributor to the *Colored American Magazine,* the first African American journal established in the twentieth century. *Colored American Magazine* published three of her serials (since reprinted as *The Magazine Novels of Pauline E. Hopkins* in the Schomburg Library of Nineteenth-Century Black Women Writers) and several short stories, among them the 1900 short story "Talma Gordon."

While clearly addressing issues of miscegenation and the then-popular theme of the "tragic mulatto," "Talma Gordon" is also a classic "locked room" mystery, popularized by Edgar Allan Poe in the 1841 short story "The Murders in the Rue Morgue." If Poe is considered the "Father of the American Detective Story," Hopkins, who utilized some of the same conventions as Poe in this and other short stories, can be arguably called the "Foremother of African American mysteries."

THE CANTERBURY CLUB of Boston was holding its regular monthly meeting at the palatial Beacon Street residence of Dr. William Thornton, expert medical practitioner and specialist. All the members were present, because some rare opinions were to be aired by men of profound thought on a question of vital importance to the life of the Republic, and because the club celebrated its anniversary in a home usually closed to society. The Doctor's winters, since his marriage, were passed at his summer home near his celebrated sanitarium. This winter found him in town with his wife and two boys. We had heard much of the beauty of the former, who was entirely unknown to social life, and about whose life and marriage we felt sure a romantic interest attached. The Doctor himself was too bright a luminary of the professional world to remain long hidden without creating comment. We had accepted the invitation to dine with alacrity, knowing that we should be welcomed to a banquet that would feast both eye and palate; but we had not been favored by even a glimpse of the hostess. The subject for discussion was "Expansion: Its Effect upon the Future Development of the Anglo-Saxon Throughout the World."

Dinner was over, but we still sat about the social board discussing the question of the hour. The Hon. Herbert Clapp, eminent jurist and politician, had painted in glowing colors the advantages to be gained by the increase of wealth and the exalted position which expansion would give the United States in the councils of the great governments of the world. In smoothly flowing sentences marshaled in rhetorical order, with compact ideas, and incisive argument, he drew an effective picture with all the persuasive eloquence of the trained orator.

Joseph Whitman, the theologian of worldwide fame, accepted the arguments of Mr. Clapp, but subordinated all to the great opportunity which expansion would give to the religious enthusiast. None could doubt the sincerity of this man, who looked once into the idealized face on which heaven had set the seal of consecration.

Various opinions were advanced by the twenty-five men present, but the host said nothing; he glanced from one to another with a look of amusement in his shrewd gray-blue eyes. "Wonderful eyes," said his patients who came under their magic spell. "A wonderful man and a wonderful mind," agreed his contemporaries, as they heard in amazement of some great cure of chronic or malignant disease which approached the supernatural.

"What do you think of this question, Doctor?" finally asked the president, turning to the silent host.

"Your arguments are good; they would convince almost anyone."

"But not Doctor Thornton," laughed the theologian.

"I acquiesce whichever way the result turns. Still, I like to view both sides of a question. We have considered but one tonight. Did you ever think that in spite of our prejudices against amalgamation, some of our descendants, indeed many of them, will inevitably intermarry among those far-off tribes of dark-skinned peoples, if they become a part of this great Union?"

"Among the lower classes that may occur, but not to any great extent," remarked a college president.

"My experience teaches me that it will occur among all classes, and to an appalling extent," replied the Doctor.

"You don't believe in intermarriage with other races?"

"Yes, most emphatically, when they possess decent moral development and physical perfection, for then we develop a superior being in the progeny born of the intermarriage. But if we are not ready to receive and assimilate the new material which will be brought to mingle with our pure Anglo-Saxon stream, we should call a halt in our expansion policy."

"I must confess, Doctor, that in the idea of amalgamation you present a new thought to my mind. Will you not favor us with a few of your main points?" asked the president of the club, breaking the silence which followed the Doctor's remarks.

"Yes, Doctor, give us your theories on the subject. We may not agree with you, but we are all open to conviction."

The Doctor removed the half-consumed cigar from his lips, drank what remained in his glass of the choice Burgundy, and leaning back in his chair contemplated the earnest faces before him.

"We may make laws, but laws are but straws in the hands of Omnipotence.

> There's a divinity that shapes our ends,
> Rough-hew them how we will.

And no man may combat fate. Given a man, propinquity, opportunity, fascinating femininity, and there you are. Black, white, green, yellow—nothing will prevent intermarriage. Position, wealth, family, friends—all sink into insignificance before the God-implanted instinct that made Adam, awakening from a deep sleep and finding the woman beside him, accept Eve as bone of his bone; he cared not nor questioned whence she came. So it is with the sons of Adam ever since, through the law of heredity which makes us all one common family. And so it will be with us in our re-formation of this old Republic. Perhaps I can make my meaning clearer by illustration, and with your permission I will tell you a story which came under my observation as a practitioner.

"Doubtless all of you heard of the terrible tragedy which occurred at Gordonville, Mass., some years ago, when Capt. Jonathan Gordon, his wife, and little son were murdered. I suppose that I am the only man on this side of the Atlantic, outside of the police, who can tell you the true story of that crime.

"I knew Captain Gordon well; it was through his persuasions that I bought a place in Gordonville and settled down to spending my summers in that charming rural neighborhood. I had rendered the Captain what he was pleased to call valuable medical help, and I became his family physician. Captain Gordon was a retired sea captain, formerly engaged in the East India trade. All his ancestors had been such; but when the bottom fell out of that business he established the Gordonville Mills with his first wife's money, and settled down as a money-making manufacturer of cotton cloth. The Gordons were old New England Puritans who had come over in the *Mayflower;* they had owned Gordon Hall for more than a hundred years. It was a baronial-like pile of granite with towers, standing on a hill which commanded a superb view of Massachusetts Bay and the surrounding country. I imagine the Gordon star was under a cloud about the time Captain Jonathan married his first wife, Miss Isabel Franklin of Boston, who brought to him the money which mended the broken fortunes of the Gordon house, and restored this old Puritan stock to its rightful position. In the person of Captain Gordon the austerity of manner and indomitable willpower that he had inherited were combined with a temper that brooked no contradiction.

"The first wife died at the birth of her third child, leaving him two daughters, Jeannette and Talma. Very soon after her death the Captain married again. I have heard it rumored that the Gordon girls did not get on very well with their stepmother. She was a woman with no fortune of her own, and envied the large portion left by the first Mrs. Gordon to her daughters.

"Jeannette was tall, dark, and stern like her father; Talma was like her dead mother, and possessed of great talent, so great that her father sent her to the American Academy at Rome, to develop the gift. It was the hottest of July days when her friends were bidden to an afternoon party on the lawn and a dance in the evening, to welcome Talma Gordon among them again. I watched her as she moved about among her guests, a fairylike blonde in floating white draperies, her face a study in delicate changing tints, like the heart of a flower, sparkling in smiles about the mouth to end in merry laughter in the clear blue eyes. There were all the subtle allurements of birth, wealth, and culture about the exquisite creature:

> 'Smiling, frowning evermore,
> Thou art perfect in love-lore,
> Ever varying Madeline,'

quoted a celebrated writer as he stood apart with me, gazing upon the scene before us. He sighed as he looked at the girl.

" 'Doctor, there is genius and passion in her face. Sometime our little friend will do wonderful things. But is it desirable to be singled out for special blessings by the gods? Genius always carries with it intense capacity for suffering: "Whom the gods love die young." '

" 'Ah,' I replied, 'do not name death and Talma Gordon together. Cease your dismal croakings; such talk is rank heresy.'

"The dazzling daylight dropped slowly into summer twilight. The merriment continued; more guests arrived; the great dancing pagoda built for the occasion was lighted by myriads of Japanese lanterns. The strains from the band grew sweeter and sweeter, and 'all went merry as a marriage bell.' It was a rare treat to have this party at Gordon Hall, for Captain Jonathan was not given to hospitality. We broke up shortly before midnight, with expressions of delight from all the guests.

"I was a bachelor then, without ties. Captain Gordon insisted upon my having a bed at the Hall. I did not fall asleep readily; there seemed to be something in the air that forbade it. I was still awake when a distant clock struck the second hour of the morning. Suddenly the heavens were lighted by a sheet of ghastly light; a terrific midsummer thunderstorm was breaking over the sleeping town. A lurid flash lit up all the landscape, painting the trees in grotesque shapes against the murky sky, and defining clearly the sullen blackness of the waters of the bay breaking in grandeur against the rocky coast. I had arisen and put back the draperies from the windows, to have an unobstructed view of the grand scene. A low muttering coming nearer and nearer, a terrific roar, and then a tremendous downpour. The storm had burst.

"Now the uncanny howling of a dog mingled with the rattling volleys of thunder. I heard the opening and closing of doors; the servants were about looking after things. It was impossible to sleep. The lightning was more vivid. There was a blinding flash of a greenish-white tinge mingled with the crash of falling timbers. Then before my startled gaze arose columns of red flames reflected against the sky. 'Heaven help us!' I cried; 'it is the left tower; it has been struck and is on fire!'

"I hurried on my clothes and stepped into the corridor; the girls were there before me. Jeannette came up to me instantly with anxious face. 'Oh, Doctor Thornton, what shall we do? Papa and Mamma and little Johnny are in the old left tower. It is on fire. I have knocked and knocked, but get no answer.'

" 'Don't be alarmed,' said I soothingly. 'Jenkins, ring the alarm bell,' I continued, turning to the butler who was standing near; 'the rest follow me. We will force the entrance to the Captain's room.'

"Instantly, it seemed to me, the bell boomed out upon the now silent air, for the storm had died down as quickly as it arose; and as our little procession paused before the entrance to the old left tower, we could distinguish the sound of the fire engines already on their way from the village.

"The door resisted all our efforts; there seemed to be a barrier against it which nothing could move. The flames were gaining headway. Still the same deathly silence within the rooms.

" 'Oh, will they never get here?' cried Talma, ringing her hands in terror. Jeannette said nothing, but her face was ashen. The servants were huddled together in a panic-stricken group. I can never tell you what a relief it was when we heard the first sound of the firemen's voices, saw their quick movements, and heard the ringing of the axes with which they cut away every obstacle to our entrance to the rooms. The neighbors who had just enjoyed the hospitality of the house were now gathered around offering all the assistance in their power. In less than fifteen minutes the fire was out, and the men began to bear the unconscious inmates from the ruins. They carried them to the pagoda so lately the scene of mirth and pleasure, and I took up my station there, ready to assume my professional duties. The Captain was nearest me; and as I stooped to make the necessary examination I reeled away from the ghastly sight which confronted me—*gentlemen, across the Captain's throat was a deep gash that severed the jugular vein!*"

The Doctor paused, and the hand with which he refilled his glass trembled violently.

" 'What is it, Doctor?' cried the men, gathering about me.

" 'Take the women away; this is murder!'

" 'Murder!' cried Jeannette, as she fell against the side of the pagoda.

" 'Murder!' screamed Talma, staring at me as if unable to grasp my meaning.

"I continued my examination of the bodies, and found that the same thing had happened to Mrs. Gordon and to little Johnny.

"The police were notified; and when the sun rose over the dripping town he found them in charge of Gordon Hall, the servants standing in excited knots talking over the crime, the friends of the family confounded, and the two girls trying to comfort each other and realize the terrible misfortune that had overtaken them.

"Nothing in the rooms of the left tower seemed to have been disturbed. The door of communication between the rooms of the husband and wife was open, as they had arranged it for the night. Little Johnny's crib was placed beside his mother's bed. In it he was found as though never awakened by the storm. It was quite evident that the assassin was no common ruffian. The chief gave strict orders for a watch to be kept on all strangers or suspicious characters who were seen in the neighborhood. He made inquiries among the servants, seeing each one separately, but there was nothing gained from them. No one had heard anything suspicious; all had been awakened by the storm. The chief was puzzled. Here was a triple crime for which no motive could be assigned.

" 'What do you think of it?' I asked him, as we stood together on the lawn.

" 'It is my opinion that the deed was committed by one of the higher classes, which makes the mystery more difficult to solve. I tell you, Doctor, there are mysteries that never come to light, and this, I think, is one of them.'

"While we were talking Jenkins, the butler, an old and trusted servant, came up to the chief and saluted respectfully. 'Want to speak with me, Jenkins?' he asked. The man nodded, and they walked away together.

"The story of the inquest was short, but appalling. It was shown that Talma had been allowed to go abroad to study because she and Mrs. Gordon did not get on well together. From the testimony of Jenkins it seemed that Talma and her father had quarreled bitterly about her lover, a young artist whom she had met at Rome, who was unknown to fame, and very poor. There had been terrible things said by each, and threats even had passed, all of which now rose up in judgment against the unhappy girl. The examination of the family solicitor revealed the fact that Captain Gordon intended to leave his daughters only a small annuity, the bulk of the fortune going to his son Jonathan, junior. This was a monstrous injustice, as everyone felt. In vain Talma protested her innocence. Someone must have done it. No one would be benefited so much by these deaths as she and her sister. Moreover, the will, together with other papers, was nowhere to be found. Not the slightest clue bearing upon the disturbing elements in this family, if any there were, was to be found. As the only surviving relatives, Jeannette and Talma became joint heirs to an immense fortune, which only for the bloody tragedy just enacted would, in all probability, have passed them by. Here was the motive. The case was very black against Talma. The foreman stood up. The silence was intense: We 'find that Captain Jonathan Gordon, Mary E. Gordon, and Jonathan Gordon, junior, all deceased, came to their deaths by means of a knife or other sharp instrument in the hands of Talma Gordon.' The girl was like one stricken with death. The flowerlike mouth was drawn and pinched; the great sapphire-blue eyes were black with passionate anguish, terror, and despair. She was placed in jail to await her trial at the fall session of the criminal court. The excitement in the hitherto quiet town rose to fever heat. Many points in the evidence seemed incomplete to thinking men. The weapon could not be found, nor could it be divined what had become of it. No reason could be given for the murder except the quarrel between Talma and her father and the ill will which existed between the girl and her stepmother.

"When the trial was called Jeannette sat beside Talma in the prisoner's dock; both were arrayed in deepest mourning. Talma was pale and careworn, but seemed uplifted, spiritualized, as it were. Upon Jeannette the full realization of her sister's peril seemed to weigh heavily. She had changed much too: hollow cheeks, tottering steps, eyes blazing with fever, all suggestive of rapid and premature decay. From far-off Italy Edward Turner, growing famous in the art world, came to stand beside his girl-love in this hour of anguish.

"The trial was a memorable one. No additional evidence had been collected to strengthen the prosecution; when the attorney-general rose to open the case against Talma he knew, as everyone else did, that he could not convict solely on the evidence adduced. What was given did not always bear upon the case, and brought out strange stories of Captain Jonathan's methods. Tales were told of sailors who had sworn to take his life, in revenge for injuries inflicted upon them by his hand. One or two clues were followed, but without avail. The judge summed up the evidence impartially, giving the prisoner the benefit of the doubt. The points in hand furnished valuable collateral evidence, but were not direct proof. Although the moral presumption was against the prisoner, legal evidence was lacking to actually convict. The jury found the prisoner 'Not Guilty,' owing to the fact that the evidence was entirely circumstantial. The verdict was received in painful silence; then a murmur of discontent ran through the great crowd.

" 'She must have done it,' said one; 'who else has been benefited by the horrible deed?'

" 'A poor woman would not have fared so well at the hands of the jury, nor a homely one either, for that matter,' said another.

"The great Gordon trial was ended; innocent or guilty, Talma Gordon could not be tried again. She was free; but her liberty, with blasted prospects and fair fame gone forever, was valueless to her. She seemed to have but one object in her mind: to find the murderer or murderers of her parents and half brother. By her direction the shrewdest of detectives were employed and money flowed like water, but to no purpose; the Gordon tragedy remained a mystery. I had consented to act as one of the trustees of the immense Gordon estates and business interests, and by my advice the Misses Gordon went abroad. A year later I received a letter from Edward Turner, saying that Jeannette Gordon had died suddenly at Rome, and that Talma, after refusing all his entreaties for an early marriage, had disappeared, leaving no clue as to her whereabouts. I could give the poor fellow no comfort, although I had been duly notified of the death of Jeannette by Talma, in a letter telling me where to forward her remittances, and at the same time requesting me to keep her present residence secret, especially from Edward.

"I had established a sanitarium for the cure of chronic diseases at Gordonville, and absorbed in the cares of my profession I gave little thought to the Gordons. I seemed fated to be involved in mysteries.

"A man claiming to be an Englishman, and fresh from the California gold fields, engaged board and professional service at my retreat. I found him suffering in the grasp of the tubercle fiend—the last stages. He called himself Simon Cameron. Seldom have I seen so fascinating and wicked a face. The lines of the mouth were cruel, the eyes cold and sharp, the smile mocking and evil. He had money in plenty but seemed to have no friends, for he had received no letters and had had no visitors in the time he had been with us. He was an enigma to me; and his nationality puzzled me, for of course I did not believe his story of being English. The peaceful influence of the house seemed to soothe him in a measure, and make his last steps to the mysterious valley as easy as possible. For a time he improved, and would sit or walk about the grounds and sing sweet songs for the pleasure of the other inmates. Strange to say, his malady only affected his voice at times. He sang quaint songs in a silvery tenor of great purity and sweetness that was delicious to the listening ear:

> 'A wet sheet and a flowing sea,
> A wind that follows fast,
> And fills the white and rustling sail
> And bends the gallant mast;
> And bends the gallant mast, my boys;
> While like the eagle free,
> Away the good ship flies, and leaves
> Old England on the lea.'

"There are few singers on the lyric stage who could surpass Simon Cameron.

"One night, a few weeks after Cameron's arrival, I sat in my office making up my accounts when the door opened and closed; I glanced up, expecting to see a servant. A lady advanced toward me. She threw back her veil, and then I saw that Talma Gordon, or her ghost, stood before me. After the first excitement of our meeting was over, she told me she had come direct from Paris, to place herself in my care. I had studied her attentively during the first moments of our meeting, and I felt that she was right; unless something unforeseen happened to arouse her from the stupor into which she seemed to have fallen, the last Gordon was doomed to an early death. The next day I told her I had cabled Edward Turner to come to her.

" 'It will do no good; I cannot marry him,' was her only comment.

" 'Have you no feeling of pity for that faithful fellow?' I asked her sternly, provoked by her seeming indifference. I shall never forget the varied emotions depicted on her speaking face. Fully revealed to my gaze was the sight of a human soul tortured beyond the point of endurance; suffering all things, enduring all things, in the silent agony of despair.

"In a few days Edward arrived, and Talma consented to see him and explain her refusal to keep her promise to him. 'You must be present, Doctor; it is due your long, tried friendship to know that I have not been fickle, but have acted from the best and strongest motives.'

"I shall never forget that day. It was directly after lunch that we met in the library. I was greatly excited, expecting I knew not what. Edward was agitated, too. Talma was the only calm one. She handed me what seemed to be a letter, with the request that I would read it. Even now I think I can repeat every word of the document, so indelibly are the words engraved upon my mind:

" 'MY DARLING SISTER TALMA: When you read these lines I shall be no more, for I shall not live to see your life blasted by the same knowledge that has blighted mine.

" 'One evening, about a year before your expected return from Rome, I climbed into a hammock in one corner of the veranda outside the breakfast-room windows, intending to spend the twilight hours in lazy comfort, for it was very hot, enervating August weather. I fell asleep. I was awakened by voices. Because of the heat the rooms had been left in semidarkness. As I lay there, lazily enjoying the beauty of the perfect summer night, my wandering thoughts were arrested by words spoken by our father to Mrs. Gordon, for they were the occupants of the breakfast room.

" ' "Never fear, Mary; Johnny shall have it all—money, houses, land, and business."

" ' "But if you do go first, Jonathan, what will happen if the girls contest the will? People will think that they ought to have the money as it appears to be theirs by law. I never could survive the terrible disgrace of the story."

" ' "Don't borrow trouble; all you would need to do would be to show them papers I have drawn up, and they would be glad to take their annuity and say nothing. After all, I do not think it is so bad. Jeannette can teach; Talma can paint; six hundred dollars a year is quite enough for them."

" 'I had been somewhat mystified by the conversation until now. This last remark solved the riddle. What could he mean? Teach, paint, six hundred a year! With my usual impetuosity I sprang from my resting place, and in a moment stood in the room confronting my father, and asking what he meant. I could see plainly that both were disconcerted by my unexpected appearance.

" ' "Ah, wretched girl! you have been listening. But what could I expect of your mother's daughter?"

" ' 'At these words I felt the indignant blood rush to my head in a torrent. So it had been all my life. Before you could remember, Talma, I had felt my little heart swell with anger at the disparaging hints and slurs concerning our mother. Now was my time. I determined that tonight I would know why she was looked upon as an outcast, and her children subjected to every humiliation. So I replied to my father in bitter anger:

" ' "I was not listening; I fell asleep in the hammock. What do you mean by a paltry six hundred a year each to Talma and to me? 'My mother's daughter' demands an explanation from you, sir, of the meaning of the monstrous injustice that you have always practiced toward my sister and me."

" ' "Speak more respectfully to your father, Jeannette," broke in Mrs. Gordon.

" ' "How is it, madam, that you look for respect from one whom you have delighted to torment ever since you came into this most unhappy family?"

" ' "Hush, both of you," said Captain Gordon, who seemed to have recovered from the dismay into which my sudden appearance and passionate words had plunged him. "I think I may as well tell you as to wait. Since you know so much, you may as well know the whole miserable story." He motioned me to a seat. I could see that he was deeply agitated. I seated myself in a chair he pointed out, in wonder and expectation—expectation of I knew not what. I trembled. This was a supreme moment in my life; I felt it. The air was heavy with the intense stillness that had settled over us as the common sounds of day gave place to the early quiet of the rural evening. I could see Mrs. Gordon's face as she sat within the radius of the lighted hallway. There was a smile of triumph upon it. I clinched my hands and bit my lips until the blood came, in the effort to keep from screaming. What was I about to hear? At last he spoke:

" ' "I was disappointed at your birth, and also at the birth of Talma. I wanted a male heir. When I knew that I should again be a father I was torn by hope and fear, but I comforted myself with the thought that luck would be with me in the birth of the third child. When the doctor brought me word that a son was born to the house of Gordon, I was wild with delight, and did not notice his disturbed countenance. In the midst of my joy he said to me:

" ' " 'Captain Gordon, there is something strange about this birth. I want you to see this child.'

" ' " "Quelling my exultation I followed him to the nursery, and there, lying in the cradle, I saw a child dark as a mulatto, with the characteristic features of the Negro! I was stunned. Gradually it dawned upon me that there was something radically wrong. I turned to the doctor for an explanation.

" ' " 'There is but one explanation, Captain Gordon; there is Negro blood in this child.'

" ' " 'There is no Negro blood in my veins,' I said proudly. Then I paused—*the mother!*—I glanced at the doctor. He was watching me intently. The same thought was in his mind. I must have lived a thousand years in that cursed five seconds that I stood there confronting the physician and trying to think. 'Come,' said I to him, 'let us end this suspense.' Without thinking of consequences, I hurried away to your mother and accused her of infidelity to her marriage vows. I raved like a madman. Your mother fell into convulsions; her life was despaired of. I sent for Mr. and Mrs. Franklin, and then I learned the truth. They were childless. One year while on a Southern tour, they befriended an octoroon girl who had been abandoned by her white lover. Her child was a beautiful girl baby. They, being Northern born, thought little of caste distinction because the child showed no trace of Negro blood. They determined to adopt it. They went abroad, secretly sending back word to their friends at a proper time of the birth of a little daughter. No one doubted the truth of the statement. They made Isabel their heiress, and all went well until the birth of your brother. Your mother and the unfortunate babe died. This is the story which, if known, would bring dire disgrace upon the Gordon family.

" ' "To appease my righteous wrath, Mr. Franklin left a codicil to his will by which all the property is left at my disposal save a small annuity to you and your sister."

" 'I sat there after he had finished his story, stunned by what I had heard. I understood, now, Mrs. Gordon's half contemptuous toleration and lack of consideration for us both. As I rose from my seat to leave the room I said to Captain Gordon:

" ' "Still, in spite of all, sir, I am a Gordon, legally born. I will not tamely give up my birthright."

" 'I left that room a broken-hearted girl, filled with a desire for revenge upon this man, my father, who by his manner disowned us without a regret. Not once in that remarkable interview did he speak of our mother as his wife; he quietly repudiated her and us with all the cold cruelty of relentless caste prejudice. I heard the treatment of your lover's proposal; I knew why Captain Gordon's consent to your marriage was withheld.

" 'The night of the reception and dance was the chance for which I had waited, planned, and watched. I crept from my window into the ivy vines, and so down, down, until I stood upon the windowsill of Captain Gordon's room in the old left tower. How did I do it, you ask? I do not know. The house was silent after the revel; the darkness of the gathering storm favored me, too. The lawyer was there that day. The will was signed and put safely away among my father's papers. I was determined to have the will and the other documents bearing upon the case, and I would have revenge, too, for the cruelties we had suffered. With the old East Indian dagger firmly grasped I entered the room and found—that my revenge had been forestalled! The horror of the discovery I made that night restored me to reason and a realization of the crime I meditated. Scarce knowing what I did, I sought and found the papers, and crept back to my room as I had come. Do you wonder that my disease is past medical aid?'

"I looked at Edward as I finished. He sat, his face covered with his hands. Finally he looked up with a glance of haggard despair: 'God! Doctor, but this is too much. I could stand the stigma of murder, but add to that the pollution of Negro blood! No man is brave enough to face such a situation.'

" 'It is as I thought it would be,' said Talma sadly, while the tears poured over her white face. 'I do not blame you, Edward.'

"He rose from his chair, wrung my hand in a convulsive clasp, turned to Talma and bowed profoundly, with his eyes fixed upon the floor, hesitated, turned, paused, bowed again, and abruptly left the room. So those two who had been lovers parted. I turned to Talma, expecting her to give way. She smiled a pitiful smile, and said: 'You see, Doctor, I knew best.'

"From that on she failed rapidly. I was restless. If only I could rouse her to an interest in life, she might live to old age. So rich, so young, so beautiful, so talented, so pure; I grew savage thinking of the injustice of the world. I had not reckoned on the power that never sleeps. Something was about to happen.

"On visiting Cameron next morning I found him approaching the end. He had been sinking for a week very rapidly. As I sat by the bedside holding his emaciated hand, he fixed his bright, wicked eyes on me, and asked: 'How long have I got to live?'

" 'Candidly, but a few hours.'

" 'Thank you; well, I want death; I am not afraid to die. Doctor, Cameron is not my name.'

" 'I never supposed it was.'

" 'No? You are sharper than I thought. I heard all your talk yesterday with Talma Gordon. Curse the whole race!'

"He clasped his bony fingers around my arm and gasped: *'I murdered the Gordons!'*

"Had I the pen of a Dumas I could not paint Cameron as he told his story. It is a question with me whether this wheeling planet, home of the suffering, doubting, dying, may not hold worse agonies on its smiling surface than those of the conventional hell. I sent for Talma and a lawyer. We gave him stimulants, and then with broken intervals of coughing and prostration we got the story of the Gordon murder. I give it to you in a few words:

" 'I am an East Indian, but my name does not matter, Cameron is as good as any. There is many a soul crying in heaven and hell for vengeance on Jonathan Gordon. Gold was his idol; and many a good man walked the plank, and many a gallant ship was stripped of her treasure, to satisfy his lust for gold. His blackest crime was the murder of my father, who was his friend, and had sailed with him for many a year as mate. One night these two went ashore together to bury their treasure. My father never returned from that expedition. His body was afterward found with a bullet through the heart on the shore where the vessel stopped that night. It was the custom then among pirates for the captain to kill the men who helped bury their treasure. Captain Gordon was no better than a pirate. An East Indian never forgets, and I swore by my mother's deathbed to hunt Captain Gordon down until I had avenged my father's murder. I had the plans of the Gordon estate, and fixed on the night of the reception in honor of Talma as the time for my vengeance. There is a secret entrance from the shore to the chambers where Captain Gordon slept; no one knew of it save the Captain and trusted members of his crew. My mother gave me the plans, and entrance and escape were easy.'

"So the great mystery was solved. In a few hours Cameron was no more. We placed the confession in the hands of the police, and there the matter ended."

"But what became of Talma Gordon?" questioned the president. "Did she die?"

"Gentlemen," said the Doctor, rising to his feet and sweeping the faces of the company with his eagle gaze, "gentlemen, if you will follow me to the drawing room, I shall have much pleasure in introducing you to my wife—née Talma Gordon."

Rudolph Fisher

From

The Conjure-Man Dies

Radiologist, musician, and writer, RUDOLPH FISHER (1897–1934) was a multitalented luminary of the first African American arts movement popularly called the Harlem Renaissance. He wrote his first short story, "The City of Refuge," while in his senior year of medical school at Howard University. News of its publication by the *Atlantic Monthly* in 1925 spread among the principal Negro writers and figures of the day: Arna Bontemps noted that the story, the first by an African American writer published in the magazine, created "something of a sensation"; Langston Hughes would call Fisher the "wittiest" of the Harlem Renaissance figures, and Alain Locke heralded him as one of the "new generation not because of years only, but because of a new aesthetic and a new philosophy of life."

Fisher moved from Washington, D.C., to New York in 1927 to set up his medical practice; his first novel, *The Walls of Jericho*, was published the following year. The novel introduced Jinx Jenkins and Bubber Brown, characters who would later appear in Fisher's second novel, *The Conjure-Man Dies: A Mystery Tale of Dark Harlem*, published in 1932. More importantly, however, *The Conjure-Man Dies* introduced the first black detective duo, Dr. John Archer and his sidekick, New York police detective Perry Dart. While not the first mystery by a black writer (it was preceded by W. Adolphe Roberts's 1926 novel *The Haunting*

Hand), Fisher's was the first by an African American writer to feature black characters.

The Conjure-Man Dies received brief but positive reviews in *Opportunity* and *Time* magazines, but because mysteries were not taken seriously by most African American intellectuals or by literary critics in general, the novel has generally been omitted from serious literary criticism—a critique in a *Dictionary of Literary Biography* entry on Fisher and in John McCluskey Jr.'s fine analysis of Fisher's work, *The City of Refuge: The Collected Stories of Rudolph Fisher,* being two notable exceptions.

Fisher made the analogy between his detective duo and a bowman (Archer) and his arrow (Dart): "the vision of the former gives direction and aim to the action of the latter," a statement true of many classic pairings of amateur sleuth and police detective before and after Fisher's time, including Sherlock Holmes and Inspector Lestrade, Hercule Poirot and Inspector Japp, Philo Vance and Sergeant Heath. While in intellect, learned discourse, and powers of deduction a clear descendent of Sir Arthur Conan Doyle's Sherlock Holmes and an equal of S. S. Van Dine's Philo Vance, Fisher's Dr. Archer was intimately involved in his community and culture in a way that has been emulated by African American mystery writers ever since. And *The Conjure-Man Dies,* Rudolph Fisher's landmark in detective fiction, put black characters and themes squarely in the middle of the dramatic action, where heretofore they had been only minor characters in novels by whites.

Sadly, Dr. Archer and Perry Dart appeared only twice more, in the 1935 novella, "John Archer's Nose," and in a stage version of the novel *Conjur' Man Dies,* which premiered in 1936. Both were written before their creator, Rudolph Fisher, fell ill and succumbed, apparently to the effects of chronic exposure to his own X-ray machinery, on December 26, 1934.

Chapter One

ENCOUNTERING the bright-lighted gaiety of Harlem's Seventh Avenue, the frigid midwinter night seemed to relent a little. She had given Battery Park a chill stare and she would undoubtedly freeze the

Bronx. But here in this mid-realm of rhythm and laughter she seemed to grow warmer and friendlier, observing, perhaps, that those who dwelt here were mysteriously dark like herself.

Of this favor the Avenue promptly took advantage. Sidewalks barren throughout the cold white day now sprouted life like fields in spring. Along swung boys in camel's hair beside girls in bunny and muskrat; broad, flat heels clacked, high narrow ones clicked, reluctantly leaving the disgorging theaters or eagerly seeking the voracious dance halls. There was loud jest and louder laughter and the frequent uplifting of merry voices in the moment's most popular song:

> "I'll be glad when you're dead, you rascal you,
>   I'll be glad when you're dead, you rascal you.
>   What is it that you've got
>   Makes my wife think you so hot?
>   Oh you dog—I'll be glad when you're gone!"

But all of black Harlem was not thus gay and bright. Any number of dark, chill, silent side streets declined the relenting night's favor. 130th Street, for example, east of Lenox Avenue, was at this moment cold, still, and narrowly forbidding; one glanced down this block and was glad one's destination lay elsewhere. Its concentrated gloom was only intensified by an occasional spangle of electric light, splashed ineffectually against the blackness, or by the unearthly pallor of the sky, into which a wall of dwellings rose to hide the moon.

Among the houses in this looming row, one reared a little taller and gaunter than its fellows, so that the others appeared to shrink from it and huddle together in the shadow on either side. The basement of this house was quite black; its first floor, high above the sidewalk and approached by a long graystone stoop, was only dimly lighted; its second floor was lighted more dimly still, while the third, which was the top, was vacantly dark again like the basement. About the place hovered an oppressive silence, as if those who entered here were warned beforehand not to speak above a whisper. There was, like a footnote, in one of the two first-floor windows to the left of the entrance a black-on-white sign reading: "Samuel Crouch, Undertaker."

On the narrow panel to the right of the doorway the silver letters of another sign obscurely glittered on an onyx background: "N. Frimbo, Psychist."

Between the two signs receded the high, narrow vestibule, terminating in a pair of tall glass-paneled doors. Glass curtains, tightly stretched in vertical folds, dimmed the already too-subdued illumination beyond.

2

It was about an hour before midnight that one of the doors rattled and flew open, revealing the bareheaded, short, round figure of a young man who manifestly was profoundly agitated and in a great hurry. Without closing the door behind him, he rushed down the stairs, sped straight across the street, and in a moment was frantically pushing the bell of the dwelling directly opposite. A tall, slender, light-skinned man of obviously habitual composure answered the excited summons.

"Is—is you him?" stammered the agitated one, pointing to a shingle labeled "John Archer, M.D."

"Yes—I'm Dr. Archer."

"Well, arch on over here, will you, doc?" urged the caller. "Sump'm done happened to Frimbo."

"Frimbo? The fortune-teller?"

"Step on it, will you, doc?"

Shortly, the physician, bag in hand, was hurrying up the graystone stoop behind his guide. They passed through the still open door into a hallway and mounted a flight of thickly carpeted stairs.

At the head of the staircase a tall, lank, angular figure awaited them. To this person the short, round, black, and by now quite breathless guide panted, "I got one, boy! This here's the doc from 'cross the street. Come on, doc. Right in here."

Dr. Archer, in passing, had an impression of a young man as long and lean as himself, of a similarly light complexion except for a profusion of dark brown freckles, and of a curiously scowling countenance that glowered from either ill humor or apprehension. The doctor rounded the banister head and strode behind his pilot toward the front of the house along the upper hallway, midway of which, still following the excited short one, he turned and swung into a room that opened into the hall at that point. The tall fellow brought up the rear.

Within the room the physician stopped, looking about in surprise. The chamber was almost entirely in darkness. The walls appeared to be hung from ceiling to floor with black velvet drapes. Even the ceiling was covered, the heavy folds of cloth converging from the four corners to gather at a central point above, from which dropped a chain suspending the single strange source of light, a device which hung low over a chair behind a large desklike table, yet left these things and indeed most of the room unlighted. This was because, instead of shedding its radiance downward and outward as would an ordinary shaded droplight, this mechanism focused a horizontal beam upon a second chair on the opposite side of the table. Clearly the person who used the chair beneath the odd spotlight could remain in relative darkness while the occupant of the other chair was brightly illuminated.

"There he is—jes' like Jinx found him."

And now in the dark chair beneath the odd lamp the doctor made out a huddled, shadowy form. Quickly he stepped forward.

"Is this the only light?"

"Only one I've seen."

Dr. Archer procured a flashlight from his bag and swept its faint beam over the walls and ceiling. Finding no sign of another lighting fixture, he directed the instrument in his hand toward the figure in the chair and saw a bare black head inclined limply sidewise, a flaccid countenance with open mouth and fixed eyes staring from under drooping lids.

"Can't do much in here. Anybody up front?"

"Yes, suh. Two ladies."

"Have to get him outside. Let's see. I know. Downstairs. Down in Crouch's. There's a sofa. You men take hold and get him down there. This way."

There was some hesitancy. "Mean us, doc?"

"Of course. Hurry. He doesn't look so hot now."

"I ain't none too warm, myself," murmured the short one. But he and his friend obeyed, carrying out their task with a dispatch born of distaste. Down the stairs they followed Dr. Archer, and into the undertaker's dimly lighted front room.

"Oh, Crouch!" called the doctor. "Mr. Crouch!"

"That 'mister' ought to get him."

But there was no answer. "Guess he's out. That's right—put him on the sofa. Push that other switch by the door. Good."

Dr. Archer inspected the supine figure as he reached into his bag. "Not so good," he commented. Beneath his black satin robe the patient wore ordinary clothing—trousers, vest, shirt, collar, and tie. Deftly the physician bared the chest; with one hand he palpated the heart area while with the other he adjusted the earpieces of his stethoscope. He bent over, placed the bell of his instrument on the motionless dark chest, and listened a long time. He removed the instrument, disconnected first one, then the other, rubber tube at their junction with the bell, blew vigorously through them in turn, replaced them, and repeated the operation of listening. At last he stood erect.

"Not a twitch," he said.

"Long gone, huh?"

"Not so long. Still warm. But gone."

The short young man looked at his scowling freckled companion.

"What'd I tell you?" he whispered. "Was I right or wasn't I?"

The tall one did not answer but watched the doctor. The doctor put aside his stethoscope and inspected the patient's head more closely, the parted lips and half-open eyes. He extended a hand and with his extremely long fingers gently palpated the scalp. "Hello," he said. He turned the far side of the head toward him and looked first at that side, then at his fingers.

"Wh-what?"

"Blood in his hair," announced the physician. He procured a gauze dressing from his bag, wiped his moist fingers, thoroughly sponged and reinspected the wound. Abruptly he turned to the two men, whom until now he had treated quite impersonally. Still imperturbably, but incisively, in the manner of lancing an abscess, he asked, "Who are you two gentlemen?"

"Why—uh—this here's Jinx Jenkins, doc. He's my buddy, see? Him and me—"

"And you—if I don't presume?"

"Me? I'm Bubber Brown—"

"Well, how did this happen, Mr. Brown?"

" 'Deed I don' know, doc. What you mean—is somebody killed him?"

"You don't know?" Dr. Archer regarded the pair curiously a moment, then turned back to examine further. From an instrument case he took a probe and proceeded to explore the wound in the dead man's scalp. "Well—what do you know about it, then?" he asked, still probing. "Who found him?"

"Jinx," answered the one who called himself Bubber. "We jes' come here to get this Frimbo's advice 'bout a little business project we thought up. Jinx went in to see him. I waited in the waitin' room. Presently Jinx come bustin' out pop-eyed and beckoned to me. I went back with him—and there was Frimbo, jes' like you found him. We didn't even know he was over the river."

"Did he fall against anything and strike his head?"

"No, suh, doc." Jinx became articulate. "He didn't do nothin' the whole time I was in there. Nothin' but talk. He tol' me who I was and what I wanted befo' I could open my mouth. Well, I said that I knowed that much already and that I come to find out sump'm I didn't know. Then he went on talkin', tellin' me plenty. He knowed his stuff all right. But all of a sudden he stopped talkin' and mumbled sump'm 'bout not bein' able to see. Seem like he got scared, and he say, 'Frimbo, why don't you see?' Then he didn't say no more. He sound so funny I got scared myself and jumped up and grabbed that light and turned it on him—and there he was."

"M-m."

Dr. Archer, pursuing his examination, now indulged in what appeared to be a characteristic habit: he began to talk as he worked, to talk rather absently and wordily on a matter which at first seemed inapropos.

"I," said he, "am an exceedingly curious fellow." Deftly, delicately, with half-closed eyes, he was manipulating his probe. "Questions are forever popping into my head. For example, which of you two gentlemen, if either, stands responsible for the expenses of medical attention in this unfortunate instance?"

"Mean who go'n' pay you?"

"That," smiled the doctor, "makes it rather a bald question."

Bubber grinned understandingly.

"Well here's one with hair on it, doc," he said. "Who got the medical attention?"

"M-m," murmured the doctor. "I was afraid of that. Not," he added, "that I am moved by mercenary motives. Oh, not at all. But if I am not to be paid in the usual way, in coin of the realm, then of course I must derive my compensation in some other form of satisfaction. Which, after all, is the end of all our getting and spending, is it not?"

"Oh, sho'," agreed Bubber.

"Now this case"—the doctor dropped the gauze dressing into his bag—"even robbed of its material promise, still bids well to feed my native curiosity—if not my cellular protoplasm. You follow me, of course?"

"With my tongue hangin' out," said Bubber.

But that part of his mind which was directing this discourse did not give rise to the puzzled expression on the physician's lean, light-skinned countenance as he absently moistened another dressing with alcohol, wiped off his fingers and his probe, and stood up again.

"We'd better notify the police," he said. "You men"—he looked at them again—"you men call up the precinct."

They promptly started for the door.

"No—you don't have to go out. The cops, you see"—he was almost confidential—"the cops will want to question all of us. Mr. Crouch has a phone back there. Use that."

They exchanged glances but obeyed.

"I'll be thinking over my findings."

Through the next room they scuffled and into the back of the long first-floor suite. There they abruptly came to a halt and again looked at each other, but now for an entirely different reason. Along one side of this room, hidden from view until their entrance, stretched a long narrow table draped with a white sheet that covered an unmistakably human form. There was not much light. The two young men stood quite still.

"Seem like it's—occupied," murmured Bubber.

"Another one," mumbled Jinx.

"Where's the phone?"

"Don't ask me. I got both eyes full."

"There 'tis—on that desk. Go on—use it."

"Use it yo' own black self," suggested Jinx. "I'm goin' back."

"No you ain't. Come on. We use it together."

"All right. But if that whosis says 'Howdy' tell it I said 'Goo'by.' "

"And where the hell you think I'll be if it says 'Howdy'?"

"What a place to have a telephone!"

"Step on it, slow motion."

"Hello!—Hello!" Bubber rattled the hook. "Hey, operator! Operator!"

"My Gawd," said Jinx, "is the phone dead too?"

"Operator—gimme the station—quick. . . . Pennsylvania? No ma'am—New York—Harlem—listen, lady, not railroad. Police. *Please,* ma'am. . . . Hello—hey—send a flock o' cops around here—Frimbo's—the fortune-teller's—yea—13 West 130th—yea—somebody done put that thing on him! . . . Yea—OK."

Hurriedly they returned to the front room where Dr. Archer was pacing back and forth, his hands thrust into his pockets, his brow pleated into troubled furrows.

"They say hold everything, doc. Be right over."

"Good." The doctor went on pacing.

Jinx and Bubber surveyed the recumbent form. Said Bubber, "If he could keep folks from dyin', how come he didn't keep hisself from it?"

"Reckon he didn't have time to put no spell on hisself," Jinx surmised.

"No," returned Bubber grimly. "But somebody else had time to put one on him. I knowed sump'm was comin'. I told you. First time I seen death on the moon since I been grown. And they's two mo' yet."

"How you reckon it happened?"

"You askin' me?" Bubber said. "You was closer to him than I was."

"It was plumb dark all around. Somebody could'a snook up behind him and crowned him while he was talkin' to me. But I didn't hear a sound. Say—I better catch air. This thing's puttin' me on the well-known spot, ain't it?"

"All right, dumbo. Run away and prove you done it. Wouldn't that be a bright move?"

Dr. Archer said, "The wisest thing for you men to do is stay here and help solve this puzzle. You'd be called in anyway—you found the body, you see. Running away looks as if you were—well—running away."

"What'd I tell you?" said Bubber.

"All right," growled Jinx. "But I can't see how they could blame anybody for runnin' away from this place. Graveyard's a playground side o' this."

Chapter Two

OF THE TEN Negro members of Harlem's police force to be promoted from the rank of patrolman to that of detective, Perry Dart was one of the first. As if the city administration had wished to leave no doubt in the public mind as to its intention in the matter, they had chosen, in him, a man who could not have been under any circumstances mistaken for aught but a Negro; or perhaps, as Dart's intimates insisted, they had chosen him because his generously pigmented skin rendered him invisible in the dark, a conceivably great advantage to a detective who did most of his work at night. In any case, the somber hue of his integument in no wise reflected the complexion of his brain, which was bright, alert, and practical within such territory as it embraced. He was a Manhattanite by birth, had come up through the public schools, distinguished himself in athletics at the high school he attended, and, having himself grown up with the black colony, knew

Harlem from lowest dive to loftiest temple. He was rather small of stature, with unusually thin, fine features, which falsely accentuated the slightness of his slender but wiry body.

It was Perry Dart's turn for a case when Bubber Brown's call came in to the station, and to it Dart, with four uniformed men, was assigned.

Five minutes later he was in the entrance of 13 West 130th Street, greeting Dr. Archer, whom he knew. His men, one black, two brown, and one yellow, loomed in the hallway about him large and ominous, but there was no doubt as to who was in command.

"Hello, Dart," the physician responded to his greeting. "I'm glad you're on this one. It'll take a little active cerebration."

"Come on down, doc," the little detective grinned with a flash of white teeth. "You're talking to a cop now, not a college professor. What've you got?"

"A man that'll tell no tales." The physician motioned to the undertaker's front room. "He's in there."

Dart turned to his men. "Day, you cover the front of the place. Green, take the roof and cover the backyard. Johnson, search the house and get everybody you find into one room. Leave a light everywhere you go if possible—I'll want to check up. Brady, you stay with me." Then he turned back and followed the doctor into the undertaker's parlor. They stepped over to the sofa, which was in a shallow alcove formed by the front bay windows of the room.

"How'd he get it, doc?" he asked.

"To tell you the truth, I haven't the slightest idea."

"Somebody crowned him," Bubber helpfully volunteered.

"Has anybody ast you anything?" Jinx inquired gruffly.

Dart bent over the victim.

The physician said, "There is a scalp wound all right. See it?"

"Yea—now that you mentioned it."

"But that didn't kill him."

"No? How do you know it didn't, doc?"

"That wound is too slight. It's not in a spot that would upset any vital center. And there isn't any fracture under it."

"Couldn't a man be killed by a blow on the head that didn't fracture his skull?"

"Well—yes. If it fell just so that its force was concentrated on certain parts of the brain. I've never heard of such a case, but it's conceivable. But this blow didn't land in the right place for that. A blow at this point would cause death only by producing intracranial hemorrhage—"

"Couldn't you manage to say it in English, doc?"

"Sure. He'd have to bleed inside his head."

"That's more like it."

"The resulting accumulation of blood would raise the intra—the pressure inside his head to such a point that vital centers would be paralyzed. The power would be shut down. His heart and lungs would quit cold. See? Just like turning off a light."

"OK if you say so. But how do you know he didn't bleed inside his head?"

"Well, there aren't but two things that would cause him to."

"I'm learning, doc. Go on."

"Brittle arteries with no give in them—no elasticity. If he had them, he wouldn't even have to be hit—just excitement might shoot up the blood pressure and pop an artery. See what I mean?"

"That's apoplexy, isn't it?"

"Right. And the other thing would be a blow heavy enough to fracture the skull and so rupture the blood vessels beneath. Now this man is about your age or mine—somewhere in his middle thirties. His arteries are soft—feel his wrists. For a blow to kill this man outright, it would have had to fracture his skull."

"Hot damn!" whispered Bubber admiringly. "Listen to the doc do his stuff!"

"And his skull isn't fractured?" said Dart.

"Not if probing means anything."

"Don't tell me you've x-rayed him too?" grinned the detective.

"Any fracture that would kill this man outright wouldn't have to be x-rayed."

"Then you're sure the blow didn't kill him?"

"Not by itself, it didn't."

"Do you mean that maybe he was killed first and hit afterward?"

"Why would anybody do that?" Dr. Archer asked.

"To make it seem like violence when it was really something else."

"I see. But no. If this man had been dead when the blow was struck, he wouldn't have bled at all. Circulation would already have stopped."

"That's right."

"But of one thing I'm sure: that wound is evidence of too slight a blow to kill."

"Specially," interpolated Bubber, "a hard-headed cullud man—"

"There you go ag'in," growled his lanky companion.

"He's right," the doctor said. "It takes a pretty hefty impact to bash in a skull. With a padded weapon," he went on, "a fatal blow would have had to be crushing to make even so slight a scalp wound as this. That's out. And a hard, unpadded weapon that would break the scalp just slightly like this, with only a little bleeding and without even cracking the skull, could at most have delivered only a stunning blow, not a fatal one. Do you see what I mean?"

"Sure. You mean this man was just stunned by the blow and actually died from something else."

"That's the way it looks to me."

"Well—anyhow he's dead and the circumstances indicate at least a possibility of death by violence. That justifies notifying us, all right. And it makes it a case for the medical examiner. But we really don't know that he's been killed, do we?"

"No. Not yet."

"All the more a case for the medical examiner, then. Is there a phone here, doc? Good. Brady, go back there and call the precinct. Tell 'em to get the medical examiner here double time and to send me four more men—doesn't matter who. Now tell me, doc. What time did this man go out of the picture?"

The physician smiled.

"Call Meridian 7-1212."

"OK, doc. But approximately?"

"Well, he was certainly alive an hour ago. Perhaps even half an hour ago. Hardly less."

"How long have you been here?"

"About fifteen minutes."

"Then he must have been killed—if he was killed—say anywhere from five to thirty-five minutes before you got here?"

"Yes."

Bubber, the insuppressible, commented to Jinx, "Damn! That's trimming it down to a gnat's heel, ain't it?"

But Jinx only responded, "Fool, will you hush?"

"Who discovered him—do you know?"

"These two men."

"Both of you?" Dart asked the pair.

"No, suh," Bubber answered. "Jinx here discovered the man. I discovered the doctor."

Dart started to question them further, but just then Johnson, the officer who had been directed to search the house, reappeared.

"Been all over," he reported. "Only two people in the place. Women—both scared green."

"All right," the detective said. "Take these two men up to the same room. I'll be up presently."

Officer Brady returned. "Medical examiner's comin' right up."

The detective said, "Was he on this sofa when you got here, doc?"

"No. He was upstairs in his—his consultation room, I guess you'd call it. Queer place. Dark as sin. Sitting slumped down in a chair. The light was impossible. You see, I thought I'd been called to a patient, not a corpse. So I had him brought where I knew I could examine him. Of course, if I had thought of murder—"

"Never mind. There's no law against your moving him or examining him, even if you had suspected murder—as long as you weren't trying to hide anything. People think there's some such law, but there isn't."

"The medical examiner'll probably be sore, though."

"Let him. We've got more than the medical examiner to worry about."

"Yes. You've got a few questions to ask."

"And answer. How, when, where, why, and who? Oh, I'm great at questions. But the answers—"

"Well, we've the 'when' narrowed down to a half-hour period." Dr. Archer glanced at his watch. "That would be between ten-thirty and eleven. And 'where' shouldn't be hard to verify—right here in his own chair, if those two fellows are telling it straight. 'Why' and 'who'— those'll be your little red wagon. 'How' right now is mine. I can't imagine—"

Again he turned to the supine figure, staring. Suddenly his lean countenance grew blanker than usual. Still staring, he took the detective by the arm. "Dart," he said reflectively, "we smart people are often amazingly—dumb."

"You're telling me?"

"We waste precious moments in useless speculation. We indulge ourselves in the extravagance of reason when a frugal bit of observation would suffice."

"Does prescription liquor affect you like that, doc?"

"Look at that face."

"Well—if you insist—"

"Just the general appearance of that face—the eyes—the open mouth. What does it look like?"

"Looks like he's gasping for breath."

"Exactly. Dart, this man might—might, you understand—have been choked."

"Ch—"

"Stunned by a blow over the ear—"

"To prevent a struggle!"

"—and choked to death. As simple as that."

"Choked! But just how?"

Eagerly, Dr. Archer once more bent over the lifeless countenance. "There are two ways," he dissertated in his roundabout fashion, "of interrupting respiration." He was peering into the mouth. "What we shall call, for simplicity, the external and the internal. In this case the external would be rather indeterminate, since we could hardly make out the usual bluish discolorations on a neck of this complexion." He procured two tongue depressors and, one in each hand, examined as far back into the throat as he could. He stopped talking as some discovery further elevated his already high interest. He discarded one depressor, reached for his flashlight with the hand thus freed, and, still holding the first depressor in place, directed his light into the mouth as if he were examining tonsils. With a little grunt of discovery, he now discarded the flashlight also, took a pair of long steel thumb forceps from a flap in the side of his bag, and inserted the instrument into the victim's mouth alongside the guiding tongue depressor. Dart and the uniformed officer watched silently as the doctor apparently tried to remove something from the throat of the corpse. Once, twice, the prongs snapped together, and he withdrew the instrument empty. But the next time the forceps caught hold of the physician's discovery and drew it forth.

It was a large, blue-bordered, white handkerchief.

George S. Schuyler
writing as William Stockton

The Shoemaker Murder

GEORGE S. SCHUYLER (1895–1977) was a well-known Harlem
Renaissance journalist, novelist, and critic. His early articles
appeared in H. L. Mencken's *American Mercury,* and he worked
as a journalist, first with A. Philip Randolph's *Messenger* and
later as the New York correspondent and associate editor for
the *Pittsburgh Courier,* where he was employed from 1924
through 1966.

Schuyler had a reputation as an iconoclast and was noted for
his scathing articles and fiction, which exposed corruption and
fraud among whites and blacks. He is probably best known for
his 1931 novel satirizing American racism, *Black No More: Being
an Account of the Strange and Wonderful Workings of Science in the
Land of the Free.* Another, lesser-known novel published in the
same year, *Slaves Today,* is a fictionalized account of the enslave-
ment of native Africans by the descendants of American blacks
who were ruling Liberia, a story Schuyler had reported for the
New York Evening Post while on assignment there.

Using his own name, as well as several pseudonyms, Schuyler
also wrote a prodigious amount of mystery and crime fiction,
most of it serialized in the *Pittsburgh Courier* between 1933 and
1939, as well as some of the earliest known political thrillers by
a black author, most notably the 1936–37 serial "The Black
Internationale: Story of Black Genius Against the World" and
its 1937–38 sequel "Black Empire: An Imaginative Story of a

Great New Civilization in Modern Africa" (reprinted as *Black Empire* in 1991). Another serialized mystery, *The Ethiopian Murder Mystery,* was reprinted as a novel in 1994. While many of his mysteries and thrillers address issues of African liberation, the story reprinted here, "The Shoemaker Murder" (written under the pseudonym William Stockton), is set in Harlem. The story has not been reprinted since its original publication in 1933.

DETECTIVE SERGEANT HENRY BURNS knelt over the prostrate corpse in the dingy shoe shop on 126th Street in black Harlem. He looked at the gaping, fatal wound in the back of the shoemaker's skull. Brains and blood had gushed from it onto the dirty wooden floor. The tall Negro detective rose, brushed the knees of his meticulously creased trousers, and lit a cigarette. The two patrolmen, an Irishman and a brown-skin lad, waited expectantly for him to speak.

"Well, it's murder all right," he declared. "They got him with the first blow. They used that hammer. Whoever did it had a terrible wallop, all right . . . Keep that crowd away from the window, Clancy, and keep the door fastened. The inspector and the coroner will be here soon."

He flicked the ash from his cigarette and swept the little shoe shop with his keen glance.

"It's going to be a tough assignment," he observed to the colored policeman. "The door was locked from the inside. The transom was nailed down. There is no way to get from this room into the rag shop behind, opening on the little alley. Let's go around and question the old lady in the rag shop."

They went out and around the corner to the shop in the rear. The windows were covered with burlap bagging, the place was piled high with sacks of rags, bundles of old newspapers, and assorted junk. In an old broken-down chair near the door sat an aged Mrs. Ferguson, the proprietress.

"We're officers," began the detective, looking sharply at the old woman, who glanced back indifferently. "Did you hear any noise or voices in the shoe shop around noon?"

"Naw suh, Ah ain't heered nuthin'," she replied, "an' Ah bin sittin' heah since long befo' noon."

"Did you know Johnson, the shoemaker?"

"Yassah, Ah knowed him. He bin rentin' fum me foh nigh on tuh six year."

"So you own this building, eh?"

"Yassuh, my husban' left hit tuh me when he died."

"How long has that partition between your shop and the shoe shop been there?"

" 'Bout ten yeahs."

Burns worked his way through the bundles and bags back to the wooden partition. He surveyed it minutely, pressing here and there with his hand and knocking with his knuckles. There was evidently no opening.

"Is there a basement under this space?" he asked the old woman.

"Yassuh, they's ah cellar."

"How do you get down to it?"

"They's a doah outside."

The detective stood silent for a moment looking all over the room. "Have you got a furnace downstairs?"

"Yassuh."

"Who takes care of it?"

"Jerry. He's tha janitor. An' he helps me aroun' heah with mah business."

"Where is he?"

"He's downstaahs, Ah guesses."

"Stay here, Williams," commanded Burns, turning on his heel. Going outside he walked down the four steps to the basement door. Trying it, he found it fastened. He beat on it. There was no reply.

Alert now, he put his broad shoulder against the flimsy door. After a couple of lusty lunges, the door gave way. He found himself standing in the dark cellar.

Whipping out his flashlight, he lighted his way forward until he found the electric light switch. He pulled it up and flooded the place with light. He noted immediately that there was no partition in the cellar separating the two parts of the building as there was upstairs. In the center was the rusty furnace. To one side was a rickety cot with two or three dirty quilts and a filthy pillow. The rest of the cellar was filled with bags of rags, bundles of paper, and various odds and ends. Far forward was a coal bin right under the street. There was no sign of Jerry, the janitor.

Carefully the detective examined every foot of the basement floor. It had been freshly swept in the open space where there were no bags or bundles. He turned the beam of his flashlight on the ceiling. There was apparently no opening there. Burns frowned.

He was about to leave the basement when it occurred to him that there might be an opening after all. He looked again at the pile of bags against one wall reaching clear to the ceiling. He got to work immediately moving them to one side. Yes, there it was, a narrow wooden staircase leading, of all things, into the shoe shop through a trapdoor. Strange that he had not noticed the door when he was in the shoe shop. He now ascended the little stairway and examined the narrow trapdoor. It was hooked. He examined each step but there was absolutely no clue, no mark, nothing.

Then he saw two broom straws on the top step caught in a crack. He grunted, smiled grimly, and pocketed them.

He descended the stairway, stepped over the bags of rags, and was about to switch off the light when the outer doorway was darkened. Looking up quickly he saw standing there a huge elderly mulatto man in tattered overalls, scowling at him.

"Whatchu doin' here?" asked the man.

"I'm an officer," the tall Negro detective replied. "Who are you and what are you doing here?"

"I'm the janitor here," replied the man suspiciously. He looked intoxicated and the odor coming from him confirmed it.

"So you're Jerry, eh?"

"Yea, I'm Jerry. Whatchu doin' here, an' whatchu mean breakin' down that door?"

"Never mind that," snapped the detective. "You sit down there and answer my questions."

Jerry shuffled in reluctantly and sank heavily down on the cot.

"Now where have you been since before noon?" began Burns, standing over the hulking form of the man.

"Oh, I jus' bin over tuh git uh drink or two."

"So I see. What time did you leave here?"

" 'Bout eleven."

"Was Johnson the shoemaker working in his shop when you went out?"

"Yassuh. I heered him tappin' up there."

"Do you always lock that door when you go out?"

"Yassuh, allus do. Some o' these boys aroun' heah might steal our rags and papers."

"Hummph. Well, how long have those bags been up against that staircase?"

" 'Bout two weeks."

"And you haven't cleaned up this place—swept it out since then?"

"Nawsuh," replied Jerry, "I don't bothah sweepin' out 'cept once in uh while."

"Where's your broom?"

"Ovah b'hind the furnace."

Burns stepped quickly behind the furnace to get the broom. It was not there. Alert now, he looked carefully everywhere. Finally he found it alongside the coal bin.

"Did you put this broom here?" he asked sharply.

"Nawsuh," replied Jerry, "I ain't had that broom in two weeks an' w'en I got through with it, then I hung it up behin' th' furnace."

Detective Burns grunted with satisfaction. Taking Jerry with him, he returned to the shoe shop. The place was crowded with high police officials and the coroner. Burns reported immediately to Inspector Sullivan.

"What have you found, Burns?" asked the inspector.

"It's a tough case, Inspector," replied the Negro. "This man Johnson has had this shop here for six years. He was found murdered at 12:30 P.M., when a woman came here to get a pair of shoes heeled. The door was locked from the inside. The transom is nailed shut. There's no door connecting this shop with the rag shop behind. However, there is a stairway leading from the basement into this shop. I found it covered up by a big pile of bags filled with rags and bundles of paper. The pile has been there two weeks. Now here's something funny. The janitor says he hasn't swept the basement for two weeks, since the last shipment of rags and papers, and yet the basement has been swept but only the space underneath this shop. I found these two broom straws caught in the top step of the stairway. There are no footprints and no fingerprints as far as I could see. The trapdoor leading from this room to the basement is hooked from the basement side. Jerry, that's the janitor, heard Johnson working at eleven o'clock when he went out to the speakeasy around the corner. The old lady who owns this dump, Mrs. Ferguson, says she has sat in her place since long before noon. And yet this fellow was murdered in here. And the murderer must have been a powerful fellow because Johnson was a big guy. But there was no way for a big man to get in the place. Everything was locked from the inside."

"It's a puzzler, all right," said the inspector, scratching his head. "Did this guy, Johnson, ever have any visitors?"

"The neighbors say not," Burns answered. "He stayed in here most of the time. Ate here, too, but whenever he did go out he hung up his little sign saying when he'd be back. It was hanging there when we broke in. Either he was planning to go right out, which was unusual this time of day, or else he had just come back. The woman looked in and saw him on the floor at twelve-thirty. He was murdered sometime between eleven and twelve-thirty."

"Did he have any money on him?"

"Yes, that's the funny thing about it, Chief. He had twenty-five bucks in his pocket. So you see, it wasn't robbery. There's quite a bit of money in the cash register."

"Well, somebody did it," declared the inspector. "Keep hunting. I'll send a couple of men to help you. There've been too many murders around here lately."

"All right, sir. I'll stay on the job."

The coroner soon departed with the body of the shoemaker. The high police officials left soon after. Patrolman Clancy kept the curious away from the door. Detective Burns sat in the shoemaker's chair near the door, smoking cigarette after cigarette and frowning in thought.

Finally, with an exclamation, he jumped up and ran out to the street. Stopping near the curb, he closely examined the coal hole in the cement sidewalk. Then, much agitated, he returned to the shop and telephoned several places. Then he rushed out, shouting back over his shoulder to Clancy to let no one into the shop.

Two hours later Detective Burns sat in the office of Inspector Sullivan with several white detectives. Before the semicircle of officers sat a Negro, very black and hunchbacked. The man sullenly watched the men as they sat silently before him.

"What's the idea of having us pick up this fellow, Burns?" asked the inspector. "He don't know nothing about it."

"Well, I think he does, Chief," insisted Burns. "I took a long chance but I'm sure I'm right."

"Where's your evidence?" asked the inspector.

"You see this little strand of cloth? Well that came off this fellow's coat. He was wearing a different coat, just this color of brown, when he murdered Johnson this noon. It caught in a nail when he went in the cellar door. It's a cinch, Chief."

"It's a dirty frame-up," yelled the hunchback, snarling at Burns. "I never had a coat like that. This is the only coat I've got. You've got nothing on me."

"He went in the cellar door, Chief," repeated Burns, ignoring the man's denial. "I've got the fingerprints."

The little man grinned but said nothing.

"You should have been smart enough to wear gloves," said Burns, speaking directly to the accused man. "Now you'll burn for neglecting to do so."

"That's all stuff," jeered the man, "there wasn't no fingerprints."

"Oh, yes there were," accused Burns, swiftly showing a sheet with photostatted prints, "and they're yours, too."

"Well, I guess that cinches it, all right," commented the inspector, with a tone of decision, rising.

"Yes, that's all we need," commented the other officers, moving back their chairs and rising.

The little black man looked puzzled, then frightened, then panic-stricken. He swallowed a couple of times, then licked his lips.

"That was good work, Burns," said the inspector, placing his hand on the detective's shoulder. "Those fingerprints on that cellar door settle everything. We can get a conviction on that."

"Say, listen, Chief," wailed the alarmed little black man, "honest, them ain't my fingerprints. You can't put that on me. I—I—I didn't do it. I didn't kill him."

"You didn't kill who?" snapped Burns.

"Why Johnson," replied the suspect.

"How did you know he was dead?" shouted the inspector. "Who told you? We didn't. We picked you up but we didn't say what for. Why did you think we wanted you for that?"

Trapped! Tracked! The hunchback sat speechless for a minute, then alternately plied with questions and threatened, he confessed.

"That was fine work, Burns," commented the inspector afterward, "but how did you ever conceive the idea of having us pick up the hunchback?"

"Well, Chief," explained the other. "I could see we were up against a clever fellow. In the first place, he had almost committed a perfect crime. There were no fingerprints, no evidence of any kind. The murder had obviously been committed coolly and with premeditation. It showed the murderer was familiar not only with the building but with the habits of the occupants. Business was always slack in the shop around noon. The old lady in the rear usually read her morning papers about that time. Jerry, the janitor, generally spent his noon hour in. Johnson would be alone.

"Now it was impossible for the murderer to have got out of the cellar door, assuming he had gone down through the trapdoor after killing Johnson, because the cellar door was locked. He must have come through the coal hole. I found all the dirt around the coal hole cover had been jarred away by the cover being removed.

"Now here's the way I built up the case: the fellow had studied the layout. He knew the block was almost deserted just before school lets out at noon. He entered the coal hole, being short, and immediately placed the cover back on behind him. Then he descended the coal chute into the bin, threw the bags away from the trapdoor, unhooked it, entered Johnson's shop, and killed him. He retraced his steps, piled the bags back, but not before he had swept the steps to remove the coal dust footprints. That's also the reason why he swept the cellar floor, from the furnace to the coal bin. Unfortunately for him, he couldn't hang Jerry's broom back in its place without tracking up the cellar floor again, so he just threw it back. He left the cellar by the same way he entered, taking a chance that no one would see him. No one did. I figured that only a small fellow could get through that coal hole, and I was sure it was a man and not a boy. It had to be a small man but yet a powerful one because Johnson was a pretty big fellow. I took a chance on it being a hunchback."

"Fine!" exclaimed the inspector. "But what did he kill him for? He didn't rob him, as you know."

"Revenge. That's the answer. He confessed as much. Eight years ago Morgan, that's the hunchback, and Johnson were gold mining in British Guyana. They struck it pretty rich but they got to quarreling and in the fight that ensued, Johnson seriously injured Morgan's back, causing that hump on it. He left Morgan for dead and came here to the States. Morgan followed him here after he got well but just located him this week."

"Yes, but why didn't he just bump him off with a gun and beat it?"

"This," said Burns, displaying a piece of worn, folded paper. "It is a map showing the location of a gold mine in British Guyana. Johnson had it in his cash register. It is the only thing Morgan took. He wanted to get back to find that mine. He knew beforehand that Johnson had it."

"Smart work, Burns," smiled the inspector.

"Yes, I did some pretty good guessing," the Negro replied.

Alice Dunbar-Nelson

Summer Session

While her status as the widow of famed poet Paul Laurence Dunbar often overshadowed her own career, ALICE DUNBAR-NELSON (1875–1935) was an accomplished poet and writer whose fiction works included *Violets and Other Tales* (1895) and *The Goodness of St. Rocque and Other Stories* (1899), the latter credited by scholar Ann Allen Shockley as the first published collection of short stories by an African American woman. She was also the editor of two nonfiction works, *Masterpieces of Negro Eloquence: The Best Speeches Delivered by the Negro from the Days of Slavery to the Present Time* (1914) and *The Dunbar Speaker and Entertainer* (1920). Additionally, *Give Us Each Day: The Diary of Alice Dunbar-Nelson,* edited by Gloria T. Hull, was published in 1984. Her poetry and short stories were also published and anthologized throughout her lifetime and her collected work is the subject of three volumes in the Schomburg Library of Nineteenth-Century Black Women Writers.

"YOU WERE FLIRTING with him!"

"I was not. I don't know how to flirt."

"So you say, but you can put up a pretty good imitation."

"You're mistaken."

"I am not. And a man you never saw before in your life. And a common taxi driver."

"He's not a common taxi driver."

"How do you know?"

"I just know."

"Strange exchange of intimacies for the first meeting."

"I tell you—"

"Shut up!"

"I won't shut up, and don't you dare tell me that again!"

There was a warning note in her usually gentle voice; an ominous tightening of her soft lips; a steely glint in her violet eyes. Logan heeded the warning and sat in grim silence, while Elise ground gears and otherwise mishandled her little car through the snarled traffic of Amsterdam Avenue.

"You told me 114th Street, and I waited for you there for a half hour, and I got jammed in the traffic and things went wrong, and this young man got out of his taxi, and straightened me out. And while I waited for you he just stayed and talked."

"To your delight."

"What was I to do? Push him away from the running board? I was standing still, and I couldn't drive away since I was waiting for you."

"I told you 115th Street, and there I stood on the corner in the broiling sun for a half hour, while you were carrying on a flirtation with a taxi driver, until I walked back, thinking you might have had an accident."

"Don't you say flirtation to me again. You said 114th Street. You never speak plain over the telephone anyhow."

"Anything else wrong with me since you've met your new friend— the Taxi Adonis?"

Elise brought the car to a grinding, screeching pause in front of the movie house which was their objective. They sat through the two hours of feature and news and cartoons and comedy and prevues in stony silence. They ate a grim meal together in the usual cafeteria, and she set him down at the men's dormitory of the university in the same polite and frigid silence. Logan glanced at her now and then just a trifle apprehensively. He had never seen just this trace of hardness in her, like the glint of unexpected steel beneath soft chiffon. But his manly dignity would not permit him to unbend. He answered her cold good night with one as cold, and for the first time in that summer session, during which they had grown to know and like one another, they parted without making a future date.

He waited for her next day at luncheon hour, as she came from her class with a half-dozen other chattering summer-school teacher-students. His manner was graciously condescending.

"Shall we have luncheon together?" Lordly and superior as usual.

She flashed her usual violet-eyed smile of delight, but he felt, rather than saw, that the smile did not quite reach the eyes; that the violets were touched as by premature frost.

"What I can't quite understand," he pursued, after he had brought her tray, deftly removed the salad, tea, and crackers, and placed the tray behind the next chair, "is, if you are skillful enough to drive from Portland, Maine, to New York alone and without disaster, how you can get mixed up in a mere traffic jam on Amsterdam Avenue, and have to have a taxi driver get you out."

Elise's brows went up at the awkward English, so at variance with his usual meticulous and precise phrasing, and a haunting query clouded her eyes. Logan quenched an embarrassed "Hem" in iced tea.

"I did not drive from Portland," was her final response. "I came from my own town, twenty-seven miles beyond Portland."

There was no particular reason for Elise's driving down Amsterdam Avenue after classes that afternoon, but she did and a friendly red light brought her to a halt at 114th Street. Adonis—Logan's sneering cognomen stuck in her mind, and she realized with a guilty start how ruggedly applicable it was—stuck his face in her car window. Poppies suffused her cheeks and dewy violets swam in a sea of flame.

"All right?" he queried.

"Quite, thank you." The light was happily green, and she meshed her gears.

"What's the hurry?" He put a protesting hand on the wheel.

"I have an engagement!" She sped away frantically. Adonis whistled at the wabbling career of her little coupé down the street.

She saw him just ahead of her in the cafeteria line next evening at dinnertime. She reached for her tray with hands that insisted upon trembling, though she shook them angrily. He smiled daringly back at her. He was even handsomer out of his taxi uniform than in it, and the absence of the cap revealed crisp auburn curls of undoubted pugnaciousness.

"You get a seat, I'll bring your dinner."

"But I—"

"Go on—"

There was a difference between Adonis' ordering of her movements and that of Logan's. A sureness of merry audacity against prim didacticism. She sat at a window table and meekly arranged silver and napkins.

"But I could never eat all that," she protested at the tray, "beef and potatoes and—and—all that food."

"I knew that's what's the trouble—diet of salads and iced tea and crackers, mentally, spiritually, physically."

Elise ate roast beef and corn on the cob and pie à la mode and laughed at Adonis' jokes, and his whimsical descriptions of man and his appetites. Over their cigarettes she chuckled at his deft characterizations of their fellow diners.

"Eat hay and think hay," he was saying, "thin diets and thin souls. You need a red-blooded chap like me to make you eat food, put flesh on your bones, and reconstruct your thinking from New England inhibitions to New York acceptance and enjoyment of life."

Elise's world rocked. School principals used muddled English. Taxi drivers talked like college professors.

Adonis paused and regarded something on his shoulder as if it were a tarantula. Logan's hand quivered in rage, and veins stood up on its pallor "like long blue whips," Elise found herself thinking.

"Aren't you taking a lot of liberties with a young lady to whom you've not been introduced?" snarled the owner of pallor and veins.

Adonis brushed off the hand and the remark with a careless gesture. He arose and bowed elaborately. "Miss Stone and I have been introduced, thank you, by ourselves—and you?"

Elise looked perilously near tears, "Oh, er—Logan—Mr. Long—this is—er—Mr. McShane."

Logan looked stonily through Adonis, "I don't accept introductions to taxi drivers, even if you do eat with them, Elise."

"Oh, please—" she began.

"That's all right," Adonis gathered up the checks. "Just let me settle this with the cashier, and then if you don't mind, we'll go outside, and settle the physical difference between a taxi driver and—" He did not finish the sentence, but the sinister drawl and contemptuous pause made Elise's scalp prickle with shame for Logan.

"You would suggest a common brawl; quite true to type. I hope, Elise, you have seen enough of such ruffianly conduct to be satisfied."

"Quite the contrary," she answered coolly, "I am going out with

Mr. McShane in his taxi." It was pure spite, and she had a sinking feeling that she might not be wanted.

"Terry to you," he retorted, "and let's be going. We've got a busy evening before us."

Logan was beside them on the sidewalk, blocking the way to the taxi parked at the curb.

"Elise, don't be a fool." He grasped her arm and wrenched it, so that she gave an involuntary cry of pain. Terence McShane's next three moves were so violently consecutive as to seem simultaneous. His right hand caught Logan neatly on the point of the chin, so that he went down with amazing swiftness; his left encircled Elise's waist and lifted her into the taxi, and both hands swung the machine with a roar and sputter in the general direction of the Washington Bridge.

"But you're losing fares," Elise protested.

"Nonsense. If you can stand this bumpety-bump, what's the dif?"

"It's entrancing," she murmured at the river, the sky, the stars, the electric signs on the Jersey shore, at Terry's hatless curls.

"Police call," the radio protested, "calling all police cars. Look out for taxi license Y327D. Driver abducted summer-school student. Watch for taxi. Arrest driver. Kidnapping charge."

From their leafy shelter, where somehow the taxi had parked itself— neither could have told when or how it stopped under those particularly umbrageous trees, they stared at the radio's accusing dial.

"Well, I'll be—" Terry swore softly. "What do you think of that worm putting in such a charge at headquarters?"

"Oh, Terry, you'll be arrested and put in jail!"

"Will you go to jail with me?"

"You know I will—oh, what am I saying?"

"Words of wisdom, me darlin'. Let's go. Anyhow I'm glad we didn't cross the bridge and get into Jersey."

Through circuitous ways and dark streets, avoiding police, taxis, inquisitive small boys and reporters on the loose, they drew up in front of police headquarters.

Elise sat demurely on a bench, and began to repair damages to her hair, complexion, and neck frills. The little pocket mirror wavered ever so slightly as Logan stood accusingly in front of her, but her eyes did not leave the scrutiny of their mirrored counterpart.

"A pretty mess you've made of your life and reputation," he thundered. "Your chances for any position in my school are gone."

Elise put back a refractory curl behind her ear, then tried it out on her cheek again, surveying it critically in the mirror.

"Won't you recommend me for a job, Mr. Principal, after I've studied so hard all summer?"

Terry's gales of unrestrained mirth at the desk made them both look up in amazement. Laughter rocked the walls of the station house, rolled out into the summer street. Captain and Sergeant and Lieutenant and just plain officers roared lustily, all save one quiet plainclothes man, who laid an iron grip on Logan's arm.

"Terence McShane, you were always the best detective in the city," roared the Captain. "And you made him bring himself right into our outstretched arms."

The iron grip on Logan's arm terminated into steel bracelets.

"Okeh, Longjim Webb, alias Prof. Logan Long, the school principal, looking the summer students over for teaching material in his consolidated upstate school, we'll give you a chance in the Big House to meditate on the law against white slavery."

"Your zeal to corral this particular choice bit of femininity made you throw caution to the winds," suggested Detective Terence McShane.

Incredulity, disgust, anger swept the violet eyes. Elise flared into Terry's face.

"You—you—pretending to be a taxi driver. You just used me for a decoy," she raged.

Terry held her protesting hands tight as he whispered below the hubbub of Logan's protestations,

"Never a bit of it, my dear. I loved you the first day you stalled your car in the thick of things on 125th Street, before you even saw me, and I got in the habit of following you around while I was impersonating a taxi driver, to get a chance to know you. Then when I found this"—a wave toward the still-voluble Logan—"had marked you for another one of his prey—well you don't mind if I combined a bit of business with my pleasure?"

Elise's faint "No" was visible, rather than audible.

"It's all right then? Shall it be beefsteak for two?"

"Yes."

"And you won't take back what you promised up there on the Drive?"

"How can I," she laughed, "when my middle name is McBride?"

Chester Himes

His Last Day

CHESTER HIMES (1909–84) remains one of the reigning forces in
African American detective fiction. His career spanned over
fifty years and included eighteen novels, two volumes of autobiography, and over fifty short stories.

Himes, who began writing fiction during a seven-
and-a-half-year incarceration for armed robbery, wrote three
underappreciated novels before immigrating to France in 1953.
Although he remained unrecognized in his homeland during
much of his lifetime, Himes was popular in France and was
later noted on both sides of the Atlantic for his unique ability to
interweave issues of black rage, race, and crime unlike any
other author of his time.

In 1956 Himes wrote to a friend that he was "trying desperately to write a detective story to get a little money." The result
was *La Reine des pommes* or *For Love of Imabelle* (also called *A
Rage in Harlem* in the U.S.). It was the first novel in his "Har-
lem domestic series," which featured black detectives Coffin
Ed Johnson and Grave Digger Jones. *A Rage in Harlem* won
France's Grand Prix de la Littérature Policière in 1958, a first
for an African American writer. Coffin Ed Johnson and Grave
Digger Jones appeared in eight other novels including *Cotton
Comes to Harlem, The Heat's On, Blind Man with a Pistol,* and
Plan B, the last published posthumously in France in 1984 and
in the U.S. in 1993.

"His Last Day," the 1933 short story published here, was one of those written while Himes was serving time in the Ohio State Penitentiary. It is reprinted here, complete with ellipses to denote missing text, as it was in *The Collected Works of Chester Himes* (Thunder's Mouth Press, 1990).

THE SMALL, BRIGHT LIGHTS screwed to the sockets in the ceiling of the corridor, one in front of each cell, illumined the narrow passageway, the dead-white walls and ceiling, the grayish concrete floor with a brilliant eye-stabbing glare. The first five cells were bare and empty. On one of the horizontal bars of the sixth hung a white wooden label with the name Wilson painted in a black arc across the top and underneath it the number 13289 connected the edges of the arc.

Immediately outside the cell, across the four-foot corridor, a uniformed guard sat tilted back against the wall in an unsympathetic straight-back chair. His cap visor was pulled low over his forehead to shade his eyes from the overhead glare, and his head nodded slowly up and down as he dozed fitfully. When his chin sagged below a subconscious danger point he would awake with a jerk and glance sharply about him as if to recall where he was and what it was that he was supposed to be doing. The dull black stock of a pistol appeared projecting from a holster at his side.

The corridor light shone obliquely within the cell forming a checkerboard pattern by the shadow of the bars halfway across the smooth concrete floor and illumined the entire cell with a sharp twilight. A chair stood beside the bunk partly within the light, laden with clothes strung over its back in careless disorder. The bunk abutted the right wall, extending from within two feet of the rear wall to within two feet of the bars which comprised the front of the cell. A washbasin and a sanitary commode were built out from the rear wall opposite the bunk and immediately above them was a small, narrow tin shelf. The cell was devoid of any other furnishings.

A man lay stretched out on the grayish-white sheet of the narrow bunk snoring slightly. His full-length, dingy white underwear were twisted about his body as if he had been turning over in his sleep. But now he lay on his back, perfectly still except for the rhythmic rising and falling of his chest as he breathed. His left arm was flung across his chest, the hand clenched in a tight fist. The other arm rested at his side, the fingers curled loosely inward. His left leg was twisted under his right.

The sheet was creased in a hundred places and the drab gray blanket lay in a heap on the floor at the foot of the bunk.

An oblique shaft of light struck across the man's face, throwing his features into relief. Tiny beads of perspiration glistened on his forehead, and his dark brown skin shone with a film of perspiration and oil that had seeped through its pores.

His short, black hair curled over his head in disorder. Tiny lines had begun to form in crow's-feet at the corners of his eyes, otherwise his face was smooth as a baby's, giving to him a youthful appearance that he did not merit. His forehead was high and [. . .], his nose was large and prominent with wide, flaring nostrils, and his mouth was thick-lipped and sensuous. There was an indefinable sense of weakness about his mouth. One felt it rather than saw it. A stubble of thick, blue beard decorated his square, bulldog chin.

His large, powerful body reached the full length of the bunk and his head rested on the very edge of a lumpy pillow. One would have received the impression of jungle strength and animal cunning by careful observation.

The man moved his hand across his face as if some imaginary object was bothering him. Suddenly his eyes opened wide. He lay without moving for a moment, staring about the cell with his muddy, sleep-heavy eyes. After a while he turned over on his side and pushed the chair away from the bed. He reached his hand underneath the bed, took out a red coffee can, and rolled a cigarette from the tobacco flakes and rice papers within it.

He sprawled back obliquely across the bed with his hands resting on the wall at his side and his torso lying flat, and stuck the cigarette in his mouth. He struck a match from a safety box and applied it to his cigarette. The flame painted the white walls a flickering crimson and outlined grotesque shadows of his cupped hands on the rear wall. He blew the match out, inhaled deeply on the cigarette, and thumbed the match in the direction of the guard.

The guard was sitting straight in his chair now, and peering intently into the cell.

"Taking a drag, eh, Spats?" he asked, trying to keep his voice from betraying the uneasiness he was feeling.

The warden had instructed him to keep a sharp eye on the condemned men to prevent them from committing suicide. Burning was effective even if it was rather gruesome and some guys would try anything to beat the chair, the guard reasoned. Jobs were scarce and he didn't want to have to look for another one.

Spats took another deep inhalation and let smoke dribble through his nostrils.

"Just takin' my mawnin's mawnin', Bill," he replied. His voice was as harsh as the foghorn on a Duluth-bound ore ship.

Things were different now, he thought idly. When he was in before on that robbery rap over in the regular cells a guard would have marched him across the yard to the "hole" and probably have stood him up for four or five hours had he seen him smoking in bed at any time while the cell lights were off. Now he could smoke in bed all he wanted to and they didn't make a peep. Well, that's progress, he mused and gave a harsh snort of laughter at the thought.

The guard jumped at the unmirthful sound. He stared at the side of Spats's face as if to read his mind, but he could only see the red glow of the cigarette as Spats [. . . . . .]

"Well, today's the day, eh, Spats," he remarked.

Spats's thoughts swerved sharply back again to the immediate present.

"Yep, if the governor don't change his mind and give me a last-minute reprieve, which ain't likely. He ain't got any reason to do it, anyway."

"Wel-l-l?" the guard questioned. He was curious to know how Spats was taking it.

"Oh, I'm ready," Spats explained. "I don't give a damn now that all chance is gone. I just made the fight for a new trial because I didn't want to overlook any bets. I'm too good a gambler for that. I never would feel just right taking the lightning ride if I thought that I'd had a chance to beat it and then overlooked it."

The guard nodded understandingly.

Spats relapsed again into silence. He reviewed the chain of circumstances that led up to his present confinement in the death row at Big Meadows where he had spent ten years on a robbery charge, and had returned in less than a year after his release to ride the lightning in the hot-squat.

His mind turned back to that Sunday morning out in the Texas Club in Center City. He hadn't intended to pull off that bit of shooting, but he had been wary and sort of prison scared too. Ten years in the big house had taught him not to take any chances, to shoot when the occasion called for shooting, and shoot straight, and pay for his blanks with his freedom.

He'd been heisting the manager of the Club in the ground-floor foyer as he came down from the Club above with the Saturday night's receipts.

His mouth crooked in a mocking grin as he thought of the wide, frightened eyes of the little Jew when he commanded him to get 'em up. Why, the little sucker trembled so that he could hardly hold his arms above his shoulders, and just because a guy had a heat in his face.

Then the dicks busted in like rosy-cheeked heroes in an 1890 melodrama. He didn't even have time to clip the little tyke for his layers. One dick stepped in from the street and the other came thumping down the stairs. And he, Spats, standing in the floor with his heat in his hand. It was a tight squeeze and he had to smoke his way out. But of all the tough breaks that he ever had had, the one who lived was the one who saw his fawn-colored spats and remembered them. He'd been a fool for wearing spats on the job but then he thought it safe as a drink of water.

He always would believe that the tip-off came from a frail, one whom he had gone nuts over the night before and spilled his plans about the job trying to impress her.

He frowned and flipped the cigarette against the wall at the back of the cell. He was conscious of a dull burning resentment at having been sold by a lousy frail. He didn't claim to be smart but he didn't usually act that dumb. Well, a jane had been many a con's Waterloo, but that didn't ease the choking, self-contemptuous intensity of the chagrin.

Suddenly the small round globe in the exact center of the ceiling flashed on, flooding the cell with brilliant yellow light.

Spats stretched and yawned loudly and tested the cold concrete floor with his bare feet. He pulled the chair containing his clothes over to the bunk and began to dress. Heavy cotton socks, dark blue trousers wrinkled and bagged, blue cotton shirt freshly laundered and given to him the night before to wear to the chair—to the chair.

And he wouldn't be doing this tomorrow. He would be dead—burnt to death in the chair—and crammed into one of those small wooden coffins that fundless executed men were buried in. A stifling sensation came in his chest and his breath whistled through his mouth. His fingers turned to thumbs and he found it impossible to button his shirt.

Then the disturbing thought left as suddenly as it had come. Jeeze, he would be glad to get it over with, he thought. This suspense was giving him the jitters. He had lived long enough, anyway.

When he finished dressing he washed his face and hands in the bowl and dried himself with the towel that had been given him at his bath a few days before. He took his toothbrush from his vest pocket and lathered some soap on it. Then a little voice whispered in his ear, mocking him. "What are you cleaning up so much for?" it asked. "You're not going anywhere but to hell, and it don't make any difference how you look going there."

He broke the handle of the brush with a savage snap and hurled the pieces through the bars, cursing horribly under his breath.

The guard got up from his chair and kicked the pieces to one side of the corridor.

"Take it e-e-easy, take it e-easy, Spats," he cautioned. "You'll just make a fool of yourself and have the papers poking fun at you in the late editions."

Spats quickly got himself under control and managed a smile. "Just got a toothache," he defended.

The guard's words made him conscious of his most fervid desire other than that of beating the rap altogether—which was very improbable—and that was for the papers to say that he had gone to the chair with a smile. He wanted to take the last stroll down the stone-flagged corridor with a sneer on his lips and a mocking, devil-may-care spirit in his stride, and the other inmates seeing him pass would say:

"Jeeze, there goes Spats as cool as if he was taking an afternoon stroll —and damned if he ain't grinning. Jeeze, what-a-nerve, what-a-man."

He understood the convicts' intense curiosity concerning the condemned men and knew that their topic of conversation for days after an electrocution would be how the condemned man acted when he walked across the yard.

He turned back to his bed, carefully folding and spreading the blanket over the sheet, then drew the chair to the center of the floor and slumped down into it, cocking his feet on the bars at the front of the cell.

"I hope it don't rain today, Bill. I'd hate to get wet when we crossed the yard on the way to the chair," he joked.

"Aw, a little water won't hurt you. Just make the juice shoot through you that much quicker," Bill informed him with the self-satisfied assurance born of complete ignorance.

"Well, if that's the case I guess I'll wet my head before I go out. They tell me that a man lives two or three seconds after they turn the juice on him," Spats said. He shuddered involuntarily at the thought.

"Well," opined the guard, "they'll leave your head kinda damp when they shave it. But you'll have firsthand information concerning how long a man lives after they turn the juice on you." He chuckled at his grim humor.

Spats jumped to his feet. Beads of perspiration formed on his forehead and his face turned three shades paler. "What the hell are you trying to do, get my goat?" he snarled hoarsely.

The guard eyed him indifferently. "Well, here comes your breakfast. After you get a belly full you might feel better," he remarked as a blue-clad convict approached, carrying a heavy aluminum plate and a small aluminum bucket of coffee.

The attendant slid the plate and bucket through a cutout in the bars at the base of the door.

"What do you want for dinner, old kid?" he asked Spats.

Spats remembered the condemned men were given whatever they desired for their last meal and he didn't want to think about last meals.

"Just bring the regular dinner," he replied.

The attendant stuck a spoon through the bars. "OK. That'll be chicken. That's the regular last meal."

Last meal. The phrase kept popping up. It had a disturbing effect on Spats's appetite. "Beat it, rat," he snarled at the attendant.

The man hastened away.

Spats eyed his breakfast with a complete absence of enthusiasm. There were two doughnuts, some fried potatoes and gravy, two thick slices of bread and a chip of butter. The coffee was sugarless and slightly muddied with milk.

He wolfed the food, not tasting it, kicked the tins through the door, tossed the spoon out on the corridor floor and rolled and lighted a cigarette. He took several deep inhalations before taking the cigarette from his lips and explained to the guard, "I guess I must've been hungry, Bill. That slop sure tasted good this morning."

The guard looked up and nodded.

And then the thought suddenly assailed Spats that this was the last breakfast he would eat, ever. His hands began trembling. He quickly stuck the cigarette back into his mouth and jammed them into his pockets. He glanced sharply toward the guard to see if he had noticed the action.

But the guard was preparing to leave. His hours were over. Another guard took his place in the chair and nodded a good morning to Spats.

"The time nears, young man," he observed.

"Sure be glad when it's over with," Spats rejoined.

"Young man," the guard asked in a soft, sympathetic voice, "have you got right with God?"

Spats's lips curled in a sneer. "Has God got right with me?" he argued. "I didn't ask to come here into this world. He brought me here. He didn't make any provision for me to eat or to get the things I needed to live, so I got them the best way I could." His voice relieved the congestion that was forming in his lungs, the tautness that was pulling at his muscles. He continued, speaking faster: "That way was robbery. A sucker got in my way and I bumped him, maybe. I didn't ask that dick to come after me that Sunday morning. Perhaps God sent him there. If he did he sure as hell got him killed. I ain't a damn bit sorry to see a meddling dick get croaked. It was him or me or whoever the guy was who bumped him. You kept me here ten years and then turned me out into the world where I was ten years late to make a living and because I get accused of bumping a dick making that living you say: 'Young man, have you got right with God?' To hell . . ."

"Young man, young man, I wouldn't say that if I were you," the guard remonstrated gently. "You are on the brink of eternity and you have done enough already without adding to your other sins that of unforgivable profanity."

"All right, all right, deacon, if you're scared to listen to facts," Spats sneered. "But I want you to know that I ain't a damn bit worried, anyway," he added and lapsed into silence.

He took his hands from his pockets and struck a match to relight the dead butt in his lips. He noticed that his hands were still trembling so he held them in his lap and forced the muscles to steadiness through an exertion of his will.

Trembling like a panicky rat, he upbraided himself. Just like that tyke he had lined that Sunday morning in the Texas Club.

His mind spanned the months and returned to that Sunday morning. He remembered how he had made a panicky retreat from the scene of the shooting and beat it to Pony Boy's flat on Thackery Avenue.

The same Pony Boy who had given him that moniker, Spats, years ago when he was a kid in his teens and used to gamble in Pony Boy's dive. That had been long before he had taken his first tumble and got the sawbuck in the big house. The name stuck through the years just as had his exaggerated fondness for fawn-colored spats.

He and Pony Boy had been the best of friends then. He brought plenty players to fatten the games in Pony Boy's joint.

Later, when he saw Pony Boy kill an unwilling dame one night in a rented room by striking her on the temple with his fist, they became better friends. He had dangled the sharp edge of a prison sentence over Pony Boy's head and made him dance to his tunes.

That had been the only place in the entire city where he felt safe to go that morning. He got there hungry and broke just as the sun began to turn red in the eastern sky. His luck had served him well for he had found Pony Boy alone in the flat. His wife was away on a visit at the time.

He had been safe enough there but he got to thinking about five grand he had left with his pal, the manager of a nearby cabaret. A couple of nights later, when he thought the hunt had dimmed a little, he slipped down to the cabaret. He told himself that he needed the dough in case he should get a chance to clear the city.

"Someone to see you," the guard called, interrupting his chain of reminiscences.

Spats lifted his gaze and scowled at the bars. Two neatly dressed men came up and nodded to him.

The guard moved his chair in closer so that he could keep a sharper watch.

"We're from the *Graphic*," one of the men explained. "Want to interview you."

Spats forced a smile to his face. "How do you do, gentlemen," he greeted.

"Fine day for an electrocution," the reporter remarked, testing Spats's nerve.

Spats paled slightly, but his smile remained, frozen.

"Do you want a picture of him, Dan?" the other reporter asked. He took a small camera from his pocket and began to adjust it.

"No don't bother. He isn't that important," Dan replied.

"Do you still maintain your innocence?" he questioned Spats.

"Sure do," Spats contended. "I was home and in bed when that killing jumped off."

"That's what I told this kid here," Dan smiled, nodding toward his companion. "They haven't electrocuted a guilty man during the twenty-two years I've been on the sheet. Do you hold any ill feelings toward the people who sent you here? The judge, the prosecutor, the cop who testified against you?"

"No, I don't. I know that the judge and the prosecutor were just doing their duty. And that dumb copper was just mistaken. I believe that he was sincere in thinking that the party he saw was me," Spats conceded. "You know my record influenced the jury. Just a chain of circumstances that an ex-con hadn't a chance to beat."

"Yeah, that's copy. Smiling Joe Collotti said the same thing seventeen years ago. Well, I see that you're not afraid of the chair, anyway," Dan noted.

"Afraid of what? Why I'm laughing," Spats assured them, and let out a snort of unclassifiable noise to prove it.

"Well, I'll give you a line about going to the hot seat with a smile on your lips. How'll that suit you?"

"Fine, Dan."

"Now don't break down and make me out a liar," Dan cautioned, as he closed his notebook and turned to go.

"I'll be smiling when the juice is turned on," Spats called after him. "I'm a man."

No sooner had the reporters left than a little, sallow-faced man with nose glasses attached to a ribbon around his neck appeared before the bars, as if he had been waiting his turn.

"This must be your busy day, Spats," he greeted, wearing a mechanical smile.

"Hello, Zanny. Any news?" Spats asked. He couldn't quite keep the note of desperate hope from his voice.

"Nope. I just came over to tell you goodbye. I did everything that I could for you. The appellate court was almost compelled to uphold the verdict. You're so conspicuously guilty. And then there wasn't a flaw in the prosecution to get a grip on. You didn't expect any aid from the governor, anyway."

The hope died in Spats's eyes. "Nope, I didn't expect to beat it but I was just playing my hand to the end." His voice was resigned. "Well, so long, Zanny. I'll pick you up later in hell." He tried to smile. He failed.

"By the way, Spats," Zanny spoke as if a sudden thought had flashed to his mind, "where is that jewelry that you promised to turn over to me for fighting your case? You said it was in a safety box in the Guardian Trust Company. I have a statement for you to sign so that I can get it. Then you can tell me the number of the box. The guard here will witness the transaction, won't you, sir?" He turned to the guard.

The guard nodded.

Spats gave a snort of mirthless laughter. "There ain't any jewelry, Zanny. You got beat that time. You'll remember me when everybody else has forgotten me, because I stung you."

Blood surged to the attorney's face, mottling it with a dirty red. "Well, you'll get burnt yourself, Spats," he sneered.

Spats jumped toward the bars, a savage snarl issuing from his lips. The attorney retreated hastily as if he thought that Spats might get out through the bars. He kept on down the corridor and didn't slacken his pace until he was out of sight.

Spats indulged in a fit of bloodcurdling, insane laughter. "That's one lousy tyke fixer who gave his services for nothing," he muttered.

A few minutes later the same attendant who had brought him his breakfast appeared with a large tray covered with a white linen napkin. Spats wondered what it was that they were feeding him today.

And then he remembered that this was his last meal. Last meal. The words stuck in his mind, leechlike, and a hollow feeling came to his stomach. His appetite was suddenly dissipated. He felt that the least tiny crumb would stick in his throat and choke him.

But when the attendant stuck the food through the door and the savory odors wafted across his nostrils his appetite returned. He examined the dinner, picked up the different plates and laid them on his bunk. There was chicken, dressing, candied sweet potatoes, salad, celery, ice cream and cake—and a spoon to eat it with. Spats ate as much as he could hold and shoved the dishes back through the door.

A feeling of well-being pervaded him. He lit a cigarette and found to his surprise that it really tasted good. That was all he had needed, he told himself, just something good to eat. He had been hungry and had thought he was turning yellow.

Sure, he was going tonight. What the hell did he care? He wouldn't let a little thing like that faze him. He exploded with a snort of mirthless laughter and the guard looked up to see what the trouble was.

"I guess you think that because a man is going to die he should be crying and praying, eh, brother," Spats sneered, noting the guard's quick interest. "Well, I'm not like those sniveling rats. I'm a man."

He stretched out on his bunk, feeling drowsy, and slowly puffed on his cigarette.

A whiskey glass and a woman, he mused. Well, he had steered pretty clear of whiskey, but he hadn't always been able to keep clear of the women.

Like that night when he went to the cabaret to get the five grand from his pal. He had gone in and seen his pal and got by the two dicks that were there on the lookout for him, trying to corral that five grand reward the citizens had put out for him, dead or alive.

He could remember it as plain as if it had just happened.

He had bumped into Eloise coming out of the cabaret and she had recognized him. But he had her number. She liked money well enough to sell him to the first policeman who hove into view, but she was yellow. However, he had chilled her monetary ambitions with a few sharp threats and she had beat it down the street one way while he beat it another.

But it was when he had returned to Pony Boy's that the bottom dropped out of his world.

Pony Boy was dead, shot by a woman named Margaret, whom he had been keeping. Margaret said that Pony Boy had been jealous of the attention she gave her twelve-year-old boy and had taken him away from her. And she had come down and demanded him to tell her where the boy was. One word led to another, and that led to the shot that killed Pony Boy.

Spats had recognized Margaret. He knew her well. They had been childhood sweethearts wrapped up in each other, once. But he had left her flat—with the callous indifference of youth—when she told him that she was going to have a baby. Remorse from that action, burning in his soul like an eternal fuse down through the years, goading him to deeds of extreme recklessness and cruelty, had made his name a byword in police headquarters for crimes of unusual viciousness.

It was this baby, now a twelve-year-old boy, whom Margaret called Little Spats, that Pony Boy had taken away from her.

It was funny, Spats thought, how he had always been a sucker for a good sob story.

If at that moment, Margaret had said, "Let's go unicorn hunting," he would have put on his unicorn clothes.

But she just stood and looked at him through her large, dumb-animal eyes so he had given her the five grand that he had got from his pal and sent her out to look for the kid. Then he cleaned all traces that she might have left in the flat and left a trademark of his own—fingerprints and a fawn-colored spat.

And a few minutes later he had taken hot lead in the guts from a tommy gun wielded by a squad of coppers.

His trial, four months later, when he had recovered from his wounds, was merely a formality of justice. The jury had convicted him long before.

He lit another cigarette and turned over on his side, puffing leisurely. Well, he thought, he had had his day, anyway. He was living on some-one else's time now. He'd hoisted many a guy and had beat some tough raps. He had even put a few guys to sleep with a spade in their face, too. But he had known that he wouldn't beat that last rap, cop-killing. He had known it ever since that Sunday morning when he made that panicky getaway from the Texas Club. He had known he would burn —if he lived.

He'd been a lone wolf: no friends, one woman, and he never would be quite sure that she didn't turn him up for that other five grand. Not even a mother to grieve for him when he was gone. Well, he was glad for that.

He'd just been a good spender, a fast liver, a hard guy.

And now he was in the condemned men's row in the state prison. And today was his last day.

His throat felt suddenly dry. He jumped from the bed and gulped great swallows of water, spilling some of it down his shirtfront.

The guard eyed him speculatively.

Spats noticed the guard's gaze. "Just had a nice nap," he lied, trying vainly to keep his voice casual.

"You'll have a long nap directly," the guard reminded him.

Blind panic boiled up within him at the words. His last day. In just a few hours he would be dead. Fear increased in him in cold stifling waves. A definite sensation of ice chilled him. He began to tremble all over as if he had the ague. His thoughts became vague beyond endur-ance and his craven fear intensified to the point where it would break beyond all control.

He tried to steady himself. If this kept up he would go to the chair like a blubbering, sniveling rat. He might even have to be carried, for now his legs were so weak that he could hardly stand.

The thought brought some semblance of control back to his dis-traught senses. He thought of the article they would have about him in the papers—"He went to the chair with a smile on his lips." He be-came more calm and even experimented with a smile. Why, what the hell was the matter with him? He was a man, he wasn't scared.

A shadow appeared in front of him. He looked up and noticed a tall, gray-headed man with the garb of the clergy standing by his door.

Deep brown eyes which gleamed with infinite pity shone from the minister's seamed, tan face. The prison chaplain stood at his side.

The prison chaplain said, "I've brought Reverend Brown from one of the city churches to give you a few words of consolation. I thought that perhaps you would like to have one of your own race to spend the last few hours with you."

"Last few hours!" The words seared Spats's mind like tongues of flame. He tried to rise from the chair but his knees buckled together and collapsed under him. His teeth began to chatter and the words "last few hours" raced through his mind like white fire, expelling all other thought. He tried to speak but his tongue stuck to the roof of his mouth.

The guard pushed his chair forward to the minister. Reverend Brown seated himself and moved nearer the bars so that he could be heard without having to raise his voice.

"Mr. Wilson," he began, addressing Spats, "have you got a mother, sir?" Spats trembled visibly.

"If you have," Reverend Brown continued, "she would want you to get right with God this day."

"Stop! Stop!" Spats cried, his voice rising to a shrill yell. "Get away! Get away! I don't want to hear it."

"I'm not trying to make you feel bad, Mr. Wilson," Reverend Brown explained in sterling sincerity. "My heart goes out to you. You're a young man. Perhaps society hasn't given you the breaks that you have deserved. I can't remedy that, I have no control over the machinery of society. Perhaps at times you have wanted to go straight and live according to the word of God, and the callous and ungodly peoples of your environment would not let you.

"But the glory of it all is that there is a forgiving God. He will give you a chance to do better in the next world, a chance to atone for the mistakes you have made in this one—if you only confess Him, my son, if you only confess Him and have faith in Him. Get on your knees, humble your spirit and ask His forgiveness. I'm sure he won't deny it."

"Get away, get away, I say!" Spats yelled, springing to his feet and raising his clenched hand as if he would smash the bars and tear the good minister limb from limb. "Take him away, take him away," he commanded the chaplain standing nearby. "I don't want to hear his sniveling prattle about God."

The chaplain shook his head.

The minister slowly arose from his seat. He placed one hand on the bars and leaned forward trying to look Spats in the eyes. "My son," he said, "I would gladly take your place; your mother, if she is living, would gladly take your place in that chair of death, if this day you would confess God and ask His forgiveness." There was the ring of unalloyed truth in the minister's voice.

Spats flung himself on his bunk and turned his face toward the wall. "I'm a man," he muttered. "I don't need God to go to the chair with me. I didn't have Him when I croaked that lousy meddling dick and I don't need Him now."

A look of infinite sadness spread over the old minister's face. "Son, isn't there anything I can say that may give you comfort in your last few minutes of life? Isn't there anything that will influence you to see the light, and show that you are taking the wrong attitude? Isn't there any way or anything that I can do that will persuade you to take God into your heart before it is too late?" he pleaded.

Spats maintained a sullen silence. The old minister turned away with drooping shoulders and departed. "This is the saddest day of my life. I have failed," he confessed to the chaplain.

The guard resumed his seat eyeing Spats with unveiled contempt. "I'd like to tell you what I think of you," he said.

But Spats didn't hear him. The words "LAST FEW MINUTES OF LIFE" were disseminating through his blood like tiny crystals of ice. He felt numb, drenched with a sense of unspeakable shame. He shouldn't have treated the old minister like he had, he regretted. He should have listened to him politely and after his sermon he should have told him that he confessed God. It wouldn't have hurt him and it would have made the old minister so happy.

But then people reading that he had got religion on his last day would have thought him yellow, and said that he had had to go to God to get the nerve to go to the chair. Nope, he would take his medicine just as it came.

But the words "LAST FEW MINUTES OF LIFE" drew his mind back like great fingers, to the horrible death that awaited him. He could visualize himself sitting in the chair with his head shaved. He could feel the officers strapping his arms down to the metal arms of the chair. He could feel the black cap slipping down over his head, over his eyes.

He sprang from his bunk with a muttered curse on his lips and a driving, haunting fear in his eyes.

Maybe there was some truth in this hereafter stuff, after all. Most of the people of the civilized world believed in some kind of hereafter. And he had scorned the idea, turned down a chance to get in line for a ticket to this everlasting paradise. Now, perhaps he would have to burn through eternity in hell. But then the fact that everybody believed in it didn't prove it to be so. How the hell did they know, anyway?

He began to fight for control as the fear increased within him. He forced all thoughts from his mind by a strenuous exertion of his will. He then rolled a cigarette, his hands moving in short, jerky movements as he exerted great control to keep them from trembling.

He took a dozen deep inhalations before he removed the cigarette from his lips. The smoke tasted like burning straw in his mouth, but after a while it created a sort of dullness in his mind. He threw the cigarette from him and rolled and lit another one.

"What time is it, captain?" he questioned the guard.

The guard took his watch out of his pocket, glanced at it and said, "A quarter to two." He put his watch back in his pocket, folded his arms and maintained a distinct attitude of silence toward Spats.

"I guess they'll be around directly to take me out," Spats remarked. His voice relieved that freezing, gnawing fear that was creeping through his heart and slowly deadening his muscles.

The guard didn't show any inclination to talk.

"You don't have to talk to me, brother," Spats sneered, noticing his attitude.

He rolled and lit another cigarette and slumped down into his chair eyeing the guard through hate-laden eyes.

In a few minutes the officials came and took him out of the cell and marched him across the yard to the little brick house at the end of the road.

Spats walked rigidly erect, like a drunken man trying to keep from staggering. He said a few words to the deputy warden in a snarling whisper through the corner of his mouth. He gave a snort of harsh mirthless laughter, once. And on his lips he wore a frozen, sneering, mocking smile. But in his eyes there was the subtle hint of utter fear.

Ann Petry

On Saturday the Siren
Sounds at Noon

ANN PETRY (1911–   ) achieved wide critical acclaim with her
first novel, *The Street,* a story of life in Harlem told in a realistic
and painfully honest style. The 1946 novel was the first book by
an African American woman to sell over a million copies. Her
other books include *Country Place, The Narrows,* and *Miss Mu-
riel and Other Stories,* as well as several successful children's
books.

Her stories have appeared in *The New Yorker, Redbook,* and
The Crisis, the last of which published one of her earlier short
stories, "On Saturday the Siren Sounds at Noon." Echoing
some of the same issues as *The Street,* "On Saturday the Siren
Sounds at Noon" is published here for the first time since its
original appearance in *The Crisis* magazine in December 1943.

Mrs. Petry still lives in the same small Connecticut town
where her family once owned a drugstore, and where she
worked as a licensed pharmacist.

AT FIVE MINUTES of twelve on Saturday there was only a handful of
people waiting for the 241st Street train. Most of them were at the far
end of the wooden platform where they could look down on the street
and soak up some of the winter sun at the same time.

A Negro in faded blue overalls leaned against a post at the upper end of the station. He was on his way to work in the Bronx. He had decided to change trains above ground so he could get a breath of fresh air. In one hand he carried a worn metal lunch box.

As he waited for the train, he shifted his weight from one foot to the other. He watched the way the sun shone on the metal tracks—they gleamed as far as he could see in the distance.

The train's worn 'em shiny, he thought idly. Trains run up and down 'em so many times they're shined up like a spittoon. He tried to force his thoughts to the weather. Spittoons. Why'd I have to think about something like that?

He had worked in a hotel barroom once as a porter. It was his job to keep all the brass shining. The doorknobs and the rails around the bar and the spittoons. When he left the job he took one of the spittoons home with him. He used to keep it shined up so that it reflected everything in his room. Sometimes he'd put it on the windowsill and it would reflect in miniature the church across the street.

He'd think about spring—it was on the way. He could feel it in the air. There was a softness that hadn't been there before. Wish the train would hurry up and come, he thought. He turned his back on the tracks to avoid looking at the way they shone. He stared at the posters on the walls of the platform. After a few minutes he turned away impatiently. The pictures were filled with the shine of metal, too. A silver punch bowl in a Coca-Cola ad and brass candlesticks that fairly jumped off a table. A family was sitting around the table. They were eating.

He covered his eyes with his hands. That would shut it out until he got hold of himself. And it did. But he thought he felt something soft clinging to his hands and he started trembling.

Then the siren went off. He jumped nearly a foot when it first sounded. That old air raid alarm, he thought contemptuously—always putting it off on Saturdays. Yet it made him uneasy. He'd always been underground in the subway when it sounded. Or in Harlem where the street noises dulled the sound of its wail.

Why, that thing must be right on top of this station, he thought. It started as a low, weird moan. Then it gained in volume. Then it added a higher screaming note, and a little later a low, louder blast. It was everywhere around him, plucking at him, pounding at his ears. It was inside of him. It was his heart and it was beating faster and harder and faster and harder. He bent forward because it was making a pounding pressure against his chest. It was hitting him in the stomach.

He covered his ears with his hands. The lunch box dangling from one hand nudged against his body. He jumped away from it, his nerves raw, ready to scream. He opened his eyes and saw that it was the lunch box that had prodded him and he let it drop to the wooden floor.

It's almost as though I can smell that sound, he told himself. It's the smell and the sound of death—cops and ambulances and fire trucks—

A shudder ran through him. Fire. It was Monday that he'd gone to work extra early. Lilly Belle was still asleep. He remembered how he'd frowned down at her before he left. Even sleeping she was untidy and bedraggled.

The kids were asleep in the front room. He'd stared at them for a brief moment. He remembered having told Lilly Belle the night before, "Just one more time I come home and find you ain't here and these kids by themselves, and I'll kill you—"

All she'd said was, "I'm goin' to have me some fun—"

Whyn't they shut that thing off, he thought. I'll be deaf. I can't stand it. It's breaking my eardrums. If only there were some folks near here. He looked toward the other end of the platform. He'd walk down that way and stand near those people. That might help a little bit.

The siren pinioned him where he was when he took the first step. He'd straightened up and it hit him all over so that he doubled up again like a jackknife.

The sound throbbed in the air around him. It'll stop pretty soon, he thought. It's got to. But it grew louder. He couldn't see the tracks anymore. When he looked again they were pulsating to the sound and his eardrums were keeping time to the tracks.

"God in Heaven," he moaned, "make it stop." And then in alarm, "I can't even hear my own voice. My voice is gone."

If I could stop thinking about fire—fire—fire. Standing there with the sound of the siren around him, he could see himself coming home on Monday afternoon. It was just about three o'clock. He could see himself come out of the subway and start walking down Lenox Avenue, past the bakery on the corner. He stopped and bought a big bag of oranges from the pushcart on the corner. Eloise, the little one, liked oranges. They were kind of heavy in his arms.

He went in the butcher store near 133rd Street. He got some hamburger to cook for dinner. It seemed to him that the butcher looked at him queerly and he could see himself walking along puzzling about it.

Then he turned into 133rd Street. Funny. Standing here with this noise tearing inside him, he could see himself as clearly as though by some miracle he'd been transformed into another person. The bag of oranges, the packages of meat—the meat was soft, and he could feel it cold through the paper wrapping, and the oranges were hard and knobby. And his lunch box was empty and it was swinging light from his hand.

There he was turning the corner, going down his own street. There were little knots of people talking. They nodded at him. Sarah Lee who ran the beauty shop—funny she'd be out in the street gossiping this time of day. And Mrs. Smith who had the hand laundry. Why, they were all there. He turned and looked back at them. They turned their eyes away from him quickly when he looked at them.

He could see himself approaching the stoop at 219. Cora, the janitress, was leaning against the railing, her fat hips spilling over the top. She was talking to the priest from the church across the way. He felt excitement stir inside him. The priest's hands were bandaged and there was blood on the bandages.

The woman next door was standing on the lower step. She saw him first and she nudged Cora.

"Oh—" Cora stopped talking.

The silence alarmed him. "What's the matter?" he asked.

"There was a fire," Cora said.

He could see himself running up the dark narrow stairs. Even the hall was filled with the smell of dead smoke. The door of his apartment sagged on its hinges. He stepped inside and stood perfectly still, gasping for breath. There was nothing left but charred wood and ashes. The walls were gutted and blackened. That had been the radio, and there was a piece of what had been a chair. He walked into the bedroom. The bed was a twisted mass of metal. The spittoon had melted down. It was a black rim with a shapeless mass under it. Everywhere was the acrid, choking smell of burned wood.

He turned to find Cora watching him.

"The children—" he said, "and Lilly Belle—"

"Lilly Belle's all right," she said coldly. "The kids are at Harlem Hospital. They're all right. Lilly Belle wasn't home."

He could see himself run blindly down the stairs. He ran to the corner and in exciting agony to the Harlem Hospital. All the way to the hospital his feet kept saying, "Wasn't home." "Wasn't home." "Wasn't home."

They let him see the kids at the hospital. They were covered with clean white bandages, lying in narrow white cots.

First time they've ever been really clean, he thought bitterly. A crisp, starched nurse told him that they'd be all right.

"Where's the little one?" he asked. "Where's Eloise?"

The nurse's eyes widened. "Why, she's dead," she stammered.

"Where is she?"

He could see himself leaning over the small body in the morgue. He still had the oranges and the meat and the empty lunch box in his arms. When he went back to the ward, Lilly Belle was there with the kids.

She was dressed in black. Black shoes and stockings and a long black veil that billowed around her when she moved. He was thinking about her black clothes so that he only half heard her as she told him she'd just gone around the corner that morning, and that she'd expected to come right back.

"But I ran into Alice—and when I came back," she licked her lips as though they were suddenly dry.

He could see himself going to work. The next day and all the other days after that. Going to the hospital every day. Living in an apartment across the hall. The neighbors brought in furniture for them. He could hear the neighbors trying to console him.

He could see himself that very morning. He'd slept late because on Saturdays he went to work later than on other days. When he woke up he heard voices. And as he listened they came clear to his ears like a victrola record or the radio.

Cora was talking. "You ain't never been no damn good. And if you don't quit runnin' to that bar with that dressed up monkey and stayin' away from here all day long, I'm goin' to tell that poor fool you're married to where you were when your kid burned up in here." She said it fast as though she wanted to get it out before Lilly Belle could stop her. "You walkin' around in mournin' and everybody but him knows you locked them kids in here that day. They was locked in—"

Lilly Belle said something he couldn't hear. He heard Cora's heavy footsteps cross the kitchen. And then the door slammed.

He got out of bed very quietly. He could see himself as he walked barefooted across the room. The black veil was hanging over a chair. He ran it through his fingers. The soft stuff clung and caught on the rough places on his hands as though it were alive.

Lilly Belle was in the kitchen reading a newspaper. Her dark hands were silhouetted against its pink outside sheets. Her hair wasn't combed and she had her feet stuck in a pair of run-over mules. She barely glanced at him and then went on reading the paper.

He watched himself knot the black veil tightly around her throat. He pulled it harder and harder. Her lean body twitched two or three times and then it was very still. Standing there he could feel again the cold hard knot that formed inside him when he saw that she was dead.

If the siren would only stop. It was vibrating inside him—all the soft tissues in his stomach and in his lungs were moaning and shrieking with agony. The station trembled as the train approached. As it drew nearer and nearer the siren took on a new note—a louder, sharper, sobbing sound. It was talking. "Locked in. They were locked in." "Smoke poisoning. Third degree burns." "Eloise? Why, she's dead." "My son, don't grieve. It will probably change your wife." "You know, they say the priest's hands were all bloody where he tried to break down the door." "My son, my son—"

The train was coasting toward the station. It was coming nearer and nearer. It seemed to be jumping up and down on the track. And as it thundered in, it took up the siren's moan. "They were locked in. They were locked in."

Just as it reached the edge of the platform, he jumped. The wheels ground his body into the gleaming silver of the tracks.

The air was filled with noise—the sound of the train and the wobble of the siren as it died away to a low moan. Even after the train stopped, there was a thin echo of the siren in the air.

Hughes Allison

Corollary

HUGHES ALLISON (1908–74) began his career as a ghostwriter of
novels and later wrote radio scripts and plays. His 1937 play,
The Trial of Dr. Beck, the story of a black physician on trial for
the murder of his wife, the founder of a hair care empire, was
the first play by an African American to be produced by the
Federal Theatre on Broadway.

The short story presented here was written in response to a
statement made by Frederick Dannay, publisher of *Ellery
Queen's Mystery Magazine,* at a Mystery Writers of America
meeting that there was no subject matter considered taboo for
publication in the magazine. Allison approached Dannay in the
hotel bar and challenged him to print a serious crime story, set
in the Negro community, with a Negro as the main character.
The result was the groundbreaking "Corollary," published in
July 1948 and winner of an honorable mention in *EQMM*'s
third annual contest.

In a letter to the editors that accompanied the story, Allison
wondered, "Could tough, hard-boiled Sam Spade or suave,
gentlemanly Ellery Queen enter that dark, costly museum
room [of Negro culture] and single out the culprits? While it's
possible they could, it's improbable they really would. For neither . . . is equipped to think with his skin. Moreover,
merely apprehending the room's culprits is not the most important factor involved." The impact of black culture on crime

and its detection is a subject that would be explored by other black writers of mystery in the decades that followed.

JOE HILL should have been assigned to the case three months before its bolder principals accidentally tangled with a radio patrol car and were arrested that Wednesday morning in Oldhaven. But neither Inspector Duffy nor Chief Richard Belden had ordered Joe assigned to the case in the beginning. By that Wednesday it was late. Already a pernicious web—fashioned out of mutilation, terror, and indecision—had begun to coil itself around four unsuspecting persons: a pair of stupid, elderly grandparents; an alert but inexperienced child; and a sincere, though too-exacting, schoolteacher.

It was late Wednesday afternoon, a few hours after the arrests had been announced in the public press, that Joe was finally summoned to the Chief's third-floor office.

Belden, seated behind his desk, was in high humor. "Huh!" he growled. "One guess! What's in the cell block?"

Joe grinned, "The cure for a three months' headache."

"Right! But they're punks," Belden declared. "I've had a good look at 'em. And only one thing the papers have said in the last three months really fits."

"What's that, Chief?" Joe asked.

"Their handle—'the Bandit Quintet.' "

"The Chief means," Inspector Duffy explained, "we've caught ourselves five yellow jerks with a yen to sing."

Joe said, "With or without persuasion?"

"Without," Duffy replied. "And plenty loud, in a good key, for as long as we want."

Belden said, "I've been a cop for a long time. So I've seen lots of talkers. I don't pretend to know what makes 'em do it. But I do know how to handle 'em. Treat 'em easy, take your time, let 'em spout—and comb every bit of what comes out for leads."

"That's the play all the way," Duffy agreed.

"Not a single one of this Quintet gang seems to have a previous record," the Chief said. "That may be why our stools failed to produce. But just the same. Dig—easy and gently—for crook connections. Lots of cases are still wide-open. Joe, you draw the chauffeur. Says his name

is Albert Johnson. Claims he's a powerful church-going fellow. Still, he
—watch him, huh?"

"I'll watch him," Joe promised.

Duffy said, "How about the men to work with Hill, Chief?"

One of the telephones on Belden's desk jangled.

"Give him boys with Middle Ward experience," Belden said. Picking up the phone, he growled, "Yes?"

In an aside to Joe, Duffy said, "Make it Shaw from Homicide, Carlton from the Bandit Squad—"

Chuckling at the phone, Belden told it, "Sure. Put *him* on."

"—Swenson from Auto—" Duffy continued.

"Ah! Mr. Prosecutor!" Belden exclaimed at the phone.

"—and Goldberg from Identification," Duffy concluded, matching
the grin on Belden's face.

"We're happy as kids about it!" Belden told the phone. "Right this
minute Detective Hill's on his way to the cell block for a session with
their chauffeur."

Joe looked at Duffy.

"Take a peep at all five of 'em," the Inspector told him. "Skip the
murders for the time being. Just touch your man for the overall number
of stickups. Then come back here."

Joe had seen the same kind of scared, repentant men before. They were
in separate cells. Four were pale-faced nonentities who stared at him as
he slowly walked past their barred cages, out of solemn eyes that begged
for pity. The fifth man—the chauffeur—was exactly like his confeder-
ates. Except that his skin was black.

Stepping close to the bars, Joe said, "I'm Detective Hill."

A trace of surprise showed through the worry, shame, and fear
etched in the ebony face.

"I knowed," the chauffeur said, "a few of our folks in Oldhaven was
cops. But I thought they was all just street cops."

Joe said, "They tell me you're in a little trouble, Johnson."

The man nodded. "Th' Chief—he come to see me. I said I'd talk."

"Chief Belden's not a bad fellow to talk to."

"I seen you now. So—Well, our people is always so far behind. I was
just trying to—to catch up a little bit."

"No regular work?"

"I had been chauffeuring for a rich woman—named Mrs. Stevens.
But th' job—it was running out. And I met them other four."

Joe smiled encouragingly. "Yes. The others."

"You see—it was like this," the chauffeur said. "Mrs. Stevens—she's a very old lady. She got sick. Before she let 'em take her to th' hospital, she said to me, 'Albert, you've been with me such a short time; I didn't make the same provisions for you. Because you're still young and healthy.' Well, that made me—"

Joe interrupted. "Ever pull a holdup all by yourself?"

"Naw, sir! Only with them other four."

"How many jobs did you do?"

"We done—lemme figure. Yeah. Twenty. And I just driv th' car. That's all I done. Ever!"

Backing away from the bars, Joe said, "Johnson, we'll talk again—in a little while. Huh?"

A talker, it would be a long time before the chauffeur's confessional jag wore off. Joe left the cell block.

When he reentered the office, the Chief was still on the phone with the Prosecutor. But joy had vanished. Belden was in a rage, shouting, "Yes, I said th' punks would talk! But they've been on a three-month stickup spree. So how'n hell can we feel 'em for leads if we rush 'em off to that alley-house office you run?"

As the Chief paused, Duffy told Joe, "That Prosecutor's loaded with a tom-cat's nerve. He's pushing us to arraign these five bums—like we'd jugged 'em for loitering!"

"Huh!" Belden yelled at the phone. "I don't have the men to do it that quick. You said *Monday* morning first. Now you switch it to *Saturday* morning—so they'll be in court *by* Monday!"

"He's crazy!" Duffy said.

"You're crazy!" Belden said. "But I'll do it! Now get th' hell off my line!" He jammed the phone in its cradle with a bang.

"Try to be nice to some people!" Duffy said. "Try it!"

"Lowell will do anything to be Governor!" Belden said. "He's after headlines. No skin off *his* political beak if *we* mess it up."

Duffy said, "Well, we just got to try and deliver—"

"You listen!" Belden interrupted. "I want the last scrap of information pumped out of that mob. By Saturday morning too! See?"

Duffy said, "Yes, sir."

"You'll proceed from the first to the last stickup. And—"

"In *that* order?" Duffy asked, interrupting.

"Huh! We're only the police!" Belden said. "Will a spread in Sunday's papers land us in the Governor's mansion?"

Duffy said, "Oh! *Lowell* wants it that way."

"Huh! So no sleep for the men you put on it till it's all tied and wrapped up. Understand?"

Homicide's Shaw, Bandit's Carlton, Auto's Swenson, and Identification's Goldberg—the men Inspector Duffy had named to work with Joe in connection with processing the Quintet chauffeur for arraignment—were agreed that meeting the Prosecutor's deadline was one thing. It was another thing, they said, not to miss an important lead in the insane race to beat the exacting hands of the Prosecutor's arbitrary watch. Something would go wrong.

Four other crews—each a duplicate in unit composition—stood with Joe and his particular colleagues and listened grimly to Duffy's procedural instructions.

"Yes, you gotta finish this job by Saturday morning," the Inspector said. "And if you think you can skip being thorough, think some more. See? Comb every word these punks speak, run down every name, every place they mention. For leads. Lots of cases are still wide-open. At all times," he continued, "keep our five guests separated. Be informal, gentle, sympathetic. They'll cooperate. First, let 'em spill their guts. Then ease 'em into handing you the date and location of their first robbery. Clear that with me, so that all of you will be certain about that point. Same procedure with murder. Next, get the overall number of jobs they did together. Then work forward. Get the relevant, material details of each successive crime: holdup and/or robbery-murder. End with the last stickup. See?"

The processing began at seven o'clock Wednesday night.

The chauffeur insisted upon addressing himself only to Joe, who had to carry the interview. But there were no pointed questions during this stage of the game. Johnson just rambled, naming personalities, places, continuity, and chronology. Goldberg jotted down the man's more pertinent statements. At 11 P.M. Joe went to Duffy, told him the culprit's recollection of the first robbery's date and location.

"He still maintains," Joe added, "there were twenty jobs in all."

"Those three points—date, location, total jobs—check."

"Five murders. They occurred during the sixth, eighth, tenth, fifteenth, and eighteenth robberies."

"That checks. What about the car?" Duffy said.

"Just one. Belonged to his employer, Mrs. Stevens. She's in Wildwood Hospital—an incurable, he says."

"I'll check on her."

Joe said, "Before each job he'd steal a set of license plates and substitute them for the set registered in the Stevens name."

"Swenson from Auto will check that. After each job the boys looked for him down in the Middle Ward. How come they missed him?"

"When Mrs. Stevens had to go to the hospital, she told him he could use a room in her apartment."

"He'd hole up there after a job. What about his dough?"

"He says he put most of it in the Oldhaven Merchants' Bank."

"An original stash for holdup money. Check the bank first thing in the morning. Where'd he spend the rest?"

"Says he gave some to his church."

"Forget it. Where else?"

"Girls. Goldberg has their names. He'd pick 'em up in the Mattox Hotel, a place run by a woman named Big Rose."

"Goldberg is Identification. I'll have him check the women for records and send Shaw to check the hotel. That's a Middle Ward dump, Joe. Too bad we couldn't spare you when this case first got going. Ten to one, you'd have done what the other boys' faces didn't let them do —pick up Johnson's trail. Maybe you'd have run into him there—at the Mattox—before all the killings started."

Joe said, "Water over the dam now."

"Yeah. I'm going to have Carlton round up witnesses. Need 'em for lineups. You check his room in the Stevens place. Take a squad car. Collect his clothes."

When Joe returned to Headquarters, after a look at the Stevens apartment, he had the chauffeur identify the particular garments he had worn during the commission of each crime; each piece of apparel was then labeled with a date, time notation, and a stated location. Next, Joe turned his attention to a long stream of witnesses who viewed the Bandit Quintet in intermittent lineups. He visited the bank, made notes on deposits and withdrawals.

Late Thursday afternoon, during a joint conference with the five processing detective contingents, the Inspector said, "Speed it up! Get 'em out there where the action occurred. Let 'em show you how they did it—in front of a camera. Tomorrow—that's Friday—and not a second later than 4 P.M., we got to let the stenographers start taking down their formal statements. Move!"

Sleep had been a stranger to Joe on Wednesday night. Sleep and Joe remained strangers Thursday night. He kept himself going with cigarettes, sandwiches, and lots of black coffee. Friday afternoon, at ten minutes to four, he marched up to Duffy.

"We have the details and the photographed 'reenactments' of Johnson's part in nineteen successive crimes," Joe announced.

"Well?" Duffy said, frowning.

"We didn't have time to run him through job number twenty."

Duffy grinned. "Okay. The cake's yours."

"Huh?"

"The Prosecutor's really after the details on the five killings. He'll schedule the easiest and juiciest murder for quick trial, so he can grab lots of headlines. Couple of crews had to cram, skip—to get in the murders. They're three and four jobs short, Joe."

"Then I don't get the dunce cap."

"Naw. You and your boys just trot Johnson through the nineteen jobs and he'll sing the whole tune to that last stickup by ear. The Prosecutor ain't worrying about what *we* miss. It's nearly four o'clock. Get going, Joe."

Each processing detective crew herded its own Quintet culprit up to the fourth floor of Headquarters and into an enormous, open, desk-strewn, rectangular room whose facilities were officially the property of the rank and file members of the Homicide Squad. Four of the Quintet were placed, separately, in the big rectangle's corners. Joe, his crew, and a stenographer gave Johnson a chair near a cluster of battered desks in the very middle of the room. He began making his formal statement Friday at precisely 4 P.M.

It was a slow, tedious task: boring, unexciting. They started with the first crime. Deleting extraneous matter as they went along, they retained as best they could the essential, relevant facts which were material to Johnson's own acts and words, and such other acts and words as occurred or were spoken in his presence. When an original copy and a stack of carbons were typed, Goldberg read the contents aloud to the chauffeur. Johnson read it aloud, then signed the confession. Joe and his colleagues provided witnessing signatures. A notary's seal was affixed to the document. And the procedure began again in connection with crime number two.

It went on and on. The detectives and culprits alike drank coffee, chewed sandwiches, lit one cigarette from another, and wistfully toyed with the idea of climbing in a bed.

Inspector Duffy roared, "Chief Belden's at home. He just phoned me. He's been in constant contact with Prosecutor Lowell. They'll be arriving here at Headquarters in a little while. Speed it up! How far off is Saturday morning?"

Gradually, the glare from the room's blazing lights turned the working men's haggard eyes into dull rubies. Their heads ached. Joe and his crew finished with Johnson's nineteenth statement.

When Homicide's Shaw said it was already Saturday morning, Joe glanced at his wristwatch. It was 1 A.M.

Bandit's Carlton said, "I'm dead on my feet."

"These boys," Shaw said, "just didn't mix with other crooks. They ain't handed us a single lead yet. Whiz this last one along."

Carlton said, "Joe, take a squint at that Wednesday's 'squeal sheet.' Go by that—and get this job over with!"

Glancing at a piece of paper, Joe said, "Give us the facts on your last job, Johnson."

Johnson said, "Tuesday night, I stole a set of license plates. Then I went in a phone booth and called the poolroom where them other boys was at. We got a job set for next day."

"Go on," Joe said.

"I went straight home," Johnson said, "and got in bed. Next morning—Wednesday—I got up at eight o'clock. I was by myself. I never took nobody to my room—'cause ol' Mrs. Stevens trusted me. Once, her lawyer—Mr. Colbax Todd—writ a 'portant paper for her. She told me what was in it, axted me to put my name on it. So she musta trusted me. And I—"

Joe interrupted. Irrelevancies were creeping in. "You got up at 8 A.M."

Johnson said, "That paper never took care of me—lak it did them others. So I let them other boys talk me into—"

Joe interrupted again. "You got up at eight o'clock!"

"All that," Johnson said, "was before Mrs. Stevens went to th' hospital."

Shaw said, "What did you do Wednesday after eight?"

"I fixed a meal," Johnson said, "and et it. I was nervous. So I went and got th' car and driv to th' Middle Ward."

"Take time out there to talk to anybody?" Joe asked.

"I seen Prophet Hamid. He was right in front of his temple on Nickle Street. I knowed him. So when he called me, I stopped th' car.

He axted me would I go and git an ol' man by th' name of Tom Turner. And I said yes. I went."

Joe said, "Anybody go with you? Where does Turner live?"

"I was by myself. He live on Dawkins Place. I don't know th' number. I just knows th' house. I driv there. Ol' man Turner was just coming out his front door. I driv him to th' Prophet's temple. I never got out. I driv to Oldhaven Park and done what I always done in there —switched license plates on th' car."

"Go on," Joe said.

"Then I driv to Commerce Square. A loan shop we was going to rob was there. I parked a block off. Them four other boys walked past and went in th' loan shop. They run out, jumped in th' car, and I started it. A block off we run into a radio car with two cops in it. They was awful mad at us for hitting 'em. They found out we was robbers. So they 'rested all five of us."

Joe said, "It was 11 A.M. Just who is Tom Turner?"

"An ol' man what used to go to th' church where I goes at."

Shaw said, "What about Prophet Hamid?"

"Him?" Johnson said. "Everybody down in th' Middle Ward knows *him*. I seen him 'round lots."

"In the Mattox—for instance?" Shaw asked. "With Big Rose?"

"Yeah. He make lak he know what you thinking 'bout. I give him plenty chances to tell me my mind. He's just a lot of big mouf."

Shaw said, "This wraps it up, boys. I'll call Duffy." He did.

Duffy said, "You fellows all through?"

" 'Cept for one thing," Johnson said.

"Yeah?" Duffy said. "What's that?"

"I b'lieves," Johnson replied, "I deserves a break—'cause I just ain't what you can call *bad*. Before I met up with them four other boys, I had never been in no real trouble. Mrs. Stevens—she took very sick. She said to me, 'Albert, you'll need another job. Use the car to look for one if you like.' So I—"

Interrupting, Duffy said, "She didn't mean for you to use her car in twenty stickups and five murders."

"I never done th' killings," the chauffeur said. "I just driv th' car. For them other boys. Before that I had a good record. Axt my pastor, Reverend G. J. Ball. Axt Mrs. Stevens."

Duffy said, "She's comatose."

"She's *what?*" Johnson said.

"In a coma. Unconscious," Duffy explained.

"Oh," Johnson said. "But Detective Hill—he know th' real thing what made me rob folks. And I think he should help git me a break."

Duffy said, "First, give him a break. Sign this last statement."

"Okay. Sure! Didn't I sign them other statements?"

At 2 A.M. Joe got in an elevator. When he stepped out on the first floor, Chief Belden was waiting to go up.

"The arraignment is set for 1 P.M., Monday," Belden said. "You look busted up."

Joe was a big man: six feet one inch in height, with two hundred pounds of solid muscle appropriately strung along an excellently developed frame. Ordinarily, his eyes were a shade of brown in complete consonance with the chestnut hue of his skin. But now his eyes were bloodshot, his face a mat of unshaven black bristles, and his huge physique literally drooped.

He said, "I *feel* busted up too."

"I know," Belden said. "You needn't come in till noon, Monday."

Wearily, Joe stumbled out to the sidewalk in front of Headquarters just as several cars pulled up to the curb. Prosecutor Elwood Lowell and some of his assistants got out. A taxicab rounded a corner. Joe signaled its driver.

He got in the cab. "The Wallace Thurman Houses—Unit Four—on the far side of the Middle Ward."

Pulling away from the curb, the taxi driver said, "What'd they have you down to Headquarters for, huh, buddy?"

Tired, on edge, Joe snatched a gold-plated shield out of his pocket. Sticking it over the driver's shoulder and under the man's nose, he said, "Cop! Central Bureau. See? I'm in a hurry."

The tiny three-room apartment on the fourth floor of the model housing development where Joe maintained bachelor quarters was a welcome sight. Joe took one look at himself in the bathroom mirror. Then he stumbled into the bedroom and collapsed across the bed without removing anything except his hat.

The telephone awakened him. Rolling over, he picked up the jangling instrument and heard Chief Belden's voice say: "Lad, Joe, my boy! This is a helluva crime, and I should be eternally incarcerated for committing it. But you've got to come back to Headquarters. Right away."

"Huh?" Joe grunted. "What time is it?"

"Four A.M.," Belden replied. "I know you just left here. But listen:

an old-fashioned schoolteacher, named Middlesexton, brought a little colored kid down here just now. The kid says she don't trust white cops. Her teacher backs her up about that. If it wasn't for that teacher —wait'll you see her—we'd take the box."

Joe said, "Box?"

"Yes. The kid's got something in a box."

"There're ten other Negro cops in Oldhaven," Joe said.

"Yeah! In uniform," Belden said. "You know they can't—get th' hell down here, Detective Hill!"

"Yes, sir," Joe said, adding, "as soon as I put on my hat!"

Luck brought a cab for Joe in ten minutes. At fifteen minutes to five Saturday morning he entered Chief Belden's office where he found the Chief, a freshly shaven Inspector Duffy, Prosecutor Elwood Lowell, and two other people. One was a gray-haired little old lady, dressed in a style years and years out of date, whose chalk-white countenance was a combination of grim sternness and prim stubbornness. The other was a very small black girl. She was shabbily clothed, but clean. Her eyes were big, round, packed with frank suspicion, and jammed with naked fear. With trembling hands she clutched a package about five inches long, three inches wide, two inches deep—wrapped in white paper, tied with a green string.

The Chief was seated behind his desk. Duffy and the Prosecutor occupied chairs near Belden. Their faces seemed unusually pink. The child and the little old lady sat side by side in straight-back chairs against one of the room's walls. The little old lady favored Joe's rumpled clothes, bearded face, and red eyes with one glance. She reacted unfavorably.

Looking at the little old lady, the child said, "He's colored. But is he a real policeman? He don't wear clothes lak none."

"He *doesn't* wear clothes *like one,* June," the old lady replied.

"Yes, ma'am," the child said. *"Doesn't—like—one."*

The little old lady fixed Chief Belden with a stern stare. "Is this the person we've been waiting for?"

Belden gulped, sputtering, "Er—madam—he—"

"Miss Middlesexton, please."

"Yes, ma'am," Belden said. "Miss Middlesexton."

Duffy said, "This person—as Miss Middlesexton calls Detective Hill —has been continuously at work since Wednesday afternoon. He hasn't had time to bathe, shave, or put on clean clothing."

The Inspector had addressed the Chief who regained enough composure to say, "Detective Hill, ma'am, is a graduate of a most reputable university where he was a high-ranking student and an ace athlete. He won—and I do mean *won*—a post in our Department when he was twenty-two years old. He spent seven and a half years in uniform before we had the good sense to upgrade him to plainclothes status. For more than a year now he's been a member of my own personal organization, the Central Bureau."

"And we think," Duffy added, "he's a nicely balanced piece of physical and mental machinery."

"June," Miss Middlesexton told the child, "I'm satisfied that this man is an authentic officer. You may tell him your story."

Belden said, "Ma'am, let's hear a word from you first."

"Thank you," Miss Middlesexton said. "June, whose last name is Jones, is a second-grade pupil of mine at Public School Twenty. Early Friday morning she came to my desk and asked me to escort her to a policeman, adding that he must be colored. Unfortunately, Chief Belden, some Middle Ward children are afraid of—"

Belden said hastily, "Please continue, ma'am."

"I didn't care to become involved in a trifling matter," Miss Middlesexton said. "I demanded that June tell me why she needed a policeman."

"She wouldn't talk?" Belden said.

Miss Middlesexton nodded. "I know now I was too exacting. At one o'clock this morning June rang my doorbell at 54 Wilson Avenue."

Belden interrupted. "Where does June live?"

The child said, "Sixty-eight Dawkins Place. Top floor. Rear."

Belden leaned forward. "Miss Middlesexton, June is a mere child. Dawkins Place and Wilson Avenue are five miles apart. How'd she know where you live? How'd she get there?"

"Once a semester for the past thirty years," Miss Middlesexton explained, "I entertain my school charges in my home. Of course, on those occasions, I escort them there. June attended the last party a month ago. I presume she—"

Looking at Joe, June interrupted. "I walked to where she lives at."

Miss Middlesexton said, "June showed me the contents of the box—" The little old lady swallowed hard, her pale face turning gray.

Belden smiled at June. "Let's see what's in your box. Hmmn?"

The child looked at Joe.

"Chief Belden," he said, "is a nice man. Cross my heart!"

The child got out of her chair and sat on the floor. She untied her package's green string, stripped off its white paper, holding the underside up so Joe could see it.

Wearily, he sat down on the floor beside the child. "Letters apparently cut out of newspapers," he said, "are pasted here, saying, 'Talk only to the Lord's True Messenger.'"

Duffy got out of his chair. "It's an ordinary matchbox," he said. "Slide it open, kid."

As enormous tears welled up in her eyes, the child said, "Pa Tom never come home Wednesday night. Nor Thursday night. Nor before I slipped off from Ma Grace, and—and—"

Miss Middlesexton said, "I understand June's parents were killed some time ago in an automobile accident. She lives with an elderly pair of grandparents. Her maternal grandparents."

Duffy said, "Come on, kid. Open the box."

The child said, "There was another box—before this one. Me and Ma Grace found it Thursday morning laying on th' floor in th' hall—jes' outside th' door. Ma Grace acted real scared. 'Chile,' she told me, 'don't you talk to nobody 'bout this!' When I come back from school, Ma Grace was laying on her bed, crying, moaning, and praying to God to tell her what to do. Friday morning I found this here box. Pa Tom—he was still gone. So I never tole Ma Grace I had done found it. Miss Middlesexton—she's white. But I trusts her. So I axted her to help me."

Joe said, "Pa Tom. Tom. Dawkins Place."

"He my grandpa," the child said. "And that's where I lives at."

Miss Middlesexton said, "Her grandparents are Thomas and Grace Turner."

Belden picked up one of the telephones on his desk. "Rush this," he said. "Steer a prowl to 68 Dawkins Place, top floor, rear flat. Investigate the absence of Thomas Turner."

Miss Middlesexton said, "June, you must—must open it now."

"Yes, ma'am," the child said. Then she slid the box open.

Inspector Duffy said, "Good God!"

"What is it?" Belden said.

Joe said, "A finger. It's black. A piece of cotton is stuck on the spot where it was cut off from—"

He stopped talking because the child had burst into loud hysterical sobs. His weariness seemed to evaporate. Anger rose up inside of him, heating his brain, stimulating it, making bits of images and word pictures rush through his mind. He stayed right where he was—on the floor—and took the screaming little girl in his arms, cradling her, rocking with her from side to side.

He was only half aware that Miss Middlesexton had seated herself beside him to help soothe the child with a woman's voice and hand. He hardly noticed the routine fashion with which Belden and Duffy and Prosecutor Elwood Lowell were handling the telephones on the Chief's desk—summoning Homicide Squad Lieutenant O'Hara, photographers, fingerprint technicians, an Assistant Police Surgeon, Prosecutor's Investigators. Joe gave practically all his attention to the assembly of image and word fragments so that he could examine the result for a clue to what he knew would be missing.

He heard Belden saying, "Joe! Joe! Snap out of it!"

"Yes, sir." He looked at his wristwatch. It said 5:45 A.M.

"This is your case, Joe," Belden said. "Looks like a nasty one."

Duffy said, "Joe needs rest."

One of the telephones on the Chief's desk jangled. When Belden replaced the instrument, he said, "Prowl car boys reporting on the trip to Dawkins Place. They found another box outside the Turners' hall door. They broke into the flat and found Grace Turner—she was very old—a D-O-A."

"D-O-A?" Miss Middlesexton said. "What does that mean?"

Duffy glanced at the child whom Joe was still cradling in his arms. She had quieted down. "Do it mean," she said, "that Ma Grace done been scared so—she's dead?"

"D-O-A," Duffy told Miss Middlesexton, "means dead on arrival."

"Frightened into her grave!" the little old lady exclaimed. "Can't you *do* something?"

Joe said, "I think I'm on to what it's about, ma'am. I want June to answer a few questions. What work do your grandparents do, June?"

"They worked," the child replied, "a long time ago. But not now. Because of th' Gov'ment checks and my state check."

"Do you mean," Joe said, "that your grandparents get old age pension checks, and that you—"

June interrupted. "Yes, sir. And I'm what they call a 'State Child'— 'cause my parents is dead. Th' state—it gives Pa Tom and Ma Grace money for my keep."

Belden said, "That kind of money isn't big enough for a motive—"

Joe interrupted. "June, where'd your grandparents *used* to work?"

"Pa Tom—he driv th' carriage. Ma Grace—she done th' cooking. It was for a rich lady. Then she got a automobile. And she give up her big estate. And Pa Tom and Ma Grace—they was too old to do much more work. So then my father and mother—they chauffeured and cooked for—"

"Now this is it!" Joe said. "What was the rich lady's name?"

"I don't rightly know her name," the child replied. "Pa Tom and Ma Grace—they got mad at th' lady. Because she said they was too old to work. And Pa Tom wanted th' rich lady to keep th' carriage. But she got th' car. That was how my mother and father was killed—in the car one day, going somewhere. And Pa Tom—he said he never wanted to hear that rich lady's name called in front of his ears."

Joe said, "Where do you go to church, June?"

"I still goes to Reverend G. J. Ball's church. Pa Tom and Ma Grace —they quit going there. Only old people can go where they go. Reverend Ball—he used to come to th' house to axt Pa Tom and Ma Grace to come back to his church. But Pa Tom—he said that all his life he'd been going to Reverend Ball's kind of church and that his kind of church weren't doing our people no good. Reverend Ball—he said no cult was going to help our people either."

"I wonder," Joe said, "if Prosecutor Lowell will telephone a lawyer for us. If the Prosecutor does it, we'll save time."

"Anything," Lowell said. "What's the lawyer's name?"

Duffy said, "Have you got something, Joe?"

"I'll know after the Prosecutor makes that phone call," Joe replied. "His name now. It's in our files. But maybe I can remember it. Bard? Hodge? No. Rod? Doesn't fit."

"You'd better use the files," Belden said.

"I've got it," Joe said. "The name's Colbax Todd."

"Todd?" Prosecutor Lowell said. "What's Colbax Todd got to do with this?"

Joe said, "Ask him if he has a Mrs. Stevens as a client. Ask him if he recently drew up a will for her in which Thomas and Grace Turner appear among the beneficiaries. If so, for what amount?"

Lowell said, "I'll make the call. But I know Todd will insist he has to consult his client before he can give—"

Duffy interrupted. "She's comatose in Wildwood Hospital. Or was. By now, she may be dead."

"Oh!" Lowell said. "Then Todd may—I'll phone him."

"Maybe this'll add up!" Belden exclaimed, motioning Lowell to a phone on his desk.

When Lowell put down the instrument, he said, "Todd's client died about five hours ago. She left the Turners an outright bequest of fifty thousand dollars.''

"Okay, Joe," Belden said. "You've got the motive. Now what?"

Joe said, "Can we stage a couple of raids? Simultaneously? And right away?"

"I told you," Belden said, "this was your case. We raid. Now!"

Joe, Belden, and Duffy, riding in the first car of a stream of police vehicles, left Headquarters at 6:45 A.M. The last shades of night were bowing out of the sky and the city was fast discarding sleep for another day of toil and turmoil. The cars kept their sirens silent.

"I've been watching you, Joe," Chief Belden said. "I think this thing's made you mad."

Joe didn't say anything.

The police caravan swung into the section of Oldhaven known as the Middle Ward. It was not at all unlike any other Negro community in any other northern Big City. Most of it was slum area.

Duffy said, "We're on Nickle Street now. So we're almost there."

"The other raiding party, according to you, Joe," Belden said, "is more likely to find Turner than we are."

Duffy said, "As soon as we break in at our end, I'll cover the phones and call Lieutenant O'Hara at the other end of the job."

The car stopped. Belden said, "This place was once a store."

The front of the building before which they stopped had been renovated so that it resembled a combination of sectarian structures: a church, a mosque, a miniature cathedral.

Duffy said, "Give the guys a couple of seconds to get set."

"Pretty early," Belden said. "The door's probably locked."

"There's a bell," Joe said.

"Think he'll try and start something, Joe?" Belden said.

Joe replied, "I hope he does!"

"You keep your head," Belden advised. "No matter how mad you—"

Duffy said, "This is it. Let's go."

Joe rang the bell. A woman opened the door, grasped who the visitors were, and started to back away.

"Just take it easy, sister," Duffy told her. "How many phones in this place?"

"One," the woman said. "It's in the office."

"Where's Hamid?" Belden asked her.

"In the office," the woman replied.

Belden said, "No noise. Get going. Take us there."

The woman led them through a small, dark auditorium. She opened a door. Pushing her inside, they closed the door behind them. A man sat at a desk on which a telephone rested.

Belden said, "Are you Prophet Hamid?"

The man stood up. He was short and very slim. The hair on his head was long, kinky, and reddish. Some of it made a sharp, straight line just under his nose and a Vandyke on his chin. His skin was a freckled saddle-yellow. He wore a black cutaway coat with satin lapels, a clerical collar, striped pants, and shiny black shoes with pointed toes. He looked like a dressed-up bantam rooster.

"May I use your phone?" Duffy said, taking over the instrument so that the man had to step away from the desk.

"You're up early this morning," Belden told the man.

The man said, "We always have an early service on Saturdays."

"That used to be," Belden said. "But no more."

"What do you mean?" the man said. "Just who are you?"

Joe said, "The police."

"You can't come in here like this!" the man exclaimed. "This is a holy place. I'm a holy man!"

"Shut up!" Belden told him.

For a while nobody said anything. The only sound in the room was the hard breathing of the woman. Then there was a knock on the door and Duffy said, "Come in!"

A detective opened the door. "We've combed the place," he said. "Upstairs. In the cellar. We didn't find him."

Belden nodded, waved the detective out of the room, and looked at Duffy. "Phone Lieutenant O'Hara. See what he found."

After Duffy put back the phone, he said, "Joe was right, Chief. O'Hara found Turner, three fingers missing, stashed in the Mattox Hotel. The woman who runs the place—Big Rose—is talking."

Belden said, "Okay, Hamid. Now *you* talk."

"The lot of you!" Hamid said. "Get out of here!"

Joe walked over to Hamid and slapped his face.

Belden said, "For your own sake, Hamid—talk."

Standing close to Hamid, Joe said, "How long have Thomas and Grace Turner been members of your cult?"

"Don't crowd me!" Hamid said.

"Not long enough, huh?" Joe said. "Not long enough for you to work your real racket on them."

"Just how does he do it, Joe?" Duffy asked.

"As soon as old people, like the Turners, fall under the spell of his mumbo-jumbo," Joe said, "he demands the last pieces of property they have in the world—their insurance policies. He uses his temple as a front. By persuasion, by force, by tricks, by any means he can think of, Hamid makes the old people change the beneficiaries originally named in their policies so that when they die the money is bequeathed to his temple. The old people will usually sign any paper he hands them. Occasionally, he has them borrow money on their policies. Frequently, he makes them surrender the policies for their cash value. And *he* pockets the money."

"Hamid," Duffy said, "we've been questioning one of the Quintet Bandits. I mean Albert Johnson. We know that Johnson told you that a wealthy woman, Mrs. Stevens, had named Thomas and Grace Turner in her will. We also know that Johnson told you that Mrs. Stevens was dying. You take it from there, Joe."

"There's a clincher—a big payoff—to Hamid's racket," Joe said. "He cuts the whole hog. He knows his own people—Negroes. He draws his cult membership from the most ignorant, the most superstitious, the most stupid of them. He knows they regard all public institutions—including law-enforcement agencies and the courts—as hostile to their interests. So he inveigles his ancient cultists into signing an agreement giving all they own to his temple."

Duffy said, "Hmmn-huh. When he learned that the Turners were beneficiaries in the Stevens will and Mrs. Stevens was dying, he moved fast."

Moving still closer to Hamid, Joe said, "He got his hands on old man Turner, got Big Rose to stash the man in the Mattox Hotel. But Turner held out. Time was short. Hamid cut off the old man's fingers, one by one. He sent the fingers to Grace Turner to terrorize her into coming to him to beg for mercy."

"Move away from me!" Hamid screamed at Joe.

Joe's right shoulder moved suddenly. His right fist smashed hard against Hamid's mouth. Hamid went down on the floor, mouthing profanity and blood.

Belden said, "Easy, Joe. Easy, boy. Don't lose your head."

Duffy said, "Want to talk now, Hamid? Before Detective Hill really goes to work on you? The Chief may try and stop Hill but I won't!"

Belden said, "Hamid, Mrs. Stevens is dead. Bet you didn't know."

Duffy said, "And guess what? The County Prosecutor is going into the courts to have Tom Turner declared incompetent. The Turners' grandchild will get the Stevens dough."

"She wouldn't have got it," Hamid said, "if the old man had signed!"

"The terrorizing you gave Grace Turner," Belden said, "killed her."

Duffy laughed. "Prosecutor Lowell says we can't make a murder rap stick to you, Hamid. But we insist that he have you indicted for murder. Not long ago he asked us—the police—to do the impossible. We did it. Now we want him to do it. After all, no matter how you did it, you murdered Grace Turner. We want you, Hamid—for murder."

"Tell me just one thing," Hamid said. "Johnson—that chauffeur—didn't know. He said he thought it would be about a thousand dollars. But just how much did that Mrs. Stevens leave the Turners?"

Belden said, "Huh! This is funny. This is going to give this rat a bigger thrill than the chair. Tell him, Joe."

Joe said, "Fifty thousand dollars."

Richard Wright

The Man Who Killed
a Shadow

RICHARD WRIGHT (1908–60) was born in Mississippi and lived
there, and in Memphis, Tennessee; Chicago, Illinois; and New
York City, before immigrating to France in 1946, where he
lived until his death. Wright is best known for the novel *Native
Son,* which was published in 1940 to wide acclaim. *Native Son*
was a best-seller and a Book-of-the-Month Club selection,
making it the first novel by an African American to attain such
mainstream success. Wright wrote other novels, nonfiction,
and short stories as well as the best-selling 1945 autobiography
Black Boy.

The same themes that were explored in *Native Son,* namely
the consequences to society of slavery, segregation, and class-
ism, the implications of such practices for race relations and
justice for African Americans, are also present in "The Man
Who Killed a Shadow," which was published in 1946 in France
and 1949 in the United States. It was later included in Wright's
short story collection *Eight Men,* published posthumously in
1961.

Richard Wright was an inspiration to generations of African
American writers, including Chester Himes, Ralph Ellison,
and James Baldwin.

IT ALL BEGAN long ago when he was a tiny boy who was already used, in a fearful sort of way, to living with shadows. But what were the shadows that made him afraid? Surely they were not those beautiful silhouettes of objects cast upon the earth by the sun. Shadows of that kind are innocent and he loved trying to catch them as he ran along sunlit paths in summer. But there were subtler shadows which he saw and which others could not see: the shadows of his fears. And this boy had such shadows and he lived to kill one of them.

Saul Saunders was born black in a little Southern town, not many miles from Washington, the nation's capital, which means that he came into a world that was split in two, a white world and a black one, the white one being separated from the black by a million psychological miles. So, from the very beginning, Saul, looking timidly out from his black world, saw the shadowy outlines of a white world that was unreal to him and not his own.

It so happened that even Saul's mother was but a vague, shadowy thing to him, for she died long before his memory could form an image of her. And the same thing happened to Saul's father, who died before the boy could retain a clear picture of him in his mind.

People really never became personalities to Saul, for hardly had he ever got to know them before they vanished. So people became for Saul symbols of uneasiness, of a deprivation that evoked in him a sense of the transitory quality of life, which always made him feel that some invisible, unexplainable event was about to descend upon him.

He had five brothers and two sisters who remained strangers to him. There was, of course, no adult in his family with enough money to support them all, and the children were rationed out to various cousins, uncles, aunts, and grandparents.

It fell to Saul to live with his grandmother who moved constantly from one small Southern town to another, and even physical landscapes grew to have but little emotional meaning for the boy. Towns were places you lived in for a while, and then you moved on. When he had reached the age of twelve, all reality seemed to him to be akin to his mother and father, like the white world that surrounded the black island of his life, like the parade of dirty little towns that passed forever before his eyes, things that had names but not substance, things that happened and then retreated into an incomprehensible nothingness.

Saul was not dumb or lazy, but it took him seven years to reach the third grade in school. None of the people who came and went in Saul's life had ever prized learning and Saul did likewise. It was quite normal in his environment to reach the age of fourteen and still be in the third grade, and Saul liked being normal, liked being like other people.

Then the one person—his grandmother—who Saul had thought would endure forever passed suddenly from his life, and from that moment on Saul did not ever quite know what to do. He went to work for the white people of the South and the shadowlike quality of his world became terribly manifest, continuously present. He understood nothing of this white world into which he had been thrown; it was just there, a faint and fearful shadow cast by some object that stood between him and a hidden and powerful sun.

He quickly learned that the strange white people for whom he worked considered him inferior; he did not feel inferior and he did not think that he was. But when he looked about him he saw other black people accepting this definition of themselves, and who was he to challenge it? Outwardly he grew to accept it as part of that vast shadow world that came and went, pulled by forces which he nor nobody he knew understood.

Soon all of Saul's anxieties, fears, and irritations became focused upon this white shadow world which gave him his daily bread in exchange for his labor. Feeling unhappy and not knowing why, he projected his misery out from himself and upon the one thing that made him most constantly anxious. If this had not happened, if Saul had not found a way of putting his burden upon others, he would have early thought of suicide. He finally did, in the end, think of killing himself, but then it was too late . . .

At the age of fifteen Saul knew that the life he was then living was to be his lot, that there was no way to rid himself of his plaguing sense of unreality, no way to relax and forget. He was most self-forgetful when he was with black people, and that made things a little easier for him. But as he grew older, he became more afraid, yet none of his friends noticed it. Indeed, many of Saul's friends liked him very much. Saul was always kind, attentive; but no one suspected that his kindness, his quiet, waiting loyalty, came from his being afraid.

Then Saul changed. Maybe it was luck or misfortune; it is hard to tell. When he took a drink of whiskey, he found that it helped to banish the shadows, lessened his tensions, made the world more reasonably three-dimensional, and he grew to like drinking. When he was paid off on a Saturday night, he would drink with his friends and he would feel better. He felt that whiskey made life complete, that it stimulated him. But, of course, it did not. Whiskey really depressed him, numbed him somewhat, reduced the force and number of the shadows that made him tight inside.

When Saul was sober, he almost never laughed in the presence of the white shadow world, but when he had a drink or two he found that he could. Even when he was told about the hard lives that all Negroes lived, it did not worry him, for he would take a drink and not feel too badly. It did not even bother him when he heard that if you were alone with a white woman and she screamed, it was as good as hearing your death sentence, for, though you had done nothing, you would be killed. Saul got used to hearing the siren of the police car screaming in the Black Belt, got used to seeing white cops dragging Negroes off to jail. Once he grew wildly angry about it, felt that the shadows would someday claim him as he had seen them claim others, but his friends warned him that it was dangerous to feel that way, that always the black man lost, and the best thing to do was to take a drink. He did, and in a little while they were all laughing.

One night when he was mildly drunk—he was thirty years old and living in Washington at the time—he got married. The girl was good for Saul, for she too liked to drink and she was pretty and they got along together. Saul now felt that things were not so bad; as long as he could stifle the feeling of being hemmed in, as long as he could conquer the anxiety about the unexpected happening, life was bearable.

Saul's jobs had been many and simple. First he had worked on a farm. When he was fourteen he had gone to Washington, after his grandmother had died, where he did all kinds of odd jobs. Finally he was hired by an old white army colonel as chauffeur and butler and he averaged about twenty dollars every two weeks. He lived in and got his meals and uniform and he remained with the colonel for five years. The colonel too liked to drink, and sometimes they would both get drunk. But Saul never forgot that the colonel, though drunk and feeling fine, was still a shadow, unreal, and might suddenly change toward him.

One day, when whiskey was making him feel good, Saul asked the colonel for a raise in salary, told him that he did not have enough to live on, and that prices were rising. But the colonel was sober and hard that day and said no. Saul was so stunned that he quit the job that instant. While under the spell of whiskey he had for a quick moment felt that the world of shadows was over, but when he had asked for more money and had been refused, he knew that he had been wrong. He should not have asked for money; he should have known that the colonel was a no-good guy, a shadow.

Saul was next hired as an exterminator by a big chemical company and he found that there was something in his nature that made him like going from house to house and putting down poison for rats and mice and roaches. He liked seeing concrete evidence of his work and the dead bodies of rats were no shadows. They were real. He never felt better in his life than when he was killing with the sanction of society. And his boss even increased his salary when he asked for it. And he drank as much as he liked and no one cared.

But one morning, after a hard night of drinking which had made him irritable and high-strung, his boss said something that he did not like and he spoke up, defending himself against what he thought was a slighting remark. There was an argument and Saul left.

Two weeks of job hunting got him the position of janitor in the National Cathedral, a church and religious institution. It was the solitary kind of work he liked; he reported for duty each morning at seven o'clock and at eleven he was through. He first cleaned the Christmas card shop, next he cleaned the library, and his final chore was to clean the choir room.

But cleaning the library, with its rows and rows of books, was what caught Saul's attention, for there was a strange little shadow woman there who stared at him all the time in a most peculiar way. The library was housed in a separate building, and whenever he came to clean it, he and the white woman would be there alone. She was tiny, blond, blue-eyed, weighing about 110 pounds, and standing about five feet three inches. Saul's boss had warned him never to quarrel with the lady in charge of the library. "She's a crackpot," he had told Saul. And naturally Saul never wanted any trouble; in fact, he did not even know the woman's name. Many times, however, he would pause in his work, feeling that his eyes were being drawn to her and he would turn around and find her staring at him. Then she would look away quickly, as though ashamed. "What in hell does she want from me?" he wondered uneasily. The woman never spoke to him except to say good morning and she even said that as though she did not want to say it. Saul thought that maybe she was afraid of him; but how could that be? He could not recall when anybody had ever been afraid of him, and he had never been in any trouble in his life.

One morning while sweeping the floor he felt his eyes being drawn toward her and he paused and turned and saw her staring at him. He did not move, neither did she. They stared at each other for about ten seconds, then she went out of the room, walking with quick steps, as though angry or afraid. He was frightened, but forgot it quickly. "What the hell's wrong with that woman?" he asked himself.

Next morning Saul's boss called him and told him, in a nice, quiet tone—but it made him scared and mad just the same—that the woman in the library had complained about him, had said that he never cleaned under her desk.

"Under her desk?" Saul asked, amazed.

"Yes," his boss said, amused at Saul's astonishment.

"But I clean under her desk every morning," Saul said.

"Well, Saul, remember, I told you she was a crackpot," his boss said soothingly. "Don't argue with her. Just do your work."

"Yes, sir," Saul said.

He wanted to tell his boss how the woman always stared at him, but he could not find courage enough to do so. If he had been talking with his black friends, he would have done so quite naturally. But why talk to one shadow about another queer shadow?

That day being payday, he got his weekly wages and that night he had a hell of a good time. He drank until he was drunk, until he blotted out almost everything from his consciousness. He was getting regularly drunk now whenever he had the money. He liked it and he bothered nobody and he was happy while doing it. But dawn found him broke, exhausted, and terribly depressed, full of shadows and uneasiness, a way he never liked it. The thought of going to his job made him angry. He longed for deep, heavy sleep. But, no, he had a good job and he had to keep it. Yes, he would go.

After cleaning the Christmas card shop—he was weak and he sweated a lot—he went to the library. No one was there. He swept the floor and was about to dust the books when he heard the footsteps of the woman coming into the room. He was tired, nervous, half asleep; his hands trembled and his reflexes were overquick. "So you're the bitch who snitched on me, hunh?" he said irritably to himself. He continued dusting and all at once he had the queer feeling that she was staring at him. He fought against the impulse to look at her, but he could not resist it. He turned slowly and saw that she was sitting in her chair at her desk, staring at him with unblinking eyes. He had the impression that she was about to speak. He could not help staring back at her, waiting.

"Why don't you clean under my desk?" she asked him in a tense but controlled voice.

"Why, ma'am," he said slowly, "I just did."

"Come here and look," she said, pointing downward.

He replaced the book on the shelf. She had never spoken so many words to him before. He went and stood before her and his mind protested against what his eyes saw, and then his senses leaped in wonder. She was sitting with her knees sprawled apart and her dress was drawn halfway up her legs. He looked from her round blue eyes to her white legs whose thighs thickened as they went to a V clothed in tight, sheer, pink panties; then he looked quickly again into her eyes. Her face was a beet red, but she sat very still, rigid, as though she was being impelled into an act which she did not want to perform but was being driven to perform. Saul was so startled that he could not move.

"I just cleaned under your desk this morning," he mumbled, sensing that he was not talking about what she meant.

"There's dust there now," she said sternly, her legs still so wide apart that he felt that she was naked.

He did not know what to do; he was so baffled, humiliated, and frightened that he grew angry. But he was afraid to express his anger openly.

"Look, ma'am," he said in a tone of suppressed rage and hate, "you're making trouble for me!"

"Why don't you do your work?" she blazed at him. "That's what you're being paid to do, you black nigger!" Her legs were still spread wide and she was sitting as though about to spring upon him and throw her naked thighs about his body.

For a moment he was still and silent. Never before in his life had he been called a "black nigger." He had heard that white people used that phrase as their supreme humiliation of black people, but he had never been treated so. As the insult sank in, as he stared at her gaping thighs, he felt overwhelmed by a sense of wild danger.

"I don't like that," he said and before he knew it he had slapped her flat across her face.

She sucked in her breath, sprang up, and stepped away from him. Then she screamed sharply, and her voice was like a lash cutting into his chest. She screamed again and he backed away from her. He felt helpless, strange; he knew what he had done, knew its meaning for him; but he knew that he could not have helped it. It seemed that some part of him was there in that room watching him do things that he should not do. He drew in his breath and for a moment he felt that he could not stand upon his legs. His world was now full of all the shadows he had ever feared. He was in the worst trouble that a black man could imagine.

The woman was screaming continuously now and he was running toward the stairs. Just as he put his foot on the bottom step, he paused and looked over his shoulder. She was backing away from him, toward an open window at the far end of the room, still screaming. Oh God! In her scream he heard the sirens of the police cars that hunted down black men in the Black Belts and he heard the shrill whistles of white cops running after black men and he felt again in one rush of emotion all the wild and bitter tales he had heard of how whites always got the black who did a crime and this woman was screaming as though he had raped her.

He ran on up the steps, but her screams were coming so loud that when he neared the top of the steps he slowed. Those screams would not let him run anymore, they weakened him, tugged and pulled him. His chest felt as though it would burst. He reached the top landing and looked round aimlessly. He saw a fireplace and before it was a neat pile of wood and while he was looking at that pile of wood the screams tore at him, unnerved him. With a shaking hand he reached down and seized in his left hand—for he was left-handed—a heavy piece of oaken firewood that had jagged, sharp edges where it had been cut with an ax. He turned and ran back down the steps to where the woman stood screaming. He lifted the stick of wood as he confronted her, then paused. He wanted her to stop screaming. If she had stopped, he would have fled, but while she screamed all he could feel was a hotness bubbling in him and urging him to do something. She would fill her lungs quickly and deeply and her breath would come out at full blast. He swung down his left arm and hit her a swinging blow on the side of her head, not to hurt her, not to kill her, but to stop that awful noise, to stop that shadow from screaming a scream · that meant death . . . He felt her skull crack and give as she sank to the floor, but she still screamed. He trembled from head to feet. Goddamn that woman . . . Why didn't she stop that yelling? He lifted his arm and gave her another blow, feeling the oaken stick driving its way into her skull. But still she screamed. He was about to hit her again when he became aware that the stick he held was light. He looked at it and found that half of it had broken off, was lying on the floor. But she screamed on, with blood running down her dress, her legs sprawled nakedly out from under her. He dropped the remainder of the stick and grabbed her throat and choked her to stop her screams. That seemed to quiet her; she looked as though she had fainted. He choked her for a long time, not trying to kill her, but just to make sure that she would not scream again and make him wild and hot inside. He was not reacting to the woman, but to the feelings that her screams evoked in him.

The woman was limp and silent now and slowly he took his hands from her throat. She was quiet. He waited. He was not certain. Yes, take her downstairs into the bathroom and if she screamed again no one would hear her . . . He took her hands in his and started dragging her away from the window. His hands were wet with sweat and her hands were so tiny and soft that time and again her little fingers slipped out of his palms. He tried holding her hands tighter and only succeeded in scratching her. Her ring slid off into his hand while he was dragging her and he stood still for a moment, staring in a daze at the thin band of shimmering gold, then mechanically he put it into his pocket. Finally he dragged her down the steps to the bathroom door.

He was about to take her in when he saw that the floor was spotted with drippings of blood. That was bad . . . He had been trained to keep floors clean, just as he had been trained to fear shadows. He propped her clumsily against a wall and went into the bathroom and took wads of toilet paper and mopped up the red splashes. He even went back upstairs where he had first struck her and found blood spots and wiped them up carefully. He stiffened; she was hollering again. He ran downstairs and this time he recalled that he had a knife in his pocket. He took it out, opened it, and plunged it deep into her throat; he was frantic to stop her from hollering . . . He pulled the knife from her throat and she was quiet.

He stood, his eyes roving. He noticed a door leading down to a recess in a wall through which steam pipes ran. Yes, it would be better to put her there; then if she started yelling no one would hear her. He was not trying to hide her; he merely wanted to make sure that she would not be heard. He dragged her again and her dress came up over her knees to her chest and again he saw her pink panties. It was too hard dragging her and he lifted her in his arms and while carrying her down the short flight of steps he thought that the pink panties, if he would wet them, would make a good mop to clean up the blood. Once more he sat her against the wall, stripped her of her pink panties—and not once did he so much as glance at her groin—wetted them and swabbed up the spots, then pushed her into the recess under the pipes.

She was in full view, easily seen. He tossed the wet ball of panties in after her.

He sighed and looked around. The floor seemed clean. He went back upstairs. That stick of broken wood . . . He picked up the two shattered ends of wood and several splinters; he carefully joined the ends together and then fitted the splinters into place. He laid the mended stick back upon the pile before the fireplace. He stood listening, wondering if she would yell again, but there was no sound. It never occurred to him that he could help her, that she might be in pain; he never wondered even if she were dead. He got his coat and hat and went home.

He was nervously tired. It seemed that he had just finished doing an old and familiar job of dodging the shadows that were forever around him, shadows that he could not understand. He undressed, but paid no attention to the blood on his trousers and shirt; he was alone in the room; his wife was at work. When he pulled out his billfold, he saw the ring. He put it in the drawer of his night table, more to keep his wife from seeing it than to hide it. He climbed wearily into bed and at once fell into a deep, sound sleep from which he did not awaken until late afternoon. He lay blinking bloodshot eyes and he could not remember what he had done. Then the vague, shadowlike picture of it came before his eyes. He was puzzled, and for a moment he wondered if it had happened or had someone told him a story of it. He could not be sure. There was no fear or regret in him.

When at last the conviction of what he had done was real in him, it came only in terms of flat memory, devoid of all emotion, as though he were looking when very tired and sleepy at a scene being flashed upon the screen of a movie house. Not knowing what to do, he remained in bed. He had drifted off to sleep again when his wife came home late that night from her cooking job.

Next morning he ate the breakfast his wife prepared, rose from the table and kissed her, and started off toward the Cathedral as though nothing had happened. It was not until he actually got to the Cathedral steps that he became shaky and nervous. He stood before the door for two or three minutes, and then he realized that he could not go back in there this morning. Yet it was not danger that made him feel this way, but a queer kind of repugnance. Whether the woman was alive or not did not enter his mind. He still did not know what to do. Then he remembered that his wife, before she had left for her job, had asked him to buy some groceries. Yes, he would do that. He wanted to do that because he did not know what else on earth to do.

He bought the groceries and took them home, then spent the rest of the day wandering from bar to bar. Not once did he think of fleeing. He would go home, sit, turn on the radio, then go out into the streets and walk. Finally he would end up at a bar, drinking. On one of his many trips into the house, he changed his clothes, rolled up his bloody shirt and trousers, put the bloodstained knife inside the bundle, and pushed it into a far corner of a closet. He got his gun and put it into his pocket, for he was nervously depressed.

But he still did not know what to do. Suddenly he recalled that some months ago he had bought a cheap car which was now in a garage for repairs. He went to the garage and persuaded the owner to take it back for twenty-five dollars; the thought that he could use the car for escape never came to his mind. During that afternoon and early evening he sat in bars and drank. What he felt now was no different from what he had felt all his life.

Toward eight o'clock that night he met two friends of his and invited them for a drink. He was quite drunk now. Before him on the table was a sandwich and a small glass of whiskey. He leaned forward, listening sleepily to one of his friends tell a story about a girl, and then he heard: "Aren't you Saul Saunders?"

He looked up into the faces of two white shadows.

"Yes," he admitted readily. "What do you want?"

"You'd better come along with us. We want to ask you some questions," one of the shadows said.

"What's this all about?" Saul asked.

They grabbed his shoulders and he stood up. Then he reached down and picked up the glass of whiskey and drank it. He walked steadily out of the bar to a waiting auto, a policeman to each side of him, his mind a benign blank. It was not until they were about to put him into the car that something happened and whipped his numbed senses to an apprehension of danger. The policeman patted his waist for arms; they found nothing because his gun was strapped to his chest. Yes, he ought to kill himself . . . The thought leaped into his mind with such gladness that he shivered. It was the answer to everything. Why had he not thought of it before?

Slowly he took off his hat and held it over his chest to hide the movement of his left hand, then he reached inside of his shirt and pulled out the gun. One of the policemen pounced on him and snatched the gun.

"So, you're trying to kill us too, hunh?" one asked.

"Naw. I was trying to kill myself," he answered simply.

"Like hell you were!"

A fist came onto his jaw and he sank back limp.

Two hours later, at the police station, he told them everything, speaking in a low, listless voice without a trace of emotion, vividly describing every detail, yet feeling that it was utterly hopeless for him to try to make them understand how horrible it was for him to hear that woman screaming. His narrative sounded so brutal that the policemen's faces were chalky.

Weeks later a voice droned in a courtroom and he sat staring dully.

". . . The Grand Jurors of the United States of America, in and for the District of Columbia aforesaid, upon their oath, do present:

"That one Saul Saunders, on, to wit, the first day of March, 19———, and at and within the District of Columbia aforesaid, contriving and intending to kill one Maybelle Eva Houseman . . ."

"So *that's* her name," he said to himself in amazement.

". . . Feloniously, willfully, purposely, and of his deliberate and premeditated malice did strike, beat, and wound the said Maybelle Eva Houseman, in and upon the front of the head and in and upon the right side of the head of her, the said Maybelle Eva Houseman, two certain mortal wounds and fractures; and did fix and fasten about the neck and throat of her, the said Maybelle Eva Houseman, his hand or hands—but whether it was one of his hands or both of his hands is to the Grand Jury aforesaid unknown—and that he, the said Saul Saunders, with his hand or hands as aforesaid fixed and fastened about the throat of her, did choke and strangle the said Maybelle Eva Houseman, of which said choking and strangling the said Maybelle Eva Houseman, on, to wit, the said first day of March, 19———, and at and within the said District of Columbia, did die."

He longed for a drink, but that was impossible now. Then he took a deep breath and surrendered to the world of shadows about him, the world he had feared so long; and at once the tension went from him and he felt better than he had felt in a long time. He was amazed at how relaxed and peaceful it was when he stopped fighting the world of shadows.

". . . By force and violence and against resistance and by putting in fear, did steal, take, and carry away, from and off the person and from the immediate, actual possession of one Maybelle Eva Houseman, then and there being, a certain finger ring, of the value of, to wit, ten dollars."

He listened now with more attention but no anxiety:

"And in and while perpetrating robbery aforesaid did kill and murder the said Maybelle Eva Houseman; against the form of the statute in such case made and provided, and against the peace and government of the said United States of America."

P.S. Thereupon Dr. Herman Stein was called as a witness and being first duly sworn testified as follows:

". . . On examination of the genital organs there was no evidence of contusion, abrasion, or trauma, and the decedent's hymen ring was intact. This decedent had not been criminally assaulted or attempted to be entered. It has been ascertained that the decedent's age was forty."

Part II

Spooks at the Door

The Second
Black Arts Renaissance
and the Political Thriller

John A. Williams

From The Man Who Cried I Am

JOHN A. WILLIAMS (1925–   ), born in Jackson, Mississippi, has been a foreign correspondent for *Newsweek* as well as a professor and writer of fiction and nonfiction. His eleven novels include *Sissie; !Click Song;* and the political thrillers *The Man Who Cried I Am; Sons of Darkness, Sons of Light; Captain Blackman;* and *Jacob's Ladder.* He has also written nine books of nonfiction, including *If I Stop I'll Die: The Comedy and Tragedy of Richard Pryor* (co-authored with his son, Dennis A. Williams), and has edited numerous collections of writing.

The Man Who Cried I Am (1967), Williams's ominous vision of the consequences of the black liberation struggles and civil uprisings of the 1960s, brought him national and international attention. Although the complex story of one man's journey through one of the more turbulent periods of modern history and its evocative description of the 1950s and 1960s drew impressive reviews, the novel was almost equally noted in some circles for its description of the King Alfred Plan, posthumously revealed by author Harry Ames to his friend and fellow writer Max Reddick. The realistic representation of the Plan (it's title derived from Williams's middle name), which called for the forced removal of the black population to concentration camps in the event of a declared "Minority Emergency," left many black Americans believing in its veracity, even to this day.

Recipient of the American Book Award, The Richard

Wright-Jacques Roumain Award, among many others, Williams lives in Teaneck, New Jersey, and is the Paul Robeson Professor Emeritus of Rutgers University.

LEIDEN

YES, MAX THOUGHT. I knew Jaja Enzkwu, eagle-faced, hot-eyed Jaja with his sweating, pussy-probing fingers and perfumed agbadas; I knew him.

Max glanced at his watch again. Two o'clock. He wondered what Margrit was doing back in Amsterdam on such a beautiful day. He knew what Jaja was doing: feeding the bugs back in Onitsha where he had been sent in a box, after that deadly rendezvous with Baroness Huganot in Basel that day.

So much had happened that day, the day of the March on Washington. Margrit had left shortly after he called her. Then he had taken a plane to Washington. Du Bois had died in Ghana the night before, and so had Jaja, leaving behind an opened magnum of Piper-Heidsieck, a half-eaten partridge and a startled, voluptuous, eager-to-be-ravished Baroness. But Washington had been the place to be that day. There you could forget that the cancer tests were positive—it was malignant—and that you were going into cobalt treatment soon; you could forget with more than a quarter million people surging around you.

Max flipped up the next page of the letter and when he finished, he shook as if with a sudden chill, and yet the shaking hand had nothing to do with his illness; it was the letter itself. With trembling hands he lit a cigarette.

No, he told himself. I have not read what I just read. This cannot be. No, it's me, the way I'm thinking, the way I'm reading. He closed his eyes hard and held them for a long time. Then he opened them to reread the entire letter once again:

Dear Max:

You are there, Max? It is you reading this, right? I mean, even dead, which I must be for you to have these papers *and* be alone in the company of Michelle, I'd feel like a damned fool if someone else was reading them. I hope these lines find you in good shape and with a full life behind you, because, chances are, now that you've started reading, all that is way, way behind you, baby.

I'm sorry to get you into this mess, but in your hands right now is the biggest story you'll ever have. Big and dangerous. Unbelievable. Wow. But it's a story with consequences the editors of *Pace* may be unwilling to pay. And you, Max, baby, come to think of it, may not even get the chance to cable the story. Knowing may kill you, just as knowing killed me and a few other people you'll meet in this letter. Uh-uh! Can't quit now! It was too late when you opened the case. This is a rotten way to treat a friend. Yes, friend. We've had good and bad times together; we've both come far. I remember that first day we met at Zutkin's. We both saw something we liked in each other. What? I don't know, but it never mattered to me. Our friendship worked; it had value; it lasted. I've run out of acquaintances and other friends who never were the friend you were. So, even if this is dangerous for you—and it is—I turn to you in friendship and in the hope that you can do with this information what I could not. Quite frankly, I don't know how I got into this thing. It just happened, I guess, and like any contemporary Negro, like a ghetto Jew of the 1930s in Europe, I couldn't believe it was happening, even when the pieces fell suddenly into place. Africa . . .

God, Max, what doesn't start with Africa? What a history still to be told! The scientists are starting to say life began there. I'm no scientist. I don't know. But I do know that this letter you're reading had its origins with what happened there. Let me go back to the beginning. I doubt if you've heard of Alliance Blanc. In 1958 Guinea voted to leave the French Family of Nations, and at once formed a federation with Kwame Nkrumah, or Ghana, whichever you prefer. The British and French were shaken. How could countries only two minutes ago colonies spring to such political maturity? Would the new federation use pounds or francs? The national banks of both countries were heavily underwriting the banking systems of the two countries. There would be a temporary devaluation of both pounds and francs, whether the new federation minted new money or not. More important—and this is what really rocked Europe—if the federation worked, how many new, independent African states would follow suit? *Then,* what would happen to European interests in Africa after independence and federation? Was it *really* conceivable that all of Africa might one day unite, Cape to Cairo, Abidjan to Addis? Alliance Blanc said *Yes!* If there were a United States of Africa, a cohesiveness among the people—300,000,000 of them—should not Europeans anticipate the possibility of trouble, sometime when the population had tripled, for example? Couldn't Africa become another giant, like China, with even more hatred for the white West? It was pure guilt over what Europeans had done to Africa and the Africans that made them react in such a violent fashion to African independence.

The white man, as we well know, has never been of so single an accord as when maltreating black men. And he has had an amazing historical rapport in Africa, dividing it up arbitrarily across tribal and language boundaries. That rapport in plundering Africa never existed and never will when it requires the same passion for getting along with each other in Europe. But you know all this. All I'm trying to say is that where the black man is concerned, the white man will bury differences that have existed between them since the beginning of time, and come together. How goddamn different this would have been if there had been no Charles Martel at Tours in 732!

The Alliance first joined together not in the Hague, not in Geneva, not in London, Versailles or Washington, but in Munich, a city top-heavy with monuments and warped history. Present were representatives from France, Great Britain, Belgium, Portugal, Australia, Spain, Brazil, South Africa. The United States of America was also present. There were white observers from most of the African countries that appeared to be on their way to independence. The representation at first, with a few exceptions, was quasi-official. But you know very well that a quasi-official body can be just as effective as an official one; in fact, it is often better to use the former.

I don't have to tell you that the meetings, then and subsequently, were held in absolute secrecy. They were moved from place to place —Spain, Portugal, France, Brazil and in the United States, up around Saranac Lake—Dreiser's setting for *An American Tragedy,* that neck of the woods, remember? America, with the largest black population outside Africa, had the most need of mandatory secrecy. Things were getting damned tense following the Supreme Court decision to desegregate schools in 1954.

The disclosure of America's membership in Alliance Blanc would have touched off a racial cataclysm—but America went far, far beyond the evils the Alliance was perpetuating, but more of this later. For the moment, let me consider the Alliance.

African colonies were still becoming independent. Federations were formed only to collapse a few weeks later, like the Guinea-

Ghana combine. Good men and bad were assassinated indiscriminately; coups were a dime a dozen. Nkrumah in West Africa vied with Selassie in East Africa for leadership of the continent. The work of the Alliance agents—setting region against region and tribe against tribe, just as the colonial masters had done— was made easy by the rush to power on the part of a few African strongmen. Thus, the panic mentality that had been the catalyst for the formation of the Alliance seemed to have been tranquilized. There was diplomacy as usual, independence as usual. What, after all, did Europeans have to fear after that first flash of black unity? The Alliance became more leisurely, less belligerent, more sure that it had time and, above all, positive now that Africa was not a threat to anyone but itself. Alliance agents flowed leisurely through Africa now, and Western money poured in behind them.

From a belligerent posture, the Alliance went to one based on economics. Consider that 15 percent of Nigeria's federal budget comes from offshore oil brought in by Dutch, British, Italian, French and American oil companies; consider that the 72 percent of the world's cocoa which Africa produces would rot if the West did not import it. Palm oil, groundnuts, minerals, all for the West. Can you imagine, man, what good things could happen to Africans, if they learned to consume what they produce? It did not take the Europeans long to discover that their stake in Africa as "friends" rather than masters was more enormous than they could have imagined. Only naked desperation demanded that Spain and Portugal stay in Africa; the Iberian Peninsula hasn't been the same since the Moors and Jews left it in the fifteenth century. Time? It was the Alliance's most formidable ally.

In South Africa, the spark of revolt flickered, sputtered and now is dead. The Treason Trials killed it; oppression keeps murdering it, and those who say the spark is still alive, those successive schools of nattily tailored South African nationalists, who plunge through Paris, London and New York raising money for impossible rebellions, lie. The paradox, Max, is that, denied freedom, the black man lives better in South Africa than anywhere else on the continent; the average African. The bigshots—with their big houses and long cars, their emulation of the colonial masters—do all right. My friend Genet said it all in *Les Noirs*.

The Alliance worked. God, how it worked! And Africans themselves, dazzled by this new contraption the white man was giving them, independence, helped. Lumumba, disgracefully educated by the Belgians, was a victim of the Alliance; Olympio, dreaming dreams of federation, was another. Nkrumah and Touré have lasted for so long because their trust in the white man never was, and their trust in their own fellows only a bit deeper seated.

The Congo mess served as a valuable aid to the Alliance: it could test the world's reaction to black people in crisis. The Alliance was pleased to observe that the feeling in the West was, "Oh, well, they're only niggers, anyhow."

I could have foreseen that reaction; you could have foreseen it; any black man could have anticipated it. But, then, "niggers" are embattled everywhere, ain't they, baby? Asian "niggers," South American "niggers" . . . But let a revolt occur in East Germany and watch the newsprint fly! Let another Hungarian revolution take place and see the white nations of the world open their doors to take in refugees—Hungarian Freedom Fighters, yeah! Who takes in blacks, Pakistanis, Vietnamese, Koreans, Chinese, who?

But the picture began to change. It was quite clear that the Europeans had Africa well under control—and that was all they cared about. America, sitting on a bubbling black cauldron, felt that it had to map its own contingency plans for handling 22 million black Americans in case they became unruly; in case they wanted everything Freedom Fighters got just by stepping off the boat. So, America prepared King Alfred and submitted it to the Alliance, just as the Alliance European members had submitted their plans for operations in Africa to the Americans. King Alfred in its original form called for sending American Negroes to Africa, and this had to be cleared by the Europeans. The Europeans vetoed that plan; they remembered what excitement Garvey had caused in Africa. The details of King Alfred are in the case, and it is truly hot stuff. All this Alliance business is pretty pallid shit compared to what the Americans have come up with.

I should tell you that it was an African who discovered the Alliance and in the process came upon King Alfred. Who? Jaja Enzkwu, that cockhound, that's who. He stumbled on the Alliance the second year of its existence, while he was in Spain, which as you know has turned out to be a very hospitable place for ex-heads of African countries on the lam. Enzkwu didn't know what was going on; he simply sensed something, seeing a gathering of British,

American, Brazilian, Portuguese and South Africans at San Sebastián in winter. This was where the Alliance held its second meeting. I'll tell you about Jaja. Any halfway good-looking white woman can make a fool of him (which was what was happening, for him to be at a summer resort in winter), but he doesn't trust a gathering of more than a single white man. About the white man, Enzkwu has a nose for trouble. But you know Jaja.

Jaja died as he had lived, chasing white pussy. As soon as his nation became independent in 1960, using the various embassies and consulates his government had established in the Park Avenues, Park Lanes and Georges V's of the world, yes, those places, with the long, black limousines in front, chauffeured by large but deferential white men, those places with the waiting rooms filled with African art, Jaja started gathering material on the Alliance. He amassed all the information you have at hand.

How did they get to Jaja? It's a white man's world—so far. He had to hire white operatives, of course, to get to Alliance Blanc. A couple of these, Jaja's beloved Frenchmen, I believe, checked back through several white people fronting for Enzkwu, but, at last, they discovered old black Jaja sitting there behind it all. A black man, interesting. The bastards then sold *this* information to the Alliance. At this point, old Jaja, sitting behind an eighteen-foot desk, was cooling it, thinking he had it all covered. He planned to make use of the information. Like so many people, he had begun his investigations with a sincere desire to protect his country. But another consideration rose very, very quickly. He could use the information, to be released at a propitious time, to prove that the Nigerian premier, and African leaders generally, had failed to protect their people from the new colonialism. Jaja planned to gather all of Africa under a single ruler one day. That ruler was to be Jaja Enzkwu.

Panic in Washington ensued when it was discovered that Jaja not only had information on the Alliance, but on King Alfred, the contingency plan to detain and ultimately rid America of its Negroes. Mere American membership in the Alliance would have been sufficient to rock America, but King Alfred would have made Negroes realize, finally and angrily, that all the new moves—the laws and committees—to gain democracy for them were fraudulent, just as Minister Q and the others had been saying for years. Your own letter to me days after you left the White House only underscored what so many Negro leaders believed. The one alternative left for

Negroes would be not only to seek that democracy withheld from them as quickly and as violently as possible, but to fight for their very survival. King Alfred, as you will see, leaves no choice.

The European members of the Alliance were not as concerned as America about the leak. In fact, if King Alfred was revealed and racial violence exploded in America, America's position as world leader would be seriously undermined. There were members in the Alliance who wished for this. The danger in Africa being nullified, the white man became divided. In the U.S., the situation had worsened. There had been that second boy at Ole Miss; the dogs and fire hoses in Birmingham; kids blown up in church; little brushfire riots that came and went across the country, like wind stroking a wheat field. Minister Q's voice was now large indeed. The March on Washington appeared to have been the last time the Negroes were peacefully willing to ask for and take any old handout.

The Alliance had not counted on the efficiency of the Central Intelligence Agency, which had placed agents in Nigeria within days of receiving the report that Jaja had information. Concealing King Alfred became the top priority assignment of the National Security Council and the CIA. Jaja was not killed at once for two reasons: first, the agents were unable to ascertain where he kept the papers. Second, on a trip to Paris, the agents made a fake attempt on his life to make him go for the papers. But this only resulted in arousing Jaja's curiosity, and he began backtracking through his former operatives and discovered that the Americans knew that he knew. Then Jaja started to deal. He'd give over the papers and keep his mouth shut, if the Americans gave him Nigeria. The U.S. had no choice but to agree, when it had the opportunity. It would take time. All right, Jaja said. But not *too* much time.

Jaja moved, ate, slept and crapped with an army of bodyguards. He had only to put it out that the Hausas in the north were after him, and every Ibo in the eastern region understood.

Enzkwu came to see me two days before your March on Washington. He was thin and drawn and quite subdued. Almost a year, I learned later, had passed since making the deal with the U.S. and nothing had come of it. Even Charlotte did not bring out that old gleam to his eyes, as her presence has done for many of my friends. Jaja and I had dinner that night, surrounded by some of the biggest Ibos I've ever seen. After, a car followed us, but it was his and was filled with his men. We didn't talk too much in his hotel.

We were in one room and his guards in another. Every five minutes, one of the guards would knock on the door and ask something in Ibo, and Jaja would reply in Ibo. It was always the same question and the same answer.

Jaja was on his way to Switzerland and he gave me the key to a safe deposit box in a Paris bank and told me to get what was in it, if he did not return from Switzerland. I was puzzled and curious about his mood, but I took the key without asking questions. Of course, he was killed. I hustled to the bank and what I found was this information you now have found, plus a letter from Jaja, similar to my letter which you are now reading. The material fascinated me. I'd spent so much of my life writing about the evil machinations of Mr. Charlie without really *knowing* the truth, as this material made me know it. It was spread out before me, people, places and things. I became mired in them, and I *knew* now that the way black men live on this earth was no accident. And yet, my mind kept telling me that Jaja's death was a coincidence, a mere coincidence. I could not believe that I, too, soon would be dead. One looks at death, always moves toward it, but until the last denies its existence. I was trapped by my contempt for everything African. I made the bodyguards just a part of the African spectacle. I gripped the material, I hugged it to my chest, for now I would know; if they killed me, I would know that this great evil did exist, indeed, thrived. And Dr. Faustus came to my mind. The Americans killed Jaja, obviously because they ran out of patience, and because they thought they could find the material without him.

I didn't say anything to you when you came through Paris on your way to East Africa because I had not seen Jaja then.

It is spring. Strange, now that life seems to quicken a bit, and you can see people smiling more, and the trees starting to bloom, I feel tired, going downhill. I am sure the Americans are on to me. Perhaps the French keep them off, not wanting trouble to becloud De Gaulle's new image. At least that's what I think, and that's why I haven't made any trips outside France. I thought of giving it to the Russians, but would they even accept it from me? Even if they did, can't you see the West laughing it off as another Russian hoax, even Negroes?

But there was America itself. You and *Pace*. You must have access to outlets where this material would do the most good. The choice is yours and yours alone as to whether you want to wreck the nation or not. My opinion? No, Max, it's up to you. Think of the irony: the very nation that most wants to keep the information secret would be the very one to release it!

A personal item: Charlotte seems to have found a strange tolerance for me these days. I think she knows about the material. And she has found out about Michelle and me, at last. How, I don't know, exactly, but I think American agents have told her, to enlist her aid.

In fact, Max, old trusted friend, everybody knows everything now, past and present.

I am getting this material to Michelle tonight. She will get it to you even if she has to swim to New York. I know of no one else. And perhaps this is a sign, the ultimate sign, that I am very tired. I can only hope that no harm comes to her.

Another item, old buddy. Tomorrow I'm having lunch with a young man I understand you've met. His name is Edwards, and he's quit Uncle Sam's foreign service to write a novel about it. I can't resist these youngsters who come to see me, to sit at the feet of the father, so to speak. I guess I'll never outgrow it. I suppose you're next in line to be father . . .

HARRY

Shock, gracious, pain-absorbing shock came at once and lessened the hurt and surprise. Max, reacting normally for the moment, lit another cigarette, picked through and carefully read Enzkwu's papers.

Yes, there was explosive material here. Enough to unsettle every capital city in the West; enough to force the Africans to cut ties with Europe at once and worry about the consequences later; enough to send black Brazilians surging out of their *favelas* and *barrios* to inundate the sleek beach places of the whites. Wherever white men had been involved with black men, Enzkwu's photostats disclosed a clear and unrelenting danger. Recorded in cold black type were lists of statesmen and diplomats, the records of their deeds, what they planned to do, when, where, why and to whom. The list of people dead, Max knew, and therefore murdered, if their names appeared in Enzkwu's papers, included the residents of four continents. African airfields equipped for the handling of jets and props, along with radio and power stations, the number of men in the army of each country, plus a military critique of those armies, were set down here.

Now Max's hand held another numbered packet, but above the number were the words: THE UNITED STATES OF AMERICA—KING ALfred. Slowly, he pulled out the sheaf of photostats. So, this is King Alfred, Alfred the Great. He mused, Why is it called King Alfred? Then he saw the answer footnoted at the bottom of the first page.

KING ALFRED★

In the event of widespread and continuing and coordinated racial disturbances in the United States, KING ALFRED, at the discretion of the President, is to be put into action immediately.

PARTICIPATING FEDERAL AGENCIES

National Security Council   Department of Justice
Central Intelligence Agency   Department of Defense
Federal Bureau of Investigation   Department of Interior

PARTICIPATING STATE AGENCIES
(Under Federal Jurisdiction)

National Guard Units   State Police

PARTICIPATING LOCAL AGENCIES
(Under Federal Jurisdiction)

City Police   County Police

Memo: National Security Council

Even before 1954, when the Supreme Court of the United States of America declared unconstitutional separate educational and recreational facilities, racial unrest and discord had become very nearly a part of the American way of life. But that way of life was repugnant to most Americans. Since 1954, however, that unrest and discord have broken out into widespread violence which increasingly have placed the peace and stability of the nation in dire jeopardy. This violence has resulted in loss of life, limb and property, and has cost the taxpayers of this nation billions of dollars. And the end is not yet in sight. This same violence has raised the tremendously grave question as to whether the races can ever live in peace with each other. Each passing month has brought new intelligence that despite new laws passed to alleviate the condition

★ 849–899 (?) King of England; directed translation from the Latin of the *Anglo-Saxon Chronicle*.

of the Minority, the Minority still is not satisfied. Demonstrations and rioting have become a part of the familiar scene. Troops have been called out in city after city across the land, and our image as a world leader severely damaged. Our enemies press closer, seeking the advantage, possibly at a time during one of these outbreaks of violence. The Minority has adopted an almost military posture to gain its objectives, which are not clear to most Americans. It is expected, therefore, that when those objectives are denied the Minority, racial war must be considered inevitable. When that Emergency comes, we must expect the total involvement of all 22 million members of the Minority, men, women and children, for once this project is launched, its goal is to terminate, once and for all, the Minority threat to the whole of the American society, and, indeed, the Free World.

Chairman, National Security Council

Preliminary Memo: Department of Interior
Under KING ALFRED, the nation has been divided into 10 Regions (See accompanying map).

   In case of Emergency, Minority members will be evacuated from the cities by federalized national guard units, local and state police and, if necessary, by units of the Regular Armed Forces, using public and military transportation, and detained in nearby military installations until a further course of action has been decided.

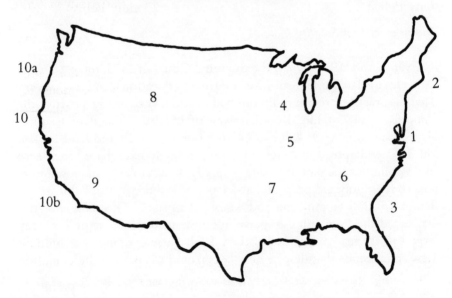

1   Capital region
2   Northeast region
3   Southeast region
4   Great Lakes Region
5   South central region
6   Deep South region
7   Deep South region II
8   Great Plains, Rocky Mountain region
9   Southwest region
10   a, b, West Coast region

No attempt will be made to seal off the Canadian and Mexican borders.

Secretary, Department of Interior

Combined Memo: Department of Justice
                  Federal Bureau of Investigation
                  Central Intelligence Agency

There are 12 major Minority organizations and all are familiar to the 22 million. Dossiers have been compiled on the leaders of the organizations, and can be studied in Washington. The material contained in many of the dossiers, and our threat to reveal that material, has considerably held in check the activities of some of the leaders. Leaders who do not have such usable material in their dossiers have been approached to take Government posts, mostly as ambassadors and primarily in African countries. The promise of these positions also has materially contributed to a temporary slowdown of Minority activities. However, we do not expect these slowdowns to be of long duration, because there are always new and dissident elements joining these organizations, with the potential power to replace the old leaders. All organizations and their leaders are under constant, 24-hour surveillance. The organizations are:

1   The Black Muslims
2   Student Nonviolent Coordinating Committee (SNCC)
3   Congress of Racial Equality (CORE)
4   Uhuru Movement
5   Group on Advanced Leadership (GOAL)
6   Freedom Now Party (FNP)
7   United Black Nationalists of America (UBNA)
8   The New Pan-African Movement (TNPAM)
9   Southern Christian Leadership Conference (SCLC)

10   The National Urban League (NUL)
11   The National Association for the Advancement of Colored People
     (NAACP)
12   Committee on Racial and Religious Progress (CORARP)

NOTE: At the appropriate time, to be designated by the President, the leaders of some of these organizations are to be detained ONLY WHEN IT IS CLEAR THAT THEY CANNOT PREVENT THE EMERGENCY, working with local public officials during the first critical hours. All other leaders are to be detained at once. Compiled lists of Minority leaders have been readied at the National Data Computer Center. It is necessary to use the Minority leaders designated by the President in much the same manner in which we use Minority members who are agents with CENTRAL and FEDERAL, and we cannot, until there is no alternative, reveal KING ALFRED in all its aspects. Minority members of Congress will be unseated at once. This move is not without precedent in American history.

Attorney General

Preliminary Memo: Department of Defense
This memo is being submitted in lieu of a full report from the Joint Chiefs of Staff. That report is now in preparation. There will be many cities where the Minority will be able to put into the street a superior number of people with a desperate and dangerous will. He will be a formidable enemy, for he is bound to the Continent by heritage and knows that political asylum will not be available to him in other countries. The greatest concentration of the Minority is in the Deep South, the Eastern Seaboard, the Great Lakes region and the West Coast. While the national population exceeds that of the Minority by more than ten times, we must realistically take into account the following:

1   An estimated 40–50 percent of the white population will not, for various reasons, engage the Minority during an Emergency.
2   American Armed Forces are spread around the world. A breakout of war abroad means fewer troops at home to handle the Emergency.
3   Local law enforcement officials must contain the Emergency until help arrives, though it may mean fighting a superior force. New York City, for example, has a 25,000-man police force, but there are about one million Minority members in the city.

We are confident that the Minority could hold any city it took for only a few hours. The lack of weapons, facilities, logistics—all put the Minority at a final disadvantage.

Since the Korean War, this Department has shifted Minority members of the Armed Forces to areas where combat is most likely to occur, with the aim of eliminating, through combat, as many combat-trained Minority servicemen as possible. Today the ratio of Minority member combat deaths in Vietnam, where they are serving as "advisers," is twice as high as the Minority population ratio to the rest of America. Below is the timetable for KING ALFRED as tentatively suggested by the JCS who recommend that the operation be made over a period of eight hours:

1. Local police and Minority leaders in action to head off the Emergency.
2. Countdown to eight hours begins at the moment the President determines the Emergency to be:

    A. National
    B. Coordinated
    C. Of Long Duration   8th Hour

3. County police join local police.   7th
4. State police join county and local forces.   6th
5. Federal marshals join state, county and local forces.   5th
6. National Guards federalized, held in readiness.   4th
7. Regular Armed Forces alerted, take up positions; Minority troops divided and detained, along with all white sympathizers, under guard.   3rd
8. All Minority leaders, national and local, detained.   2nd
9. President addresses Minority on radio-television, gives it one hour to end the Emergency.   1st
10. All units under regional commands into the Emergency.   0

"O" Committee Report:

Survey shows that during a six-year period Production created 9,000,000 objects, or 1,500,000 each year. Production could not dispose of the containers, which proved a bottleneck. However, that was

almost 20 years ago. We suggest that vaporization techniques be employed to overcome the Production problems inherent in KING ALFRED.

Secretary of Defense

Max smoked and read, read and smoked until his mouth began to
taste like wool and when he finally pushed King Alfred from him, he
felt exhausted, as if he had been running beneath a gigantic, unblinking
eye that had watched his every move and determined just when movement should stop.

Yeah. Jaja had done his work well. He could have embarrassed and
startled a lot of people, blacks and whites, but you have to weed a
garden for the flowers to grow. Those dossiers, he knew pretty much
what was in them. Well, he had known it; there are always dues to pay.
A smoldering anger coursed through Max's stomach. Yes, those leaders
clearly had left themselves vulnerable, vulnerable for the hunters who,
for a generation and more, sought Communists with such vehemence
that they skillfully obscured the growth and power of fascism. How
black skins stirred fascists! Perhaps because it was the most identifiable
kind of skin; you didn't have to wait until you got up close to see
whether a nose was hooked or not; a black skin you could see for a
block away. And in the face of the revelations in Jaja's papers, Harry
and Jaja both, made giddy by the presence of that massive, killing evil,
had dared to toy with it; had dared to set their pitiable little egos down
before that hideous juggernaut. And they had hoped to live. That hope
had revealed their inability to accurately measure what was readily mea-
surable. Jaja for greed, and you, Harry, it's just starting to come. They
didn't let their minds go out.

They did not let their minds go out to picture the instability of what
seems static; they did not see planets colliding with each other, or
picture Sahara or Kalahari as lakes, or picture plains where the Alps,
Andes and Rockies now stand; nor did they picture oceans above the
sands that crunch softly beneath the feet in the sweet-smelling paths of
the Maine or Vermont woods. No, they did not picture the extinction
of man and beast and places. If they had, *then* they could see four
million dead because they themselves, like the later nine million, refused to see evil rearing up before them, quite discernible, quite mea-
surable. Man is nature, nature man, and all crude and raw, stinking,
vicious, evil. And holding that evil lightly because the collective mind

refuses to recall the sprint of mountains, the vault of seas and, of course, beside that, the puny murder of millions.

It is still eat, drink and be murderous, for tomorrow I may be among the murdered.

This seeing precisely, Max told himself, is a bitch!

Sam Greenlee

From The Spook Who Sat by the Door

Chicago native SAM GREENLEE (1930–   ) is the author of two novels, *The Spook Who Sat by the Door* (1969) and a second thriller, *Baghdad Blues* (1986). *The Spook Who Sat by the Door,* like John A. Williams's *The Man Who Cried I Am,* was a literary response to the civil rights upheaval of the 1960s, the riots in the middle and late years of the decade, and part of the black cultural explosion commonly called the Black Arts Movement.

As segregation and discriminatory hiring practices were abolished, many African Americans gained entrance for the first time to formerly all-white organizations and corporations, although they were usually relegated to lower-level positions. Greenlee himself was a beneficiary of such changes; his statement at the beginning of *The Spook Who Sat by the Door* expressed not only his own professional position but also the status of those who are supposedly at the margins of the American workforce. "I have recently returned from four years of writing in Greece. I am employed, with fat salary and fancy title, by an otherwise white civil rights organization in Chicago. My job is to sit by the door." Freeman, the protagonist of *The Spook Who Sat by the Door,* is also about to be admitted to the then all-white bastion of the CIA, where his position as "spook by the door" will have a double meaning.

The Spook Who Sat by the Door was adapted for the screen in

1973, the movie directed by Ivan Dixon and starring Lawrence Cook and J. A. Preston.

FREEMAN watched the class reunion from a corner of the common room of the CIA training barracks. It was a black middle-class reunion. They were black bourgeoisie to a man, black nepotism personified. In addition to those who had recruited themselves upon receiving notice that the CIA was now interested in at least token integration, five were relatives or in-laws of civil-rights leaders, four others of Negro politicians. Only Freeman was not middle class, and the others knew it. Even had he not dressed as he did, not used the speech patterns and mannerisms of the Chicago ghetto slums, they would have known. His presence made them uneasy and insecure; they were members of the black elite, and a product of the ghetto streets did not belong among them.

They carefully ignored Freeman and it was as he wished; he had no more love for the black middle class than they for him. He watched them establishing the pecking order as he sat sipping a scotch highball. It was their first day in the training camp after months of exhaustive screening, testing, security checks. Of the hundreds considered, only the twenty-three present in the room had survived and been selected for preliminary training and, constantly reminded of it since they had reported, they pranced, posed and preened in mutual and self-admiration. To be a "Negro firster" was considered a big thing, but Freeman didn't think so.

"Man, you know how much this twelve-year-old scotch cost me in the commissary? Three bills and a little change! Chivhead Regal! As long as I can put my mouth around this kind of whiskey at that price, I'm in love with being a spy."

"You know they call CIA agents spooks? First time we'll ever get paid for that title."

"Man, the fringe benefits—they just don't stop coming in! Nothing to say of the base pay and stuff. We got it made."

"Say, baby, didn't we meet at the Penn Relays a couple of years ago? In that motel on the edge of Philly? You remember that chick you was with, Lurlean? Well, she's teaching school in Camden now and I get a little bit of that from time to time. Now, man, don't freeze on me. I'm married, too, and you know Lurlean don't give a damn. I'll tell her I saw you when we get out of here."

Where'd you go to school, man? Fisk? I went to Morris Brown. You frat? Q? You got a couple brothers here, those two cats over there. What you major in? What your father do? Your mother working, too? Where your wife go to school? What sorority? What kind of work you do before you made this scene? How much bread you make? Where's your home? What kind of car you got? How much you pay for that suit? You got your own pad, or you live in an apartment? Co-op apartment? Tell me that's the new thing nowadays. Clue me in. You got color TV? Component stereo, or console?

Drop those names: doctors I have known, lawyers, judges, business-men, dentists, politicians, and Great Negro Leaders I have known. Drop those brand names: GE, Magnavox, Ford, GM, Chrysler, Zenith, Brooks Brothers, Florsheim. Johnnie Walker, Chivas Regal, Jack Daniel's. Imported beer. Du Pont carpeting, wall-to-wall. Wall-to-wall drags with split-level minds, remote-control color TV souls and credit-card hearts.

Play who-do-you-know and who-have-you-screwed. Blow your bourgeois blues, your nigger soul sold for a mess of materialistic pot-tage. You can't ever catch Charlie, but you can ape him and keep the gap widening between you and those other niggers. You have a ceiling on you and yours, your ambitions; but the others are in the basement and you will help Mr. Charlie keep them there. If they get out and move up to your level, then what will you have?

They eyed Freeman uneasily; he was an alien in this crowd. Some-how, he had escaped the basement. He had moved up to their level and he was a threat. He must be put in his place. He would not last, breeding told, but he should know that he was among his betters.

The tall, good-looking one with the curly black hair and light skin approached Freeman. He was from Howard and wore his clothes How-ard-style, the cuffless pants stopping at his ankles. His tie was very skinny and the knot almost unnoticeable, his shoulder padding nonex-istent. He had known these arrogant, Chicago niggers like Freeman before, thinking they owned Howard's campus, moving in with their down-home ways, their Mississippi mannerisms, loud laughter, no manners, elbowing their way into the fraternities, trying to steal the women, making more noise than anyone else at the football games and rallies. One of those diddy-bop niggers from Chicago had almost stolen his present wife.

"Where you from, man? You don't seem to talk much."

"No, I don't."

"Don't what?"

"Don't talk much. I'm from Chicago."

"Chicago? Where you from before that? Way back, Georgia, Snatchback, Mississippi? You look like you just got off the train, man. Where's the paper bag with your sack of fried chicken?"

Freeman looked at him and sipped his drink.

"No, seriously, my man, where you from? Lot of boys here from the South; how come you got to pretend? I bet you don't even know where State Street and the Loop is. How you sneak into this group? This is supposed to be the cream, man. You sure you don't clean up around here?"

Freeman stood up slowly, still holding his drink. The tall one was standing very close to his armchair and had to step back when Freeman rose.

"Baby, I will kick your ass. Go away and leave me to hell alone."

The tall one opened his mouth to speak; a fraternity brother sidled up, took his arm and led him away. Freeman freshened his drink and sat down in front of the television set. After a lull, the black middle-class reunion resumed.

He had not made a mistake, he thought. All niggers looked alike to whites and he had thought it to his advantage to set himself apart from this group in a way that would make the whites overlook him until too late. They would automatically assume that the others—who looked and acted so much like their black representatives and spokesmen who appeared on the television panels, spoke in the halls of Congress, made the covers of *Time* and *Life* and ran the Negro newspapers and magazines, who formed the only link with the white world—would threaten to survive this test. Both the whites and these saddity niggers, Freeman thought, would ignore him until too late. And, he thought, Whitey will be more likely to ignore a nigger who approaches the stereotype than these others who think imitation the sincerest form of flattery.

He smiled when he thought about walking into his friend's dental office that day.

"Hey, Freebee, what's happening, baby? Ain't seen you in the Boulevard Lounge lately. Where you been hiding? Got something new on the string?"

"No, been working. Look, you know the cap you put on after I got hung up in the Iowa game? I want a new one. With an edge of gold around it."

"Gold? You must be kidding. And where you get that refugee from Robert Hall suit?"

"That's where I bought it. I'm going out to Washington for a final interview panel and I want to please the crackers." His friend nodded. He understood.

Freeman did not spend much time socializing with the rest of the Negro pioneers, those chosen to be the first to integrate a segregated institution. He felt none of the gratitude, awe, pride and arrogance of the Negro "firsts" and he did not think after the first few days that many of them would be around very long; and Freeman had come to stay.

They had calisthenics in the morning and then six hours of classes. Exams were scheduled for each Saturday morning. They were not allowed to leave the area, but there was a different movie screened each night in a plush, small theater. There was a small PX, a swimming pool, a bar and a soda fountain. There was a social area at each end of the building in which they lived that included pool tables, Ping-Pong, a television room with color TV, chess and checker sets. There was a small library, containing technical material related to their classes and light fiction, magazines and periodicals. There was a music room with a stereo console containing an AM-FM receiver and with records consisting mostly of show tunes from Broadway hits of the last decade. There were Coke machines. It was like a very plush bachelor officers' quarter.

There were basketball courts, badminton courts, a nine-hole golf course, squash courts, a gym, a 220-yard rubberized track, a touch-football field. After the intensive screening which they had undergone prior to their selection, none of the rest thought that the classes and examinations were anything more than window dressing. They settled down to enjoy their plush confinement during the training period after which they would be given offices in the vast building in Langley, Virginia, down by the river.

Freeman combined a program of calisthenics, weight training, isometrics, running and swimming, which never took more than an hour, usually less than half that time. He would watch television or read until dinner, take an hour's nap and then study until midnight.

No one at the training camp, white or colored, thought it strange that Freeman, a product of the Chicago ghetto, where Negroes spend more time, money and care in the selection of their wardrobe than even in Harlem, should be so badly dressed. Or that, although he had attended two first-rate educational institutions, he should speak with so limited a vocabulary, so pronounced an accent and such Uncle Tom humor. They put it down to the fact that he had been an athlete who had skated through college on his fame. Freeman did not worry about the whites because he was being exactly what they wished. The Negroes of the class would be ashamed of him, yet flattered by the contrast; but there might be a shrewd one among them.

There was only one. He approached Freeman several times with penetrating questions. The fraternity thing put him off.

"You a fraternity man, Freeman?" he asked once over lunch.

"Naw. I was once because of the chicks. You had to have that pin, you know. Almost as good as a letter in football. But I thought that kinda stuff was silly. I used to be a Kappa."

He looked at Freeman coldly. "I'm still a Kappa," he said. He finished lunch and never spoke to Freeman again.

Midway through the fourth week, three of the group were cut. They were called into the front office and informed that their grades were not up to standard, and that same evening they were gone. Panic hit the group and there were several conferences concerning what should be done. Several long-distance phone calls were made, three to politicians, five to civil-rights bureaucrats. The group was informed that they were on their own and that after the time, energy, money and effort that had gone into their integration, they should feel obligated to perform up to the highest standards. Freeman had received the best grades in each of the exams, but no one was concerned with that fact.

Two others left the following weekend, although their grades were among the highest in the group. Freeman guessed correctly that it was for homosexuality and became convinced that in addition to being bugged for sound, the rooms were monitored by closed-circuit TV. He was right. The telephones, even the ones in the booths with coin boxes, were bugged as well. The general received a weekly report regarding the progress of the group. It appeared that those intellectually qualified could be cut on physical grounds. They were already lagging at the increasing demands of the morning calisthenics and were not likely to survive the rigors of hand-to-hand combat. The director of the school confidently predicted that not one of the Negroes would survive the ten weeks of the school, which would then be completely free for a new group of recruits presently going through preliminary screening. It was to the credit of Freeman's unobtrusive demeanor that the school's director did not even think of him, in spite of his excellent grades and physical condition, when making his report to the general. If he had, he might have qualified his report somewhat.

The general instructed his school's director to forward complete reports to the full senatorial committee. He intended to head off any possible criticism from Senator Hennington. He could not know that the senator was not in the least concerned with the success or failure of the Negro pioneers to integrate the Central Intelligence Agency. He had won his election and for another six years he was safe.

"When this group is finished, I want you to begin screening another. Don't bother to select Negroes who are obviously not competent; they have already demonstrated their inability to close the cultural gap and no one is in a position seriously to challenge our insistence not to lower standards for anyone. It will cost us a bit to flunk out six or eight a year, but we needn't worry about harassment on this race thing again in the future if we do. It's a sound investment," said the general. He was pleased and again convinced that he was not personally prejudiced. Social and scientific facts were social and scientific facts. He ate a pleasant meal in his club that evening and noted that there were both white and colored present. The whites were members and guests; the Negroes served them. The general did not reflect that this was the proper order of things. He seldom approved of the rising of the sun, either.

Two more were cut for poor marksmanship. Freeman had obtained an ROTC commission at college and had served in Korea during the police action. He was familiar with all of the weapons except the foreign ones, and a weapon is a weapon. Only the extremely high cyclic rate of the Schmeisser machine pistol bothered him and that did not last very long.

"Mr. Freeman," the retired marine gunnery sergeant said, "that is an automatic weapon and designed to be fired in bursts. Why are you firing it single-shot?"

"It's to get its rhythm, Sergeant. I couldn't control the length of the bursts at first and I was wasting ammo, but I think I have it now."

The sergeant knew that Freeman had been an infantryman, and marines, in spite of what they claim, have at least a modicum of respect for any fighting man. "OK, Mr. Freeman. Show me what you mean. Targets one through five, and use only one clip."

"Call the bursts, Sergeant."

"Three. Five. Five . . ." He called the number of rounds he wanted in rapid succession, as fast as Freeman could fire them. There were rounds left for the final target and, on inspection, they found that one five-round burst had been six instead.

"That is very good shooting, Mr. Freeman. Were you a machine gunner in Korea?"

"No. I was in a heavy weapons company for a while and got to know MGs fairly well, but I spent most of my time in a line infantry company. I like automatic weapons, though. I learned it's not marksmanship but firepower that wins a firefight. I want to know as much as I can about these things."

"All right, Mr. Freeman, I'll teach you what I know. You can have all the extra practice and ammo you want. Just let me know a day ahead of time and I'll set it up. We'll leave the Schmeisser for a while and start with the simpler jobs, and then work up. Pistols, too?"

"Yes, I'd like that, Sergeant. And I'd rather your maintenance section didn't clean them for me. I'd rather do it myself. No better way I know of to learn a weapon than to break it down, clean and reassemble it."

The gunnery sergeant nodded his head and something rather like a smile crossed his face.

Freeman read everything in the library on gunnery, demolition, subversion, sabotage and terrorism. He continued to head the class in examination results. There was much more study among the group now and they eyed one another uneasily, wondering who would be the next to go. They had no taste for returning to the jobs they had left: civil-rights bureaucracies, social welfare agencies, selling insurance, heading a playground in the ghetto, teaching school—all of the grinding little jobs open to a nonprofessional, middle-class Negro with a college degree. Long after Freeman retired, between midnight and one, his program not varying from the schedule he had established during the first week, the rest of the class studied far into the night. The group was given the army physical aptitude test, consisting of squat jumps, push-ups, pull-ups, sit-ups and a 300-yard run.

Freeman headed the group with a score of 482 out of a possible 500. The men finishing second and third to him in academics were released when they scored less than 300 points. There were only two other athletes in the group, one a former star end at Florida A and M, the other a sprinter from Texas Southern. They were far down on the list academically, although they studied each night until dawn. It was just a matter of time before they left. In two months there were five of the group left, including Freeman. Hand-to-hand combat rid them of two more.

The instructor was a Korean named Soo, but Calhoun, his supervisor, was an American from North Carolina. The niggers would leave or Calhoun would break their necks. He broke no necks, but he did break one man's leg and dislocated another's shoulder. He was surprised and angered to find that Freeman had studied both judo and jujitsu and had a brown belt in the former and a blue stripe in the latter. He would throw Freeman with all the fury and strength he could muster, each time Freeman took the fall expertly. He dismissed the rest of the class one day and asked Freeman to remain.

"Freeman, I'm going to be honest with you. I don't think your people belong in our outfit. I don't have anything against the rest of the group; I just don't think they belong. But you I don't like."

"Well, I guess that's your hang-up."

"I don't like your goddamn phony humility and I don't like your style. This is a team for men, not for misplaced cottonpickers. I'm going to give you a chance. You just walk up to the head office and resign and that will be it. Otherwise, we fight until you do. And you will not leave this room until I have whipped you and you walk out of here, or crawl out of here, or are carried out of here and resign. Do I make myself clear?"

"Yes, whitey, you make yourself clear. But you ain't running me nowhere. You're not man enough for that." Freeman felt the adrenaline begin coursing through his body and he began to get that limp, drowsy feeling, his mouth turning dry. I can't back away from this one, he thought.

"Mr. Soo will referee. International judo rules. No chops, kicks or hand blows. Falls and chokeholds only. After a fall, you get three minutes' rest and we fight again and I keep throwing you, Freeman, until you walk out of this outfit for good."

"Mr. Soo?"

They bowed formally and circled one another, each reaching gingerly for handholds on the other's jacket. He had fifteen pounds on Freeman and wore a black belt; but a black belt signifies only that the wearer has studied judo techniques enough to instruct others. The highest degree for actual combat is the brown belt Freeman wore. Calhoun was not a natural athlete and had learned his technique through relentless and painstaking practice. His balance was not impressive and he compensated with a wide stance. Freeman figured his edge in speed all but nullified his weight disadvantage. He had studied Calhoun throughout the courses; he had watched him when he demonstrated throws and when he fought exhibition performances with Soo. Freeman was familiar with his technique and habits and knew that he favored two throws above all others, a hip throw and a shoulder throw, both right-handed.

He came immediately to the attack. Freeman avoided him easily, feeling him out, testing his strength. Calhoun was very strong in the shoulders and arms, but as slow as Freeman had anticipated. He compensated by bulling his opponent and keeping him on the defensive.

Calhoun tried a foot sweep to Freeman's left calf, a feint, then immediately swung full around for the right-handed hip throw. Freeman moved to his right to avoid the sweep, as the North Carolinian had wanted, then, when Calhoun swung into position for the hip throw, his back to Freeman, Freeman simply placed his hand on his back and, before he could be pulled off balance and onto the fulcrum of Calhoun's hip, pushed hard with his left hand, breaking contact. It had been a simple and effective defensive move, requiring speed and expert timing. They circled and regained their handholds on each other's jackets. After a few minutes of fighting, realizing that he was outsped, Calhoun began bulling Freeman in an effort to exhaust him.

Soo signaled the end of the first five-minute period. They would take a three-minute rest. By now, Freeman knew his opponent.

You'd be dangerous in an alley, thought Freeman, but you hung yourself up with judo. Karate, or jujitsu, maybe, to slow me down with the chops and kicks. But there is just no way you can throw me in judo, white boy. He wondered whether to fight, or to continue on the defense. He looked at Calhoun, squatting Japanese style on the other side of the mat, the hatred and contempt naked on his face. No, he thought, even if I blow my scene, I got to kick this ofay's ass. When you grab me again, whitey, you are going to have two handfuls of 168 pounds of pure black hell. He took slow, deep breaths and waited for the three minutes to end.

Soo nodded to them, they strode to the center of the mat, bowed and reached for one another.

Freeman changed from the standard judo stance, with feet parallel, body squared away and facing the opponent, to a variation: right foot and hand advanced, identical to a southpaw boxing stance. It is an attacker's stance, the entire right side being exposed to attack and counter from the opponent. Freeman relied on speed, aggressiveness, natural reflexes and defensive ability to protect himself in the less defensive position. He wanted only one thing: to throw this white man. He moved immediately to the attack.

Freeman tried a foot sweep, his right foot to Calhoun's left, followed up with a leg throw, *osoto-gare,* then switched from right to left, turning his back completely to his opponent, whose rhythm he had timed, and threw him savagely with a right-handed hip throw.

Calhoun lay there and looked at Freeman in surprise. He got slowly to his feet, rearranging his judo jacket and retying his belt. Freeman did the same, then, facing him, he bowed as is the tradition. Calhoun remained erect, staring at Freeman coldly. Freeman maintained the position of the bow, hands on thighs, torso lowered from the hips.

"Calhoun-san. You a judoka. You will return bow of Freeman-san," hissed Soo. Reluctantly, Calhoun bowed. They returned to their places on the mat, squatting Japanese style, waiting for the three minutes to end. Freeman wondered if he could keep from killing this white man. No, he thought, he's not worth it and it would really blow the scene. But he does have an ass-kicking coming and he can't handle it. This cat can't believe a nigger can whip him. Well, he'll believe it when I'm through . . .

Soo signaled them to the center of the mat.

Freeman methodically chopped Calhoun down. He threw him with a right-foot sweep, a left-handed leg throw, another hip throw and finally a right-handed shoulder throw. Calhoun, exhausted by now, but refusing to quit, reacted too slowly and landed heavily on his right shoulder, dislocating it. Soo forced the shoulder back into the socket and the contest was finished. Saying nothing, they bowed formally and Freeman walked slowly to the locker room. It was the end of the day, Friday, and he would have the weekend to recuperate. He would need it.

Calhoun asked for an overseas assignment. Within three days he left for leave at his family home in North Carolina, then disappeared into the Middle East.

Freeman would have to be more careful; there were holes in his mask. He would have to repair them.

Part III

The New Renaissance in Black Mystery Fiction

Walter Mosley

Fearless

WALTER MOSLEY (1952–   ) is the author of four mystery novels
that have been acclaimed as "a snapshot social history of the
black experience in postwar L.A." Mosley's protagonist, Easy
Rawlins, who has been described as "a tough guy with a good
heart [who] . . . combines the moral realism of a Humphrey
Bogart gumshoe with the barely checked race rage of a Richard
Wright antihero," first appeared in *Devil in a Blue Dress*. Nominated for an Edgar for best first mystery and winner of a John
Creasy Award in Great Britain for best first novel, *Devil in a
Blue Dress* was followed by *A Red Death* and *White Butterfly,*
both of which were nominated for the Golden Dagger Award,
among others. *Black Betty,* the fourth novel in the series, was
published in 1994. The movie version of *Devil in a Blue Dress,*
starring Denzel Washington and Jennifer Beals, was released in
1995, the year that also saw publication of his first nonmystery
novel, *R.L.'s Dream.*

Mosley has said of his Easy Rawlins series, "My idea as a
writer at this point is to write about black male heroes . . . a
black man who is heroic in a flawed way; of course, black men
in America have to be." While he was speaking of Easy, the
description also applies to Paris Minton and Fearless Jones of
the story published here for the first time. "Fearless" has been
adapted for broadcast on the Showtime cable network.

Born in South Central Los Angeles, Walter Mosley lives in

New York City. He is a member of the Executive Board of the PEN American Center, where he chairs the Open Book Committee, and is on the Board of Directors of the National Book Awards. He is also the current president of Mystery Writers of America, the first African American to hold that position.

1

DEAR PARIS MINTON, the letter began.

Fearless didn't write letters very often and was overly formal when he did. But I understood that he was trying to write a good letter and was therefore following the rules that he had learned in his brief childhood education.

I hope that you are fine and well up there in San Francisco. I am fine. My leg never really healed too good but other than that I cannot complain. Well I could complain but complaining never helped any Negro that I ever knew so I do not waste much time talking about what I know cannot change.

I skipped his apologies about not writing for three years and the list of a dozen or so jobs he had held since running down to L.A. At the bottom of the page is where he got down to business:

You once told me, Paris, that you would come if I called. I never thought that I would call. I mean you and me are straight up even and you don't owe me a thing. But I could use your help with something down here. I got troubles that no fist or pistol could solve. I need a good friend and you are the best friend that I ever had. I cannot write why I need your help in a letter. I cannot write it down. But if you could come I surely would be grateful.

That letter was why I was standing out on the sidewalk in Oxnard at five o'clock in the morning, waiting for the last connecting bus to L.A. A black man. Alone. Every car that drove by was driven by somebody white, and every one of them slowed down to see what a Negro might be doing in their town—on their property.

Back down in Fayette, Louisiana, where I was born, they had definite rules about where a colored man could stand—and where he couldn't. They had signs that told you where to go. I hated it but at least I knew what to expect.

Up north, in California, they didn't have signs. They *did* have rules —but rules that didn't jibe, rules that folks had brought with them from Michigan and New York and Mississippi, and every other state in the union. A white man from Georgia would get mad at a Negro for sitting next to him at a dinette counter. But the short order cook was from Maine and had had his life saved by a colored medic from South Carolina during World War Two. So instead of those two white men agreeing—they fought.

Fought over the rights of a Negro!

Now all of that was well and good but it made for a hard time when I was first in California. One man tells you to sit at the table and then the next one says that he'll tear your head off if you do.

I'm not a brave man. So I mainly stayed in neighborhoods where we all knew the same rules and where we were all the same color.

But I learned that I couldn't hide—even down among my own people.

One night after a heavy rain I ventured out on "Little" Smith Street —which was no more than an alley in the Filmore district of San Francisco—to catch my friend Fearless Jones after his short-order shift at the Lazy Spoon Diner. I wanted to go with him to hear some jazz. I liked running with Fearless because he was a war hero and all the good-looking women would come around when he'd be there. And if one of those women realized that she wasn't going to get with Fearless that night she might hang out with me just to be around him.

It was late and I was dapper—with a few dollars in my pocket, too. Nothing in the world could have gone wrong that night; at least that was what I thought.

"Hey, nigger!" a cop yelled from his patrol car. "You better start cluckin' 'cause you already walk like a goddamned rooster."

"Yessir, officer. I'm sure 'nuff bound to crow tonight!" I'd heard the word *nigger,* I'd heard it my whole life long, but I swallowed the shame and told that man the truth: I was out for a good time—that's all.

"What you say, boy?" one of the cops growled. They both got out of their car brandishing police sticks.

"Uh . . . uh . . . What's the thing . . . I mean, uh . . . the problem, officers?"

Those mean-looking cops scared the talk right out of my mouth. As they advanced and I could feel the darkness of the street settle around me, I felt like a bug when the great shadow of a foot comes over him.

"Excuse me, officers," somebody said.

The policemen looked to their right. I looked too. And what I saw just heaped more fear on top of what I already felt.

Fearless Jones was standing there in full sergeant's dress. He had fifteen medals across his left breast—medals he'd been given for killing dozens of white Germans.

"Excuse me, officers," he said again. "But you got some kinda trouble wit' Paris here?"

I felt my left leg take a half step backward. I didn't want to but I couldn't help myself.

The police turned from me and I took another half step.

"Well, well, well," one of the cops said. "One'a those circus monkeys. The kind that the organ grinder fucks up the ass after every show."

Fearless was a solid, if slender, six-footer with small eyes and the capacity for a big smile. He smiled when the policeman offended him like that. He smiled even wider as they came toward him.

I should have gone up and stood next to my friend but instead I moved backward, deeper into shadow, and mouthed silently, "Run, fool! Run!"

But Fearless was true to his name.

"What you want wit' me, officers? I ain't done a thing, not a damn thing."

One of the cops slapped Fearless across the face with his billy stick. Maybe he expected Fearless to fall down or back away but he was disappointed whatever he thought, because when he swung again Jones wrested the club out of his hand and poked him in the diaphragm with it. The other cop went for his gun but he was too close to Fearless and was disarmed with a solid whack across the back of his hand. Fearless kicked that cop in the gut, picked up his gun, and went over to disarm the other one.

The policemen, when they saw that Fearless had them disarmed, looked like they knew what was coming. This wasn't the first time they came spitting and swinging at a black man for walking too straight. Now they saw Retribution towering over them.

All of a sudden I started to shake. I was scared to the point of tears but I was happy, too. "Kill 'em," I whispered so that nobody could hear; so that nobody could blame me for the revenge that burned in my soul.

But Fearless didn't shoot. As much as I was afraid that he would, and as much as I wished that he would—Fearless just smiled. He looked down at the pistols, one in each hand, and a surprised look came across his face.

"Lawd, Lawd," he said. "You know I gotta lotta practice killin' you white boys. Whole lotta practice." Then he threw the guns far away over his back. I didn't hear anything for a long time and then I heard the clatter far up the street.

"You think I'm just a niggah and you bad men with them guns. Well, now it's all equal," Fearless said, and those cops swarmed up at him.

The fools should have run the other way.

Fearless was having a grand time. He took their punches and gave back just as good. One cop hit him a terrible blow to the head but all Fearless said was, "Hotcha! All right!" and then he hit that cop so hard that the poor soul did a backward somersault when he hit the ground.

Fearless taunted them and then swung in hard. In less than two minutes both cops were on the pavement, breathing hard and barely conscious. One of them had rolled facedown into a pool of water that had gathered after the rains.

"Better get up outta that water, boy," Fearless said as he lifted the man by his collar. He didn't see the other cop rising up behind him with the knife that he pulled out of his pocket.

"Watch it, Fearless!" I cried, and then I clapped my hand over my mouth, afraid of my own words.

Words that were almost too late.

Fearless shifted and the blade took him in the arm. He went down and my heart sank. But then Fearless slashed out with his elbow and knocked the cop to the ground. But that cop had the strength of fear in him. He leaped up and slashed Fearless's thigh. That was his last mistake.

I wanted to stop Fearless. I didn't want to see that man choked to death. Murder is a sin. But by the time I found my legs, both those policemen were dead. One drowned in the gutter and the other strangled with Fearless's blood flowing into his eyes.

"Fearless! Let go, man. Let go!" I yelled, trying to pull him off of the wide-eyed corpse.

Fearless slumped to the side, bleeding and panting with rage. I hustled off my shoes and then my long nylon socks. I used the socks as tourniquets for his wounds.

Fearless swooned and I half dragged him down four blocks to our flophouse hotel. At that late hour only Old Man Onceit sat at the desk —and Old Man Onceit never saw a thing that could cause him trouble.

The police scoured the neighborhood looking for the cop killers. They came to the men's hotel that Onceit ran but he got rid of them.

Onceit was from the old school of Negro life. He bowed his head and lied his butt off.

"Yeah, they come in here last night, Paris," he told me. "But I says, 'Nawsir, Mr. Officer. Nawsir, I ain't seened a thing an' you know I been sittin' here all night long.' " Then Onceit pulled out a gallon jar with about a quart of yellow urine in it. "I told 'em I didn't even leave my desk to take a piss an' them white boys laughed and left."

Fearless almost died. He got a high fever and I had to give him alcohol rubdowns and feed him aspirin.

"Don't let 'em get me, Paris," Fearless would rave sometimes. "Shoot me if they come up in here!"

He'd grab me and beg for me to kill him rather than to let them take him in. I don't know what he was thinking. Maybe he thought that the cops were like the Germans.

Maybe he was right.

After about a week, the fever went down and I gave him my last twenty dollars and got him on a late night train to L.A. He had a cousin down there—Ella May.

"I owe you, Fearless," I told him at the train. We had him dressed in a big trench coat and a wide, floppy-brimmed hat. "I owe you my life."

"How you figger you owe me anything, Paris? You the one nursed me."

"That was easy. Anybody could do that. But you did somethin' more. You stood up for me even when I wouldn't do it for myself. I owe you for that, Fearless. You can call on me anytime."

2

On that lonely morning, waiting for my connection, I was sorry I had ever made Fearless that promise.

The bus squealed up on time. I was the only passenger getting on at Oxnard.

The dark bus was half-full. It smelled of sweat and cigarettes and stale thermos coffee. I looked around for some black faces but didn't see any. A white woman wearing a yellow hat smiled as I went past her. She must have seen how nervous I was and wanted to make me feel welcome.

"Hey, nigger, watch it!" a white man, who sat one row behind her, said.

I didn't know if he was yelling at me because I'd nudged him or because that woman smiled hello. I went all the way back and sat in the last seat. That was next to the toilet.

I moved as far away from the smell as I could and rested my head against the cold window. There was a promise of dawn from over the mountains but not enough light for me to read my copy of Dante's *Inferno*.

I loved reading books by the great thinkers. I had loved reading ever since I was a child in church. I read so well that Sister Bernice would have me read from the Bible at every Sunday School meeting. I had read the whole Bible, both testaments, by the time I was thirteen. After that I had all kinds of questions about what I had read. But the minister and his deacons didn't want to be asked too many questions. They told me to have faith in the words of the Lord, that I should read his words over and over until I came to understand his truth in my heart.

That's when I started reading other books. I found that there had always been philosophers in Europe who had questions about the Bible —and God. I had made it kind of a hobby to read those thinkers. Actually, that's why I moved to California. I was told by a man I met in New Iberia that anybody could go into a library in California and take out a book.

Anybody.

In Louisiana and Mississippi, Texas and Arkansas, a Negro needed special permission to get a book out of the library. He had to show some special need to read those tomes of knowledge that the Europeans had stored for more than two thousand years.

"Niggers think they own the world today. Yes they do."

I was half dozing and couldn't really make out the angry words but I knew that they were aimed at me.

"They went to war. They carried guns and shot down white men. They raped our women over there. And now they're back and they think that they can do it here."

I looked up the aisle. One or two men shot glances back at me.

"There he is," the white man that had cursed me before stood up and pointed me out. "He winked at this woman right here. This white woman."

The woman didn't stand up and deny it. It was better that she didn't. A white woman putting herself anywhere in proximity of a black man, even if she meant to protect him, only caused more trouble.

"Here he is thinkin' that he can kiss your girlfriend and kick you in the behind. Isn't that right, mister?"

When he tried to include the man across the aisle from him I took the knife out of my bag. It was only four inches long but it was sharp as a razor and almost two and a half inches wide. It was a fighting knife made for a close quarters argument—but I was no fighter. I'd never cut a man. I had rarely even used my fists.

"Yeah," the angry man said as if the man across from him had agreed with his foolish talk. "I was over there. I was in Germany. Why the Germans threw down their guns when they saw white soldiers because they had intelligence that the black soldiers ate their prisoners."

Intelligence.

I had never been drafted, never gone to the war, but I didn't say anything about that. All I could do was grip my knife and hope that the white people on that bus didn't need to kill me.

I was scared again. I had spent so much of my life being afraid that it left me sick at heart. Here I was a self-educated man. I had read Aristotle and Aquinas. I could talk to almost anybody about almost anything because I read the newspapers every day. I wasn't trying to hurt that man but that didn't matter. He hated me and he was willing to tell me and everybody else about it. I had raped his women because he believed that I did. I had cannibalized his white Nazi brothers because they said so.

And if I wasn't careful I'd be dead because he said that was for the best.

"What we should do is go on back there and teach him a lesson."

Fearless would have stood up and said, "Come on then! Bring your pale flat ass back here and see if I don't chew it off for you." That's what Fearless would have said.

I whispered those words, sweating and shaking so hard that I might have had a fever.

"Come on," he said. "Let's go back there and teach him a lesson." But nobody wanted to get involved with it. They were all doing their business, and regardless what they felt about Negroes, they weren't ready to lynch me.

"I'll see you when we get to L.A.," he said. I wasn't looking at him but I knew he was addressing me.

———

The bus wound its way into downtown Los Angeles by seven-thirty. We came to a stop beside the station and everybody got out. Everybody but the driver, the angry white man, and me.

I sat there for a couple of minutes hoping that that crazy man would just leave. But when he didn't I took my bag in my left hand and palmed the blade with my right.

When I got near the white man he sprung up and started to say something. I don't know what he wanted to say because I was so scared I grabbed him and shoved my knife up next to his throat.

"Open your mouth and I cut yo' th'oat, boy. C-c-cut it," I said. I held him there for a long time—a full minute or more. His face turned the color of bone and he made a funny little humming noise, but he didn't say a word.

My hand wasn't any too steady; I could have shivered him to death.

Finally I pushed him and he fell backward into his seat. I moved quickly then. I had put myself into jeopardy and the only thing left was to run.

I went for the front but found the driver standing in the well of the door. I came up to him quickly, bag in one hand and knife in the other. The driver looked down at my blade and then at my face—he wasn't scared of me. Then he looked over his shoulder at the angry-man-turned-coward who was still trying to catch his breath back in his chair.

The driver, who was very large and corpulent, smiled then. He backed out of the door and made a gesture with his hand that said, *after you.*

I didn't know what was in the driver's mind—I didn't care either. I hot-footed it for four blocks without pausing or looking back. On Alameda I saw an older Negro man walking and carrying a brown lunch sack. I went toward him, to ask him if he knew how I could catch a bus down to 112th and Avalon. But when he saw me coming he shied to the side and sped up his pace.

I didn't know what was wrong with him until I looked down at my hand and saw that I was still carrying the knife.

3

An hour later I was walking down the block that Fearless lived on. It was back in the days when there weren't all that many proper apartment buildings in L.A. That block was mainly houses. Most of them were small homes with big yards sporting fruit trees and surrounded by neatly trimmed grass.

But Fearless's house was large and rambling. It was slapped together from unpainted and weathered planks—three floors high, with a room or two stuck up on the roof. The lawn was wild with half-dead passion fruit vines that draped themselves over everything giving the impression of an abandoned spider's web.

There was a stately eucalyptus tree in the front yard that had a hand-painted sign nailed to it: NO CHILDREN. NO DOGS.

An old woman was sitting on the porch in a straight-backed wooden chair.

"Mornin'," I said to her.

"It is that," she said back.

She was a Negro woman, with skin the color and luster of mud. Her eyes were tired and she didn't make a move that she didn't have to.

"Fearless Jones live here?" I asked.

"Mmm-hm," she hummed.

"What apartment?"

"Up to the top an' on your left."

I waited for more but there wasn't any more coming.

There were people here and there along the halls of the rooming house. Some doors were decorated with photographs or ribbons. Somebody had laundry drying on the banister that went along the stairs. I ran into her on the third floor. She was trying to find a place for a large bath towel in the midst of her bloomers, bras, and skirts.

"Hi," I said.

"Hi." She had small bones and a thin face but her eyes and lips were very large.

"You know where Fearless Jones live?"

"Right down through that door at the end of the hall. It's a ladder leads up to that illegal add-on Mrs. Banks put in. Fearless the left door," she said. And then with some bad taste in her mouth, "Deletha on the right."

"Thanks," I said. I went down toward the door she pointed to, I even opened it up. But then I went back and asked, "Why you puttin' your laundry on this dusty old banister when it's so nice outside?"

" 'Cause if I put it outside somebody gonna take it."

"You think somebody gonna steal yo' draws?"

She didn't answer in words but her face told me that I better sleep with my socks on if I wanted to wear them in the morning.

I got up the ladder and into the small makeshift add-on that the land-lady had put there to catch some extra rent. The door to the left was closed and locked. Nobody answered my knock.

"Fearless! Fearless!" I thought he might have been asleep.

The door behind me came open. I turned and saw her. I looked into her eyes and things started happening in my body. I had the feeling of motion like one gets on a ship at sea.

Her eyes and skin were the same color brown. And that skin was so smooth that she must have just finished rubbing lotion into it. She had on a dark cotton dress but she could have been wearing a burlap sack and that body would have shown through.

I wanted to ask her a question but I had forgotten what it was.

Duke Ellington's band was playing in the room behind her. It was just a radio but it felt like the Duke was really there.

I looked over her head—just to see.

Her eyes looked to the side and then back to me.

"You wanna dance?" Those were the first words that Deletha Mason ever said to me.

And I was a young man then. That is to say—a fool.

There were windows on three walls of her room. They were all un-shaded and open too. Birds sang in the eucalyptus branches, the Duke played from the radio. Nobody could see us up there because Fearless's house was the tallest thing around.

I took this woman-dream into my arms. When she pressed her body against mine she felt my excitement.

"Oh," she said softly. The look she gave me said that it was okay.

We danced for a while. The music changed. We danced some more. Our hands moved around. I explored her body while she moved her fingers on my face. She came the first time with her long nails circling my eyes. Then her hands went down my body.

"Could we, we go over there?" I asked, looking at her bed. Her hands had been something I'd missed for my whole life.

Deletha looked over there but then she looked back at me and shook her head no.

"I wanna dance, baby," she said and then she did something with her fingertips that made me hunch over her and say something that was in no language I had ever heard.

By the time the music had changed again we were on our knees. She was smiling, almost laughing at me, and swaying to the music. I went wherever she wanted me to go.

"These the only pants I got, momma," I said, hoping that she'd understand. And she did understand me, but not like I wanted her to. Her smile got vicious and her hands got busy. I was on my back crying out and certain that I knew what every verse I had ever read had meant. We were both fully clothed with Deletha on top still working her hands.

"Stop, baby. Stop," I begged.

"What? What you say?"

"Pl-please stop."

"Can't you stop me?"

"No," I whispered and she took pity.

I was lying there with the bright California sun shining in. The birds were still singing. Benny Tyler had picked up the pace on the radio.

"You better get them pants off," Deletha said. "I'll rinse 'em out."

I did what she said and asked, "You got a towel I could wrap around me?"

"You just get in the bed." She was smiling again. "I be right there."

4

"You can't fall in love in no minute." That's what my Aunt Alberta used to say. I loved my auntie and I always said, "Yes, ma'am," and I always believed her; until that day with Deletha.

If it was just her body against mine I would have liked it but I wouldn't have called it love. But in the bed I lost my mind. She talked to me in the bed. Not the usual kind of talk about how good I was or how good that felt. She would kiss me and hold me, ride me and whisper in my ear. At one point she went in my bag. She didn't care about the knife but Dante she lingered over.

"You wanna read t'me, Paris?"

It was as if she knew what was in my heart, what I needed from a woman. It was the same question Sister Bernice used to ask me after Sunday School. We'd go into the minister's room and I'd read verses that she called out.

I read to Deletha.

Deletha scrubbed my soul.

Much later on we were napping in the bed when all of a sudden Deletha jumped up. She grabbed my pants that were drying on the windowsill.

"Get dressed quick!"

"What? Why?"

"Fearless might be your friend now but he won't be no more if he find you in my bed."

"Fearless? . . . and you?"

I could hear the sound of someone walking down the hall on the floor below. I didn't say another word to Deletha. I just hurried on my pants and shirt, my socks and shoes. I was stuffing the laces under the tongues of my brogans while Deletha was making the bed. She finished that and went across the room to grab a beer bottle from the shelf. She popped off the top just as Fearless came in the door.

He was a little older and gaunt about the face, but the effect made him seem even more powerful—even more deadly than he had been right after the war.

"Paris!" That big smile came out and I was almost glad. I saw when he walked in that Fearless had a slight limp. He noticed my stare and looked down at his leg.

"I cain't chase down no bear but I could whip his ass if he get close enough."

We hugged and shook hands.

" 'Bout time you got home, Fearless Jones. Your boy Paris been drinkin' my beers and bendin' my ear since this mornin'. Hm!" Deletha was a different woman. She had turned from my dream to his in just seconds. All of the guilt building up in me went away then. I realized that I was a mere mortal in the presence of a goddess and her whims.

Fearless gathered her up in his arms. She was pliant with him. His baby. Never to be mine again.

Fearless had brought ribs and cold beer and potato salad. He was a Texan and so even though he had only brought food for two there was more than enough left over for me.

I learned that Fearless did construction labor for a day job and was a bouncer in the club where Deletha sang on the weekend. That's where he and Deletha met. We didn't talk too much about work though.

Mostly he was happy to see me and I was pretending that I was happy to be there.

"Yeah, Paris, it sure is good to see you," Fearless said. "You know, 'Letha. This man here has got to have read more books than the whole white population of Tuscaloosa County."

Deletha just smiled and leaned against her man's chest. I didn't look into her eyes—I wasn't strong enough for that.

"Yeah," I said. "And Fearless could whip any three men in that county."

"Maybe I should go on outta the room an' let you boys stay alone together," Deletha said.

"No, don't do that, baby. Don't do that. You know I can't stand to be away from my sugar too long."

Fearless gave Deletha a deep kiss.

"What you call me down here for, Fearless?" I asked.

"Huh? Oh yeah. Right. We don't have to talk about it tonight."

"I wanna talk about it."

"Okay. Don't bite my head off now. Sure."

"We should tell 'im, baby," Deletha said.

"You go on then. You got words better'n me."

Deletha sat down on Fearless's lap because there were only two chairs in her room. When she looked me in the eye I let myself enjoy it.

Love with a young man; it's worse than a moody drunk with a gun.

"You ever hear about Johnny Truelove?" she asked me.

I shook my head.

"He used to play trombone. He was good too but then he got into this fight an' got his lips cut up bad. That's when he started managing the Playpen."

"That's where you sing?"

"Yeah."

"I'd like to hear you sing."

That brought out a smile that Deletha didn't plan on. I was happy, a fool really, because I got Deletha to smile.

"Johnny heard me sing in a church in Compton four years ago. He give me twenty-five dollars and had me sign a seven-year contract . . ."

"You hear that shit?" Fearless said. "Twenty-fi'e dollars for seven years. That man is a slave holder an' you know he's colored too."

"But last month Willie Niles come through an' heard me."

"Willie Niles the band leader?"

Deletha nodded. "He told me t'be in Chicago when he gets back off the road in two months. He said that I could sing with his band. But Johnny never gonna let me go—he said so."

The hunger in Deletha's eyes wasn't made up.

"Buy it from him."

"He won't sell," Fearless said. "He one'a them niggers from New Orleans think his shit don't stink. He like to feel better'n us."

"Why'ont you just go on up there an' beat it outta him?" I asked Fearless.

" 'Letha don't want it. She says that that could backfire an' get me in trouble."

"I don't want my baby goin' t'jail."

"Okay," I said instead. "You can't buy it and you can't beat it out of him. I give up."

"We could steal it." Deletha smiled.

I waited.

"He's got it in a hole under his desk."

"So?"

"All we got to do is get in there when he ain't there an' steal it," Fearless said.

"Okay. Okay, let's say you right. Why did I just spend eighteen hours on three buses comin' down here for that? You wanna take them papers—take 'em." I was very mad. It was like they were playing with my life for no good reason.

"We can't get to it, Paris," Deletha said. "Johnny don't trust me since I said I wanted to leave. Fearless don't have no excuse to be back in Johnny's room. And Johnny always keeps his door locked."

"Hell then," I said. "Break in."

"Naw, man," Fearless said. "He gots all kindsa bolts and locks on that place. And he got this shepherd police dog he lets loose in the bar at night."

"Shoot the damn dog."

Fearless got a hurt look on his face. "You know me, Paris. I cain't kill no dog."

Deletha looked up at the ceiling and shook her head softly.

"So what can I do?"

Fearless showed me his big grin, the same grin he showed those cops before they died.

"They need a bartender and all I gotta do is say your name. Bartender gets the key to Johnny's office 'cause he gots the bar supplies in there."

"Why he gonna listen to you if he don't trust your girlfriend?"

The grin widened. "He don't know she wit' me. She told 'im that she hates me 'cause I'm so dark. An' you know he light enough t'pass."

It was a plan, maybe a good one, but not something that Fearless would have ever cooked up. I looked at Deletha and took in her smile.

I remember thinking that I owed Fearless something—and that trouble was my only currency.

5

Johnny Truelove liked me. I shook his hand and told him that I could make my numbers. He asked me if I could read and I said, "Well enough to sign my name and go into the right toilet."

Johnny was a tall man, taller than Fearless, skinny, and mean. He was that mulatto white that they get to be down in Creole country. He was deadly handsome except for a slashing scar across his lips. When you looked him in the eye he covered his mouth with his left hand as if he were thinking.

There was nothing in the world that Johnny loved more than an ignorant Negro.

My first week on the job he lorded over me correcting my slightest mistakes and chewing me out if I was too slow.

"Paris, make this man here a gimlet," he'd say. "And remember, a gimlet is gin not scotch." Then he'd laugh and laugh.

His bar was small and stingy. The floors smelt from spilt beer. The walls were green, and not from paint. It was a hovel that would never be clean. I suffered every minute I was there.

I worked hard at the Playpen and I'd come home tired and mad. Fearless let me have his room while he stayed with Deletha. I spent the nights listening to her radio across the hall interrupted by loud sighs and shaking through the walls.

By the time Thursday came I was ready to quit and go home. I told Fearless that I had the key to Truelove's office but that he was always in there.

"And if he ain't in there and I try to get in, he follows me up to the door an' ask me what I'm lookin' for."

"Just give it another day, Paris," my friend begged. "Deletha got a plan."

"What plan?"

"She like to keep quiet on things till they happen. She's a woman." Fearless was amazed by women. Anything they did he could explain away by the fact of their gender.

"Okay," I told him. "Just try and keep it down with Deletha tonight."

I was glad for Friday though. Because Friday was payday and on Friday I got to hear Deletha sing. Her singing voice had nothing to do with the way she spoke. Deletha sang the way she made love. Her words were what every man, and woman, wanted to hear. Her "Man Done Gone" made me want to cry. And "Hard Road Home" left me in tears. All the ways she was and everything I'd seen her do made sense when Deletha sang. She had seen the pain that we all knew, every one of us. Even her laughter broke your heart.

"Get ready tonight, Paris," Fearless told me when he came up to the bar for a drink at his break. "Just be ready."

I couldn't see anything different. Truelove spent half of the time in his office and the other half watching his locked door. I was busy because it was Friday and it seemed like everybody in L.A. loved to hear Deletha sing.

She was giving the eye to this one big guy who was seated at a table near the stage. One time she winked at him and another she blew him a kiss.

At a break I was making a quart of screwdrivers when I heard this scream.

"Git yo' hands off'a me, niggah!" It was Deletha slapping her big admirer.

"What you say?" he answered in a voice too high for his stature.

"You heard me!" Deletha screamed back.

She picked up a beer glass and slammed it into the big man's face. He put his hands up and when he brought them back down he saw the blood wrought by broken glass. He was about to slug Deletha when Fearless came up. Behind Fearless came Johnny Truelove.

But the big man had friends too.

Johnny and Fearless were outnumbered but they were sober where the other men were drunk. It took me a moment to get the courage to pick up the baseball bat that lay under the counter but I got it and I came around the bar ready to stand up—for once.

"Not that way, fool," a woman said into my ear. Deletha was standing there next to me.

"The office," she said.

Johnny's office was small and stank of cigars. He had a signed photograph of Myrna Loy on the wall and a bottle of good whiskey on the table. There was a three-hundred-pound safe on the floor in the corner, but it was shut tight.

"Move the desk," Deletha ordered.

It was a heavy oak job and I had trouble moving it. The noise from the fight was escalating outside. In the distance I could hear sirens. I started to sweat.

When I got the desk moved aside all I saw was the cracked linoleum underneath.

"Rip it off!" said Deletha.

I obeyed.

The floor underneath was good wood, almost new. It was a trapdoor with a recessed padlock holding it closed. I didn't need Deletha to tell me to break the lock. I started banging away but the lock was solid and my blows didn't do a thing.

"Keep on," Deletha urged. "Keep on."

Outside the cops were coming in the bar.

I started hitting the floor with all my might. Deletha propped a chair under the doorknob. I hit the lock again—it hardly even jumped in its hole.

Then the doorknob jiggled and Johnny cried, "Who's in there? Officers! Officers! Somebody robbin' me in there!"

Fear is what makes men their strongest. Fear gets rid of all thought and all you got left is muscle and bone. I hit that lock so hard it broke down through the floor. I ripped the splintered trapdoor from its moorings and Deletha, moving like a cat, scooped up the tin strongbox that lay inside.

Following her lead I went out the window. Behind me I heard the door giving way. All I remember after that was flight.

I caught up with Deletha two blocks from the bar. She was huffing and straining but she wouldn't let me carry the box.

"We should split up, Paris," she said when neither one of us could run any farther.

"Long as you let me have that box you could go where you want, girl."

"This is mine."

"Then you hold on to it," I said. "And I'll hold on to you."

6

We ran into Fearless heading back toward their place. He was limping at a quick gait down the misty street. I called out, "Fearless Jones."

He turned and grinned. "Hey! Hey, yeah!"

We were all there in the street about two blocks down from the rooming house.

"I cut out when the cops came," Fearless said. "Let's go on home." He put his arm around Deletha but she was in no mood for love.

"We better not, man," I said. "Truelove knows where you live and he knows it was us took his box by now. The cops'll be here any minute."

"Johnny won't send any cops," Deletha said.

"Why not, baby?" Fearless asked. "We did steal this thing."

Instead of answering Deletha said, "Paris is right. We should get down to the Dunbar and spend the night. In the morning we could take care of this here."

For a long time the Dunbar was the only good hotel in L.A. that let colored people stay in it. It was down on Central Avenue. We got a room for three. We lied saying that we were all cousins in town for a funeral.

In the room we cracked open the strongbox but there wasn't any contract in there. There was a key, a pistol, and a handwritten letter signed by Johnny Truelove.

The letter was Johnny's confession as an accessory to the murder of Calvin Plough, the previous manager of the Playpen. Johnny said that he was with Sidney "the Shark" Stein the night Stein shot Calvin for cheating at cards. Sidney and Johnny got rid of the body on a garlic farm in Pomona. Johnny took the gun, told Sidney that he'd ditched it. In return Stein gave Johnny Calvin's job.

"So you figger to trade this here letter and pistol for your contract?" I asked Deletha.

Deletha smiled and nodded; I knew she was lying. I didn't know what she was lying about, or why, but there was more to this strongbox than she was letting on.

"Tomorrow," she said. "We call Johnny and make a meeting for the trade. Fearless and I will go to meet him and I'll give him this box and he'll set me free."

"I'll go with you," I said.

"No."

"Why not?"

"Because . . ." she faltered. "Because too many people would make Johnny nervous and it would just be better this way. And, anyway, Fearless is all I need against Johnny."

I knew from the look on Fearless's face that it was no good to argue. He was her protector and savior—I was a third wheel at best.

7

Early in the morning, when Deletha went down to the lobby to call Truelove, I tried to talk sense to Fearless.

"You got to let me come wit' you, man," I told him.

He shook his head slowly and said, "No, Paris. It's better wit' just two."

"Better! Why the hell it gonna be better wit' two? He could be bringin' some gunmen wit' 'im. You shouldn't even be goin'."

" 'Letha say no, man. No gunmen and no you."

But that didn't mean I couldn't follow them.

Fearless and Deletha left the hotel after breakfast and I pretended to go back to the room. But instead I ran down the back stairs and out the front. I went up to a car parked on the street down from the hotel. There was a guy sitting there smoking a cigarette and reading *The Sentinel*, L.A.'s Negro newspaper.

"You see them?" I asked the man when Deletha and Fearless came out of the hotel.

"Uh-huh," he answered, none too sure he wanted to know any more.

"That's my best friend's wife and his buddy, Bill." I pulled out a twenty-dollar bill. Twenty dollars was a fortune in 1949.

Deletha and Fearless took a bus all the way down Central until they came to Ninety-sixth Street. At the corner there was a big cafeteria where all kinds of folks sat and ate sandwiches and stew. I jumped out of my ride and loitered around the door of the restaurant.

At a seat in the middle of the place was Johnny. He was dressed to the nines and as mean-looking as a human can get. He glared at the couple.

They didn't even sit down.

Deletha said something and Johnny took a thick envelope from his pocket. Deletha looked inside the envelope. It looked more like she was counting than reading a contract.

When she was satisfied she handed the strongbox to Johnny. Instead of looking in the box Johnny put his hand in his back pocket. Deletha screamed. That's when Fearless clocked him—hit him so hard that I could hear it at the door.

A commotion started up. Deletha and Fearless made a run for the back door.

I cut out, too.

Down the street and around the corner was an alley that seemed to run behind the restaurant. When I made it to the back door I found Fearless on the ground reeling—somebody had hit him in the head.

I started to run. I ran straight down that alley. When it came to a fork I just naturally went right. If she had taken the other way I had lost her but she didn't.

"Hold it, girl," I said, coming up behind her and catching her by the arm.

"Let me loose!" she shouted and then she started to scream, but I grabbed her and pushed her through a fence into a backyard, a garden really, full of sweet peas, tomato bushes, and sunflowers. The owners were probably at church.

I should have been at church.

"Let me loose!" she shouted again but not so loud.

"You better shut up, girl! I ain't done nuthin' to you to make you scream—not yet!"

Deletha calmed down a little and asked, "What you want?"

"What you got in that envelope?"

"Seven thousand five hundred dollars and my contract to Johnny."

Sweating must have been a natural expression for me in my youth. Any denomination over twenty dollars made me wet.

"From Johnny?" I asked.

"He told me about that gun and that confession when he was blind drunk one night. He was swaggerin' an' blusterin' an' he said about

how he was stealin' from Stein and how he had all that money in a
secret safe-deposit box that he kept under a secret name. I needed
money to go out to Chicago, Paris. Johnny didn't pay me shit."

"I'ma pay you somethin' now though, bitch." Johnny was at the
gate, .38 in his hand. His nose was bloody and his eyes were wide.

That was the most important moment of my life—up to that time.

When I saw Johnny I thought about those dead cops and that angry
man on the bus, about the sneer on that bus driver's face and about Old
Man Onceit making his way as if he still lived on a plantation down
South. All of that, and about a thousand things more is why I jumped at
Johnny—I wanted to erase all those bad feelings by dying a hero's
death. With death sure to come anyway—it wasn't too hard to be
brave.

I took the big man by surprise. We wrestled to the ground. I was
trying to keep the pistol away from my face while Johnny, the stronger
man, was intent on blowing my head off.

The muzzle was moving toward my head and all I could do was delay
it. I wasn't scared though. I didn't have time to be scared. All I could do
was to struggle for my survival and all I could do was to die.

When the shot fired and the hole appeared in the top of Johnny's
forehead I was confused. My mind floundered around for a reason and
a way that Johnny could have shot himself.

When I looked up I realized that it was Deletha, that it was a gun she
had. Now she was pointing her gun at me. I was too tired to fight
anymore and I figured that Deletha was a good shot and it wouldn't
hurt long.

When she didn't shoot I got up on one knee. Johnny was lying there
next to me—his eyes unblinking against the sun.

"Come wit' me, Paris." It wasn't the words, it was her smile that got
me.

"What?"

"Come wit' me."

"To Chicago?"

"Yeah. Come read to me."

Deletha put her gun down and all I saw was the sun through her
windows. All I heard was a thousand nights of jazz.

I still wake up at night sometimes and think that I should have gone
with her.

"Naw, baby. You too much for me. An' Fearless is my friend. We owe him somethin'."

My chances with Deletha were over with those words.

"I don't owe nobody nuthin'," she said.

"You were his girlfriend. He helped you."

"He helped hisself to my pussy, that's what he did. I gave him somethin' an' he did for me. I see it even."

"Lemme have twenty-five hundred," I said. "Let me have that and then it will be even."

I could have jumped her and taken all the money. But she was smiling at me. And like my Aunt Alberta always said, "You smart, Paris, but you still a fool."

8

I took over Deletha's room and decided to stay in Los Angeles. I told Fearless that it was Johnny who sapped him and that Deletha had killed Johnny to save my life.

"I told her to wait," I told Fearless. "But she was too scared with a dead man on her hands and ran. She said that she'd write when she felt safe again."

"She ain't never gonna write," Fearless said.

"Why you say that?"

" 'Cause she gonna be thinkin' 'bout that dead man every time she think about me and you know Deletha too sensitive to handle that."

I nodded my agreement not trusting my mouth for words.

Gar Anthony Haywood

And Pray Nobody Sees You

A Los Angeles native, GAR ANTHONY HAYWOOD (1954–   ) is the author of three novels featuring the contemporary L.A. private investigator Aaron Gunner. The first novel, *Fear of the Dark,* won the Private Eye Writers of America Award for 1987, which resulted in its publication the following year. It was followed by *Not Long for This World* and *You Can Die Trying.* His next Aaron Gunner novel, *It's Not a Pretty Sight,* will be published in 1996.

"And Pray Nobody Sees You," like the Aaron Gunner novels, is full of streetwise characters and moral ambiguity. It also features the Deuce, a bar the detective frequents and the site of the opening scene in *Fear of the Dark.* Unlike the novels, however, "And Pray Nobody Sees You" is written in the first person, allowing the reader to get more insight into gumshoe Gunner's thoughts.

Gar is also the author of *Going Nowhere Fast* (1994), a second mystery series featuring retired cop Joe Loudermilk and his wife, Dottie, an ex-schoolteacher. The couple's latest escapades can be found in *Bad News Travels Fast* (1995).

IT DOESN'T HAPPEN OFTEN, but every now and then a good story will buy you a free drink at the Deuce. Lilly has to be feeling charitable and business has to be slow, say, down to three lifeless regulars and maybe another new face, somebody who likes to treat a single shot of Myers's like a lover they're afraid to part with. Lilly will get tired of watching Howard Gaines slide dominoes across her bar, or listening to Eggy Jones whine about the latest indignity he's suffered at the hands of his wife Camille, and will demand that somebody tell her a story entertaining enough to hold her interest. Lilly calls herself asking but she's too big to ask for anything; everything she says sounds like a demand, whether it comes with a "please" or not.

She was in the mood for a story a couple of Tuesdays back and, as usual, looked to me first to do the honors. I don't always take the prize on these occasions, but I manage to get my share. Maybe it's the line of work I'm in.

This particular evening I answered Lilly's call with the following.

And watched the Wild Turkey flow afterward.

It started with a U-turn.

Brother driving a blue Chrysler did a one-eighty in the middle of Wilmington Avenue, two o'clock on a Thursday afternoon, in broad daylight. Mickey Moore, Weldon Foley, and me were standing outside Mickey's barbershop when we saw him go by on the eastbound side of the street, stop, then yank the Chrysler around like he'd just seen somebody who owed him money. We would have all ducked for cover, smelling the week's latest drive-by in the making, except that the driver looked too old to be a gangbanger and the three of us were the only people on the street. That left us nothing else to believe but that we'd just seen the act of a fool, nothing more and nothing less.

"You see that? That nigger's crazy," Mickey said.

"Sure is," Foley agreed, nodding his hairless head. I sometimes suspect Mickey keeps him around precisely for that purpose; he sure as hell never has to take his clippers to him.

"And look: not a goddamn cop in sight. Now, if that was *me*—"

"Or me," I said, thinking the same thing my landlord was thinking. I'd never gotten away with a U-turn in my life.

The Chrysler was now headed back in our direction on the westbound side of the street, cruising in the right lane the way cars do when the people driving them are looking for a parking space. It was an old '71 Barracuda, a clean and chromed-out borderline classic with a throaty exhaust and tires you could hide a small country in. It was grumbling like a California earthquake when it finally pulled to a stop at the curb, directly in front of us.

The driver got out of the car and approached us, his left arm folded up in a white sling. We let him come without saying a word.

"One of you Aaron Gunner?" he asked. He was a wiry twenty-something, six-one or six-two, with razor lines cut all along the sides and back of his head, something I imagined he'd had done in hopes of drawing attention from his face. It was sad to say, but the boy looked like a black Mr. Potato Head with bad skin.

"That's me," I told him, before Weldon or Mickey could point me out. "What can I do for you?"

He openly examined the front of Mickey's shop, as if he were looking for the fine print on the sign above the door, and said, "This is your office, right?"

"That's right. I've got a room in the back."

He glanced at my companions briefly. "All right if we go back there to talk?"

I shrugged. "Sure. Come on in."

Mickey was insulted by the slight of not being introduced, but he didn't say anything.

I led my homely visitor past Mickey's three empty barber chairs, through the beaded curtains in the open doorway beyond, and into the near-vacant space that has passed for my office for the last four years. The lamp on my desk was already on, so all I had to do was sit down and wait for my friend to find the couch and do the same.

He never did.

He just stood in front of my desk and said, "You're a private detective."

"Yes. Can't you tell?"

"I want to hire you."

"To do what?"

"I want you to find a car for me."

"A car?"

"Yeah." He nodded. "A '65 Ford Mustang, tangerine orange. Two-plus-two fastback, fully restored and cherried out."

"A '65?"

"Yeah. First year they were made. Probably ain't but fifty of 'em in the whole country still on the road."

"Two-eighty-nine, or six?"

"Come on. If it was the six, man, I'd let 'em have the damn car."

He had a point. A '65 Mustang two-plus-two without the V-eight under the hood might have been worth a few dollars to somebody, but any true collector would've considered it a stiff. Cherried out or no.

"It sounds nice," I told him.

"Man, fuck 'nice.' It's a classic. There ain't but fifty of 'em still in existence, like I said."

I nodded my head to show him I was finally paying attention. "And your name was . . . ?"

"Purdy. David Purdy. Look—"

"This car we're talking about, Mr. Purdy. I take it it belongs to you?"

"Does it belong to me? Hell, yes, it belongs to me. Why else would I be here talkin' to you?"

"I give up. Why *are* you here talking to me?"

"Because I got *jacked* last night, man. What else? Over on Imperial and Hoover, over by my girl's house. Little motherfucker shot me at the stoplight and took my goddamn car."

"You call the police?"

"The police? Of course. I told you, man, I got shot." He tried to gesture with his left arm, but just moving the sling an inch from his side seemed to bring tears to his eyes.

"So? What do you need with me?" I asked him.

Purdy answered the question with a crooked, toothy grin meant to convey incredulity. "Man, you're jokin', right? What do I need with *you?* I need you to get the goddamn car back for me. What do you think?"

He'd been looking for a foot in his ass since he'd stepped out of the Chrysler, and now he'd finally earned it. Still, I let the comment pass. I'd spent the retainers of rude jackasses before, and their money went just as far as anyone else's. Purdy's would be no different.

"You don't think the police can find the car," I said.

"Let's just say I'm not countin' on it," Purdy said. "Least, not until there ain't nothin' left of it but a goddamn frame."

"I take it you didn't have one of those electronic tracking devices on it. The kind the police can home in on?"

"No. I didn't."

"That's too bad."

"Yeah, it is. I fucked up. I put a lot of time and money in that car, then turned around and didn't protect it right. So it's gone. But that don't mean I gotta forget about it, like the cops said I should. Hell, no.

I want that car back, Mr. Gunner, and I want it back *now,* 'fore some fuckin' chop shop can hack it all to pieces."

"If that's possible, you mean," I said.

"It's possible. It just ain't gonna be easy. I'd find the car myself if the shit was easy."

I fell silent, pretending to be mulling things over, when all I was really doing was deciding on a fee.

"Somebody said you were the man for the job, so I looked you up. But if you're not—"

"What do you figure the car's worth? Ten, fifteen grand?" I asked.

"Shit. Try twenty-five," Purdy said.

"Okay, twenty-five. Here's the deal. I locate the car within forty-eight hours, in its original condition, you owe me twenty-five hundred. Ten percent of its worth, cash on delivery. If I don't find it, or I do and it's already been chopped up, you only owe me for my time. Three hundred dollars a day, plus expenses, half of which you've got to pay me now, just to get me started."

"No problem," Purdy said. Nothing I'd said had made him so much as blink.

"No problem?"

"No, man, no problem. I told you: I want the car back, and you're supposed to be the man can get it for me." He was already peeling some bills off a wad of green he'd removed from his pocket.

"I'm gonna need a description of the carjacker and the license plate of the car. And a phone number where you can be reached at any time, day or night."

Purdy threw four hundred dollars on the desk in front of me and said, "You've got it."

I still had my reservations about the man, but now I was bought and paid for.

It was time to go to work.

The first thing I did was go see Mopar.

Mopar used to steal cars. Lots of them. It was what he did for fifteen years, from the time we were in high school together right up until his last bust, when a fight in the joint left him crippled for life and scared the thief right out of him, for good. His mother still called him Jerome, but he was Mopar to everyone else; back in high school, he could steal any car you cared to name, but he did all his racing in Chryslers.

Today, Mopar was in the body shop business.

He had his own place over on Florence Avenue, between Denker and La Salle. He'd started out working there, hammering dents out of Buicks and Oldsmobiles, then slowly bought into the business, buying bigger and bigger chunks as the years went by until finally, little over a year ago, he became the man holding all the paper. And all with only one good leg.

He was standing behind the counter in the office when I came in, just hanging up the phone. He was damn near as fat as Lilly these days, and only twice as jolly. The sight of my approach brought a broad grin to his face, same one he used to wear as a kid.

"Tail Gunner! What it be like?"

That was what he used to call me back in school, Tail Gunner. I can't tell you how glad I was that the nickname never caught on with anyone else.

"It's your world, Mopar," I said, burying my right hand deep in his. "I'm just livin' in it."

"Shit, you ain't livin' in *my* world. Otherwise, I'd see you more often 'round here."

I shrugged apologetically. "What can I say? I'm a busy man."

Mopar just laughed. "So what can I do you, man? This business or pleasure?"

"Afraid it's business. I'm looking for somebody I think you might be able to help me find."

"Yeah? Who's that?"

"A 'jacker. Boy about fifteen to eighteen years old, five-seven, five-eight, 130 pounds. Dark skin and dark eyes, with braces on his teeth. Likes to wear striped clothes and a San Antonio Spurs baseball cap turned sideways on his head, bill facing east. At least, that's how he was dressed last night."

"A 'jacker? Why you wanna ask me about a 'jacker?"

"Because you used to be one, Mopar. It hasn't been that long ago, man."

"Man, I wasn't never a 'jacker! I never pulled nobody out of a car in my life!"

"No, but—"

"These kids today, man, they're crazy! Shootin' people to steal a goddamn car. Man, I never even owned a gun 'til I got this place!"

"Okay, so you weren't a 'jacker. You're right, that was the wrong thing for me to say."

"Damn right it was."

"But your objective was still the same, right? To steal cars?"

Mopar didn't say anything.

"Look. I'm not saying you know the kid. I just thought you might, that's all. Because I know you've put a few of 'em to work for you in the past, tryin' to help 'em go straight like you did, and I thought, maybe this kid I'm lookin' for was one of 'em. Or maybe you've seen him hanging around somewhere, I don't know. It was just a thought."

Mopar just glared at me, his jovial mood a thing of the past. "You say this boy 'jacked a car last night?"

I nodded. "Orange '65 Mustang fastback, in primo condition. Owner says it happened over on Imperial and Hoover, a few minutes past midnight."

"A '65 fastback? You shittin' me?"

"Afraid not. Now you know why the man wants it found before somebody takes an air wrench to it."

"You mean the fool don't know they already did that eight hours ago?"

"I guess he's the optimistic type. I tried to tell him to save his money, but he's emotionally attached. So . . ."

I waited for the big man to make up his mind, but he seemed in no hurry to do so.

"Did I mention the fact that my client got shot? Clipped in the left wing, but it could've been worse. This kid who 'jacked him isn't just in it for the rides, Mopar. He likes to shoot people, too."

Still, Mopar offered me nothing but silence.

"Tell you what. Forget it," I said. "This was a bad idea, bothering you with this. Come by and see us at the Deuce sometime, huh?"

I turned and started out of the room.

"You say the kid wears braces?" Mopar asked.

I turned back around. "That's right."

He hesitated a moment longer, then said, "I can't give you a name. But I can tell you where to look."

I told him that would be fine.

Mopar said the kid liked to hang out in front of a liquor store on Western and Eighty-first Street. Mopar remembered him because he'd had to chase him out of his shop once, when the kid had come around looking for one of Mopar's employees and had taken the news of the employee's recent dismissal badly. Every now and then since, Mopar'd see him at the liquor store, kicking it with his homies out on the sidewalk.

But he wasn't there Thursday night.

I know. I waited there six hours for him to show up. Three members of his crew were there—teenage boys dressed in oversized khaki pants and giant plaid jackets—but they were all the wrong size for the kid I was looking for, and none of them had braces on their teeth. I sat in my car across the street and thought about approaching them, but I knew all they'd do with my questions was tell me where I could stick them, so I decided to spare myself the aggravation and just stayed put.

When I'd inevitably given up watching the liquor store, I cruised the 'hood indiscriminately, hitting all the major intersections I could think of, but my results were the same. No kid with braces looking like a 'jacker on the prowl, no classic Mustangs in tangerine orange. I saw a howling parade of black-and-whites cut a swath through traffic on Normandie and Manchester, an old man roll off a bus bench into the gutter on Slauson and Vermont, and two hookers change a flat tire on a run-down convertible Pontiac on Prairie and 108th—but I didn't see any carjackers anywhere.

So I went home.

The next morning, I called Matthew Poole with the L.A.P.D. and asked him if he knew anybody in Auto. Poole doesn't owe me any favors, but the homicide man helps me out when he can all the same, I don't really know why. Maybe it's because he thinks we're friends.

The man Poole eventually put me in touch with was a cop named Link, first name Sam. Over the phone he sounded like one of those cops who came out of the womb flashing a badge and reading the obstetrician his rights; he was cordial enough, but you could tell he was of the opinion I was standing between him and his pension. I got right to the point and told him about Purdy, then asked him afterward if the story sounded familiar. The Mustang had been stolen only two nights before, I figured he ought to have heard something about the investigation, even if he himself hadn't been called out on it.

But Link said it was all news to him.

Nothing about the Mustang or Purdy struck him as familiar. And if a shooting had taken place during a 'jacking Wednesday night, he assured me he'd have known about it. In fact, he would have convinced me altogether that the whole of Purdy's story was a lie had my description of the kid I'd spent the previous night looking for not rung a bell with him.

"Striped clothes?" he asked me.

"Yeah."

"That could be Squealer. He's into stripes. You want to talk to him?"

He was offering to go pick him up for me.

"Yeah, but not formally. I need him conversant," I said, hoping he wouldn't be insulted by the insinuation the kid wouldn't talk downtown.

"You just want to know where to find him, then."

"If that wouldn't be too much trouble."

Link said it wouldn't be any trouble at all.

It took me all day to find him.

He wasn't at home and he wasn't at school. Link had given me a list of about a half-dozen places he liked to frequent, from the Baldwin Hills Crenshaw Plaza to the basketball courts at Jesse Owens Park, but he never appeared at any of them until a few minutes after 7 P.M., when he showed up at a Baskin and Robbins ice cream parlor in a mini-mall on Budlong and Fifty-sixth Street, during my second visit to the site. His pants were black denim, no stripes, but his shirt was an oversized tee with alternating blue and green horizontal bands, and the cap turned sideways on his head was silver and black, the primary colors of the San Antonio Spurs. He had arrived on foot with two other kids who looked roughly the same age, a boy and a girl, and I had to watch the three of them eat ice cream and throw napkins at each other for well over an hour before he was ready to leave again.

I had hoped when the time came he'd leave alone, but I wasn't that lucky. He left the same way he came, with his two friends in tow. The trio walked northbound along Budlong and I trailed behind them in my car, keeping a good block, block and a half between us at all times. I was prepared to go on like this all night if I had to, but I wasn't looking forward to it. Of the forty-eight hours I'd given myself to find Purdy's Mustang, more than thirty were already gone, and the clock was still running. I had to get the kid alone, or he had to lead me to the car, one or the other. And fast.

Things were looking dark when Squealer and his homies led me to a house on Fiftieth Street between Harvard and Denker, then disappeared inside. There was light in only one window, and the place was as quiet as an empty grave. The thought occurred to me they might have crashed there for the night, and an hour later nothing had happened to rule that possibility out—until the porch light winked back on and Squealer emerged from the house again.

Alone.

I got out of my car on the passenger side and ducked low to hide behind it, waiting for the kid to saunter past on the opposite side of the street. I was going to make this quick. He'd already shot Purdy and I had no reason to think he wouldn't shoot me, given the chance, so getting the drop on him first seemed to be the wise thing to do. He was stepping off the curb to cross Harvard when I closed the distance between us and put him down, rapping the base of his skull with the butt of my Ruger P-85. He fell like a house of cards. I caught him on his way down, dragged him over to my car, and tossed him in.

Then we went somewhere to talk.

There was nobody on the beach.

It was too cold for romance, and too dark for sightseeing. The moon was heavily shielded behind a thick mask of cloud cover, and a mist hung over the water like a frozen gray curse. The kid and I would not be disturbed.

I had him trussed up like a calf at a rodeo. He was bound, gagged, and blindfolded, stretched out flat upon the wooden-plank walkway that ran beneath the Santa Monica Pier. His gun was in my back pocket, a small twenty-two I'd found shoved into the waistband of his pants. Down here, the sound of the crashing waves echoed between the pier's pylons like thunder in a bottle, thoroughly directionless, and you could taste the salt of the ocean spray with every intake of breath.

When I was certain he was awake, I knelt down beside the kid and said, "I want my car."

He took that as a cue to start thrashing around, but it didn't take him long to see the futility in it. He wasn't going anywhere.

"You haven't guessed by now, we're on the Santa Monica Pier," I said. "Down at the beach. Hear the waves down there? Care for a swim?"

I rolled him over a little.

He got the gist of my phony threat right away, and bought into it completely. I had to hold him down with both hands to keep him still.

"Okay. You get the picture. You don't tell me where my car is, I push you off this fucking pier and into the Pacific. Understand?"

He started to struggle again. I put my hand on his throat and asked him one more time: "Understand?"

Finally, he grew quiet and slowly nodded his head.

"Very good. Car I'm looking for is a '65 Ford Mustang. Orange. You shot me in the arm and stole it from me Wednesday night, out on the corner of Imperial and Hoover. Remember?"

Squealer made no move to answer, so I rolled him over again, one full revolution.

"You're runnin' out of pier, homeboy," I said. Then, after a while, I asked him again, "Do you remember the car?"

This time he nodded his head.

"Good. Now—I'm going to take your gag off, and you're going to tell me where I can find it. You're not going to scream, or cry, or call for your mama—you're just going to tell me where my car is. Otherwise . . ."

I let him think about that a moment, then peeled his gag away from his mouth.

"*At the mall! At the mall, man!*" he said, gasping to get the words out.

"What mall?"

"Fox Hills Mall, man! The Fox Hills Mall!"

"What, in the parking lot?"

"Yeah! In the parkin' lot! You know, the buildin'!"

"The building?" I had to think about that a moment. "You mean the parking structure?"

He nodded his head frantically. "Yeah, that's it! The parkin' structure!"

"What floor?"

"What floor? I don't know, man. Four, I think. Don't kill me, man, please!"

"Why'd you put it there?"

"Why? I don't . . ."

"Why didn't you take it in for chopping? Why'd you park it instead?"

"Shit, I wasn't gonna chop that ride, man! It was too sweet!"

"Too sweet?"

He nodded his head again.

"What were you going to do with it, you weren't going to chop it?" I asked him.

"I was gonna *keep* it. Just . . . let it chill at the mall for a while, then change it up. Get new papers on it, an' shit, so's it could be *my* ride."

I should have guessed.

I put the gag back in his mouth and stood up. Where this kid had found the courage to shoot a man, I couldn't begin to guess. He was scared shitless and seemingly willing to do whatever was asked of him to stay alive.

Odd.

I was going to leave him as he was, anticipating the worst, bouncing about on the wooden walkway floor like a beached whale waiting to die . . . and then I thought of one more question to ask him.

Kneeling beside him again, I said, "Tell me something, June bug: What'd you shoot me for?"

And then he told me exactly what I'd thought he might.

He said I'd made him do it.

The Mustang was on the third floor.

Parked in a distant corner all by itself and covered with a tarp. I peeled the tarp off to look it over carefully, but I knew it was the car I was after inside of ten seconds. Everything about it matched Purdy's description: model, color, license plate number. With one notable exception.

It was a '66.

The '65s had a crosshairs grill; this one had the eggcrate grill of a '66. Which made it a rarity, yes, but not a classic. A man who knew cars might conceivably spend a small fortune to recover a stolen '65, but a '66? I didn't think so. Any more than I thought a man would take a bullet fighting to hold on to a '66, as Squealer the 'jacker had claimed Purdy had done Wednesday night.

Obviously, there was more to this car than met the eye.

When I finally found out what it was, a little over ninety minutes later, I called Purdy to tell him the good news.

"It's over there," I said, pointing. "Across the street."

Purdy turned and saw the Mustang parked on the other side of La Brea Avenue, directly opposite the Pink's hot dog stand in Hollywood where we were sitting. I'd used the keys I'd taken off Squealer to come here, and had been well into my second chili dog when Purdy showed up.

"I don't believe it," he said now, eyeing the car.

"We were lucky," I said, feigning weary humility.

"Where did you find it?"

I shrugged. "Does it matter?"

"No. Not really. I just thought—"

"You have my money, Mr. Purdy?"

"Of course." He took an envelope from his coat pocket and opened it so I could see the bills inside, but didn't hand it over. "You mind if I look the car over first?" he asked.

"Not at all," I said, wiping chili from the sides of my mouth. "I'll just hold on to the keys."

That wasn't what he'd had in mind, but he could see the point was nonnegotiable. Without saying another word, he left to inspect the car, then returned a few minutes later.

"Twenty-five hundred dollars," he said, handing me the envelope he'd shown me earlier. He seemed infinitely relieved.

I told him thanks and gave him his keys.

He stood there for a moment, wanting to say more, then just turned and went back to the car. He got in, started the engine, and pulled away from the curb.

Halfway down the block, he made a U-turn.

And then his rearview mirror turned red.

Some people would say I set him up, but I don't look at it that way.

Purdy had hidden a two-pound bag of crack cocaine behind the Mustang's driver's side door panel, and when I found it out at the Fox Hills Mall parking lot that night, I knew I owed him. He'd played me for a sucker. Fed me some line about his classic car getting 'jacked, just so I could run down the small fortune in rock he'd stashed inside it.

And yet . . .

Technically, no harm had been done. The man had hired me to do a job, and I'd done it. I'd found his car, delivered it on time, and been paid the agreed-upon fee. So what if the whole thing was a lie? I'd still held up my end of the bargain, and Purdy had held up his.

I owed him, and yet I didn't owe him.

So I let him go. Sort of.

I put a little of his stash in his glove compartment with his registration, then put the rest back where I'd found it. I parked the car on the same street, in the same place where, only six weeks before, I'd gotten my last ticket for making a U-turn, on La Brea Avenue near Pink's. And finally, I parked his car on the northbound side of the street, facing away from the Gardena address printed on the business card Purdy had given me.

A setup? Not hardly.

All Purdy would have had to do to get off that night was not make that U-turn.

See? He screwed himself.

All I did was watch.

Later, at the Deuce, Lilly nearly busted a gut laughing. In the proper frame of mind, the giant barkeep's as appreciative of my cleverness as I am myself. Sometimes even more so.

"Tell me one thing, Gunner," she said.

"Shoot."

"You made any U-turns yourself since then? Or you out of the habit for good?"

I grinned at her, winked, and downed the last of my free drink, though all it was by now was ice water. "Naw," I said.

"Naw, what?"

"Naw, I'm not out of the habit. I just know how to do 'em right now, that's all."

"Do 'em *right?* And what way is *that?*"

"That's where you turn the wheel," I said, demonstrating, "and pray nobody sees you."

I pushed myself away from the bar and called it a night.

Mike Phillips

Personal Woman

MIKE PHILLIPS (1946–) is the author of three novels featuring reporter Sam Dean—*Blood Rights, The Late Candidate* (which won a Silver Dagger from the British Crime Writers' Association in 1991), and the recently published *Point of Darkness,* which is set in the United States.

Born in British Guyana, Phillips immigrated to Britain in 1956. The keen awareness of the black immigrant experience in Britain reflected in Phillips's novels is in part based on his own background. He also brings a wide range of experiences to his work, including early jobs in hospitals, factories, garages, the post office, and operating a hostel for homeless black youths in London. Since the 1970s he has worked as a journalist for British newspapers and periodicals as well as BBC radio and television, and was a lecturer in media studies and journalism at the University of Westminster before turning to writing full-time.

"A Personal Woman" is a classic Sam Dean mystery in which the reporter/sleuth agrees to help a friend and is reluctantly drawn into black West Indian cultures of London and Birmingham seldom seen by outsiders. The story also displays Sam's weakness for the ladies, which gets him into trouble more often than not.

Mike Phillips lives in London, England, where he is working on the further adventures of Sam Dean.

AS SOON as I saw her I felt guilty, mainly because I hadn't seen her since the funeral and although she'd phoned me a number of times and left messages, I hadn't replied. Now here she was, waiting outside my door, and there was no escape.

I went up to her, bouncing a little in my Nikes, rehearsing the naughty grin which used to charm her out of her wits, and working out excuses in my head. She looked worried, and when she turned and saw me, her expression only lightened a little.

I gave her a big hug, trying to get my arms right round her and not succeeding because she was fatter than ever.

"Sammy, you dog," she said.

"Nina," I replied, putting as much sincerity as I could muster into my voice, "I've been meaning to get in touch with you. But you know how it is."

"I know how it is," she said. "So you can skip the excuses, you dog."

"Let's go inside," I told her, changing the subject.

She nodded, and I unlocked the door and went up the stairs first. I suspected it would be embarrassing for both of us if I was behind her, watching while she hauled herself up the three flights, and things were bad enough.

I gave her the sofa and went to put the kettle on, so that I could have a moment to think about her and adjust.

I needed the time because there was actually something overwhelming about her size, and, thinking back, I couldn't remember her being quite so big.

I'd met her husband, Charlie, at my first job, on a local paper in South London. That was twenty years ago, and I was the first black trainee on the paper. That made me the first of my kind in London, as the editor pointed out in several interviews for radio and TV. He won an award for his contribution to race relations that year, but the publicity didn't help my situation, and during the routine operation of the office, Charlie was the only one of my white colleagues who didn't treat me with indifference or suspicion. I'd been expecting hostility, so it didn't worry me much, but I was at a loss to explain Charlie's ease and friendliness, until, one day, a pretty mixed-race girl had turned up to meet him after work. Her father was from my own country in the Caribbean and she'd greeted me like a long-lost friend. We got on like a house on fire, and if she hadn't been married to Charlie I'd have tried my luck. She'd been slim then, and looking back, it was hard to identify her with the woman she'd become. Perhaps it was something to do with living in Australia, where she and Charlie had gone about ten years back. He'd done well and they'd come over about a year ago for a holiday, and to look up old friends, which was what Charlie was doing as he drove up the motorway to Leeds and ran into a jackknifing lorry. At the funeral I hadn't recognized Nina until she came up to me.

Whatever it was she wanted now, it must have been something serious to make a woman who carried so much flesh come looking for me, knowing that there were three flights of stairs waiting at the end of the trip.

"What's the problem?" I asked her.

"Claudette," she said immediately. "You remember her. My daughter."

Now that she mentioned it, the girl had been at the back of my mind. Nina and Charlie had been unable to have children and they'd adopted a boy, who, at the age of thirteen, had been stabbed to death by a gang of white kids while walking home from school. After that they'd fostered a series of mixed-race children. Young Claudette had been the latest. As a toddler, her mother had dumped her in a Liverpool convent and promptly disappeared. By the time she fetched up with Charlie and Nina she'd been through a number of foster homes, none of which had worked out. Somehow she'd hit it off with Nina, and by the time they went off to Australia, she was their adopted daughter. When I saw them ten years later Claudette and Nina looked so much alike that it would have been impossible for a stranger to guess that the relationship wasn't biological. The irony was that Claudette was more or less twice the size that Nina had been at her age, and somehow, the saddest thing at the funeral had been seeing these two fat women crying in each other's arms. That same day I had told Nina how well I remembered Charlie's kindness when things were tough, and promised that if she was staying in England, I'd help her as much as I could, for his sake. Since then I hadn't seen her.

"She's getting married tomorrow," Nina said. "I've been trying to get you for a fortnight now."

A wedding invitation. For a moment I wondered why they hadn't just sent it to me, then I began thinking about what I'd wear.

"Oh great," I said, then I stopped when the expression on her face told me there was nothing great about it.

"I'm really worried, Sammy. I can't stop her, but something tells me it's a disaster."

"People get married every day," I told her, "and she's a big girl now. What is she? Twenty-two? Twenty-three?"

She frowned angrily.

"Come off it. I'm not stupid. I don't want to stop her growing up."

I had no reply, and she stared at me, deep in thought for a minute. I waited, and after a few seconds she twisted round and dug into her bag.

"Look at this picture."

It was a photo of Claudette. She hadn't started out with Nina's pretty looks, and she had a dull, square face with a blotchy skin in which splashes of dark pigment alternated with a lighter brown. The picture had probably been taken while she was mourning Charlie, and the sadness of her mood made her look miserable and unappetizing.

"Okay," I said. "What's the point?"

Instead of replying, she handed me another photo, and in the moment I looked at it I had a flash which told me exactly what she was worried about and why.

The man in the photo was black, young, in his early twenties, and good-looking. But that wasn't all. He had a style and presence which must have been the result of careful grooming and which gave him the look of a secondhand movie idol. His hair had been straightened and teased into shiny waves, he was wearing a gray check suit which looked like a Valentino, and his arms were folded in front of him to display three gold rings and a large Rolex.

I blinked.

"Wow," I said, "he'd better have a rich daddy."

It wasn't likely, because very few of us had rich daddies, and the rich kids among us didn't look like the boy in the photo. In any case I was dodging the first question that had occurred to me, which was why a boy who looked and dressed like that would want to go out with Claudette, never mind marry her. I didn't want to be the first to say it, but Nina came out with a contemptuous grunt, as if she could read what I had on my mind.

"He drives a BMW. Everything about him is flash. I was happy when I heard she had a boyfriend. But it all happened so fast. One minute she met him. Next minute they're getting married and when I met him I couldn't work it out. I love Claudette and I want her to be happy, but try as hard as you can, you can't put these two together."

"Well," I said. "The thing is that if they like each other, it doesn't matter. That's the great thing about love. It alters every perspective. People in love don't care about differences or logic, stuff like that."

Sometimes I surprised myself. I didn't believe a word of the platitudes I'd just uttered. But even so, when I said it, not believing it, I still meant it.

"Jeeze," Nina bellowed scornfully. "I don't have to take that balls from a man who puts on his running shoes every time somebody says marriage. Besides, that's not it. Listen, Sammy, I'm not some hysterical old bag coming to you for a cup of tea and some reassuring bullshit. There's more to it than that."

I should have known. She'd never been the sort to waste her time.

"All right," I said, "have another cup of tea and tell me."

It wasn't an extraordinary story, but she told it with all the drama it had acquired in her imagination. I had composed myself to listen patiently, but it was only a few seconds before I was gripped; and I began to feel, somewhere in between my gut and the back of my mind, an odd sparkle of heat that told me I would have to go out and chase this one down.

Claudette worked in a Citizens Advice Bureau, and the young man, whose name turned out to be Vernon King, had come in one day asking for advice about an insurance matter. They had got to talking, and he had returned next day to thank her. This was unusual and when he asked her out that night she had jumped at the offer. She was a little suspicious, of course, because this was a rare event, but going out with Vernon was too good to miss.

They'd slept together right away, and by the end of the week they were planning to get married soon. This was the first that her mother had heard of the matter, and at the time she'd been delighted, because her secret fear was that Claudette would become, as she grew older, more and more isolated and alone.

Her attitude changed when she met Vernon. She'd been expecting someone different. Perhaps a hardworking, ambitious young man who needed a quiet and industrious partner—someone who wouldn't be extravagant or demanding. Or perhaps a man who was a little older in search of someone steady.

Instead, she found Vernon, with his showy clothes and car and his showbiz patter, more or less alarming. He came from Birmingham, or at least he talked like a Brummie.

"He said he was a law student."

She rolled her eyes at me and I laughed. Being a law student used to be the favorite occupation of many of the black hustlers of our youth. The real joke, though, was that many of them had made it, and were now conning people legally. Even so, it was a bad sign.

"I rang the college," she said, "and they said he had left the course. When I told her she said that she knew all about it. He dropped out for a year to make some money, and he was working as assistant manager at a wine bar in the City."

Nina persevered. She rang the wine bar and was told Vernon had worked briefly behind the bar but wasn't there anymore. When she told Claudette this bit of news the girl reacted angrily, accused her of spying and interfering, and threatened never to speak to her again if she kept on trying to sabotage their happiness.

"She was brainwashed. I could hear him talking."

I shrugged. In any case Vernon looked the type who might exaggerate his prospects and none of this seemed sinister. But Nina had saved the best for last.

After the row with Claudette she had resolved to accept Vernon at face value. The very next day, while waiting at a bus stop on the way to work, she had seen his car pull up to drop off a woman. The woman was black, young, and sexy. Nina noticed her because she was so striking, then she saw Vernon get out and give her a farewell kiss, so passionate and at the same time so familiar that she just knew they were established lovers.

Vernon had been so absorbed in gazing adoringly at her that he hadn't noticed Nina staring at him from a few yards away.

"So what did Claudette say about this?"

She sighed heavily.

"I didn't tell her. I didn't think she'd believe me, and anyway he'd probably say I was lying or mistaken. I don't know. I thought maybe it was better keeping quiet and trying to find out what's really going on. I want to know where he gets his money for a start."

She stopped and looked intensely at me, her big brown eyes moist.

"You'll help me, won't you, Sammy? I couldn't think of anybody else to turn to."

I agreed quickly, because I knew that I would sooner or later and I didn't want to draw the process out any longer than necessary. The problem was that coming from the Caribbean I'd been brought up in a culture where middle-aged women ruled the roost, and it was hard to say no. Besides, all she wanted was to find out about the boy's background and how he earned his living. If anything bad was going to happen she wanted to know where it was coming from, so that she could protect Claudette. That's what she said, anyway, and I could sympathize with all that.

The next day was the wedding.

They did it at the registry in the old Town Hall at Marylebone. It wasn't particularly romantic. It wasn't particularly unromantic. It wasn't anything. Claudette was supported by half a dozen of her chums from the CAB, all of them white and female. Most of them were around forty or older, dressed in tarted-up versions of their work clothes— three-quarter-length skirts, shirts, and sweaters—with only one hat and one suit between them. You could tell just by looking that they were workmates rather than close friends, but they were behaving with the sprightliness appropriate to the occasion, one or two furtively clutching bags of rice. All of which made an interesting contrast to Nina, massively gloomy and dignified in a pumpkin-colored dress and a white hat with flowers round the brim.

There had been something nagging away in the back of my mind, and studying Vernon, I suddenly got it. Twenty years ago when young black people got married, there would have been a gaggle of relations, toddlers, distant uncles, family quarrels, the lot, all presided over by an old granny. Since then we'd become English, and these kids were isolated in a way we used to think of as belonging to the whites.

I managed a few words with Nina on the pavement before we all went our separate ways. She didn't say much, except that she still wanted me to do what I'd promised.

It wasn't till late in the evening that I thought about Nina's troubles again.

It was half past ten and I'd just woken up, passing from one kind of stupor to another. The difference being that in the second stage I was no longer at the mercy of my spinning dreams and I could begin to control the roaring darkness in my head.

I was downing a couple of aspirins when it struck me that I was thinking about the wedding. I had been dreaming about it but I had that infuriating sense of not being able to remember. In between getting up and fetching the aspirins the whole thing had faded, leaving me only with an odd feeling of apprehension.

At that point I determined to make one phone call, so that I could tell Nina I'd done something and then forget about it.

I rang Wolverhampton, almost hoping that Wally wouldn't be in so that I could lie back on the sofa and fade to black.

He answered on the first ring.

"Wally," I said, "my old spa. How's business?"

He sussed me immediately.

"Sam? Sam Dean?"

"That's right. I just rang you for a little favor. There's a few bob in it for you."

An essential precondition.

Wally described himself as a freelance photographer, and it was true that he spent half his time, camera in hand, roaming the Midlands looking for setups he could sell to the local papers and agencies.

Once upon a time, during the riots of the eighties, he'd even got a couple of police brutality pics on the front page of three of the tabloids. But his real occupation was snapping girls. His productions varied from expensive portfolios for naive and pretty black kids who wanted to get into the model business, to soft porn for the lower end of the dirty magazine trade. On the side he organized a gospel choir and preached occasionally on the local fundamentalist circuit.

When I did stories in the Midlands I'd always hire him for the photos, because he was a hustler with a beautiful voice, a smarmily persuasive presence, and he seemed to know everyone and everything in the black communities there. Tell Wally what you wanted and he'd get it done.

I told him about Vernon King and he interrupted me as soon as he heard the name.

"I know the guy," he said.

"What about him?"

"I did some nice pics for him. He's into martial arts, and I've got some good bare chest photos. He was going to send them to radio stations for a DJ job. He made it? You're doing a story? I've got the negatives."

I should have known. Radio was the magic magnet for hustlers with an ego, a line of chat, and no talent.

"I don't think so," I said. "He's in London now."

"I thought I hadn't seen him around."

"Do you know anything about him? How he makes his living? Stuff like that?"

"I don't know. He used to live with a girl. A nurse. Something like that."

"Know anything about her?"

"No. But look. I'll find out, okay? Gimme a couple of days."

I put the phone down with a feeling of relief. Wally would cost me money, but I could probably get it back from Nina, if I could get up the resolution to ask her, and in any case whatever he came up with would get her off my back.

I lay on the sofa and went back to sleep. Round about one o'clock I woke up and ran *The Searchers,* a movie my son had lent me on his last visit. I'd first seen it, over twenty years ago, at a cinema in Hackney which had long since disappeared, but he was becoming a movie freak, and I knew it would please him if I watched it again and talked about my reactions.

I fell asleep again before the end. It was a normal night.

The phone rang just after nine in the morning, and Nina's voice emerged, sounding breathless and agitated.

"He's gone," she said. "Disappeared."

"Hold on a minute," I said.

I put the phone down, went into the kitchen, and looked out of the window. This was it. Something told me I'd have to shut the door firmly in Nina's face now, to avoid being sucked into some kind of trouble that was nothing to do with me. The two people closest to me, my son, and Sophie, my photographer friend, would disapprove.

Sophie was in Canada with a feature writer on a travel assignment, and I hadn't heard from her for a fortnight. I didn't want to think about that, but the last time we'd argued about the things I did, she'd said that she could understand about devoting your life to a cause, even dying for something important. After all she was Argentinian, she knew about such things.

At that point her bosom heaved and she gave me her angry Spanish look, reducing me to total submission. She couldn't understand, she went on, her tone softening, what made a man like me persist in getting mixed up in the sordid and petty affairs of people I didn't even care about.

"What percentage?" she shouted, her English deserting her a little. "What percentage?"

My son was more cautious in what he said, but it amounted to the same thing. Sometimes, I thought, when he forgot about not liking her, they seemed to be joined in a conspiracy to change most things about me.

I backed away from the window and picked up the phone.

"Nina?"

Now was the time to tell her.

"Sammy? Are you there? Sammy, I don't know what to do. I'm so worried."

"Don't worry," I said. "Tell me what's happened."

There wasn't much to tell. They'd gone back to Claudette's flat, because they weren't going on honeymoon for another month. This was what they said, although Nina reckoned he was broke and they couldn't afford it anyway. They'd consummated the marriage. This was a coy bit.

"Yes, I can imagine," I said. "Tell me why you're so worried."

A few hours later I was on my way to the City. I was wearing a gray YSL suit, a shirt with wide gray stripes, a blue on blue Balmain tie with matching hankie and white shoes. No one would take me for a stockbroker, but I didn't look like a bum either.

The wine bar where Vernon had worked was a cellar near Ludgate Circus in a little maze of narrow twisting streets in front of St. Paul's. Not quite the center of the City, but close enough.

The place was full of customers, nearly all of them wearing suits, and the din of their quiet lunchtime conversation was almost enough to drown out the Muzak. I took my place in the queue at the bar and when the barman raised his eyebrows at me I leaned over and shouted that I was looking for Vernon King.

He looked puzzled.

"He works here sometimes."

He shrugged his shoulders, then lifted a finger and hurried over to a man loitering at the end of the bar, who motioned to me. I followed him over to a corner of the room, near the door, where it was quieter, but not much. Once I was up close to him I realized that I'd been deceived by his mop of iron-gray curls. He was actually quite young, probably in his late twenties, but he had a thin white face which lived underground.

"Vernon worked here occasionally, but not anymore. Who are you?"

"I'm his uncle. I come from Wolverhampton, and I'm only here for a couple of days and I wanted to see the boy. See that he's okay."

I didn't risk a Midlands accent. Instead, I broadened my vowels and slowed down my delivery, giving it the sort of generalized Caribbean tinge which makes the English assume they're talking to a dumb peasant. He looked sympathetic, as if he believed me and understood what a trial it would be to have Vernon as a nephew. I put on an air that I hoped was credibly pathetic. He studied my tie, my suit, my shoes, his eyes shifting up and down.

"Look," I said. "I'll be honest with you. His mother's not well. I guess if you know him you know there's a few problems in his background."

I cocked my head and smiled ruefully at him, a man of the world plagued by family duties. He didn't smile back.

"She threw him out of the house," I confided. "Now she's sick. She's confined to bed or she'd have been here herself. She wants me to give him a letter. I can understand it if you don't want to give out your employees' addresses, but can you forward a letter?"

He was falling for it. He nodded.

"Yes. I'll do that."

I put my hand in my pocket, felt around, and swore angrily.

"Bugger it. I left the letter back at my friend's flat. I'll have to go back there, then bring it to you later. How do I get to Balham from here? What time do you close?"

Instead of giving it the correct pronunciation, Ballum, I said Balham, which was really too much even for the dummy I was pretending to be, but it seemed to convince him.

"Wait a minute," he said. "I'll give you the forwarding address. You can send it yourself."

He disappeared behind the bar, and I felt a surge of exhilaration, which lifted the depression I'd been feeling ever since Nina told me that Vernon had walked out of Claudette's flat at nine o'clock the night before, to do some late night shopping, and hadn't come back. That morning they'd tried the hospitals and the police. But no luck. She'd known it all along, she said.

When the manager brought me the address scribbled on a scrap of paper I didn't need any acting to show that I was pleased, and this time he really did smile.

Back in the flat I rang Nina at the Building Society where she worked. I told her I had something to follow up.

"The thing is," I said, "I'm not sure exactly what you want to do about him. You can't drag the man back to Claudette if he's left."

"No. I don't want to do that. But I want the situation settled. We have to know what his intentions are. If he's coming back. Or what the hell he really wants. He can't mess her about like this."

I asked her what Claudette thought about it.

"What do you think? She's a bit disillusioned."

The rest was business. I told her that locating Vernon might take time and money. I would have to get some help.

"Go ahead," she said immediately. "Spend what you have to and let me know."

I cut her off and rang Maman Nightingale.

"Sammy," she said accusingly. "Where you been?" She still spoke with the accent of the French dialect she'd brought with her from St. Lucia.

I'd known her ever since I was about nineteen, when I was courting her sixteen-year-old daughter, Francine, along with half a dozen other boys. None of us captured Francine, because she got pregnant by a reggae drummer who played with a group that had once topped the black music charts, and she lived round the corner from her mum with a gaggle of kids. But, in any case, most of us used to hang around Maman Nightingale as much for the food and the company as for the chance of squeezing up Francine.

Maman cooked the home food our own mothers had either given up or couldn't go to the trouble of going down to the market to get. Black puddings and pigs' feet, long sweet fruit drinks and pepperpot stew. The moment she saw one of her boys, as she called us, she'd go to the kitchen and get a plate.

She was one of the fattest women I knew, but she had no shortage of suitors. Her sex and vigor were legendary, and she had her last baby after Francine left. This was Aubrey, the youngest and the biggest of her four sons.

"Where's Aubrey, Maman?" I asked when the greetings were over.

"Upstairs, playing with his computer. You want him?"

I did. Aubrey had grown up like his brothers, in and out of a series of residential homes and juvenile lockups. He was built like Arnold Schwarzenegger, one of his early heroes, and although he had a reputation for sudden violence, he was a nice polite boy with a gentle, courteous air. He spent his mornings at the gym, his afternoons watching videos, and his evenings round a variety of clubs. Occasionally he was arrested. Years before this, I used to watch over Aubrey while his mum was out shopping, I'd taken him to the park to stumble over his first football, and he did errands for me with an uncomplaining tolerance. At a price.

When he came on the line I told him what I wanted and he agreed, in his pleasant way, to meet me later on outside Finsbury Park station.

I rang Wally in Wolverhampton next, but this time there was no reply.

That didn't surprise me, and I lay back on the sofa, feeling like a general at rest, running over the setup in my mind. My strategy was simple. I would take shifts with Aubrey watching the address the manager of the wine bar had given me, in the hope that Vernon would show up sooner or later. If we could be sure he lived there, the women could come along and do the business—tell him off or whatever it was they had in mind. If he didn't live there, we could follow him until we knew where he was staying. Risky, but I couldn't think of anything else.

I spent the afternoon dozing, in preparation for what I thought would be a wakeful night. It would be lunchtime in North America, and I wondered what Sophie was doing.

Suddenly the day had gone and the evening was following it, moving fast. I got down to Finsbury Park with a few minutes to spare before ten, and parked outside the hall near the station.

I knew the spot because my family had lived not far away, back down toward Highbury, and I'd gone to school there. I'd never liked it very much and I'd promised myself long ago to shake the dust of these ugly streets from my feet without regret, but even so, the memories kept flooding in.

Those days the pavement I was looking at would be swarming with kids waiting to go into the hall. A cinema at first, it had become a rock club during the heyday of the music, then it turned into an Irish dance hall. As the area and the times changed, it closed and then reopened as a bingo palace. Now it was boarded up, dark, awaiting its next transformation.

The door of the car squeaked, and Aubrey got in smoothly, considering his size. The old banger sighed and squatted lower on its tires.

"Hi," Aubrey said. "Looks like you're dreaming."

He was wearing a sleeveless pullover and 501s, and carrying a denim jacket and a sports bag. He looked like the bad boy that he was.

I described Vernon and told him about the setup while we drove east toward the street where we were going to watch for Vernon. A little way up we stopped at a fast food joint run by a Trinidadian Indian and bought some fried fish to supplement the patties that Aubrey's mum had given him for the night. I left him sitting in the car, with strict instructions to ring me from the phone booth on the corner if Vernon showed up, and to drive carefully if he had to follow him anywhere. He nodded calmly, humoring me, while he plugged in his Walkman and fitted the headphones over his ears. As I walked away he was munching contentedly, his head nodding in time to the music.

I wasn't worried about him, though. Aubrey started getting into trouble as a ten-year-old lookout for a gang of pickpockets, and he'd worked his way up since then through car theft, and breaking and entering. If Vernon showed up, Aubrey wouldn't miss him, and he'd stick to his quarry wherever he went.

Back home I rang Wally again.

"It's late, man," he grumbled. "I was in bed."

That meant he had company.

"Okay," I said. "Make it quick."

"There's nothing much. Seems like he split up with the nurse girl months ago and went to London."

"Anything else?"

"No. I didn't know what you wanted. He wasn't in no trouble."

"What about the girl? You saw her?"

"No. She's in London too. I think."

"What about her? Any trouble?"

"Well. Not exactly. Except that she got sacked from her job a while back. It was a big thing. Some old guy she was looking after fell out a window. They were going to charge her with neglect or something, but there was no evidence and they dropped it. She lost her job, though."

He gave me her name, Norma Chambers, and described her. I couldn't see what it all had to do with Claudette, but I was clutching at straws. Maybe the girlfriend had bumped into Vernon and spirited him away. These things happen, I told myself.

After that I waited and I must have gone to sleep because when the phone rang it was about two in the morning, and I came up fighting the blackness with an agonizing pain in my arm where I'd been lying on it. I stood up and fell over because my leg had gone to sleep too. Groaning and cursing, I got on my hands and knees and crawled to the phone.

"He's here, a BMW," Aubrey said. "What do you want me to do?"

"Just watch and see if he stays there. If he doesn't, follow him till he goes home and then ring me. If he does, just wait till I come."

"Okay."

He sounded cool and unconcerned, as if all this was in a night's work, and maybe it was.

I decided to give it till the morning before going down. He might be just visiting. Besides, it would have to be Claudette who went barging in. All I had to do was establish where he was.

I settled down to sleep again, but I was too charged up, so I put *The Searchers* on again to catch the bit I'd slept through the night before. After an hour or so it was coming to an end when the phone rang again. I picked it up, expecting Aubrey to tell me he was on the move, but this time it was Nina.

"Sammy." She sounded breathless, with a note I hadn't so far heard in her voice. "Can you come over? Please. Something's happened."

"What?"

"Just come. I'll tell you."

Less than half an hour later the taxi was pulling up outside her house in Tottenham, one of those dinky little redbrick two-story hutches off Black Boy Lane which they'd built after the war to accommodate working-class people with an itch for ownership, complete with a garden and access to a stretch of allotments running behind the houses. Back then, before they'd run the Victoria Line out there, this had been cheapo housing. Now Nina was mortgaged up to the throat to pay for it.

She was up and waiting, because the door swung open before I could ring.

"She's in there," she whispered hoarsely. Her eyes rolled. "They tried to kill her tonight."

"What? Who tried to kill her?"

She shushed me, putting her finger to her lips.

"We don't know. Someone got in tonight and they turned the gas on. It's only luck she's alive."

"Ma," Claudette's voice called from the living room.

Nina inclined her head and we went in. Claudette was sitting huddled up on the big sofa. She was wearing a dressing gown with a nightdress under it, but she had the French windows open, and I could hear the early birds beginning to sing in the back gardens.

"Uncle Sammy," she said tearfully and I went across and embraced as much of her as I could.

"What happened?" I asked her.

"I don't really know," she said. "I might have left the gas on, Ma."

She looked at Nina hopefully, as if she wanted her to say that it had all been a mistake.

"Hold on," I said. "Tell me what happened."

"I'll tell you," Nina said fiercely. "I couldn't sleep thinking about the whole situation, and round about two o'clock I rang her to see how she was."

"Wait a minute, Ma," Claudette said. She wasn't going to be deprived of her share of the drama, I could tell. I looked at her and she picked up the story.

"I was waiting up just in case."

She paused. She didn't say in case of what, but I guessed it must have been in case Vernon came back or a hospital rang to say he was a patient or the police to say that they were holding him.

"I didn't get to sleep till half past one, and I don't know how long I was asleep, but something must have woken me. I was sort of half asleep and I felt like there was someone moving about. At first I thought I was imagining it, like a dream. Then after I thought it had to be Vernon, so I didn't say anything. I thought any minute he would come in and tell me what was going on. Then it went quiet, and I started calling out, but there was no answer. So you know how it is when you're half asleep already, I just kind of dropped off. I don't know how long, then the phone rang. I got up. I felt kind of funny, and when I realized it was Ma, I was going to tell her to ring in the morning, then I smelled this gas."

"That's what she said," Nina piped up. "Oh my God, Ma, the gas. I told her to go and turn it off without switching on the lights. By luck she hadn't touched the electricity because sometimes these things blow up. So she turned it off and opened the windows, and I went straight round and fetched her home."

"Could she have left it on?"

"No. She had dinner here with me. She didn't cook at all tonight."

Claudette nodded in confirmation. I thought about it. Claudette might have been screwed up and overweight, but she wasn't stupid. If things had happened as she described, then it was possible someone was trying to kill her. But it was about two in the morning when Aubrey rang me. It couldn't be Vernon.

"Are you sure about the time? When you heard someone in the flat."

"About two. I know because I was going to ring Ma before I went to sleep, and I looked at my watch about half past one and decided it was too late."

"Was anything missing?"

"Nothing special. Just some old papers and souvenirs. Photos and my birth certificate."

I'd heard the story before. All Claudette possessed was a birth certificate with the names of her mother and father on it. But she'd never been able to trace them.

"It's Vernon," Nina said. "Isn't it?"

I said I didn't think so. Then I told them where he was and what time he'd got there.

Claudette began heaving herself to her feet.

"I'm going there, Ma."

"No," I said quickly. I raised my eyebrows at Nina, enlisting her support. "It's too late and I don't even know if he's still there. Leave it till the morning. That's best."

"He might be in trouble."

She was close to tears, and in spite of myself, I was feeling a kind of admiration for her. Her husband had walked out, someone was trying to kill her, and yet her first concern was for him. Nina stepped in then, and together we talked her out of going out and coaxed her upstairs to bed. By then she'd stopped crying because she knew that her beloved Vernon was safe and she'd probably see him in a matter of hours. All was right with the world.

Afterward Nina insisted on cooking breakfast and talking over the situation. If Vernon was still there in a few hours, she thought, she would take Claudette to see him. I sat listening to her, relaxing into the coming day. Occasionally Aubrey crossed my mind, but there was no point, I thought, in both of us being out there. That was my excuse, anyway.

It was gone seven and the sun was coming up over the allotments at the back of the houses before I brought myself to make a move. I walked down to the High Street and caught a bus down to Finsbury Park. Going in this direction, toward Camden Town and the West End, the bus was already almost full, and I began to worry that I'd left too late.

I was right. When I walked down the street where I'd left Aubrey, my car was gone, and so was Vernon's BMW. I swore aloud, and when that didn't help I stood staring at the front of the house. The blank curtained windows didn't give me any inspiration. A ginger-haired woman came hurrying out and stared at me for a moment as if she wanted to ask why I was standing there gazing, but then she changed her mind and hustled off. I gave up and went home.

He was there waiting for me, and he had a rueful air which told me what had happened before he opened his mouth.

"I lost him," he said immediately. "A taxi came. He got in and they went to Camden Town. He got out and by the time I parked he'd gone. Sorry."

I told him not to worry, and to go home and get some sleep so he could repeat the exercise later on. He gave me the clenched fist and went. I rang Nina and told her. We agreed it was time to stop pussy-footing. If Vernon showed up again that night she had to go in and confront him, no matter what happened. Get it over with. Tonight would be the night. As for the strange affair of the gas being turned on, unless Vernon could shed light on it, there was nothing to be done except keep an eye on Claudette and hope for the best. I made it cut and dried because I wanted to be done with the whole business, and later on, thinking about it, I never could get rid of the feeling of regret and guilt that our last conversation had been like this.

I spent the day mooching around. I started work on an article I'd been putting off till the deadline, gave it up and went to the shops, came back and read a couple of chapters of a book about the Crusades, watched a soap opera on telly, fell asleep, worked on the article, gave it up again. I didn't get going until well into the evening. They say you can have premonitions. When my granny died my mother saw her coming down the stairs, thousands of miles away. My sister woke up crying in the night. In the Caribbean all that is normal, and sometimes I felt as if I was missing a sense. When the phone rang I picked it up without suspicion.

"Uncle Sammy?"

Claudette. Who else?

"Is she with you?"

"Nina? With me? No."

She was tearful. Ma had insisted that she stayed at the house in Tottenham for a while and she'd gone over to the flat a few hours ago to fetch some of Claudette's belongings. She hadn't come back and the telephone wasn't answering.

I looked at the typewriter and groaned inwardly.

"Okay," I said. "Don't worry. I'll go and see. She's probably stopped off somewhere."

But I was alarmed.

Claudette's flat was near the top of a block in Paddington, six stories up, and not too far from where Maman Nightingale lived. It had been built by the local council, but in recent years it had been acquired by a group of the tenants, backed by a couple of housing associations. Since then the amenities had improved and the graffiti had gone.

I parked in the courtyard and went up in the lift. Claudette's flat showed dark through the glass at the top of the door and when I rang there was no answer. I kept ringing. Suddenly the door behind me opened.

"You from the police?"

A skinny white woman with graying hair and haggard features was looking at me from the doorway of the flat opposite.

"No. I'm a friend of hers."

A tortoiseshell cat sprang out from behind her legs and streaked down the corridor.

"Come back, Sheba," she shouted. She walked down the corridor and turned to look back at me. "She fell down the stairs. They took her to St. Mary's. They came round earlier asking about her next of kin but I didn't really know her."

I stood there stupidly. I'd just talked to her. The woman came back down the corridor closer to me.

"I've said all along them stairs are dangerous. It'll take this for them to do something about it."

"You mean she's . . ." I'd sneered at actors in the movies a thousand times for doing the same thing, but I could not at the moment bring myself to say the word. Dead.

The woman looked at me sympathetically.

"Yes, dear. I'm sorry. It was an accident. I'd get round the hospital if I were you."

Till then I hadn't noticed that the area round the head of the stairs was cordoned off with a rope. Or maybe I had, without realizing the significance.

I got back into the lift and I was halfway down before it struck me that if Claudette was alive and well in Tottenham the person who had fallen down the stairs must be Nina.

There were a couple of police at the hospital, a man and a woman, and when I told them what I thought, they called a nurse and took me into a room where Nina was lying. Her face was gray and her features were set firm as if she were about to do something difficult. She had broken her neck and her skull, they said, and her heart had stopped.

I rang Claudette and told her, and asked her not to come, but she insisted. That was how it was that night. Sitting in the corridor cuddling Claudette I kept thinking about myself and what my son would feel in the same circumstances and whether Sophie would come back soon, and somehow my mind kept chasing round the fact that with her size Nina wouldn't go anywhere near those steep concrete stairs. She'd told me that more than once about tall buildings. It was a joke. "If there's no lift, baby, I ain't going," she'd say.

A young doctor gave me some tablets for Claudette. She was in shock, he said, and had to rest. I took her home then. On the way, the weeping sounds she made tore at my nerves like a rusty rasp. I felt myself getting angrier and angrier, as if the next move, the next sound from the seat beside me would drive me over some sort of edge.

Somehow we got down to Tottenham. Claudette didn't stop crying. The funny thing was that I half expected her to lay into some food the moment we got in, but she didn't, and thinking about it, I couldn't remember having seen her eating.

The other funny thing was that when she called me Uncle Sammy, I realized that I was now the nearest thing to a relative she had, and in the short term anyway, I was going to be partly responsible for her life. It wasn't a responsibility I wanted.

It was early in the morning before Claudette nodded off, and then I stretched myself out on the sofa downstairs and went to sleep. It had been a bad night and my sleep was full of nightmares, but I didn't wake till halfway through the morning. I climbed the stairs and listened. No sound from Claudette, so I went back down and started the phone calls.

Aubrey first. He had gone to Finsbury Park the night before and watched long enough to see Vernon arrive with a woman. When I didn't turn up, he'd figured something else was going on, or I'd changed my mind, and he went home.

I thanked him and asked him to come over to Nina's. Sometime during the night it had struck me that Nina might have been killed in place of Claudette. If that was so, a little protection would be a good idea, and Aubrey could crunch anyone who came near her. No worries. Besides, I needed to get out of there, and his company would probably do her good.

Next I rang Inspector Borelli, the only policeman I knew. It was Saturday, but he was on duty.

"Franco," I said. "I need a favor."

"No," he grunted immediately.

Borelli was an old classmate at my school in Islington. We weren't friends. Far from it. I'd thought he was a racist lout who I was glad to see the back of. But by the time we'd met again, he was wearing suits and struggling to master the sociological jargon which would give him the protective coloring needed for the senior jobs. I still didn't like him but he was a good contact I couldn't afford to throw away.

Today he was going to be awkward. I guessed that he would eventually do what I asked but I'd have to beg. At school I'd been quick and clever enough with words to beat him up in the classroom the way he'd done to me with his fists in the playground. My suspicion was that now we were grown-up, he'd have done quite a lot to keep me coming back, my sarky tongue smoothed into gracious forms of flattery. It wasn't just that it made him feel clever and superior. He knew it hurt a little.

"Franco. This is nothing, man."

I told him about Nina's accident and asked him to find out whether the police suspected foul play. That was easy and it wasn't really inside information, but I was only softening him up.

"If I've got time," he said.

"Just one more thing."

I gave him the names. Vernon King and Norma Chambers and told him I wanted to know if they were known in Brum.

"You must be joking."

"Nothing confidential," I said hurriedly. "No details. All I want to know is if there's anything out of order. Generally."

He sniggered. "What's in it for me?"

I was on firm ground here. "If it works out a couple of serious arrests. You'll be a hero."

"Bullshit." But he was interested. "What's the connection?"

Blowed if I'd tell him that. "I don't know yet."

"I'll think about it," he said.

I told him that I needed to know right away and I'd ring him back, and he grumbled a little before agreeing. So far so good.

I went up to see if Claudette was stirring and found her wide awake gazing tearfully into space. I told her about Aubrey and why I had asked him to come over and she nodded vacantly. I had the feeling she'd forgotten about Vernon and all that.

"It's funny," she said, sniffling. "I always used to want my real parents. Even when I knew Nina and Charlie really loved me. Now I couldn't care less, if I could just have them back."

She wailed aloud then and burst into tears. I made soothing noises, but it didn't do any good, so I made some tea and sat with her while she wept, till the doorbell rang.

Aubrey was standing there grinning. Behind him a taxi stood with its engine running.

"Pay the man," Aubrey said.

I paid, while he went into the house, and when I went back in he'd already made himself comfortable in an armchair, his headphones in place, nodding and tapping his feet.

I told him what to do and left without going back upstairs.

Finsbury Park was crowded with weekend shoppers, but when I got on to Vernon's street it was quiet, almost deserted. I marched straight up to the house and rang the first bell I saw. The ginger-haired woman answered, and I think she recognized me, because she shuffled backward a little and her expression was suspicious and unfriendly. I didn't ham it up.

"I'm looking for Vernon King," I said.

"There's no one by that name living here," she said. At the same time she made a motion as if to shut the door.

"Norma Chambers?"

"She's upstairs," she said unwillingly. "Third floor. Ring the bell."

This time she did slam the door before I could shove my way in, and I rang the third-floor bell, and rang it again when no one answered. Eventually, just as I was about to give up the door swung open.

The black woman who stood there was tall, her hair cut short in a style that gave her thin strong features a haughty Amazonian look. She was wearing a loose white blouse and a short leather skirt from which emerged a pair of shapely legs which seemed to go on forever. There didn't seem to be anything whatsoever wrong with her.

"Yes?"

I nearly stammered before I caught myself.

"I'm looking for Vernon. Vernon King."

"Why have you come here? He doesn't live here."

Her eyes looked as if it wouldn't take a lot to make them angry.

"You know him. He's been here two nights."

"So what? Who are you?"

I told her who I was and why I was looking for Vernon. When she heard about the marriage she frowned, and when I'd finished she stood aside.

"Come in."

It was an elegant flat for the area, with a spareness that suited her. We sat opposite each other round a small dining table.

"We went together in Birmingham," she said, "but I packed all that in when I left. I'll be honest with you. I've had enough of Vernon and men like him."

She gave me a sudden smile that was frank and open and charming. I'd thought she was in her late twenties, but now she looked younger.

"I don't know how he found me," she continued, "but he turned up the other night, drunk, demanding to speak to me. I had to let him in. I know him. He wouldn't have gone away before everyone around here had woken up and fetched the police."

"So you let him in."

She looked rueful. "I shouldn't have, but I did. Then I realized he was too drunk to drive, so I let him stay till the morning. Then he left."

"You haven't seen him again?"

I was offering her the chance to lie, but she didn't take it.

"He came back last night. He wouldn't go the other morning till I'd promised to talk to him. About us."

Her mouth twisted scornfully on the words.

"There was no us, but I saw him. We came back and talked. He wasn't too sober, and he'd brought a bottle of champagne. Any excuse. This time he tried to rape me."

She shifted her eyes to the tabletop.

"That was it. He never told me he was married or anything like that. The bastard."

"Any idea where he is?"

"No. I didn't want to know. I told you. I don't want anything to do with him. I don't suppose a man like you would understand but he's just a boy without a future."

She smiled at me again, with a lot of warmth, and I began wondering what life would be like with a woman like this.

As if she could read my mind, she smiled at me again.

"Want some coffee?"

I did, and we sat talking for a while. She told me about herself. She'd been a nurse, then dropped that when she left Birmingham, and now she was a receptionist at an advertising agency. She was excited to meet a reporter like me, she said, because she was interested in public relations. Maybe I could give her some advice. She hadn't many friends in London, and sometimes she got confused and lonely.

"Not lonely enough, though," she said, laughing, "to start up again with a bastard like Vernon."

The morning wore on, while I worked at tearing myself away. At first I'd thought she was aloof, beautiful, and sexy. Now she put me in mind of a younger sister. It was like talking to a different woman. I could see exactly why Vernon would come back, but that didn't solve any of the puzzles I was wrestling with.

In the end I arranged to see her again, to let her know what was going on. We exchanged phone numbers.

"Don't forget," she said at the door. Her eyes shone, then she leaned forward impulsively and kissed me, a soft dry pressure that was like a promise.

By the time I got home I'd calmed down sufficiently to ring Borelli.

"Where've you been, you prat? I've rung twice already."

"Legwork," I told him. I only wished.

"Well, the bloke's a wanker. Nothing on him. Parking tickets. Bollocks. But this Norma, though. She's a bit tasty. You know what I mean?"

I had a sinking feeling when I thought of the hour I'd spent gazing into her candid brown eyes.

"What's she done?"

He told me the story briefly, using general terms and euphemisms, but I got the gist of it.

Norma had been working in a nursing home near Coventry, and one of her patients, a geriatric white man named George Armstrong, had taken a great liking to her. That was normal. His family had been wiped out in a plane crash years before, and like a lot of old people in those circumstances, he needed someone on whom to fix his affections. So there were no problems until the old man fell out of a top-floor window one dark evening. He shouldn't have been in that spot, and Norma had been on duty. The nursing home, worried about taking the rap, blamed Norma and sacked her.

"What made it worse," Borelli said, "was that he turned out to have loads of money, loads. Just before his little accident he changed his will and left Norma a sizable chunk of it, nearly a hundred grand. Most of that had been coming to the nursing home under the old will, so they challenged it and got it set aside."

"What about the bulk of it?"

"He left it to a daughter. But he'd lost touch with her long ago and they couldn't find her. That was what Norma said about the will. He left her a few bob because she reminded him of his long-lost daughter. It could have been. But the real story was that he was more or less senile and totally dependent on her. And she was more than a nurse. She called herself his personal woman."

I laughed. The last time I'd heard the term was in Jamaica. I'd been talking to a taxi driver who was telling me about the children he had by three different mothers. I told him he was real bad, and he gave me a cheeky grin. "And I have a personal woman too," he said.

Norma was operating in a very different culture, but hearing the term, I began getting a sense of a woman who possessed an insolent and defiant humor.

"Those were the words she used?" I asked Borelli.

"That's right. She said what she liked around him. Like she bossed him around. They said she kept him happy by doing his naughties. The old hand jobs. Don't know how he lasted as long as he did."

"So all she got was the sack?"

"That's right. I wouldn't repeat this if I was you, but some of my colleagues feel she was lucky to get away with it."

Something he'd said was careering through my head like a stream of wayward bubbles.

"Franco. Who would know the details of this stuff? The will and everything."

"Can't help you there. Try the lawyers."

"Thanks."

His tone changed.

"I hope you haven't been wasting my time."

"I haven't. You'll hear from me soon."

"See that I do."

I rang Wally.

"Wally. Norma Chambers, Vernon's girlfriend. The case she was involved in when she got the sack. The old bloke. I want to know the solicitor who represented him. Drew up his will and that."

"Bloody hell," Wally said. "I've got a job on."

"Come on, Wally. It's no big thing. Just ring the local paper. You know guys there."

"Okay."

I put the phone down and thought over what Borelli had said about Norma. The woman I'd met had been nothing like that. Except that, thinking back, she'd fallen for my charms a little too readily. I was as willing as the next man to believe I was irresistible, but a lady like

Norma would have too many choices to be swept off her feet by an over-the-hill hack.

The phone rang. It was Wally with the name of Armstrong's solicitor and his home number.

"Wally, you're a prince."

"Don't worry about the compliments. Send me some money."

I called the number. A woman answered and told me that Mr. Hibbert was away.

"Am I speaking to Mrs. Hibbert? Where can I contact him? It's urgent."

"Yes. I'm Mrs. Hibbert. Who are you?"

Her voice was cool, but I was ready.

"I'm ringing from Birmingham radio." I gave my voice a self-important tone. "We're doing a phone-in on the changes in legal aid and what it will mean to the public and the profession. We wondered whether your husband could be on the panel."

She didn't hesitate.

"He's at a conference in London. I'll give you the number of his hotel."

After she'd done that there was a tiny pause.

"Birmingham Radio. Which one is that? BBC or independent?"

"Both actually," I said firmly.

I rang Claudette. Aubrey answered. He was fine. Claudette was fine. Everything was cool you know, Sammy. I told him I would want him later if things worked out and he said yes. He had a calm I envied.

The hotel was one of those respectable old-fashioned ones in Marylebone. The desk clerk eyed me coldly when I asked for Hibbert.

"They're both out."

"Both?"

"Mr. and Mrs. Hibbert."

"I'll wait. Can you tell me when he arrives?"

He nodded and waved to one of the padded seats in the lobby.

I found a three-month-old copy of *Vogue* and read it carefully. I could hear the clattering of cutlery when the door to the dining room opened. Teatime, so I guessed he might be back soon. But he wasn't, and round about five I was beginning to worry that Hibbert wasn't coming back for his tea when I saw the desk clerk pointing me out to a couple who had just walked in.

They looked at me. I smiled and nodded, then the couple exchanged a few words and Hibbert handed the woman a room key. She walked into the back of the lobby toward the lifts, while he approached me. He had reddish-blond hair and a short mustache, and he was wearing a smart light gray suit. He looked like a man who liked a bit of a laugh and a glass of whiskey.

I shook his hand and told him who I was. When I told him what I wanted to know about George Armstrong he frowned.

"I was under the impression you had a message for me. If you want to talk about this, make an appointment with my secretary and see me at my office. But I warn you, I don't discuss the confidential affairs of my clients."

"This isn't confidential, Mr. Hibbert. I can find out in other ways, but I need to know quickly."

He raised his eyebrows.

"Good afternoon to you," he said.

He turned and made to walk away, but I moved in front of him.

"Mr. Hibbert. This is dead serious. Life and death. I think you should know that I spoke to Mrs. Hibbert on the telephone a short time ago, and she was in Birmingham."

His gaze flicked toward the lifts, and then he looked around rapidly as if checking to see if anyone was listening. Then he stared at me again, his eyes angry and intent.

"I don't want to know anything confidential. I really don't. But you can save us both some trouble by giving me just a few minutes. Do you want to tell Mrs. Hibbert you'll be a couple of minutes?"

He would have dearly loved to have kicked me in the pants. But I was betting on the respectability I'd read from knowing his profession and from the tone of the hotel. He'd brought his small-town stuffiness with him and he didn't want it disturbed, even at the price of a few minutes' conversation with an untouchable, especially when the un-touchable had caught him bang to rights in a London hotel with a woman who was not his wife. A couple of clergymen walked past and looked at us curiously, as if they were wondering what we were doing together. I smiled at them. But it rattled Hibbert.

"Come into the bar," he said.

Our little chat took less than fifteen minutes.

"I want you to understand," Mr. Hibbert said when he'd finished, "that none of this is privileged information. But neither is it for publi-cation, and if you mention my name in connection with any of this I shall sue you back to the gutter."

"I understand," I said, smiling warmly at him. "Thank you very much, and give my love to Mrs. H. Okay? You know what I mean?"

He breathed out sharply. If looks could kill.

People were on their way out for the night and the pubs were filling up by the time I got back home. I climbed the stairs tiredly, thinking about being out with a woman, at a party or a restaurant, but I had too much to do tonight, and even if I hadn't, I wouldn't know who to ask, now Sophie was away.

On the phone Claudette sounded as dispirited as I felt. I asked her whether she and Vernon had made their wills before they got married.

"Yes. In case anything happened to either of us."

There was a long pause while this sunk in. I only had one more question, and then I asked her to get Aubrey. It had taken me a long time to get there, but now I knew what was going on and what I wanted to do.

I drove fast to Finsbury Park, but as I had half expected, there was no one there and Norma didn't answer her bell. I got back in and drove up to Tottenham. By now I felt like the Ancient Mariner.

Aubrey answered the doorbell. Claudette was upstairs lying down, he said. I waited till he was sitting opposite me and came straight to the point.

"I think I know what these people are doing and why they're doing it. But they can't really be stopped, 'cause I don't have any evidence. I mean I think they did her mum, but it's impossible to prove. I have to try and get them to give themselves away somehow, to panic them into giving me some kind of edge on them."

He grinned skeptically.

"You think they'll do that?"

"I don't know, but maybe I can get them to lay off her, Claudette, before anything else happens. The thing is they're not at Finsbury Park anymore. I might have blown it by going to see her today and they'll make themselves scarce for a while. Just in case. If they do that it's the end. No one's going to chase after them because I'm suspicious. So I have to find them."

He was sitting up straight, nodding intelligently, like a little kid.

"Okay. The only thing I can think of is having a look in her flat to see if we can find anything to tell us where they've gone. That's where you come in."

His face went through some interesting changes when he realized what I was asking him. First he looked puzzled, then amused, and finally he frowned. Embarrassed.

"No," he said. "I don't do that anymore. After the last time I promised Maman."

"I'm not asking you to steal," I said, "just go in and take a look."

But nothing I could say would shift him. Finally I had an inspiration.

"Suppose Maman says it's okay?"

His face cleared up.

"Oh. If she does. No problem."

"Let's go talk to Maman."

He hesitated.

"What's the matter now?"

He pointed to the ceiling.

"You leaving her on her own?"

I hadn't thought of that, and eventually we decided to take her with us to Maman's.

It turned out to be easier than I thought it would be. I took Maman into the kitchen and explained the problem. I swore Aubrey would come to no harm, and after a little thought, she told me that her heart had gone out to Claudette and she would like to help.

"But if anything happens to that boy"—she waved a spoon—"is you I come looking for, Mr. Sammy."

I swore again to look after him, and we left. Claudette was sitting in Maman's favorite chair being fussed over, and she looked, in spite of everything, as if she was enjoying it.

Norma's flat was dark and Vernon's car was not in sight. Aubrey slipped out and walked across the pavement. He walked confidently with a soft, springy tread, and although I was watching him he seemed to disappear into the hedge. The next quarter of an hour was bad. I sweated and trembled and every couple of minutes I wished I hadn't thought of such a stupid idea. Then suddenly he was there again, crossing the road, as if he'd just been for a quiet stroll.

He got in the car and handed me a piece of paper.

"This is all I could find," he said. "It was next to the phone and it looked new."

It was an address near Hyde Park. I knew the place too. It was a huge block of luxury flats which were owned by the Church of England and let to transients, usually from the Middle East, at massive and inflated rents. I could imagine Vernon in such a place.

"This could be it," I said, my excitement rising.

On the way I talked over my options with Aubrey. I talked. He listened. If I could kid them into thinking I knew more than I did, maybe they'd do something stupid. It didn't occur to me that they might do anything dangerous, which just shows how stupid I was being.

The building was in a quiet square. At this time, about ten, it was still choked with cars, and we only found a parking space after a few circuits. I left Aubrey in the car and went up in the lift, which whirred softly. When I got out, my feet seemed to sink into the carpet. There were soft and discreet lights up and down the length of the corridor. It was that sort of place.

Flat 31 had a white door and a gleaming brass knocker. I knocked and a man's voice called out.

"Who is it?"

I tried a high and affected delivery.

"Room service."

It was the first reply to come into my head, and I had no idea whether or not the building had such a thing, but I was almost sure that Vernon wouldn't know either.

I must have been right, because the door opened almost immediately, and he was standing there. He was wearing a white short-sleeved silk shirt and baggy blue trousers, cinched in tight round his narrow waist. Up close I noticed his big brown eyes and long eyelashes.

"Evening," I said, just the way I'd rehearsed it on the way up. "Can I come in. I'm from downstairs."

He'd only seen me briefly at the wedding, and I was banking on his not remembering for a bit. Something flickered round his eyes, though, but he gave way. I went in quickly, guessing that he realized he'd seen me before, without being able to place the occasion.

The room was bigger than I'd have expected from outside, stretching away to end in windows which gave a view of the square, its lights gleaming through the trees in luminescent green haloes. At the far end was an archway which led to a large kitchen, and nearest me was a closed door which I guessed concealed a bedroom. The furniture was cream-colored leather grouped round a big round coffee table.

He was behind me, but somehow I felt the moment when it struck him where he'd seen me before.

"You," he shouted suddenly. "Out."

So he'd recognized me. Big deal.

"Claudette, your wife, sent me," I said, facing him. "I've got to talk to you."

"What goes on between me and her is our business," he said. "Get out. Now."

He gestured with his thumb, but I backed away from him farther into the room. Like Norma, he had the singsong inflection and the tight vowels of a Brummie, and that reminded me. There were two glasses on the coffee table.

"It was just between the two of you when you got married. That's right," I said. "Even though you didn't tell her about all that money she'd inherited."

I rubbed my thumb and finger together in his face. Now I'd started I didn't have to pretend anger.

"Yeah. I'm not too bothered about you ripping her off. But someone pushed her mum down the stairs and that's a different ball game. I'm going to get you for that."

He was worried. I could see that from the way his forehead creased up, but then the rest of his face screwed up angrily and he growled at me.

"Piss off."

I didn't wait to hear the rest of what he said, because I took a couple of quick steps to the bedroom door and banged on it.

"Norma," I shouted. "Come out here, Norma."

Out of the corner of my eye I saw him winding up to kick me and I moved fast enough to deflect it. Even so his foot grazed my thigh and I stumbled against the wall.

"Yeeagh," he screamed, and came at me in a sort of springing dance that I recognized from the martial arts movies. I scrambled to get behind the sofa, but I wouldn't have made it if Norma hadn't opened the bedroom door and come out just then.

"Vernon," she said sharply and he stopped and stood still, like an action man doll whose battery had run out of juice.

"Hello, Norma," I said. "Fancy seeing you here."

She smiled at me, the smile that I guessed she used when she wanted people to roll over with their paws in the air. She was wearing the same leather skirt with a shirt that was open almost to the waist. The way she looked made me want, even in the circumstances, to lie at her feet with a silly smile.

"Piss off," Vernon said. He pointed at the door again.

"No," Norma told him. "Let him talk. I want to hear this."

She crossed to the sofa, sat down, and patted the spot next to her. She leaned forward and I could see her big brown breasts moving inside the shirt.

"Come on," she said softly.

"Leave it out, Norma," I told her, sitting down. "I'm not a randy old-age pensioner yet. I just came to talk to you and get a few things sorted out."

Her expression changed, and a pair of hot and angry eyes bored into mine. Obviously, she didn't much like the direct approach, but after everything that had happened I didn't have what it took to be subtle.

"I want Claudette left alone, and I want to know how her mother died."

She smiled again, almost lazily. The rapidity of her mood swings had me confused.

"Vernon's left her alone. I thought that was the problem. He didn't realize what a pig she was until after the wedding, then he left. There's no crime in that, and we don't know anything at all about the other thing you mentioned."

She paused, watching me with a feline calculation. I had the feeling that she knew her words were cruel and that the cruelty gave her pleasure.

"Besides, whatever happened, nobody can prove that Vernon had anything to do with it."

"For a clever person," I said, "you're dead stupid. I saw the old man's solicitor today. Mr. Hibbert. You remember him?"

I saw that she did.

"Well, he told me a story about this white businessman named George Armstrong. In Wolverhampton. It seems that he gave this black girl a job back in the sixties. That was in the days when old Enoch was still making speeches about race and immigration that got the skinheads around there all stirred up, and in the circumstances George Armstrong got himself a big reputation as a decent liberal. But when she got pregnant, he threw her out without thinking about it. This should interest you, Vernon."

It must have done, because he didn't even snarl at me. Norma was still watching with her cat's eyes, and I hurried on in case anyone was encouraged by the pause to interrupt.

"He didn't show any signs of worrying about it when she moved out of the area and disappeared, but years later his wife and two daughters flew into a mountain in Spain, and his conscience began to bug him.

But he still didn't do anything until he began to twitch and dribble and drool and forget who he was and he bought himself into the nursing home where he met you. You know the rest."

"Don't stop," she said. "Make it up as you go along."

She couldn't have been happy. But I couldn't read her expression.

"You were really good to him, like a daughter, he thought. Which is why I suppose he empowered you to do some business for him, like hiring somebody to find his daughter. But, surprise, surprise, surprise, the agency couldn't find her. Not with you giving them their instructions. I don't know whether you had everything planned then or whether you hoped that once the old man believed his daughter was lost you'd come in for all that money."

She shrugged, her eyes far away.

"Maybe you'd located Claudette before you killed him. It doesn't matter because it worked either way. Claudette had her birth certificate with her parents' names on it. I asked her about her father's name today and she told me what was on the certificate. George Armstrong. She didn't know, but she'd have had no problem proving who she was, and once Vernon married her and they'd made those wills he had a good claim on any property she inherited. Providing she was dead."

I paused. I was getting into a lot of guesswork now and I was hoping they'd help me out but neither of them made any comment. Norma's eyes were fixed on mine with an expression that I couldn't read.

"What I don't understand is why you tried to kill Claudette before she claimed her inheritance. As far as I could make out Vernon could still claim it, but it would have been a lot easier to wait. Wouldn't it?"

Suddenly her eyes slid away from mine and flicked toward Vernon, and this time I understood the look on her face.

"Bloody hell," I said. "Is that what it's all about? You spend all that time playing with a senile old man and then push him out a window for his money. Then you can't bear to wait a few more weeks because you're too jealous to stand the thought of your boyfriend shagging Claudette. Or maybe it was the marriage. You had to go along with it, but you couldn't stand it?"

Her composure broke then. Her face twisted with fury and she made an abrupt gesture. I pulled back to dodge the blow I thought was coming, but as I moved, Vernon grabbed me from behind and began squeezing my throat. He must have got hold of a nerve, because the pain was excruciating. My eyes began to mist over and I heard a roaring in my ears. Norma said something and the pain subsided a little.

Vernon had let go of my throat, but he still held my chin delicately in one hand, with the other poised on the back of my neck.

"Don't move," Norma said. "He can break your neck before you can wink."

I grunted. I had no intention of moving. My heart was thumping in my chest like a sledgehammer and the pain in my neck had spread.

She got up and moved to the armchair opposite. She leaned back and crossed her legs. Now she was at ease I could see she was wearing nothing at all under the leather skirt, but by now the fact meant nothing at all to me.

"What else?"

She was smiling again.

"I can't talk like this," I said in a thin, strangled tone.

Her smile broadened and she nodded at Vernon. He took his hands away, but they stayed resting, on either side of my head, on the back of the sofa.

Suddenly she burst out with it.

"I did everything for that old git. He wanted me to have that money. Me. It was mine till those greedy bastards robbed me. You know what that feels like? You know how it feels?"

"What about Claudette? How do you think she would feel about being robbed?"

"What about her? She was getting value for money. Besides, she'd never know, would she?" She gave me a sweet smile, her eyes dreamy. "You've got no proof of anything, anyway."

This was my cue.

"You're right," I said. "I shouldn't have accused you."

I made to get up and Vernon's hands were back on my throat.

"I'm not that stupid," Norma said. "Once you start talking to other people, they'll start making connections the way you did. No one's going to bother us right now, but if you go around telling lies about us anything could happen."

"The police know I'm here," I said desperately. "Detective Inspector Borelli. Paddington. I'm supposed to check back with him."

She laughed merrily.

"Pull the other one," she said.

She got up and went into the other room. Vernon's grip didn't relax. When she came back she was holding a syringe.

She held it up.

"Smack," she said. "It's got a hell of an effect if you're not used to it. At this strength it'll kill you."

"There's a bloke downstairs," I croaked. "Waiting in my car."

I described the car, and she went to the window and looked out.

"I can see the car," she said. "But there's nobody in it."

"He must have gone to phone or for a drink or something. He'll be back."

"Sure," she said.

She didn't believe a word I said, and I had a hunch that even if she did, she didn't care. In my head I cursed Aubrey for not being on the job. She came toward me with the needle, and I braced myself to try and pull Vernon over my head, broken neck and all.

Just then there was an almighty crash. In my desperate state it sounded like a thunderclap. The wrath of God. But it was only the front door slamming open halfway off its hinges. Simultaneously, Aubrey was leaping into the room, a marvelous, beautiful sight.

I'll give Vernon credit. He went for Aubrey like a dog off the leash, and I didn't bother to sit around rubbing my neck. As he let me go I lashed out at Norma, who was still staring at the door as if transfixed. I caught her on the jaw and she went down, so I took the needle out of her hand and threw it across the room. By the time I looked up to see if Aubrey needed my help, he had Vernon down on the ground and was kicking him methodically. Fortunately he was wearing sneakers, but I shouted at him to stop. Just in case. Then I went over and embraced him. He took it stoically, with a little bashful grin.

"That was great," I said. "I was never so grateful to see anyone in my life."

"I thought I'd better come up," he said, "and look through the letter box."

No one had noticed.

"And how did you do that?" I pointed at Vernon lying in a heap on the floor, and Aubrey's expression turned scornful.

"He's into Tae Kwan Do," he said. "But he doesn't train. He's a wally."

I rang Borelli then, and while I was talking Norma got up and stretched out on the sofa. I put the phone down and looked at her when I was finished.

"I'm sorry, Norma," I said. And I was.

Hugh Holton

The Thirtieth Amendment

HUGH HOLTON (1946–   ) is a commander in the Chicago Police Department and the highest-ranking mystery writer active in law enforcement. His fictional hero, Commander Larry Cole, has appeared in two novels, *Presumed Dead* (1994) and *Windy City* (1995).

Hugh's contribution to this anthology, "The Thirtieth Amendment," set in the not-too-distant future, is equal parts detective story and science fiction. Moreover, "The Thirtieth Amendment" is a chilling projection of our society's current anger toward a judicial system that is seen as being overly protective of criminals and the increasing demand for a crackdown on crime and the criminal element.

Holton is chairman of the Midwest chapter of Mystery Writers of America and also publishes a regular column in *Mystery Scene* magazine entitled "Cop's Corner."

The Future

CONGRESS repealed the Bill of Rights with the Thirtieth Amendment. Instead of playing games with idealistic crap about search and seizure, rights against self-incrimination and protection from double jeopardy, the Gingrich White House took aim at the criminal element which was turning America into a wasteland. The Tri-X Law, as it was called, made the death penalty not only legal but mandatory for the maggots, drug dealers, child molesters, and social undesirables who murdered, kidnapped, and played treasonous games with scum like the Iraqi dictator Saddam Hussein.

Mr. Law and Order himself, President Newt Gingrich, supported a broader interpretation of the Tri-X Law at the state level. So in California bikers who engaged in violent acts on public highways were added to the list. In New York and Chicago punks engaged in illegal acts on rapid transit lines were added to the list. In Texas, which I always thought was a pretty progressive state, corrupt politicians were added to the list. The other sixty-three states, with the exception of Old Mexico, soon followed suit.

This caused a remarkable increase in executions, which became the growth industry in the U.S.A. for the twenty-first century. My name is Jules Freitag and I managed to get in on the ground floor, so to speak. I majored in Public Executions and Human Terminations at Harvard. The course took six years to complete at a cost of $600,000. The first three years were spent on Law and Sociology, as these subjects relate to the Tri-X Law. The last three years were devoted exclusively to an intricate study of Physiology, not from a medical standpoint, but rather from the termination end. Efficiency was our aim and by efficiency I don't mean just speed, as at times it is decreed that pain must be as much an integral part of the sentence as the death itself.

I am a master of my art.

Randolph Nimrod, the Deputy Commissioner of the National Bureau of Executions and Public Terminations in Miami, called me into his office. He was an intense man of sixty who had given his all to our profession and was considered a living legend. A man with no family or friends, he had risen within the Bureau to the rank of deputy because of his supreme devotion to the field and his administrative skill. For some reason, though, he didn't like me, which made what he had to say that much harder to understand.

"I've selected you for a special assignment, Freitag."

I am usually not a very demonstrative fellow. My vocation demands this. But Nimrod did get my eyes to widen a bit. "Me?"

"Yes, you!" He frowned, grimacing as if he had just been administered a Xyclon cube, which tastes like a sugar cookie and kills in eight seconds.

I stood at attention and waited, as there was nothing else I could do.

"There's an inmate in Chicago named Darka Paris. A vicious convicted murderess. Cut off her lover's head with a butcher knife. I want you to size her."

I stared at him. As a Bureau Deputy Commissioner, he had a staff of over a thousand professional executioners to choose from. There were any number of them beholden to him for their positions who would be eager to do as he asked. My pride told me I was selected because I was the best. But I knew Nimrod would never admit it.

The Jetstar got me from Miami to Chicago in twenty minutes. The state prison was in the inner city. The walls stretched from Thirty-fifth Street on the north near the old ball park, down what had once been an expressway for ground vehicles called the Dan Ryan, to Fifty-third Street on the south and west over to State Street. The surrounding area had become an urban desert.

I was admitted through the seven normal security gates leading into the prison. The buildings had originally been high-rise, low-income housing which social neglect had transformed into human zoos. So, during the final year of the Quayle presidency, remaining residents were ordered out and the maximum security penitentiary was established in the sixteen-story monstrosities near the center of what had once been the second largest city in the United States.

The Tri-X inmates were held at the center of the complex in the 4444 Building. As I stood in the shadow of the imposing edifice, surrounded by machine guns, electrified barbed wire, and guards recruited primarily for their ability to inflict violence on their fellow man rather than for their intellect, I recalled a phrase from a high school literature class: "Abandon hope all ye who enter here." Very appropriate, I thought, as I was admitted inside. But then I was a professional who had no time for poetry.

Inside the Tri-X section it was bright, clean, and terrifying, especially if one were an inmate forced to spend the last moments of one's life on Earth here. The thick-foreheaded guard escorted me to a private room where I could check my equipment and put on my work clothing. There was a surliness in his manner initially which was quickly erased when I exited wearing the black hood which displayed only my eyes and mouth.

It was the same everywhere I went. The hood generated a fear so intense it tended to manifest itself as a separate physical entity. This made my work much easier.

"The girl is in Block L," he said, staunchly refusing to look at me. "She's a real looker. Keeps saying she's innocent, but they all say that." He laughed, glancing sideways at me to see if I had enjoyed his little joke. All he could see was the outside of the hood, which revealed no more emotion than my face beneath it.

We came to her cell and he started to open the door.

"Stop!" I ordered so abruptly he jumped. "You must properly prepare the inmate before I enter."

He caught on quick enough and took the garments I gave him before slipping inside the cell. I waited in the corridor studying the cracked plaster on the walls of the high-rise gallery until he came out.

"She's ready," he said, still refusing to look at me.

I entered to find the inmate securely chained to a chair. Her head was covered with a hood, very much like my own, and her body was shrouded in a black full-length robe. The only flesh exposed was that of her hands, arms, and neck, which I would need to work with directly.

I prided myself on the efficiency of my sizings, which involved the taking of vital statistics about the inmate to aid in the selection of the method I would choose for her death. I could generally do an accurate, very thorough sizing in less than two hours. With her it would take longer because she violated the regulations by talking continuously.

"I know you're here to kill me and that you're trained to ignore what I say but, for the love of God, you must listen!"

It was strictly forbidden by the Executioner's Code of Conduct for me to speak to her. We wore the hoods to maintain mutual anonymity and to prevent any buildup of sympathies between inmate and executioner. Talking could engender some degree of sympathy, but in Executioner Psychology 412, it was plainly established that condemned inmates were liars. It was simple self-preservation to try to maintain one's existence as long as possible by whatever means necessary. So they lied.

"I *am* innocent!"

Of course you are, my thoughts mocked her. How many times had I heard that before. I could have her gagged, but then she had a nice voice. One that could even be called sexy. I scolded myself for my lack of professionalism and concentrated on my work.

"I would never kill Arthur! I loved him! Someone followed us and executed him! It happened so quickly only one of you people could have done it!"

The last statement got through to me. She was making me angry by impugning the integrity of one of the last truly noble professions on Earth. My job was to kill her and her crime limited the means by which I could do it. But then there were always certain tricks of the trade that could be used to make my method of dispatch pure agony for a very long time.

"It had to be an executioner!" Her anger bubbled on the edge of hysteria. "Who else has the knowledge and ability to kill like that?"

Like what? But I forced the question out of my mind. I didn't care.

"What kind of people kill without warning? Would kill Arthur without giving him a chance to defend himself?"

I wanted to ask how it happened but I figured she'd tell me soon enough at the rate she was going.

"You people are cowards! You hide behind your black masks and slaughter people like animals! You're nothing but murderers!"

Look who was talking? I could do the sizing procedure in the order I chose. Now I felt it was time to slow her down a bit. I'd heard all of this before.

Judging by her size, a pint should do the trick. I started drawing blood from her jugular vein.

"His head was . . . severed . . . from . . . his . . . body."

The food in this place wasn't that bad, as prisons go, but then those on death row seldom had much of an appetite. So she was weak and the way I drew blood was just a tad slower than a speed that would induce shock. She was coming down a bit too fast, so I cut the flow slightly.

She hit a plateau, which she managed to maintain for a time. "They said . . . that I . . . did it . . . with a . . ." She was starting to ramble.

Butcher knife, darling! You did it with a butcher knife. Deputy Commissioner Nimrod told me.

As a professional, educated practitioner of the fine art of Executioning, I knew such an act as severing a head cleanly to be impossible except by guillotine or at the hands of a master craftsman of the highest caliber. I studied my inmate and the stats of her sizing. If her victim were asleep . . . ?

"One stroke . . ."

I removed the tube from her neck and cleaned her up. I would have to leave word with the stupid guard to make sure she was given a proper supper with plenty of liquids to replace the blood. I was putting my needles away when something she just said intrigued me.

"One stroke . . ." she repeated in a weak, dazed voice.

One stroke? At Harvard we had studied World History of Executions I, II, III, IV and Advanced. Crucifixion, drawing and quartering, and boiling in oil were all methods we had been forced to review and write extensive research papers about. My paper had been on beheadings, and during the first year after Tri-X passed this method was quite popular.

There had been few skilled practitioners of the art of severing a head cleanly from the body. When accidents started occurring with some frequency there was a public outcry and the method was outlawed in the States, although France kept it for historical reasons.

"One stroke," she mumbled again.

As I recalled from the research I had done for my paper, to do the job cleanly, it took several things to carry one off with precision: either a guillotine or a sharp, heavy blade; a strong steady hand; and the eye of a sharpshooter. Outside of the lucky amateur, there was maybe one executioner who had really been good at it . . .

"One stroke."

She was beginning to bore me. Enough of this nonsense! I had work to do.

My sizing completed, I decided that this inmate would die in exactly twenty-four hours by being burned alive.

Back in my quarters I kept thinking about beheadings. I used my pocket 1,000 K computer to call up historical data, most of which I already knew. I'd always wanted to do a beheading myself, but by the time I completed my studies at Harvard, the law had changed. But Nimrod had said she used a butcher knife. Of course the inmate was lying, but in the Day Before Death Seminar IV it was taught that there was always motivation behind any lie. I decided to check out her story.

The Illinois Division of the two million-strong National Police Force had taken over the Merchandise Mart on the Chicago River. Although Illinois had a relatively small contingent compared to the New York and California Divisions, they were crammed into what was once the largest office building in the world and were constantly searching for more space. It was rumored the NPF would soon be taking over the old Sears Tower, which could be confiscated from its current owners under Section V, 3, C. sub. para. f. (1), 2. of the Tri-X Law, which states: "No property or possessions will be held secure from seizure by the NPF established by this Amendment, where such seizure relates to the safety, security, and peace of the United States of America."

Under Section V, the NPF could confiscate yachts, summer homes, bank accounts, and anything else they desired in the name of law and order. This was an excellent system for the NPF to utilize as a peacekeeping tool, as it was unnecessary to make many arrests. All they had to do was confiscate everything the recalcitrant owned. The only vocal critics of this section of the Tri-X Law were currently penniless, stateless street people. This was another twenty-first-century advance of the Gingrich White House.

The captain I was directed to see had an "I'm too busy for this shit" attitude until he found out who I was. He might be able to confiscate property, but I could simultaneously confiscate his life. Isn't this a great country?

"This is an unusual request coming from Executions," the captain said when the Darka Paris file was delivered to his office by a clerk.

"Oh?" I found it best to speak in soft monosyllables when I was trying to scare the red corpuscles out of someone. Especially a pompous ass from the NPF.

He coughed, stuttered, and handed over the file. "Take it with you. Don't worry about getting it back to me. In fact, you can keep it." He ushered me out the door with more than a small sigh of relief.

The photographs were beautiful. They revealed a work of art the likes of which I had never seen before. The head had been lopped off with a precision that would make a heart surgeon look like a beef boner. I was so excited I studied them for hours. Aside from my admiration for the work, I realized instantly that Darka Paris could not have killed this man. Not with a butcher knife, a chain saw, or a hyperbolic laser. There was no doubt in my mind that a razor-sharp blade had been used. A blade in the hands of a master executioner.

I read the NPF report. The assigned detective had done a slipshod investigation. The evidence was sketchy, contradictory, or circumstantial. A butcher knife with the inmate's fingerprints all over it was listed and catalogued as the murder weapon.

Putting the file down and examining the artwork in the photos once more I made a decision. I would have to find whoever did this. Just to talk briefly with such a craftsman would be a supreme honor indeed.

The same guard who had escorted me into the inmate's cell at 4444 was on duty again. He was considerably more attentive than during our first meeting and I was glad he was there because I was going to need him.

After I changed, he went into the cell to prepare the inmate. While I waited outside I thought about the girl. She was innocent but that was a secondary consideration. She would lead me to the master, then . . .

"She's ready," the guard said, stepping from the cell.

"I'll need your assistance."

"Me?" He took a step backward. "I don't know nothing about no executions."

"It's a good thing to learn, friend." I had a very difficult time talking to him like this. Especially since he wasn't wearing an inmate's hood. "Executions is the growth industry of the twenty-first century."

He seemed barely convinced, so I didn't give him a chance to think it over. "Inside—now!"

He jumped and followed me. He stood awkwardly in the corner of the cell not knowing what to do. The inmate was again hooded, robed and chained in her chair. She trembled violently.

"This is a simple procedure," I said for the guard's benefit. "Efficient and self-contained with very little mess to clean up later." I pulled a pint spray bottle containing nitroholic acid from my bag.

"It's easy. You just spray it on . . ." I pointed the nozzle first at the inmate before turning it on the guard. He screamed and went for his electric truncheon but he was far too slow. ". . . and ignite." I held the mini-torch in my gloved hand. The flame licked across the confined space and enveloped him. He ignited, flared, and burned away as fast as tissue paper. Only a few ashes remained, which would be enough to temporarily convince prison officials the execution had been carried out. It had gone off quick and efficient, the way I liked it.

"Now, my dear," I said, undoing her chains, "you and I are going to get out of here."

Hooded executioners can go anywhere without question. Together we walked out of Chicago State Prison and were given a limousine ride to the jet port on the lake. It was not until we were in my private compartment aboard the Jetstar that I permitted her to remove her hood.

"Thank you," she said, embracing me. "I could sense when you walked in the cell that you were a decent man. I knew you'd help me."

She was an attractive woman, as looks go, with soft features and a petite body. Under different circumstances I might have liked to spend some of my yearly ninety-five-day vacation time with her, but I had more important things to think about now. On top of that she was a condemned prisoner whom I had already sized and I would have to terminate anyway. After all, it was still my job. I had merely postponed implementation of sentence temporarily.

"I want you to tell me everything about Arthur's murder that you can remember. Leave nothing out. It's the only way I can help you." The lie came off my lips easily, as I had been taught by the best liars in the country in Political Terminations 343. It suddenly occurred to me that all of my instructors in the course had either been politicians or bureaucrats like Nimrod.

She was so willing to help me she made me sick. She told me everything. She and Arthur Hickey—the deceased victim—were engaged. They had taken a prenuptial vacation, as was the current custom, to Atlantis (formerly Australia). While there, Hickey began complaining that someone was following them. He became moody and withdrawn from her, constantly looking over his shoulder. He became so obsessed with the belief they were being watched, he cut short their vacation and returned to the States. A day later he was dead.

"It happened so fast I can barely recall it now," she said. "There was a knock at the door of our cubicle. Arthur opened it and . . ."

I let her cry. I knew the rest anyway. The NPF detective had probably made the erroneous connection that she murdered him with the knife simply because it was in the kitchen section of the ten-foot by ten-foot cubicle they rented for $1,000 a week and she was the only suspect because the detective didn't look for any other.

I went back to my computer. I concentrated on prenuptial vacations, divorce honeymoons, funeral excursions, and terminal illness jaunts. I matched all the names on these lists against anyone who had been beheaded under any circumstances in the past twenty years. I came up with 568 hits.

Amazing! And everything pointed in one direction. I had all the answers before we set down in Miami.

Deputy Commissioner Nimrod looked up from his desk when we walked in. When he saw Darka he stiffened. Then his eyes flared angrily at me.

"What are you doing, Freitag?" he said in a choked voice. "Are you insane? I sent you to do a simple execution. Why did you bring her back here?"

I was sorry he was taking it this way. I really had hoped we could be friends now. The reason I'd brought the girl here was to give her to Nimrod so he could work his artistic execution style on her. The computer had revealed that my esteemed leader had been at or near each of the 568 locations where the bodies with severed heads had been found. That kind of coincidence was too much for even the NPF to swallow. I could only presume that he had been doing a little practice freelancing, which I could understand. After all, he was just a deskbound executioner trying to keep his hand in.

I was starting to explain when he leaped from behind his desk swinging a very formidable-looking sixteenth-century battle ax with an edge that gleamed with terrifying sharpness. I knew that in his hands it was as lethal as a nuclear suppository.

Darka screamed and backed away into a corner, as Nimrod advanced on me. With nothing else I could do, I fumbled in my bag and came up with the spray bottle and torch I had used in the Chicago prison. I was merely going to use them to ward Nimrod off, but he feinted toward me and then drew back to hurl the ax.

In the instant he threw that blade, I knew I was being terminated with no chance of escape, but I admired his artistry to the last. I managed to spray a liberal amount of nitroholic acid on him before my head was sliced off my shoulders to drop to the floor.

I was dying at light speed, but still able to see and think. It happened so fast my headless body was still standing a few feet away with the spray bottle and mini-torch in my hands. I could see Darka over in the corner cringing in fear and Nimrod looking at me with supreme triumph etched on his face.

My last act in life was willing my hand to ignite the torch. As I blinked off into eternity I was certain I had failed because mind and body were no longer part of the same mechanism.

But the fates were kind to me, at least as far as Nimrod went. When I arrived at the Gates of Hell, he was waiting for me. It seems his being instantly cremated succeeded in making his trip to the Netherworld faster. There we found ourselves in the company of some of history's greatest killers. For the rest of time we sat around talking methodology, practice, and execution. It wasn't Heaven, but what the hell.

Gary Phillips

Dead Man's Shadow

GARY PHILLIPS (1955–) is the author of the Ivan Monk mystery *Violent Spring* (1994). Phillips says of Monk's Los Angeles, "The landscape in which Monk operates has been shaped in the post-industrial crucible of the 1990s. In particular, Monk's home state of California has wrought Proposition 13 (the tax revolt that gutted services), Proposition 187 (the anti-immigrant backlash), and Proposition 184 (three strikes, and the further criminalization of youth).

"Monk's birthplace was blue-collar, once-black South Central Los Angeles. Nowadays South Central, like other parts of the city, is home to various cultures and numerous languages. Yet many remain segregated from their neighbors and each other across its vast urban sprawl. The city is broke, its financial problems only exacerbating racial tensions. But some still make money the old-fashioned way, because avarice, lust, and larceny are great motivators, with murder the preferred method of negotiation."

The criminal intent Phillips sees in some of L.A.'s citizens certainly applies to the characters in "Dead Man's Shadow." The story is enriched through the seldom-seen glimpse it provides of the role of African American defense workers during World War II.

Phillips's commentaries and op-eds have appeared in such newspapers as the *Los Angeles Times,* the *Los Angeles Village*

> *View,* the *San Francisco Examiner,* and the *Miami Herald.* His
> weekly column "Raisin' Sand" appears in an L.A. suburban
> newspaper, the *Compton Bulletin.* He recently completed the
> second Ivan Monk novel, *Perdition U.S.A.*

THE CORPSE hung headfirst below the parapet of the factory by a
rope. Buried in the middle of its forehead was a short-handled ax.
Dried blood, the color of old copper, trailed from the fatal wound into
the salt and pepper hair of the deceased man.

"That's how he was found. That's how they found my father."

Ivan Monk looked up from the photo at the woman sitting across
from him. She was younger than he was, in her early thirties. His
potential client wore form-fitting jeans, snakeskin boots, and a loose
black T-shirt. Her hair was done in a combination dreads and plaits
prevalent among black women her age. A sort of homage to the moth-
erland by way of Alice Walker and Angela Davis.

"What have the police produced?" he asked evenly, unsure of the
emotional territory he might be treading.

"In the three weeks since the murder, not a goddamn thing." She
glowered at him unblinkingly.

"This is a particularly gruesome and brazen method of murder. Killing a man at his place of employment, then putting him on display."
He paused, unsure of how to proceed.

"What are you suggesting, Mr. Monk?"

"Who might have had it in for him this bad?"

Belinda Bolden snorted and shifted her body in the Eastlake chair in
Monk's office. "Now you sound like Tierney, that lazy slab of beef
who's supposed to be finding my dad's killer."

"The cop in charge."

"From the Foothill Division." Bolden leaned forward. "My dad
worked at Velson Aircraft Manufacturing for thirty years. He started
out there when the Machinists Union was barely letting blacks into the
skilled trades. And that was because people like him organized protests
with the help of the NAACP.

"Dad didn't take a whole lot of shit from anyone, but he was a fair
and honest man. So yeah, you figure it out. A black man who stood up
for his rights was bound to upset some white boys. You must know
what that's like, brother."

Monk smiled and his eyes drifted back to the photo. "Had your father been getting death threats?"

"No. But there are all those bikers hanging out over in Chatsworth, and white-trash heavy metalheads cruising Ventura Boulevard just spoiling for an excuse to mess with black folks. Don't you think those are logical places to start? There has been an increase in hate crimes in the Valley."

"But the police don't think that's an angle?"

A side of her mouth lifted in contempt. "They don't, but at least they don't trip like the clowns down at the Spur bar."

"What?"

Irritation pinched her face. "There's a story been going around out there since I was a kid. And now with Dad's murder, it's gotten to be the hot topic again."

Belinda Bolden didn't seem inclined to talk further on the subject, but Monk hated incompleteness. "So what's the story?"

"Alright, just to get this over with. Back in the forties, around the close of the war, some strange killings happened out there in Pacoima."

"Like this?" Monk pointed at the picture.

"Wait, I'm getting there. Velson was booming in those days. And because there was a shortage of white men to fill the shifts, women and minorities got the work despite the feelings of the companies and the unions.

"Pacoima was a bit more benign in its racism. Unlike other parts of Los Angeles, they didn't have restrictive housing covenants. My dad's people settled there when he was a kid. It was my grandmother who'd worked at Velson during the war."

"And these killings?"

"It all started in December of '44. The black and brown workers at Velson, including some hipster whites, had a club they hung out at called the Kongo Room.

"On this particular Saturday night, four drunk white Marines marched into the club and demanded a halt to this fraternization between the races. Naturally a fight erupted. Henry Swankford, a big raw-boned-so-black-he-was-blue-black man off the Delta, laid out two of the jarheads with his bare hands. The third one he killed with a blow to the temple."

"I can imagine what happened next," Monk said sympathetically.

"Despite eyewitness testimony that the third Marine had pulled a knife on Swankford, he was convicted by an all-white jury of second-degree murder."

"Swankford goes to prison," Monk finished.

"Folsom, May of '45. A couple of days after Hitler committed suicide," she noted sarcastically. "The fourth Marine said on the stand he'd seen no knife in his buddy's hand. He was lying of course. My grandmother was there that night and had testified to the truth."

"And the killings?"

"Swankford escaped in '46. Less than a week later, the Marine who'd lied was found murdered in his apartment out in Indio."

"An ax buried in his forehead," Monk visualized.

Bolden said, "In the fall of '48, one of the other surviving Marines was discovered the same way in a cab he drove over on Chandler in Burbank." The woman stared at Monk, then went on. "At each site they also found a red parrot feather."

Intrigued, Monk asked, "Which symbolizes . . . ?"

"A sacrifice to Eshu, also known as Elegba," Bolden explained. "An *orisha,* a deity of the Santeria religion. Some folks consider him to be the devil, but most certainly he is the god of tricks."

Santeria was a practice whose roots wound back to the Yoruba people of Africa and transmogrified with Catholicism in Cuba during the slave trade. In the modern world, it had followers from the South Bronx to South Central. What little Monk knew about it he'd learned from a documentary on PBS.

Bolden continued. "The rumor among those who used to frequent the Kongo Room was that Henry Swankford had made a deal with Elegba to exact his revenge on the three soldiers."

"Were Swankford's prints found on the handles of the axes?"

"I don't know. My grandmother would know the details." She stopped short, scrutinizing him. "I'm going to pay you to find out who killed my father, Mr. Monk. Not run around digging up ghost stories."

"Okay, but what happened to the last Marine?"

"I don't know, and I don't care. I only told you this so you'd know what you'd be hearing out there and not get sidetracked. There was no parrot feather found near my dad."

"It's not impossible to believe that some copycat killer chanced upon the old articles about the murders and decided to try it out. But I don't believe in goblins either, Ms. Bolden."

She rose, offering her hand as she'd done when she'd entered his office. But this time, as Monk stood to shake it, she put some effort behind the grip. "I think I'm glad I asked around and got to you."

The restored '64 Ford Galaxie 500 purred along the 210 freeway like a well-oiled sewing machine. Its midnight-blue shell gleamed like alien skin under the unforgiving afternoon sun.

He approached Pacoima in the east end of the San Fernando Valley. As he did, Monk passed through Lakeview Terrace, a section of L.A. County made infamous by the videotaped beating of black motorist Rodney King by members of the L.A.P.D.'s Foothill Division. Consciously he checked his speed and headed into the town whose name meant "rushing waters" in an American Indian tongue.

Using the directions provided by his client, he arrived at Velson Aircraft Manufacturing at the end of a row of red-brick businesses on a dead-end street called Aerodrone. It was a long three-story affair. Over the large entrance, in arched Parisian lettering, the hand-painted sign spelled out the company name. P-51 Mustangs, wind lines streaking behind them, circled around the first and last letters.

Monk parked and entered the facility. Men and women were busy at drill presses, short block stands, and the many other accoutrements of airplane engine assembly. He took a flight of metal stairs to the offices on the second floor, and gave his name to a flat-chested receptionist. After a few moments Karl Velson, one of the owners, ushered Monk into his office.

"Have a seat," Velson said, angling back behind his desk. "When Oliver's daughter called to tell me you were coming out, I made you a copy of his company file." Velson's hair was a thick, trimmed mane topping a pleasant face. The image suggested he took his children to the park, and honored his wedding anniversaries. The eyes behind the thin lenses of his glasses were observant.

"I appreciate that, Mr. Velson." Monk looked at him across a desk littered with papers, parts, and a steel model of a Cessna.

From somewhere in the swamp before him, Velson produced the file and shoved it at Monk. "All I can tell you is that everyone here at the shop was shocked at Oliver's brutal death." Idly, he moved some of the papers around.

Monk said, "Mr. Bolden's body, according to what the daughter was told, was spotted hanging from the roof around 6 A.M. I take it there's no guard at night."

"Nor in the day. We're not Hughes or Lockheed, Mr. Monk. We

ain't cranking out stuff for the Stealth Bomber. Velson hasn't manufac-
tured those kind of parts since Pop ran the operation. Now we do
finished blocks for Cessnas, Pipers, and other commuter aircraft."

"And Bolden was here the night of his death on company business?"

"Yes, he had keys to the place. I'm sure Belinda's told you he was the
shop foreman and union rep. There were some new specs on an engine
contract, which would, ah, will necessitate some shift changes. Oliver
needed to go over them to plot out how we'd swing it with our
existing personnel."

Monk remarked, "Isn't that something that you and he would have
gone over together?"

A perturbed expression flitted across the pleasant man's face. "My
brother was supposed to have done that. In fact, it was the second
meeting he'd blown."

"So what happened to him both times?"

The door to the office suddenly swung open and in stepped a man
with unkempt hair who was older and heavier than the other Velson.
That they were brothers was easy to detect. But this one's face had a
harder, cynical set to it. The eyes were wary and his color florid. Monk
sized him up as a man who took his lunch over the rocks.

The older brother appraised Monk too but said nothing. He started
toward a door to the right.

Chidingly Karl Velson addressed his sibling. "Why don't you tell Mr.
Monk here where you were the night Oliver was murdered, Otto."

Otto Velson halted in midstride, turned on his heels, and stomped
over to Monk. He glared down at him with a snarl parting his lips. "I
already told that partner of yours, Tierney, why I didn't show that
night."

Karl Velson answered for Monk. "This man isn't a police officer. Mr.
Monk's a private eye Belinda Bolden hired to find out who killed her
father."

There was a deeper reddening working up from Otto Velson's neck.
Grimacing, he swiveled his large head at his brother. "What my dear
brother is riding me about is I was down at the Spur unwinding when I
should have been here with Oliver. But that doesn't mean that I could
have prevented his death."

The head moved in Monk's direction. "It could have been me too,
you know?"

"Tell him how else you unwind." A cruel note manipulated the
younger Velson's voice.

"Fuck off." Otto Velson disappeared into his office and slammed the door.

The other brother looked at the door, then Monk. "There's a hagged-out bleached number who works the Spur. My brother is one of her steady, if not exactly favorite, customers. He was doing the horizontal bop with her that night."

"What's her name?" Monk inquired.

Karl Velson's mouth made an ugly line. "She goes by the original title of Lola." Something in Monk's manner made him rear back as if struck by lightning. "Wait a minute, I know what you're trying to do. My brother may be a drunk, but he's no murderer. He had no reason to kill Oliver."

Neutrally Monk said, "Just being thorough." With that he took hold of the file and rose. "Thanks for your time."

"Sure," Velson responded, a note of hesitation in his voice. "If there's anything else, you let me know."

Monk was almost to the door, stopped, debated with himself, then turned around. "What do you know about this Henry Swankford business?"

What could have been a laugh escaped from the younger Velson. "I think I believe that Oliver was killed by some zonked out crackhead looking for cash. Hell, man, the Valley is filled every night with runaways, Manson groupies, and God knows what else. This area is a lot different than when I was a kid. The ax in Oliver's head was from our fire box."

"Was the petty cash taken?"

"Yes, about seven hundred dollars."

"Yet," Monk pointed out, "according to what Belinda was told, there were no prints on the ax handle. It's been my experience that drug addicts aren't what you'd call advance planners."

Velson did a thing with part of his face that committed him to nothing.

Monk said goodbye again and drove over to Gloria Bolden's house. She was the mother of the deceased man and the grandmother of his client. He parked under a billowing pepper tree and got out into the oppressive still, hot air.

The house was a ubiquitous modest 1950s-era tract number with an attached garage. Its saving individual feature was an overhanging porch bordered by low hedges. The neat lawn was a mixture of fading green splotched with yellow stains like giant liver spots. A royal palm commandeered the right side of the grass divided by a flagstone walkway.

At the front door, no one answered his repeated knocking. He left a brief note on the back of one of his business cards and went away.

In nearby Arleta Monk found a public library. And despite the most recent round of county budget cuts, it was open. But the newspaper clippings they had on microfiche only went back to 1953. The librarian, a brunette in her fifties with the shoulders of a swimmer, directed him to the San Fernando Valley Historical Society for older information.

The Society was contained in a mock Tudor two-story on a quiet residential street in Van Nuys. There he went through bound clippings concerning the trial of Henry Swankford, his escape, and the subsequent murders of the two Marines. All the pieces were written by the same man, a Frank Ameson. Another article, also by Ameson, was an interview at an undisclosed location with the last Marine, who was scared witless.

"Excuse me," Monk said to the elderly gent who had helped him. "You wouldn't happen to know whatever became of Frank Ameson?"

The old man had an affliction of palsy that caused his left hand to shake slightly as he talked. "I should know, young man. Frank and me worked on the *Valley Herald* damn near thirty-five years. Frank's been dead at least another twelve. Smoked like they wouldn't make 'em no more." He shook his head in remorse.

"Do you know if he kept notes about the Swankford case?"

The older man cocked a gray brow. "You ain't one of those tabloid journalists, are you?" He spat out the question.

Monk showed him his license. This produced a chuckle from the other man.

"Yeah, you got that look. Frank's notes went the way of the dime phone call when the paper folded. Who knows? I don't have most of mine either." He seemed to be winding down but then got his second wind. "Course now, I keep my ear to the ground, Ivan Monk. Got some working reporter friends on the *Daily News* and *L.A. Times* who tell me what's going on in these parts."

The old boy was getting geared up for a long one. He injected, "Thank you for your time, Mr. . . ."

"Garrity, Homer Garrity."

Monk shook his hand warmly and started off.

"Let me know if you solve the Henry Swankford murders," Garrity cracked.

Monk drove about aimlessly, absorbed in arranging the pieces in his mind. Eventually he came across a Carrow's and got a bite to eat. Afterward, he traveled back into Pacoima. He found the Spur as the evening began to chase away the light.

The interior was a comfortable enclave of people socializing, teasing, drinking, and playing pool. Working stiffs savoring the unreality alcohol and the smell of the opposite sex afforded. But closing time always rolled around and brought you back to the grinding reality of your small life.

It was a bar like a thousand others he'd been in over the thousand years he'd been running after lost hope. Getting kicked in the ribs for his effort while trying to decipher human misery, and looking down the long drop of oblivion. Waiting for his turn to make the leap.

He found a perch on a stool. The bartender, a stout Chicano with graying temples and slitted eyes, sauntered over to him. "What'll it be, Sportin' Life?" He wiped the bar clean with a soggy cloth.

"Miller."

The bartender left and returned with the beer. "Buck and a quarter, bro."

Monk laid a ten on the counter. "I'll run a tab. Is Lola here tonight?"

Blank-faced, the bartender replied, "She'll be back in about fifteen." He picked up the note and moved off.

Eighteen minutes later a dyed-blonde in a slit skirt and low heels entered. Her hair bounced past her shoulders and was done in a perm that needed refreshing. Even in the dim light, Monk guessed her age to be late forties, but she was slim, athletic of build.

Lola carried a purse big enough to haul around a couple of phone books. She made her way to the bar where she leaned across at a gesture from the barman. They talked, and he pointed at Monk. She came over. Lola liked garish eye shadow but no lipstick.

"Hey, baby." Her breath smelled of mints and gin and something else. She hefted the purse onto the bar with a dull thud and sat next to Monk. "You're new around here, big boy." Lola sized him up and down. "With a build like yours, I bet you work construction."

Monk put a twenty on the bar between them and signaled for the bartender. "Another beer for me, and . . ."

"The usual, Enrique." She eyed Monk as Enrique filled their orders.

"If you add another thirty to that Jackson, you can put your balls on my chin."

Enrique delivered the drinks and drifted off once more.

Monk smiled. "Some other time when I'm not on the clock myself."

Lola cocked her head when he displayed his license. She held up an index finger, and with the other hand dug out a pair of half-glasses from her voluminous purse. She put them on and said, "Show me that again, honey."

She read the green-colored Bureau of Consumer Affairs-issued license to snoop slowly, silently mouthing the words as she went along. When she finished, she picked up the twenty and buried it in the bag. Lola crossed her legs and sipped her drink.

"What time were you with Otto Velson on the twenty-third of last month?" Monk had some of his beer, anticipating her response.

"Jesus, this is about the murder."

Monk said nothing.

Nervously she plucked at a corner of her full bottom lip. "Well, I was with Otto from about seven to ten."

"He get some kind of special rate?" Monk wondered if the time of death had been pinned down for Bolden.

She batted her eyes. "My regulars always do, Ivan. They don't go away unsatisfied." Her smile revealed a rotted bicuspid. "Course in Otto's case, you gotta allow for the fact he passes out a lot. Hell, I even let him stay the night sometimes."

"When he left you did he go home?" Monk gulped more brew.

"Hey, man, what are you getting at?" She laughed loudly, nervously. "Otto kill somebody? Shit." Lola sampled more of her gin.

"Otto into kinky stuff?"

"Otto ain't much on variation or technique, if you know what I'm saying. 'Sides, why you want to know, sweetie?" She winked broadly.

He let that go. "Tierney talk to you already?"

"Sure," she mumbled over another mouthful of booze. She put the empty glass on the bar. "Thanks for the drink and the twenty, handsome. If you get back to these parts, look me up."

She inclined her body and whispered to him, "I'll put some ice on your dick, we'll snort some crank, and I'll wear your big ass out."

She got off the stool and glided farther into the bar's cloud of promise, the lure of easy, hot sex coming off her in palpable waves.

Presently, Lola left with a rotund, sweating man lapping at her heels.

Monk followed them out and watched the duo walk off the lot, swallowed by the lonely streets. He went back inside to sit, think, and drink.

Time passed. Otto Velson wandered in and sat at a booth. He hadn't noticed Monk. Velson ordered a sandwich and two drinks while he looked around for Lola.

Presently, Velson got up and headed out the front door. Monk came up behind him in the parking lot. "I'd like to have a word with you, Mr. Velson."

He swung unfocused eyes onto Monk. Recognition sharpened them. "You're that private guy."

Before he could continue, Lola appeared again.

"Where you been?" Velson demanded. Jealousy crowded his slurred words.

"Guess," she said contemptuously. She sparked at noticing Monk. "Come on, linebacker. I bet ya Otto'd pay to watch you and me go at it."

Velson's face got even more purple under the blue spotlights lining the eaves of the Spur's roof. He lurched at Lola who sidestepped him effortlessly. The drunk man stumbled onto the ground.

Monk made to help him and a siren went off. A squad car coasted close, its lights pulsing. Two uniforms emerged, guns drawn. A cool anxiety chilled Monk's heart.

"This man bothering you, miss?" one of the cops asked Lola, advancing on Monk, 9mm first.

"Men been bothering me all my life." She laughed at her own joke.

Monk's hands went up.

Velson righted himself, fuming. "Arrest this cocksucker."

The other cop politely said, "He attack you, sir?"

"Yeah," Velson lied.

"He's full of shit," Lola offered.

The first cop stepped close and could now smell the liquor seeping from Velson. He glared at Monk, then Lola. "Maybe we all better sit down and sort this out."

The other cop took a glance at his partner.

"Okay, slick, looks like you know the routine," the first cop said to Monk. He motioned for him to lean against the wall.

He complied and was patted down.

"Clean. Let me see some ID."

Monk produced his wallet and handed it over to the one who'd searched him. The cop got a sour look upon reading it. He walked back to his partner, and the two conferred quietly. Lola stood apart from Velson who was sweating like he was in a contest. The first cop returned and stood close to Monk.

"You better come down to the station with us, Monk." He said it real quiet, real intense.

"What for?"

"We'd like you to come down to the station with us," the cop emphasized.

"Am I under arrest?" Monk straightened up from the wall.

"We'd appreciate your cooperation."

A beat, then, "Alright," Monk conceded.

Lola smiled crookedly at Velson. "My gravy train."

Monk got in the cruiser unhandcuffed. As the car pulled away, Lola blew him a kiss.

Detective Sergeant Hugh Francis Tierney was a tall, boxy-built white man rummaging in his early fifties. His face was jowled and topped by a bad haircut. He possessed a loud checked sport coat that was draped over a chair. The cop walked with a slight limp and talked as if his vocal cords were tied in a knot.

"Tell me once more," he demanded.

Monk fixed his gaze on the acoustic tile lining the interrogation room and sighed. For the ninth time he told the cop how he came to be at the Spur.

When he was finished the large cop asked, "Why do you think Otto Velson killed Oliver Bolden?"

"I didn't say that. I said I think it's interesting his alibi is so weak."

Tierney sat across from Monk, placing his elbows on the table. His fingers were like bloated sausages splayed across the scarred surface. "What I think is you're a second-string peeper and sometimes bounty hunter who's milking a grieving daughter for whatever you can get."

"That's what makes America great, Sarge. There's room for all kinds of opinions."

Gritting his teeth, Tierney squeezed out an "Uh-huh."

Just to annoy him further, Monk asked, "Do you think the rumors are true? An old ghost is stalking the Valley?"

Tierney grinned wickedly. "Sure, Monk. I believe Henry Swank-ford is the cause of all this like I believe private eyes serve a useful function."

They stared at one another for a few minutes. Then, "Get out of here, knob shaker. Go home if you got one."

Monk walked out. A man in overalls with a police ID badge clipped to his breast pocket entered the room he'd just left.

Monk heard what the man said as he continued walking. "I hate to tell you this, Sarge, but your car's still not ready."

The bulky cop finally let his anger out in a string of invectives at the mechanic, the city budget, and General Motors' cars in particular.

By the time Monk trudged back to his car and got to his apartment in Mar Vista, it was past four in the morning. He stripped down to his boxers and sank into bed. In a dream, Lola chased him with an ax, a red feather clutched between her teeth.

After ten he was up, showered, shaved, and got breakfast from Khan's Golden Chariot Coffee Shop on the next block. A little past one he finally got out to North Hollywood and Oliver Bolden's house.

The place was a freshly painted stucco Valley wonder done in somber beiges. Monk let himself in with the key Belinda Bolden had given him. Inside it was quiet as a sanctuary. The lights still worked; the Boldens hadn't closed the place out yet.

Some time later, after poring over the paltry yet personal material accumulated in a person's life, Monk found nothing to help him decipher Oliver Bolden's death. Just the detritus of photos, papers—including the funeral program for his wife's service, and the handwritten scraps that marked one's passage on the stone called Earth. He picked up the phone and called Gloria Bolden.

"Hello," an older female voice answered on the first ring.

"Mrs. Bolden?"

"Yes, who's this?"

"My name is Ivan Monk, your granddaughter—"

"It's Mr. Monk," Gloria Bolden announced to someone out of range of the handset. Back into it, she said, "Where are you now?" Her voice had taken on an urgency.

"I'm in the Valley." He wasn't going to tell her he was digging through her son's belongings.

Mrs. Bolden said, "Can you come over right away? Something's come up."

"I'm there."

Twenty minutes later Belinda Bolden opened the door before he was halfway up the walk.

"Harriet Stubbens has been murdered," she announced.

"Who?" Monk said, gaining the porch.

"She called herself Lola."

"Shit. Ah, excuse me, Mrs. Bolden." The grandmother, a refined woman with silver hair and a straight frame, stood just inside the door.

"I've used a lot worse, Mr. Monk. Come on in."

Belinda talked excitedly as Monk entered. "About nine this morning they found Lola dead behind the Spur. An ax buried in her forehead."

"Otto Velson's been arrested for her murder," Gloria Bolden added.

Monk sat down. "How do you two know all this?"

Mrs. Bolden stood next to the mantel over a bricked-up fireplace. "Pacoima's a small town, Mr. Monk. Something like this gets around quick." She wrung her hands, then went on. "You better see this too." Mrs. Bolden took a legal-sized envelope off of the mantel and brought it over to him. The older woman's unblemished hand extracted a red feather. "This came in the mail two days after Oliver's murder."

Illogically, the feather made Monk queasy. "Did you show this to Tierney?"

She gazed at Monk steadily. "No, I didn't. It shook me up so bad, I was scared to tell him about it. And too scared to throw it out."

"Did you know about this?" he asked Belinda.

"Not until today. Mama told me about it when I got here this morning. After she heard about Lola, she called me and I came over. We'd been calling around trying to find you."

Monk put his hands on his knees to steady himself. Reality seemed to be slipping away from beneath him. Like those times when he was in the Merchant Marines and plowing through rough seas. Land nowhere in sight. "Why would Otto Velson kill your son, Mrs. Bolden?"

"I don't know." There was a quaver in her voice. "I do know that Henry Swankford was the kind of man who didn't take a slight from black nor white."

"What are you saying, Mama?"

Gloria Bolden sat on the thick arm of the couch heavily. "Your grandfather fought in the war. The European theater. I worked at Velson with the other girls making intercoolers for B-29s. Oliver was just a big-headed boy then. Dreaming of flying secret missions with Spy Smasher on the radio."

Monk noticed the barely hidden boredom on Belinda Bolden's face. Evidently she'd heard this tale many times before.

Mrs. Bolden paused, the past seeming to overwhelm the present. "Henry Swankford also worked at Velson. He wasn't one to enlist and fight some crackers' war, no sir. 'No white man's army wants this nigger with a rifle and the right to kill other peckerwoods,' he used to say. Henry was a big-fisted vital man who could drink a quart of raw whiskey and still work a double shift. He had the eye for the ladies too."

The way she said it got Belinda's interest.

"One night all of us were at the Kongo Room, carrying on and all, you know how it gets." She looked at the floor.

Belinda Bolden sat upright, enthralled by this new chapter of the story.

Mrs. Bolden continued. "One thing led to another and me and Henry went back to his place over the garage and talked about the money he was going to make." She stole a glance at her granddaughter, then continued.

"Maybe it was the liquor I'd drank . . . but before I knew it we were . . ."

"Making love," Belinda incredulously finished.

Gloria Bolden waved a hand, failing to give it a light air.

"What money?" Monk prompted.

"Henry had some fool notion of getting enough money for us to run away with Oliver in tow. Later I told him that night we spent together was a mistake. And it was a bigger mistake if he thought he could get away with robbing the plant. He was furious that I wouldn't go away with him."

"Didn't he worry you might tell Velson what he planned to do?" Monk said.

"Henry was wild, but crafty. He knew if I told all us colored folks would be under suspicion. Shoot, they'd string him up and them white folks would've rounded up the rest of us for being saboteurs.

"See his vice was women, Mr. Monk. Money was just a means for him to get from here to there."

"So what happened?" Belinda Bolden cut in.

"Those four Marines is what happened. Henry was still set to rob the factory that Sunday night. He'd kept goading me the week before about it, about how he was going to have all that money and how I'd be sorry I didn't go with him."

Monk passed a hand over his face. "So now a mad killer on Geritol has come back to exact revenge on your son because you dumped him more than fifty years ago?"

No one responded.

Monk got up and began to pace aimlessly. "Then why kill Lola?" He held up a finger. "Ah, maybe she's the daughter of the missing Marine." He stopped, feeling disoriented. "Look, I'm not about to go around chasing some dead man's shadow. There's an answer to be found in this world, and I'll find it."

Monk started for the door, eager for forward motion. As he passed by Belinda Bolden she rose and approached her grandmother. He left them to wrestle with the onus of old sins.

He spent futile time at the Foothill Division trying to see Otto Velson. He did manage another run-in with Tierney which ended in another insult.

From Karl Velson he learned the actual facts. His brother had awakened in Lola's apartment with a crippling hangover. Beside him in the bed lay Lola cleaved in the head by a short-handled ax, a beet-red feather stuffed in her mouth. Otto threw up on the corpse, but even with the shakes managed to call his brother.

Karl, sure of his brother's innocence, called the company attorney who in turn remanded Otto to Tierney voluntarily. Unfortunately the older Velson's fingerprints were on the ax handle. And Tierney was working on the theory that Otto, in a drunken state of pent-up fury, killed Bolden. Some years ago there had been a strike and Tierney was advancing the idea there was still bad blood between the two. The younger brother said that was bullshit, but the cop was working hard to prove it.

For the moment Otto Velson was being held as a material witness with the prospect of being charged looming quite near. As for why he killed Lola, apparently everyone in town knew the late Ms. Stubbens treated Otto like a doormat.

Monk wound by the Historical Society and asked Homer Garrity to check with his newspaper friends on a couple of things. Eventually, he swung by Lola's apartment. A black-and-white had parked in front, a cop getting out. Monk watched for a few moments from down the block, then drove off in the opposite direction.

He spent the next day crisscrossing the Valley on several errands, and took a trip to Long Beach at night.

The door eased open. A figure entered; the beam of a flashlight pierced the dark like a leak of phosphorescent radiation.

"Turn the lights on, asshole."

The switch was flipped. "Monk."

A lone ceiling fixture illuminated the interior of Lola's spartan apartment. Tierney shut the door. Monk had his .45 aimed at the cop's spreading gut. "Drop the light, then take out your piece, carefully." A thrust of the automatic underscored his words. "Put your gun on the floor and kick it away," he ordered.

"A police officer never gives up his weapon."

Monk sneered, "Honest ones don't."

Tierney blanched, but did as he was told. From the flapped pocket of his tasteless coat, Tierney removed a white envelope. Protruding from its torn flap was a red feather. "You had one of Lola's ho' friends leave this with the desk sergeant." He shook the envelope accusingly at Monk.

"That's the one you sent Mrs. Bolden, but I added the note. My office administrator wrote 'I know the truth' so it would be in a feminine hand. I figured that would send you scurrying around."

Tierney's jowls got rigid like concrete. "You're talking out of your head." His ham of a fist crumpled the envelope and shoved it back into the jacket pocket.

Monk's gun remained unwavering. "Three and a half years ago there was a bust in Palmdale of a big methamphetamine lab. Bikers, some of their chicks, enough loose cash to choke a horse, and, oh yes, a couple of trunkfuls of crank and crystal ice."

Tierney passed a dry tongue over parched lips. He glanced at the door, then back to Monk. "I had nothing to do with that."

"True. But Lola was one of the women arrested. Only she was calling herself Monique that week. She goes down on one of the vice cops back at the station house and, surprise, only gets slapped with a misdemeanor."

Tierney remained motionless.

Monk went on, "Now this vice cop only wanted a blow job. But you"—Monk pointed with the .45—"wanted a different kind of piece. You and this vice cop were drinking buddies and he told you about the vivacious Harriet Stubbens."

Tierney surveyed the room, his shoulders sagging. "I didn't want to wind up in a place like this when I retired."

"Save it for *Hard Copy,* you ain't nothing but a greedy motherfuckah trying to muscle his way to the trough. You got a hold of Lola who, for a cut, provided you with leads to other amphetamine labs." Homer Garrity, at Monk's request, had checked with his crime-beat contact at the *Times*. Among other things, the reporter told Homer about Lola's past and the crowd she used to hang with.

"How'd you put it together, Monk?" Tierney's voice was toneless.

"I kept thinking about the first killing. If Otto'd done it and not left his fingerprints in a mad drunken stupor, let alone be together enough to tie a man up and suspend him from the roof, then why would he be so sloppy with Lola's?"

Tierney seemed unnaturally calm. "That still wouldn't put you on to me."

"Lola told me the night Oliver Bolden was killed Otto'd left her around ten."

"So?" Tierney challenged.

"That was the second time Otto had stood Bolden up. Needless to say he was upset. When I talked with Karl after Otto had turned himself in, he told me he'd gotten an irate call from Oliver at ten-thirty that night. He'd said two things: it was Karl's duty to look for Otto since he'd done it the first time, and he'd stay at the shop and try to get some work done on the scheduling. After that, he hung up with a slam of the receiver."

Tierney's large body stiffened.

"So Karl went out looking for his brother. It didn't take an advanced degree for him to guess that Otto was probably with Lola. Only it took him a while to find out where she lived. But he saw Otto's car out front at eleven-thirty when he arrived. He'd checked his watch. Karl left in disgust, deciding to confront his brother the following day, once he was sober."

Tierney stared straight ahead.

"You told Lola to lie about the time Otto had left her to make a tighter frame around him. You knew Otto was supposed to be working with Oliver Bolden because Lola told you. And given his increasing blackouts, there were a lot of hours Otto couldn't account for. He was the ideal fall guy for you."

"That lie made you curious to know more about Lola," Tierney said bitterly.

Monk nodded. Garrity's reporter contact had written about several unsolved robberies of meth labs and their caches in the Valley and Long Beach over the last two years. And the reporter had told Garrity that he'd heard Tierney and his drinking pal, who was one of the officers investigating these robberies, had an unexplained falling out. Maybe the vice cop suspected Tierney, or was mad he hadn't been cut in on the action.

"Lola's comment about 'gravy train' referred to you, not Otto," Monk added. "Seeing the patrol car, she figured you were keeping closer tabs on her."

Tierney rasped, "Bitch was getting sloppy with her talk. Goin' on about how her end of things wasn't sufficient all of a sudden. Hell, I was taking all the risks, doing the scores and doing the deals with out-of-town buyers." The big cop did a motion with his upper body but stopped when Monk rose.

"You saw me the other afternoon, didn't you?" Tierney asked.

"In the black-and-white, yeah. Your build and limp are hard to miss."

"I was getting nervous about you, Monk. Maybe Lola wasn't as scared and stupid as I'd hoped, and she'd left something behind to implicate me."

"Even though you'd already searched her place the night you killed her, and put Otto's hands, who was passed out, on the ax handle." Monk moved toward Tierney. "But I guess you were kinda rushed then. Let's go."

"I was thinking you might be her new partner," Tierney said, oddly in a jovial mood. "She was so goddamn friendly with you, the uniforms told me." Without the slightest indication the big cop suddenly produced a short-handled ax from beneath his coat. He took a vicious swipe at Monk's head.

Ducking and twisting his body, Monk's shot missed Tierney and struck the overhead light. Blackness eclipsed the room. Each man fought to get his breathing under control so as not to give away his position to the other.

Monk circled to his left, anticipating Tierney who'd think he'd naturally go to the right. Close to his ear he felt the whisper of the ax as he flattened his body, lashing out low with an arm. His hand latched on to the plainclothesman's leg, and he yanked it. Tierney tumbled and Monk swarmed onto him, praying he wouldn't have to find out what it felt like to have an ax buried in his skull.

The cop rolled and Monk's body went off balance. A disturbance parted the air, and tears of fire went off behind his eyes. A wet pain engulfed Monk's side where the ax had sliced into shirt and flesh. Blindly he blasted off two more rounds to drive Tierney back.

The cop pounded across the threadbare rug. Monk was sweating and he knew shock was setting in. He scuttled across the floor as Tierney got the front door open.

The beefy man was briefly outlined in the doorway, but Monk couldn't get up, he was too weak. Feebly he reached out for the fleeing man.

Tierney brought the ax down at Monk's hand, who pulled back quickly, letting off a shot in reflex. The slug bore into Tierney's calf, upsetting his balance.

There was no landing outside the door, no purchase for the cop to fall on. Tierney yelled and did a whirlygig down the stairs. Monk couldn't see anything as he elbow-crawled to the edge of the top step. A scream came from the darkness below, and Monk involuntarily gasped for breath.

"Tierney," he called out but there was no answer. Monk could barely keep his head up, it seemed like mooring lines were tugging it to the floor. In a few moments fibers from the carpet were swirling around in his slack mouth.

Monk concluded Hugh Francis Tierney had killed Oliver Bolden because the shop foreman had encountered the cop outside of Lola's apartment. That was the first time Otto and Bolden were supposed to have done the scheduling. Tierney probably went to see Lola to set up another score, or to make sure she wasn't getting any independent ideas. Otto confirmed he wasn't with her then, he was so out of it he'd been sleeping it off elsewhere.

Bolden must have asked Tierney, probably assuming he was a john, had he seen Otto. As Tierney began to implement his plan to rid himself of Lola, he realized he had to kill Bolden also. Otherwise he'd be around and would remember where he saw Tierney once Lola was dead.

The big cop got real clever and decided to put the Swankford legend to use. Just in case the setup against Otto failed, the authorities would be looking for some crazed killer imitating the past.

Tierney'd been found dead at the bottom of Lola's apartment, the ax embedded in the center of his forehead. The police department's bio-mechanical criminalist and two investigating detectives couldn't agree as to how Tierney had managed to kill himself. For one thing there was the angle, and two, the amount of force it took for the ax to penetrate the bone.

And nobody had a sound theory to explain the parrot feather leaving the envelope and Tierney's flapped pocket and jumping into the corpse's mouth.

The cops wanted to believe Monk had done it, but the paramedics swore he was unconscious when they'd arrived. The PI had been leaking blood, and there was none on the stairs.

Subsequently, Lola's garage apartment was rented to a history student taking classes at Cal State Northridge. He was doing a paper on local Valley history and thought staying in the last pad Henry Swankford had lived in before going to prison was way cool.

Percy Spurlark Parker

Death and the Point Spread

PERCY SPURLARK PARKER (1940–   ), who is active in the Midwest Chapter of the Mystery Writers of America, has been writing mysteries for over twenty years. Big Bull Benson made his first appearance in "The Wino Murder," a short story published in the Mystery Writers of America's 1973 anthology *Mirror, Mirror, Fatal Mirror*. In addition to the 1974 novel *Good Girls Don't Get Murdered*, Benson has appeared four times in *Alfred Hitchcock's Mystery Magazine*.

Parker notes that Big Bull Benson was originally a minor character in a failed short story. At that time Benson was "four hundred pounds of mass and muscle in a pink jumpsuit with a shotgun resting on his lap, guarding a high-stakes poker game. If the story had been bought, it might have been Bull's first and last appearance." Luckily it wasn't.

BIG BULL BENSON had the coffee waiting when Rod Felton came into the office. Rod took his with cream and sugar, Bull with a shot of Grand-Dad.

Rod's old man had been Lucky Felton. The big newspapers had their nationally syndicated sports writers. *The Daily Challenger,* the rag that carried the news to the black communities of the city, had Lucky Felton. Back in '78, Lucky had gone with Affirmed as a Triple Crown cinch, when most had picked Alydar to upset things. He'd had the '85 Bears all along, and had correctly predicted the '94 baseball season would be a short one.

Bull had attended Lucky's funeral earlier in the week. Hit-and-run. It had happened on the West Side, Lucky had just left a bar and was struck down as he crossed the street. He had never been a heavy drinker but he barhopped a lot. He said it helped him keep his finger on the pulse of the city's betting spirit.

The car involved was found the next day, stripped and dumped in a vacant lot. It had been stolen, the usual hot-wire job. So far the cops hadn't come up with anyone to pin it on. And from what Bull had heard it didn't look too likely that they would.

Rod didn't waste much time, taking out a small spiral scratch pad and handing it to him. He'd called earlier telling Bull he'd found something he wanted Bull to see.

"It was Dad's and it's his handwriting."

The spiral notepad was folded open to one of the back pages. There were only three words on the page, scrawled in pencil, PHARAOHS, FIX, WIZZY.

It was clear enough to Bull. The Pharaohs were the City-South College football team. They were Conference champs and the favorites heading into a bowl game in two weeks. Bets are placed on football games not so much on who wins or loses, but how much they win or lose by. The point spread. The fix was in, somebody or bodies on the Pharaohs were being paid to control the spread. And Lucky had gotten or was getting his information from Wizzy Lee.

"Well?" Rod looked a lot like his father then, the way his thin eyebrows wrinkled as he sat leaning slightly forward, his broad face at a tilt. Bull couldn't guess the number of times Lucky had occupied the same chair, debating the merits of some upcoming sporting event.

"Looks like Lucky got hold of something." He tried his coffee, the Grand-Dad giving it an edge that mildly scratched his throat.

Rod nodded. "It looked that way to me too, but I wasn't sure if I was just making up something that wasn't there. Know who or what Wizzy is?"

"Nickel and dimer. Used to be in tight with the Phil Breeden crowd. They've been splits for a while now. But if a fix was in, Wizzy would stand a damn good chance of knowing about it."

"Breeden plays kind of rough, doesn't he?"

"The man has got a temper," Bull said. "Probably the only reason

Wizzy's still walking around is he and Breeden are second or third cousins or something."

Rod straightened somewhat in the chair, several lines playing across his forehead. "Do you think maybe it wasn't an accident, Bull? Was my dad murdered?"

Bull had toyed with the idea long before Rod showed up with the scratch pad. He had no more to go on than the fact that Lucky was dead, a hit-and-run, but had it been intentional? Maybe a part of him wanted it to be that way, more than a simple accident. Maybe he wanted someone to hate for having killed Lucky and not pity some poor slob for having no business behind the wheel of a car.

"I don't know, Rod, it's something for the police to handle."

"I know you, Bull, don't hand me that. If my dad was murdered, you'd want the bastard as much as I do. Only difference is you know your way around these things. I don't."

Bull didn't argue. He had a rep, more true than false. Whether it was more good than bad depended on who was doing the judging. He'd gotten involved with murder before, helped point the cops in the right direction a few times. Some liked him for it, some wanted to push him in front of a bus. He took a good swig of his coffee, sweetened it with a splash of Grand-Dad, then put the bottle back in the bottom desk drawer.

"Okay, so what do you want me to do?"

"Find out which it is, Bull. Please."

Sam Devlin came into the office after Rod left. He'd been working the bar out front in the Bull Pen Lounge, which took up most of the first floor of the Benson Hotel. Bull had won the deed to the hotel in an all-night poker game some years back. Sam had installed himself as bartender from day one. He was old and bald, and he talked around the wooden match in the corner of his mouth.

"Well, what'd the kid have to show ya that was so important?"

Sam had been a part of Bull's life for so long, there wasn't much Bull could keep from him, or tried.

"The fix is in on the Pharaohs' game?" Sam said, after Bull explained.

"I could be wrong, but it looks that way. Seems Lucky got caught up in it."

Sam worked on his matchstick. "I don't much like the idea of someone gettin' away with bumpin' off Lucky, but you best be careful. Phil

Breeden has always been a hard ass, and he ain't had too much in the finesse department either. Piss him off and he'll go for ya quick."

Bull caught up with Sergeant Vern Wonler at the Moore Street Precinct.

"Marge was expecting you for dinner last Saturday," Vern said.

"Yeah, she got on my case when I called to see if you were home. I tried to make it but something came up."

"Female or a deck of cards?"

"A little of both."

Vern grinned, shaking his long dark face. "You'll never change."

"I hope not."

They had grown up together. Two black kids running the streets. Now one was a cop, married with twin boys. And Bull, thanks to Sam's tutoring, had done his nine to five with a deck of cards, a pair of dice, and a scratch sheet in his back pocket.

Vern sat down at his desk pushing papers and folders aside. "Murders, burglaries, muggings, another fun week at Moore Street. What can I do for you, Bull? Don't tell me you're selling tickets to the Gamblers' Ball?"

"It's about Lucky."

Vern sobered, his wide grin straightening, then turning into a frown. "I see this crap every day, but it's still hard to believe he's gone. I keep picking up the *Challenger* expecting to see his column."

"Me too. Rod came by to see me today. He found this with some of Lucky's things."

Vern studied the scratch pad for a long time. "Wizzy Lee?"

"That's my guess. If we can get hold of him, maybe we can find out for sure."

"I think we're a little late," Vern said, shifting through the papers on his desk.

He handed Bull a police report. Hit-and-run. It had occurred at 2:13 A.M. that morning outside Wizzy's apartment building on West Seventeenth Street. Witnesses described the vehicle as a four- or five-year-old Ford sedan. No one was able to tell how many people were in the car or who was driving. The victim, Leonard "Wizzy" Lee, twenty-five, was dead at the scene when the ambulance arrived.

Bull tossed the report back on the desk. "Looks like we've got an epidemic."

Bull was six-six and working on two eighty-five. Most men he came in contact with were smaller in stature. Phil Breeden was a runt, five-one at the most, and maybe 120 pounds when he strapped on his shoulder holster. But he was as mean as he was short. Word was he'd never been in a fair fight, at least not from his end. He ran the biggest book on the West Side, and dealt in a little juice action as well.

For extra muscle there was Guy Woodley or Pedro Barnes. One or the other was usually with him, and a good part of their job was holding Breeden off some jerk who was dumb enough to be late with a payment. Retribution was best handled without witnesses, but Breeden's temper rarely took that precaution into consideration.

"Tired of dealin' with the folks on the South Side, Bull?" Phil asked. He was sitting in a booth at the back of the greasy spoon he used as a front, a pad and pen on the table before him. He was sporting a box cut these days, probably an attempt to make himself look taller. A dapper dresser, his tailored dark brown jacket was a shade or two lighter than his complexion. Pedro stood next to the booth, arms folded across his thick chest, watching.

"Everything's cool on my home turf, Phil. I was close by, so I stopped to see where the heavy money's going these days," Bull said, squeezing himself in the booth across from Breeden.

"Three to five, Pharaohs by eight."

They were interesting odds. It would take three dollars to win two, if the Pharaohs won by nine or more points. But the Pharaohs had averaged twenty-four points a game their last four outings, while holding their opponents to thirteen or under. Going with the Pharaohs was still a pretty good bet.

Bull dug out a cigar and fired it up. "I guess if the Pharaohs don't make the point spread you're going to clean up."

Breeden shrugged his small shoulders. "It's the nature of the business. You can always bet against them."

"And you've got places around the country where you can do the same."

"Yeah, so? What are you trying to say, Bull?"

"I think you know, Phil. You got the fix in on the Pharaohs' game."

"Talk like that can get somebody dead."

"Yeah, I know. Lucky Felton and your cousin Wizzy so far."

"Wizzy's dead? Damn, it's about time."

"I'm supposed to believe you didn't know?"

"I don't care what you believe."

"Maybe I ought to stick with what I know."

"It's usually advisable."

"I know you've got a lot of money riding on that game. I know with the fix in you're going to clean up big time. I know that if you haven't informed certain members of the betting community of the fix, and they get wind of it, your little ass better find a good place to hide."

Bull was fishing more than anything else but it got a reaction. Breeden began breathing heavier, a slight snarl to the set of his lips, and his eyes tightened into dark little beads.

"The one thing I don't know is how many lives all this is worth to you."

"There's always room for one more," Breeden said, reaching inside of his jacket.

Pedro grabbed him. "Boss, cool it."

"Get your hands off me, Pedro, this sonofabitch got it coming," Breeden said, struggling against Pedro's grip.

"Bull," Pedro said, motioning with his head for him to leave.

Bull took a big drag on his cigar, blowing the smoke across the table as he rose. He felt more amused than threatened. It hadn't taken much to get Breeden going but if it'd come down to it, he would've knocked the runt into next week. Pedro would've taken a little more effort, but he could be handled as well. A fight wouldn't have proven anything, however, or helped him learn more than he already knew.

The City-South Pharaohs were having closed practice sessions. Bull parked at the curb by the team exit gate. He spent the better part of an hour listening to an old Motown tape of Gladys Knight and the Pips. Gladys had always been his favorite. There were a number of good women singers around, but in his estimation none of them came close. The only thing that spoiled the tape was the thought of Lucky's murder. It stayed with him, dancing out of step with each song that played.

The fix was in. Lucky and Wizzy were killed because of it. These were the obvious conclusions. Not so clear was Breeden's involvement. He was the money man alright, the one who stood to make the most out of the setup. Lucky would've been murdered to keep him quiet, but why Wizzy? And Bull couldn't say for sure Breeden had known about Wizzy's death.

A fire engine-red Dodge Neon pulled up to the curb a couple car lengths in front of Bull's Caddy. The babe that got out wore a pair of tight-fitting jeans and a gold and green City-South school jacket. Winter had been taking over the city for the past two weeks, no real snow but a lot of wind and low temperatures. The weather didn't seem to bother her as she went around to the passenger side and rested her plump rump on the Neon's fender. She was the color of strong coffee, her hair a wealth of long, tight braids. Young, late teen, early twenties. She'd never been a wallflower; it was evident in her walk as she got out of the car and perched herself on the fender. He silently congratulated whoever she was waiting for.

The second and third stringers started filing through the exit gate, some still wearing their numberless practice jerseys. There wasn't one of them who passed by her that didn't look back. She was definitely worth a second look.

Bull started out of his car when he recognized Rye Kirkland, the Pharaohs' quarterback. He was tall and rangy, and his throwing arm was one of the prime reasons the Pharaohs were heading for a bowl game. Ms. Tight Jeans got to Kirkland first, throwing her arms around his neck and smothering his lips with hers. Then they piled into the Neon, and she kicked the car to life. From the deep growl of the engine there was more under the hood than what the factory had put there. She sped off with tires screeching, exhaust vapors billowing from shiny twin chrome pipes.

"Who's the little lady?" Bull asked Mike Justin. He was offensive coach for the Pharaohs, and had been walking behind Kirkland.

"That, Bull, is Miss Takisha James. Let's see, this year's Homecoming Queen, captain and choreographer of our cheerleading squad, she carries a B average and she's on the Student Council. Word is she did the work on the Neon herself."

"I'm impressed. All that and a mechanic too."

"You must know her old man, Paul James? He owns Reliable Auto Wreckers."

Reliable was the largest black-owned auto scavenging outfit in the state, but Bull couldn't recall ever meeting its owner. "How long has she had Kirkland wrapped up?"

Justin grinned and the gray previously hidden in his stubbled beard seemed to peek through. "Right after our second game, when we buried Nohambar Central thirty-seven to nothing. She latched on to him and hasn't let go."

"Wouldn't think he'd be able to keep his mind on the game."

A bigger grin this time. "She's a hot little number alright. I had some concerns along those lines myself. But actually, Rye's been working harder since they hooked up. My hat's off to the kid. You know his story, he was in that street gang on the West Side. The gang was known for ripping off cars, keeping the chop shops supplied. Then his high school gym teacher noticed the raw talent, talked him into going out for the football team his sophomore year. Now, I've got me one of the top three quarterbacks in college ball."

Bull had heard the story a number of times from Lucky. Kirkland never admitted stealing any cars and the police never collected any hard evidence to charge against him. Football had been the turning point for Kirkland, and he had never had to look back.

There were only a few stragglers leaving the practice field now. The chill in the air was becoming more persistent, urged on by an increasing wind. Bull gathered his coat about his neck. "Mike?" He tried to pick his words carefully. "Think it's possible someone on the team might shave a few points?"

"Hell no. Not on my team."

"Think about it. It could be the reason Lucky Felton is dead."

"No way, Bull. That would mean it would have to be one of my key people. Rye, my running back Shaw, or Peters or Dubrow, my receivers."

"I don't like the idea myself, but it's the only way it adds up."

"Get a new adding machine, Bull. Somebody's lying to you."

"That's what you're going to tell the cops? They'll be coming around. Better start giving it some thought. Any of your key people acting different lately?"

"My guys are innocent, Bull. I'll tell you and I'll tell the cops. Now"—his eyes narrowed—"we got nothing else to say to each other."

With that Mike walked off mumbling something Bull couldn't make out, but he was sure it wasn't pleasant.

Smitty's was the local hangout of the City-South students. It wasn't much more than a hamburger and hot dog joint, but it was near campus so the students had made it their own. Bull swung by there, deciding to stop only when he spotted the Neon in the side lot.

The noise level in the place was definitely for younger ears. It was a combination of R. Kelly blasting through the speakers which hung from the ceiling in each corner and the occupants themselves, who had to shout to be heard across the small tables. The counter and grill took

up the back wall, flanked by worn-looking booths. Kirkland and Takisha were hugged up in one of the booths on his right.

He made his way through the maze of tables and students that filled
the floor. "That was some exit you made from the practice field." They
both looked up at him, puzzlement registering in their knotted brows.
"You parked in front of my Caddy. I was waiting to have a word with
Rye but you were too fast."

"Sorry, mister, you should've shouted or something."

"That's alright, it gave me a chance to talk to Justin."

"You know the coach?"

"Yeah, we've run into each other off and on for a couple of years
now," he said, sitting across from them. "I'm Bull Benson, Rye. I was a
good friend of Lucky Fenton's."

Kirkland smiled. It was the same wide, dimple-cheeked melter that
got plastered over the sport pages. "Lucky was my main man, ya know?
He was the first one ta put me in the papers, back when I was in high
school."

Lucky had often boasted the same.

"What can I do for ya, Mr. Benson? Ya taking over Lucky's place at
the *Challenger?*"

"Naw, I'm just trying to clear up a couple of things for the family."
It was as close to the truth as he wanted to get just now.

"Hey, man, I'm here for ya if I can help."

"Do you know a guy named Wizzy Lee?"

"Wizzy?" Takisha laughed. "Sounds like a cold. I'd remember if I'd
ever met someone like that." Close up she was even cuter, her skin
clear and smooth, her eyeliner faintly accenting her big brown eyes.

Kirkland grinned along with her, his arm slung over her shoulders.
"Sorry, I've never met him. Was he a friend of Lucky's too?"

"They knew each other. Maybe you saw him around here." It had
been a year or so since Bull had last seen Wizzy and he knew it didn't
take that much for a person's appearance to change, but he gave them
what he remembered. "Skinny, about your height, few years older,
dark, used to clear his throat a lot when he talked."

He waited as they looked at each other, shrugged. "Oh, yeah," he
added, as something else came to mind. "The bottom tip of his left ear
was missing." Hell, it had been Wizzy's most noticeable feature, funny
how it had slipped his mind.

"God, I hope I don't see him," Takisha said. "Anybody that ugly
would probably mark any baby I'll ever think about having."

They both got a good laugh out of that one, and when they settled down, Kirkland said, "I still can't help ya, man. We don't know him."

He spoke to several other people in the place, asking them straight out if they knew a Wizzy Lee. No one admitted recognizing the name or the description.

As he was leaving he ran into Tom Dubrow and Chuck Shaw. He got pretty much the same response except Dubrow thought he'd seen someone who looked like Wizzy around a time or two, either at Smitty's or at the practice field.

"I can't be positive but it sounds right." He was a little short for a wide receiver, but he had the credentials, burning speed and a pair of sure hands.

"We haven't seen anyone like that," Shaw said forcefully. He was taller than Dubrow, slower, but a clutch player.

"Which way is it, guys? You can't remember seeing him or you can?"

Dubrow started to say something, looked over to Shaw.

"We haven't seen him," Shaw said.

Dubrow shrugged, cleared his throat. "Look, mister, lately we've been getting as many strangers in here as we have students. Hell, the mayor even paraded his ass down here right after we got the bowl bid."

It was a valid point, yet it didn't explain Shaw's behavior. Prebowl jitters? Just plain tired of talking to people? Maybe. Or maybe he had something to hide.

Out in the parking lot, Bull mulled over the whole mess on his way to his car. The fix was in for the Pharaohs' bowl game. Lucky and Wizzy were killed because of it. Phil Breeden was the money man behind the fix. These things he knew. Any way he looked at it, it came out the same way. He was just lacking a little something called proof. And he hadn't learned anything so far that gave him any real hope of gaining any. Plus, he hadn't gotten any closer to who had actually committed the murders. Right now he couldn't even make a good guess.

Police work should be left for the police, they have the patience for it. Hell, he was a gambler. A deck of cards, a pair of dice, these were the things he knew the ins and outs about. Sure, he'd gotten backed into corners before, or tried to do a favor for a friend. The situations had gotten a little hairy at times but he had managed.

Still, this was different. If there was someone to grab hold of and shake the truth out of, he would. But who? It might be Kirkland, or

Dubrow, or both. Maybe it was Shaw or Peters. Who for sure was involved? Breeden. Yeah, that would be the right answer, Bull knew, but roughing him up wouldn't work. Breeden would go down for the count before he gave up any info on himself or anybody else.

He pulled his cellular phone out as he walked toward his Caddy. The little flip phone always felt like a toy in his big mitt, but he'd had it for about a year now and wouldn't be without it. He tried Vern's beeper when he couldn't reach him at the precinct, climbed into the car out of the early evening chill, and waited.

A good third of his cigar was gone by the time Vern returned his call. "Yeah, Bull?"

"Just got tired of banging my head against the wall. I'm heading back to my place, thought I'd give you what little I had."

"Go ahead, but I think I got a good leg up on closing this one out."

"How'd you do that?"

"First off, we found the car that did Wizzy. Stolen, another hot-wire job."

"Who needs a gun when a car is just as effective?"

"Something like that. Dumped in another vacant lot on the West Side. It hadn't been stripped but the report said it was wiped clean." Vern paused, as though waiting for a reply. When none was forthcoming, he continued, "I paid a visit to Breeden. What the hell did you say to him anyway? He was still boiling when I got there."

"It doesn't take much for him."

"True. Anyway, he didn't confess to any wrongdoing."

"Naturally."

"He's just a misunderstood restaurant owner who's trying to get out from under the bad label placed on him for some past indiscretions."

"I almost feel sorry for him."

"Then I tried the bar where Lucky was the night he got run down. The only question the bartender had been asked when it appeared to be a simple hit-and-run was if he'd seen anything. I asked a few more."

Bull took a pull on his cigar and waited.

"The bar is right in the heart of Wizzy's old neighborhood, and Lucky had been there twice before with Wizzy. The bartender couldn't say what they were talking about, both times they kept to themselves at a back table. Lucky was by himself that last night, he even commented on his way out that he'd been stood up."

"Set up sounds more like it."

"Exactly. But the kicker is, it's Rye Kirkland's old neighborhood too. He and Wizzy used to live in the same building. It was just something that slipped out during our conversation. Bartender used to have a lady friend who lived across the street."

"You sure of this?"

"Yeah and that's not all. I had Wizzy's file pulled. He was in the same car theft ring Kirkland was rumored to belong to. He was doing eighteen months in our downstate correctional facility when Kirkland started shining on the football field."

"Kirkland is the one Breeden's got in his pocket," Bull said. Most of the guesswork was out of it now. A few facts and the answers were lining up like his hotel patrons on a Saturday night. But there was still no answer to the big question. Who killed Lucky and Wizzy?

"I'm heading over to Kirkland's now, I think a trip down to the station is in order."

"You won't find him at home, he's here at Smitty's, the burger joint on Fifty-fifth. I just got through talking to him."

"Good, let's leave it at that. You said you were going back to your place, do it. I'll handle it from here."

"Sure thing, Vern."

"Bull, damn you. That was a little too easy. I'm warning you, just stay—"

He switched his cellular off. The connection between Kirkland, Wizzy, and Breeden was too strong to doubt Kirkland's guilt. It made sense; the one person who had the opportunity to affect the scoring most was the quarterback. The team had mainly gotten to where they were because of Kirkland. Anybody could have an off day. If Kirkland's off day happened to be bowl day, then so be it, the coaches weren't going to bench him. He'd miss a pass here, a bad hand off there, the Pharaohs could still win as long as Kirkland saw to it that it wasn't by more than eight points. The team would have the national praise, the glory of a bowl win, yet everybody who bet on them would get screwed.

He was wrestling with himself on whether to go back to his place like Vern wanted him to, or back into Smitty's and confront Kirkland, when Kirkland and Takisha came out and turned into the parking lot.

They were too wrapped up in each other to notice him. Takisha had her arm looped through Kirkland's, talking and laughing as they walked. He didn't get their attention until he stepped in front of them.

Takisha was in midsentence when she stopped abruptly and the sparkle seemed to leave her face.

"Mr. Benson," Kirkland said, still the confident young gladiator. "Thought you'd left."

"Almost, but I'm going to be waiting around a bit. You are too."

Kirkland shook his head. "Naw, I don't think so, man." He smiled down at Takisha. "Me and my baby got some other plans."

"I'm making some changes." Bull took the last drag off his cigar and flipped the butt to the ground. "You lied to me about Wizzy, you two used to run together. Cops know all about it. Fact is they're on their way over here now to talk to you. So, you won't be going anywhere until they get here."

Bull could see the confidence drain from Kirkland, in the tilt of his head, the square set of his shoulders. There wasn't even a trace of the smile left on his face. "Okay, okay. Maybe I know Wizzy, so what? What'd the cops want to see me for?"

"Taking money to fix the bowl game for starters. How much did Breeden pay you?"

There wasn't a lot of traffic on the adjacent street but Kirkland's eyes darted to the sound of each passing vehicle. "Naw, man, you're wrong. And I ain't talking to no cops."

Kirkland made a sudden move to his right, spun, reversing himself, and took off in high gear. The kid was good; by the time Bull reacted Kirkland was nearing the end of the parking lot. Bull kept himself in pretty good shape, hitting the gym at least twice a week, but chasing down quarterbacks wasn't part of his regular routine.

He took a couple of steps and Takisha latched on to his arm trying to hold him back. He easily shook her loose leaving her behind yelling for him to stop. He rounded the corner of the parking lot to find Kirkland halfway down the block. He was somewhat surprised Kirkland hadn't gotten any farther. Kirkland crossed the street, running behind a lumbering van, and just missed being hit by a taxi. Bull continued on his side of the block, keeping Kirkland in sight and actually gaining. He didn't cross over until he was sure he wasn't going to be playing tag with any oncoming traffic.

Kirkland kept looking back, which might have interfered with his gait. He broke stride a couple of times and Bull gained a little more. Another street, no traffic this time, then midway down the block Kirkland turned into an alley. Bull had done some of his best work in alleys, from crap games to fistfights. He considered the concrete canyons his home turf.

Bull hit the mouth of the alley as fast as he could, jumping to one side. It's a rarity to get a well-lit alley, most offer more shadows than anything else. Thanks to a lamppost on the street corner at the other end, he had a clear view of the center of the alley. But the path along the way was clouded with shadows. Kirkland hadn't had the chance to clear the alley. If he'd still been running Bull would've seen him, which meant he was hiding somewhere along the way with probably a brick in his hand or a broken bottle.

Bull took his time, looking from one side of the alley to the other as he proceeded. The chill night air did little to keep the stench of the garbage in check. Something scurried by, a cat or a rat he couldn't tell. In this neighborhood they came pretty much the same size.

He was nearing the end of the alley when Kirkland sprang up swinging from behind a garbage Dumpster. Bull blocked the blow with his left arm, the impact flinging the bottle Kirkland was holding against the side of the building. Bull jammed a couple of rights to Kirkland's midsection that took the wind out, and a chopping left that sent him to the pavement.

He reached down, grabbing Kirkland by his collar and hauling him to his feet. "You should've just stuck to football," Bull said.

He thought of Lucky, of the hopes Lucky had expressed for Kirkland's career, and how Kirkland had repaid him. He was about to swing again, one parting shot for Lucky, when he heard the roar of the car behind him.

He looked back into a pair of bright headlights that blinded him as they grew larger, coming closer and closer, the roar of the engine louder, nearer. He dragged Kirkland with him, flattening them both against the side of the building as a Geo Tracker sped by, the shadowy figure of the driver hunched over the wheel like an Indy pro. The Tracker's brakes screamed like hell as it roared out onto the street trying a 360, but the Tracker was too top-heavy to hold the maneuver. It flipped, bounced just once, and wrapped itself around the lamppost at the mouth of the opposite alley.

Bull poured himself a shot of Grand-Dad, put the bottle back in his desk drawer. A week had passed since the Tracker had tried to run him down. There was a *Challenger* on his desk, turned to the sports page. Rod Felton had been offered his father's old job and his first column dealt with the scheme to fix the bowl game. He did a credible job, sticking to reporting and managing to control the sentiment. But he promised his readers he'd be there when the guilty parties were brought to trial.

There were a lot of conflicting stories for the police to filter through. But they had gone with Takisha's version, mainly because she had given her statement when she thought she was going to die. It had taken the fire department a half hour to free her from the wreckage of the Tracker. It had also taken eight hours of surgery and another two days in intensive care before the doctors had given her any hope of surviving.

The whole deal had been Wizzy's idea. He took it to Breeden for backing with the promise of getting Kirkland to go along with the deal. Wizzy had started out by threatening to tie Kirkland to the old car theft ring. But it wasn't necessary, Takisha liked the idea and that was all Kirkland needed to know. Takisha had even gotten Breeden to up Kirkland's end of the take. The plan was to win the game, just control the point spread.

It had all blown up when Breeden decided to cut Wizzy out of the deal. Wizzy got mad and went to Lucky. Lucky went to Kirkland to verify the story. Kirkland denied the whole thing and Lucky took his word for it but said he would be checking into Wizzy's motive for trying to start trouble. Takisha didn't want to take the chance Lucky would discover the truth, especially her involvement in the whole thing. Working around her father's business, she'd learned how to hot-wire a car by the time she was twelve. She'd contacted Lucky to set up a meeting; he had chosen the location. Then fearing Wizzy would take his story to someone else she treated him to the same fate. When Bull ran after Kirkland, Takisha turned to her murder weapon of choice. She'd hot-wired the Tracker and followed.

Kirkland and Breeden weren't involved in the murders, but there were a half-dozen other charges they were going to be facing.

Bull folded the *Challenger,* leaning back in his chair. Rod had ended his column by predicting even with Kirkland out of the line-up, and with all the adverse publicity, the Pharaohs were going to win their bowl appearance handily.

It's the way Lucky would have done it, no sitting on the fence. Bull realized he was smiling, and figured somewhere Lucky was smiling too. He raised his glass, saying good-bye to an old friend and welcoming a new.

Njami Simon

From Coffin & Co.

Coffin & Co. (published in France as *Cerveil & Cie*, 1985; U.S. edition, 1987) was the first and only mystery written by the then twenty-four-year-old NJAMI SIMON. The novel is a masterful send-up of Chester Himes's detectives Coffin Ed Johnson and Grave Digger Jones, heroes of the "Harlem Domestic Series" Himes began in 1958.

Part of the novel's plot was inspired by the French publication of Himes's *Plan B*, after years of widespread speculation among scholars and fans that a "lost" Himes novel included the deaths of one or both of his detectives. *Coffin & Co.*'s protagonists, W. Jones Dubois and Ed Smith, have made their reputations by falsely claiming to N.Y.P.D. colleagues that they had served as role models for Himes's detectives; they fear their own disgrace with the English translation of the novel and the famous characters' death.

In reality, *Plan B* would not be published in English until the University of Mississippi Press edition of 1993.

Since *Coffin & Co.,* Simon has written six other books, including *African Gigolo* and *Les Clandestin*. A journalist for *Editions Revue Noire,* he lives in Paris, France.

Chapter One

THE DEW DROP INN, on the corner of 129th and Lenox Avenue in Harlem, was a place where you were sure to have a good time. There in

a part of the neighborhood nicknamed The Valley, blacks in their Sunday best came in little groups to have some fun. The music made the
jukebox shake, mixing with the incredible hubbub of the bar and the
improvised dance floor between the counter and the room where men
and women of all ages pranced about. In the shadows, a little withdrawn from all the action, two old men sprawled before glasses of cold
beer, lamenting the passing of a time when, instead of Michael Jackson,
the voice of Big Joe Turner made black hips sway. This part of the
black islet had been baptized the Coal Bin. It was even more dilapi-
dated than the rest of the district, though once it had been the domain,
the kingdom of dreams, through which these two black cops pursued
their scuffles and adventures. Retired now, the only things left for them
to do were drink, hum a bar of "Sometimes I Feel Like a Motherless
Child" in a throaty baritone like Louis Armstrong, blubber about past
glories and prove by way of a few sharp words that two old lions could
still terrorize the rats.

"Shit, man, we have to do something," sighed the one whose face
looked scalded with violet scars. "Anything but sit around here rotting!
I'm sick of barhopping like a couple of morons."

"Right on," the other answered. "I feel exactly the same. I'm not
going to end up like all these niggers!" His glance across the bar took in
a row of two-bit pushers, armed thieves, worn-out whores and the
bloodshot eyes of men who hadn't slept since their last fix. The solu-
tion for these burnouts, these lost souls, these addicts, was one and the
same: live and let die. Above all, survive and protect your miserable
hide through thick and thin.

"Come on, let's split," grumbled the one with the marked face.

His partner fell into step behind him. The bartender didn't charge
them for their drinks as they left. Having tough guys for guests made a
good impression, even if they had hung up their badges.

Their black sedan sat parked on the Lenox Avenue sidewalk. Every
hood in Harlem knew the car. The men climbed in. The key had not
yet turned in the ignition when a young man with a radiant face tapped
on the windshield. He was built like an athlete and held a large ghetto
blaster balanced on his shoulder. He sported the red cap of a Queens
baseball team. W. Jones Dubois, riding shotgun, opened his door.

"Get in, kid. You shouldn't be hanging around here at your age."
Dubois was forced to shout over the music that escaped the radio,
drowning his words.

"Turn that racket off!" shouted Smith in a voice loud enough to shatter the car window.

Looking contrite, the young man turned down the volume and edged across the seat behind Dubois. "You're just not with it. Bruce Springsteen's great."

"Any spade'd make that kind of music has got to be crazy. That kind of racket's not our style, boy."

"Springsteen's not black."

"That's even worse," Smith snapped.

The car rumbled off toward Central Park. Smith drove slowly, as if they were still making the rounds. Indifferent crowds moved along the sidewalks, knowing that in this neighborhood prayers were never heard. Night fell, sharpening the keenness of dark eyes. Smith burst out laughing. "Not the time to put out the whitebait now."

"No," his partner somberly agreed as the old Plymouth turned sharply left onto 126th Street.

Without slowing down, the car passed the police station where a new, young lieutenant had replaced the legendary Anderson. It continued in the direction of the Harlem River. Decrepit buildings rose toward the sky with hideous grandeur. His face pressed against the window, Dubois had the disagreeable sensation that pincers were twisting in his gut. And yet he felt certain that he knew Harlem better than anybody. During long years of service he had wallowed about in this filthy place; even so, with sixty years behind him, he was disgusted by his helplessness before it. To think that shit was the natural element of black people! The tires screeched at the intersection of First Avenue and Harlem River Drive.

"So, Grave Digger, you got the blues, or what?" asked Smith. The nickname stuck to Dubois like skin.

"Sometimes I think America isn't really our country, and that's why we're all living here like wolves. Otherwise, it just doesn't make sense."

"You're both out of your minds," scoffed Little Cassius.

Jones Dubois turned around laboriously. "You should have watched *Roots* when it was on the tube, Featherbrain."

"This is where I live," Cassius shot back, "and this is where I'm gonna make it. I don't want to spend my life dreaming about another city or another country, waiting for the white man to do something for me. I'm going to take what I can get right here."

"Swing low, sweet chariot," Smith smirked, making fun of his friend.

The Harlem River cut the black ghetto in half. To the west lay Harlem, to the east, the Bronx. The Plymouth followed the river for a moment, before reentering the heart of the forest of girders, buildings, gutted cars, billboards and burnt-out neon signs. Smith drove aimlessly, waiting until the last possible second to make his turns.

"So, kid," Dubois went on, "why aren't you at Columbia today?"

"Weren't any interesting classes. Besides, I wanted to break the news to you myself."

"It's not up to you to decide if a class is interesting, kid. You got to swallow everything they give you. You got to work hard if you're going to be secretary of state. Twice as hard as any whites," he said.

There was a moment of silence as each one meditated on these words.

"What's this news of yours, anyway?" Smith finally asked, not about to be distracted.

"I can't talk about it just like that. Let's go someplace quiet. It's serious."

"You eat yet, kid?"

"No, man! I'm hungry. As long as . . ."

"Clam up," Smith cut him off. "We haven't eaten yet either. You can tell us your story over a big plate of chicken feet and green peppers. That way when you open your trap, you won't be able to close it again."

Mama Dodge's place was located in a narrow alley between Park Avenue and Lexington. The two men knew they could find a full plate here at any hour of the day or night. The restaurant was actually a stall, just large enough to hold three tables, and Mama Dodge reigned over them as indisputable mistress. Seeing the two giants get out of their car, she walked over to them.

"Been a while since I seen you here," she said.

She tossed a murderous glance at a customer lost in contemplation behind an empty glass. "This isn't a hotel. You better move along now."

Though Mama Dodge was not herself a poet, she played the muse to local graffiti artists. With a bust that several bras could not contain, large hips still nicely rounded and the legs of a wrestler, Mama Dodge had made an impression on more than one man. The customer she'd called to stood up, paid and left without a word. Mama went over to the table, pocketed the change and wiped the Formica with a dirty towel.

"Come sit down," she said graciously to the three men in the doorway.

Noticing the young athlete, she turned to the two men, laughing. "So, the old couple's managed to make a brat. Is this one of yours?"

"Sort of," Smith answered. "He's the son of all the oppressed niggers on the planet. One day he'll be somebody too."

Mama Dodge pouted and looked uncertain. There were some bets she preferred never to make. Since the men were not there to debate this question either, they quickly sat down at the empty table. A spicy odor, strong enough to make a corpse howl, wafted through a beaded curtain from the kitchen.

Seated before the detectives' favorite dish, Cassius's tongue began to wag as Smith had predicted it would. The hot sauce made his gut burn and brought tears to his eyes. The tears blurred his vision. Enormous drops of sweat pearled under his two companions' hats. Everything conspired to make the scene appear to drip, as though the room were losing its mascara. Smith noisily licked his fingers.

"So?"

The student rubbed his eyelid with his dirty hand, then wiped his mouth, which was smeared with sauce. Dubois downed a large glass of California red. Little Cassius smiled mischievously. Mama Dodge pushed aside their empty plates and set down full ones, then she tossed her guests an anxious glance. They in turn showed a lively admiration for her cuisine by smacking their lips and grunting loudly.

"I know everything," the kid announced, once Mama, reassured, was at a distance.

"What do you know? You're still young enough to be in knickers," Smith interrupted good-naturedly. "Right, Grave Digger?"

Smith turned to the kid. "You'd better let go of your mama's tits or you'll stretch them out until she wraps them right around your neck."

"Cut the crap," exploded Little Cassius. "Don't talk to me like that. It won't work anymore. I know who you really are. I know you've never laid eyes on Chester Himes, and that you're not Coffin Ed and Grave Digger Jones. All those stories you've been spreading around Harlem are just a bunch of b.s.! I'm just as much a super-cop as you are. Books written about you—that's a lot of crap. The books exist, but you don't," said the kid.

"What's this little bastard going on about?"

Smith's voice broke; a rattle came out of his mouth. In spite of himself, his fingers tightened on the chicken leg he was sucking. Cassius gloated. He had his revenge. At nineteen he could make them walk on tiptoe. He no longer bought the scorn or lessons of these phony heroes. He didn't dare turn the other cheek now. Instead he felt like breaking Jones's jaw. As for Smith, he could eat his words about short pants. Dubois put his hat on, covering his shaved head, which looked like a relief map of the earth, complete with mountains, continents and valleys. He didn't dare look up at his accomplice.

"Don't look so glum," Cassius went on. "You've been having a good time for years. And anyone has the right to take himself for a Napoleon."

"Or for Cassius Clay," Smith said, giving him a hard look.

Caught out though they were, Smith and Jones were still old foxes. A sense of reality did not escape them for long. Once over the shock of this initial revelation, they wanted to hear more. Maybe the kid was just bluffing.

"Whatever gave you that idea?" asked Smith.

Cassius smiled a tender smile filled with emotion. "One of my buddies at Columbia is African," he said. "His parents live in France. They always send him piles of books. This month he received the latest Chester Himes. When he told me about it, I realized you've been fooling everyone around here for years."

"What's the book about?" asked Smith, a little anxious.

"Coffin Ed and Grave Digger both die. Cold, stiff, buried. They can't be up to too much now," Cassius said.

"What kind of joke is that? You'll see this stiff lay you out flat in a minute, just as soon as I finish off this plate."

"You can do whatever you want, but not those two, at least not anymore. Himes is the one who wrote it. You can bet they're not munching on chicken feet today. They're too busy pushing up daisies."

Smith let the chicken bone fall to his plate. It landed with a dull thud, like a stone fragment falling from a statue. Mama poked her nose out of the kitchen.

"Hey, you two, what's the matter? You look like you've seen a ghost."

"Nothing, Mama," Cassius said. "Something's stuck in their throats."

Unconvinced, the woman shrugged, then stepped over to an empty table armed with her dishtowel.

Jones drew a heavy breath. "Where can we find this book?" he asked.

"You'd have to go to Paris," Cassius replied.

A gleam lit up the old combatant's eyes. "You mean it's not for sale over here?"

"That's right," said the kid.

"Do you think many people have read it yet?" Smith asked.

The two detectives' mental wheels turned in tandem. For years they had strolled in step along the sidewalks of their city, copying and aping two models they had accidentally found one day between book covers. Together they saw a gap in the clouds, a light at the end of the tunnel.

"Maybe Boubacar, but he never lends his books. So, I don't think so. I haven't even read it yet myself. Anyway, I don't know enough French yet to understand it."

Smith retrieved his bone from the sauce and commenced to chew, softly crushing it between his jaws. The shadow in his eyes hadn't disappeared yet, but a shaft of sunlight struggled to replace it. Jones observed his friend. It seemed as if they hadn't seen each other for days. Smith's forehead was furrowed with deep lines.

Cassius felt a little guilty for having broken faith with these two old fools. He imagined them now as blind orphans, groping their way along like lame birds, jeered at, surrendering to the madness of the town. But why would real detectives want to act like movie stars, strutting their stuff in Harlem, posing as heroes when they were only sorry cops? He saw that they acted even more like children than he did, taking refuge in a world they had invented, unable to admit to their vanity. They're too old to start over now, he thought, I should have been more careful. He pushed aside his plate and stood. The meal they had bought him now took on a bitter taste.

"I'm gonna go get my sound machine."

"It's open," said Dubois, worn out by now. His eyes followed the young man's silhouette.

Planting her feet before the table, Mama Dodge interrupted his train of thought. They could see that she was anxious to hear the news, but the ex-cop merely took out a bill and handed it to her.

"Thanks for everything, Mama."

Smith was already standing. His face looked more sullen than ever. The customers at their tables watched them leave with a mixture of fear and admiration. They were celebrities here; a writer had even immortalized their greatest exploits in the ghetto. Out on the sidewalk, they discovered Little Cassius on the curb staring into space with his cassettes resting on his lap. He turned around to them.

"I swear, no one will find out about this. I know how to keep my mouth shut."

He tried to speak in a casual tone but neither Smith nor Jones replied. Jones opened the passenger door and slipped inside, reappearing with the giant ghetto blaster at arm's length. Smith was already taking his place behind the wheel as he handed the radio to Cassius.

"Step on it, Grave Digger," he said.

Little Cassius heard this and felt heavy. He had exposed their game, and still they went on using borrowed nicknames. Sooner or later they would take a fall. There was no room for clowns, however sad-faced, in the world waiting just around the corner. As the car pulled away, Little Cassius raised his hand in a gesture of farewell.

The most mundane details of the passing scenery caught the old cops' eyes: graveyards of abandoned cars, a shapely girl leaning on a fence, torn-up pavement, plumes of smoke that now and then unleashed layers of coal dust as if they too were taking breaths of air.

The car rolled past a section of Park Avenue called Blood Alley. They left Fifth and Marcus Garvey Park behind and turned back onto Seventh. Smith glanced at Dubois and saw at once where they were going.

The intersection of 125th and Seventh had been Harlem's Mecca during the epoch of the Black Muslims and Black Panthers. This was where they had paraded at the height of their power, with black berets clamped tightly on their heads and rifles pressed firmly to their chests. Even today this was a privileged nexus where current styles and new ideas circulated freely. Mr. Grace's bookstore was a meeting place of local black intellectuals. Grace himself was a small gentleman with shiny skin and a foxy manner. The shop was crammed with books, piled to the ceiling in stacks. To move about one edged between these chancy precipices in single file. At Mr. Grace's you could find any work related to the Cause, from near or far, whether it dealt with music, dance, painting or politics.

The Plymouth pulled up quietly beside the bookstore window, and the two old men pulled themselves out, their backs bent over by black thoughts. For forty years these two ordinary cops from a rotten neighborhood had linked their lives to two imaginary characters, whose existence they had substituted for their own. In every hovel, inside the smallest gambling den, card dealers all trembled at the sound of

"Freeze! Hold it right there!" According to them, Chester Himes had become a sort of bard or *griot* canonizing their livelier adventures. But with this latest book reality was taking its revenge, coming to claim its due. The usurped titles, the borrowed risks, the myth of two extraordinary lives, had to be restored to the fiction from which they had departed.

This was a hard blow for the two companions. Since their retirement they had lived in an enchanted past, shamelessly mixing actual adventures with dreams and fiction for the benefit of spellbound audiences. Admitting to the death of Coffin Ed and Grave Digger Jones would be to admit to their own disappearance. If Himes buried them before their time, they no longer preceded history and would be revealed for the plagiarists they were. They could not conceive of an existence where mockeries flowed freely from the mouths of punks, whores and junkies, a world wherein they commanded no respect.

These two cunning fellows invented new memories from book to book. They had tacitly agreed after thirty years of municipal service to fight to preserve this aura to the end. Without it, their lives would lose the color, strength and eccentricity they had taken so much pleasure in ever since they had discovered an author who had elevated their heroic doubles into legend. They entered the bookstore, alert.

Mr. Grace was working in his small office at the back of the bookstore. The old man removed his glasses and carefully refolded an accordionlike catalog. He smiled at his two regulars. Dubois and Smith searched his face and found it empty. There wasn't the slightest clue in his expression or his attitude. There were only the usual features, permanently animated by a kind of interior joy which the two ex-cops had never managed to figure out.

"What gives me the honor of this visit, Inspectors?"

Dubois and Smith removed their hats. They did not dare look the old fox in the eye. Did he already know? Smith took the plunge.

"Well, Mr. Grace, we've heard Chester's just published a new book . . ."

"And you'd like to know if it's in yet?" finished the bookseller. "Well, no, it's not, but I can tell you when . . ."

He stopped. His eyes twinkled.

"How is your friend Himes?"

The two cops bragged to everybody about their close ties with the writer, mingling accounts of their own adventures with those of his characters. They suddenly wondered if Grace was making fun of them.

"You will be getting it in then," said Dubois.

"Getting what in? Ah, yes, the book. Of course. It'll be here in a few weeks, maybe even in a few days."

The little man began searching through a pile of old papers littering his desk. He fished out a sheet and waved it under their noses.

"Here's the order form. Yes," he said, setting down his glasses and deciphering the paper. "You really heard that, Chester Himes . . . Wait a minute . . . Here!"

It was as if, instead of the form, he were brandishing the actual book. Dubois and Smith looked at each other. Mr. Grace, the only black man in Harlem for whom they had ever felt a degree of respect, coughed and began to clean his glasses.

"Sit down," he addressed his visitors.

He pointed to a green velvet chair. It was a sort of cross between an armchair for a very large person and a loveseat. The two detectives complied, firmly embedding themselves, hip to hip, between the arm-rests. After a long moment of silence, the bookseller smiled warmly.

"I know why you've come to see me. I have to tell you that I've been prepared for this moment for a very long time. We're about the same age, right? We just want a little peace until the day of our great voyage. I know just how you feel. I haven't read the Himes book, but someone told me what it's about. And I imagined your reaction. It's just that now, nothing can stop the machine. You have to resign your-selves to it. Absolutely nothing has changed for me though."

The ex-cops stared at the ground as if they were hoping for a sign. Dubois lifted his distracted eyes to Mr. Grace.

"Our whole world's caving in on us."

"I know," said the bookseller philosophically, "but what can you do about it? Anyway, you will have a slight respite because the book I'm going to receive will be in French. Not too many people in Harlem will be tempted. And those who do know French don't know you two."

Dubois and Smith stood up. All was not lost. Smith wanted to say something, but the bookseller stopped him.

"If you're wondering what I'm going to do, don't worry. I've been guarding your secret for nearly thirty-five years. And, you know, I've always found you more likable than your heroes! If you had been Cof-fin and Grave Digger, I might have sent you somewhere else to buy your books a long time ago. No. I won't breathe a word! Save your explanations for the others. A word to the wise is sufficient."

Dubois and Smith overflowed with apologies and thanks. Like two sleepwalkers, they left the place where their glory had been born and where it ran the risk of being irreparably tarnished. Dubois sat down behind the wheel. They headed south toward Central Park, skirted Grand Central Terminal, left the road which led to Little Italy and headed west toward Greenwich Village. Dubois ran several red lights and almost crashed into a taxi, double-parked on Fifth Avenue. Suddenly Smith seemed to wake up. He tapped his companion on the shoulder.

"Let me out here, man; I have an errand to run."

Dubois silently looked him over, then pulled the car over to the sidewalk to let Smith out.

"Don't bother to wait for me. I'll find my own way home. I'll call you tonight."

Dubois nodded and drove off without asking any questions. The street was swarming. He was surprised to see so many whites, then, coming to his senses, he realized he wasn't in Harlem anymore.

Smith waited until the black sedan had disappeared into the traffic, then hailed a cab. He gave the driver the address of Mr. Grace's bookstore. Although Grace didn't have any coordinates on the European continent for Chester Himes himself, he did manage to find the address of his Paris editor. Smith thanked him timidly a second time and returned to the waiting taxi.

That night he went home weary. He suddenly found the silence that reigned in his oversized apartment disturbing. He removed his hat and his trenchcoat, remembering a time when the house was filled with his wife's screaming and his children's racket. He turned on the television and thumbed the buttons on the remote control, unable to settle on a program. He was in the bathroom in his underwear when the doorbell rang. He hastily grabbed his bathrobe from a hook, forgetting to tie it shut, and went to the door.

Dubois laughed, leaning in the doorway.

"Is this how you dress for your guests now? Is this supposed to be the latest style?"

Smith waved him in without answering.

"I have an idea I think you're going to like," said Dubois mysteriously. "But put some clothes on your back. I can't stand to look at you like that. I feel like I'm at some kind of scar exhibit."

"Fix yourself a drink. I'll be right back."

Smith removed his robe as he walked toward the bathroom. He

glanced up at the broken window, patched with newspaper, and shrugged. For some time now he had been letting everything go. Why fix things? For whom? Since the death of his wife, life without her companionship was like whiskey with no ice. There were only memories, and even those were threatened. As he mechanically slipped on his trousers, he read the yellowed headline for the thousandth time:

DON KNIGHT, BLACK MILLIONAIRE, BUYS INTO BLACK BEAUTY SUPPLY FIRM

The celebrated businessman proposed to open a business in Paris. With the help of professional training courses, the working girls from Pigalle would be transformed into experienced hairstylists and beauticians, provided they were black. Don Knight's favorite dish, it was reported, was *escalope a la crème et aux champignons*. When in Paris, the magnate bestowed his favors not on the palaces of the Right Bank but on a discreet German-owned establishment, the Hôtel du Vieux-Colombier.

The article was accompanied by a photo showing a handsome fifty-year-old athletic-looking black man, exhibiting all his teeth. Smith finished dressing and joined his companion in the living room.

Dubois stood somberly waiting by the bar. He was still wearing his trenchcoat.

"It's not too late to stop this, Ed. It was pickling my brain until Mr. Grace gave me an idea."

"It's been eating at me too, Grave Digger," Smith replied without adding any details.

"We're going to go see Himes and convince him not to translate the book. We can at least try. After all, he owes us that much."

"Yeah," said Smith. "We can at least try."

Chapter Two

Charles de Gaulle Airport. Despite the late hour, a crowd of travelers was still bustling in the first-floor lobby. The pale neon lights, those suns that never set, made the white skin they tainted look unhealthy. White people looked afflicted by an incurable disease. An impeccably coiffed woman trotting behind a cart with a small leather trunk enthroned in the center turned suddenly around. She was startled by a burst of thundering laughter. The echo made it still more impressive: Jones Dubois was greeting France.

"Can you believe it, Ed? We're in France!"

For the first time in thirty long years, the two partners had left the territory of the stars and stripes for a little dillydallying.

Ed Smith couldn't believe it. He walked along on a sort of magic cord, afraid it might break at any moment. A taxi pulled up in front of them. The driver, bundled in a gray overcoat, was pressed against the wheel. A Gitane dangled from his lips. He watched them collect their bags and open the door.

"France seems pretty nice," said Smith before climbing into the taxi.

"Où que je vous conduis, messieurs?"

"I beg your pardon?"

"Where you go, please?" insisted the driver, resigned.

Dubois took control of the situation. He exhumed a small dictionary from his pocket, which he had lightly skimmed on the airplane, and began feebly leafing through it.

"Hotel . . . Paris," he finally uttered in a pure Harlem accent.

"Ca va. OK. Compris," said the driver, who was used to this sort of thing. He put the car into first gear and drove off slowly.

Smith smiled.

"And we thought the Plymouth was small," he commented, beaming. "What do you think about this one? Think maybe she'd move out just a little bit if we put a third cylinder in her?"

"Stop complaining. You shouldn't criticize things here," guffawed Dubois. "This isn't home."

He tried humming a few measures of "La Marseillaise," but the look he encountered in the rearview mirror dissuaded him.

Each man leaned his head against his window, absorbed by the play of passing lights. The taxi passed the Porte de Bagnolet.

Taking advantage of a red light, the driver turned back to his fares.

"C'est quoi le nom de votre hôtel? Name? Hotel?"

He tried hard to detach each syllable, but every attempt seemed doomed to failure thanks to the cigarette plugged between his lips.

"I can't just pick one out of thin air," the driver mumbled to himself in French. "Damn!"

Smith and Dubois looked at him blankly. The driver rolled his eyes. A concert of honking horns informed him that the light had been green for several seconds. Suddenly Smith, seized by inspiration, remembered the only French name which lingered in a corner of his memory.

"Hôtel du Vieux-Colombier," he said in execrable French.

Pleased with this discovery, he repeated himself several times, as if charmed by the sound of his own voice.

"The one in the sixth arrondissement?" asked the driver.

"Well?" intervened Jones, as he continued twisting his last few hairs. Smith gave him a hard look.

"Yes, sir, yes," he assured the driver.

The car drove on, while in the back seat the two cops lapsed into a contest of circumflected eyebrows. When they imagined that they had arrived, they undertook the task of extricating themselves from the Peugeot. Dubois handed the driver a five-hundred-franc note and waited patiently. The change stacked up in his open palm. At the reception desk, Smith asked him how he had calculated the exchange rate so fast.

"I didn't calculate anything," he answered. "I just waited!"

The new arrivals showed their passports to the receptionist. He was a pale, thin young man. When he realized his Oxford English was of no use with these two zombies, he straightened up a bit. They persisted in expressing themselves by gesturing and demanded two adjoining rooms. Three minutes after they went upstairs, he saw them rush by again. They hurried outside without dropping off the key. What a couple!

They were tall and stocky and had the same square jaws, short-cropped hair and graying muttonchops. What aroused the curiosity of passing Parisians was not so much their large physiques but the way they dressed: the customary felt hats they wore day and night, their long trenchcoats opening on colorful jackets. While this ensemble might create a good impression in Harlem, it raised a lot of eyebrows in the sixth arrondissement. Although eccentric clothing was not lacking in the Latin Quarter, it wasn't often sported by giant black men, curious about everything. Their ungainly appearance caused passersby to step aside, clearing a path for them through the crowds at rush hour. From time to time Ed Smith changed course slightly in order to barely graze a woman passing in the crowd.

"I like this country, man," he confided to Dubois. "We're right in the middle of a white neighborhood and people aren't looking at us like we've got the plague."

"You're right. They're not afraid we're going to stab them in the back."

"It's mellow here."

They walked into an O'Kitch near the fountain in the Place Saint-Michel. They thrust open the door with a surge of enthusiasm, and the customers froze on the spot. Although they took pleasure in their strange new surroundings, Smith and Dubois welcomed anything that reminded them of home. They had heard about filet mignon, that culinary speciality of the Seine, but failed to run it down each place they went. Now they grimly settled for two enormous hamburgers.

"You come from America?"

Screwing up his eyes, Jones turned to face the stranger who had addressed him. He was one of those African specimens who had been around, a sort of figure commonly seen in the capital but who seemed exceedingly exotic to Jones Dubois, especially because of the bone necklace he was wearing.

"I heard you speak English and I just wanted to talk with you about America."

"Where are you from?" inquired Smith in his gravelly voice.

"Africa. My name is Zigaman Fâ, Doctor of Mentaloscopic-Kinesis."

"Doctor of what?"

"Mentaloscopic-Kinesis. It's a science created to overcome the old ways imposed through the ages by the whites."

The ex-cops smiled knowingly at each other. There were plenty of these doctors hanging around the streets of Harlem. It was best to get out of the way when they took out their black bags. Even so, this one might prove useful.

"Say, Doc, you must know a lot, right?"

"That depends on what you want to know."

"We'd like to find a good place to eat. You get what I mean?"

Zigaman Fâ closed one eye and placed a long finger to his pink lips. His face lit up.

"I know exactly what you mean."

When they stood, Zigaman Fâ propelled a tall girl with amber hair and a pale complexion in front of the two Americans and introduced her to them. She was a twenty-seven-year-old student named Sylvie.

Sylvie was the proud owner of a *deux-chevaux,* which had been re-painted by hand and which she piloted like a Formula 1, lockjawed at the wheel, eyes riveted on the horizon. They drove to Mère Sophie's restaurant. She was a buxom woman from Zaire. She welcomed the doctor and his troupe with a meaty laugh, which shook her body from her toes to her flimsy brassiere, the straps of which were visible through her loose *boubou*.

The restaurant was steeped in the odor of burnt fat, which carried Smith and Jones back across the ocean to Mama Dodge's. Mère Sophie drew her whiskey from a large cask on the counter, filling wine bottles with it. She made it a point of honor to warn her clients that she didn't serve any nonalcoholic beverages. Coffin and Grave Digger's tall tales fascinated the neoscientist, although he did not entirely understand them. The conviviality of the detectives, combined with the obvious charms of Zigaman Fâ's well-endowed companion, created a most relaxed atmosphere. When the two Americans had paid the bill, which fixed catfish at the price of salmon, Zigaman Fâ opened up his arms as if to reunite two continents in his embrace.

"If there's anything you need while you're in Paris, let me know. I'm always in the café on the Boulevard Barbès after seven."

He handed them a dog-eared card before giving Sylvie's car a little slap. Pale as a corpse, she drove off more than a little drunk.

As they climbed into bed, Smith and Jones began to feel the effects of jet lag. Unless it was simply the effect of Mère Sophie's whiskey.

Chapter Three

The key turned in the lock just as the light went out in the stairwell. Amos Yebga kicked his apartment door shut.

He was a young man with an attractive stature, a dark and velvety complexion and long black eyelashes, which gave an almost feminine touch to his angular face. He was wearing a maroon suit with a light shirt, no tie and black moccasins. In the ten years of his journalist's profession, he had never felt so bored by his routine. This job was worse than the rut of a civil servant. You sat behind a desk, turning out articles on any subject so long as they were about Africa and . . . hop! On to the next one! He had even given up playing the gadfly, no longer interjecting his perpetual accusations during the editor's conferences, such as, "We're becoming a bureaucracy! We're turning bourgeois!" These objections had only raised polite smiles on the faces of his indifferent colleagues. Yebga had been dreaming of other things while wearing out the seat of his pants on the bench at journalism

school. It seemed to him at that time that the profession he was embracing incorporated adventure, danger and risk. He had chosen to
exile himself to France, because Cameroon was not ready to confront
its own corruption. Since then, he had had to change his tune. It was as
though all his accumulated hopes were about to fly away. He was
almost thirty-five, an age of reckoning, he thought.

Furious, Yebga tore off his jacket and hurled it onto a piece of
furniture that adorned the vestibule. The living-room light switch was
just to his right. He flipped it on. A warm light inundated a spacious
room furnished with discretion. At the bar, he poured out his usual
evening drink. Then he settled into an armchair beside his answering
machine. Sipping his whiskey, he played back the messages.

Legs stretched out onto a carpet of exotic motifs, he listened to a
series of voices chopped up by static on the tape:

—Hi, Amos. There's going to be a party at my place Saturday night.
If you can drop by . . .

—Hey, man, it's Bill. I finished developing the photos. So let me
know when you need them.

—Hello, Mr. Yebga. I'm taking the opportunity to call you back
regarding the book project you spoke to me about. It would be
good if you'd contact me as soon as possible. The idea interests me.

And so on.

Yebga had not set foot in his house for three days. He felt a certain
pleasure hearing these mixed voices of friends and mere acquaintances.
He paraded all these callers through his mind, thinking they made up a
strange group. They reminded him of his own vagabond life. With
each beep tone, a face or a shadow materialized in his memory. He
stood up. The urge to hear "Body and Soul" by John Coltrane moved
him. The voices continued their deaf litany:

—Amos, it's George. Could you loan me your apartment for the
weekend?

—Hey, man, I have a little problem. It's urgent. I'll call back later.

Paris white and Paris black. This was success for a black man.

Yebga crouched in front of the stereo cabinet. He did not listen
closely to the last message until he had adjusted the stereo. Something
had clicked in his head. After the joyful, calm, composed voices, this

one seemed harsh. The caller was unknown to him. What exactly had
he said? Confused, Yebga retraced his step and pushed the rewind button:

—Hello. My name is Salif Maktar Diop. Some friends told me you
could be trusted. I have some things to tell you. They must be put
in your paper. Be in front of the Café Escurial on the corner of the
Rue du Bac and the Boulevard Saint-Germain at five tomorrow.

The reporter dreamily played back the tape several times. Then he
emptied his glass, looked at his watch. There was definitely no time to
spare. He was going to be late to his girlfriend's again.

Neither Ed Smith or W. Jones Dubois slept very long. Early the next
day, they were in the street, their felt hats covering their migraines. Last
night's menu, which had fallen to their legs, made them feel like they
were wearing lead socks. They were afraid they might miss something.
They planned to spend a part of Thursday visiting Paris and the other
looking for Chester Himes. One of them selected from his wardrobe a
suit the color of fresh butter. The other opted for a midnight-blue
ensemble. Neither of them neglected to put on their eternal cop
trenchcoat. They thought that Paris was cleaner, safer and better organized than its New York counterpart; however, this did not prevent
them from getting lost. On their way to the Champs-Élysées, they
ended up at the Porte de Vanves. It was maddening that nobody seemed
capable of giving them directions. Even blacks scurried off, arms waving as if a full brigade of Harlem cops was chasing their black asses
down the street.
   "And you fed me that line about how you knew this town like the
palm of your hand," mocked Smith, jabbing his friend in the ribs.
"Where'd you pick up your French name anyway? The way things
look around here, you'd have thought we'd walked here from Harlem.
We didn't need to take a plane to see this."
   "Things have changed since the war, boy," answered the other.
"And as for giving you a line, don't forget I don't have anything to
show you here anyway."
   A fare-hunting taxi rescued them from confusion and finally dropped
them at "Champseeleezay" after having circled the city many times.
   The joy of rediscovering the handsome neighborhoods extinguished
the two detectives' mistrust, and they strolled the avenue for more than
an hour, forgetting that they had not come to Paris to play tourist.

They had themselves photographed in front of the Arc de Triomphe, wolfed down a series of Italian courses at Pino's Pizza, which would have inflicted indigestion upon any other stomach, but which just sufficed to quiet their hunger.

It was five o'clock when Smith seized his friend by the arm. The men returned up the Seine on board a tourist boat. They were the only people who dared face the open air of the immense rear deck.

"We've got to go see the publisher," Smith said regretfully.

The charm of foreign adventure fell away instantly. The monuments, the ancient stone arches, the voice of the tour guide who chattered about the curiosities of the city, the promise of pleasant evenings described in the brochures, all this vanished into thin air. Dubois bitterly recalled the motive of their trip to Paris, and the scenery around him lost its colors in a flash.

Seated on the terrace of the Escurial, Amos Yebga surveyed the horizon, staring at all the passersby. He stood up to stretch his legs. He had been seated for more than an hour, watching the play of intersection lights and breathing exhaust fumes. What could Maktar Diop look like? Who would recognize the other and how? And furthermore, how had Diop picked his coordinates? This was the first time in his career that Yebga had received this type of message. Until now, he made himself valued more for his deductions than for his investigations. Maybe Maktar Diop was an African opponent who was going to offer him ultra-secret documents. Then why speak to Yebga? He would give anything to make his editor, Glenn, see him with new eyes, rather than regarding him as a desk man, a man of routine, an intellectual. In fact he was a man of action. Often his colleagues begrudged him his diploma. Papers do not make you a reporter, they would say, it's the terrain. He was weary of waiting for a chance to put his feet on it. Maktar's call had arrived in the nick of time. It awakened hope. But it was better not to let himself be dazzled by this. Anyway, Maktar Diop was not going to show up now, Yebga was certain of it. He tried to convince himself he had only come to meet Diop out of professional conscience.

Yebga left a twenty-franc note fluttering on the table. He set out with a halting step toward the stoplight on the boulevard. He noticed two giants heading toward him. It was obvious these guys were smashed. They looked haggard and kept walking into each other. Even their exaggerated boxer's gait was not enough to steady them. Yebga saw them glancing about distractedly. The graying hair on their heads and cheeks evoked for him a confused image of his own grandfather from Yaoundé. He had died when Yebga was ten. Lost in memory, he stared unconsciously at them. They drew near, banging into the table next to where he was standing. For a handful of seconds, Yebga even thought they were going to speak to him, but they turned away at the last minute.

"Hey, sista," yelled the one with the scarred face, addressing a young woman from the Antilles. She in turn almost got herself run over trying to dodge them.

They spoke in English, apparently convinced this was the language blacks used the world over. Yebga's eyes shone with amusement; these two guys looked like they had just landed from the moon. Their long trenchcoats, felt hats and gala clothing called to mind the archaic uniforms of the Congolese sappers. They flailed their arms about like drowning men.

"Yes, can I help you?"

Doubtless the guy who addressed them was from the political science department, with this display. He stopped, a large smile smeared across his face.

"Wow! Hey, man, we're in luck," sighed Dubois. "I thought no one in France spoke English."

"Yeah," added Smith. "And there's only a little ocean between us."

The two blacks stood planted side by side on the sidewalk. The stream of passersby elbowed each other trying to avoid them, not without occasional complaints. Yebga watched them exhibit a sheet of crumpled paper under the eyes of their new savior. What could they be looking for with those faces like half-reformed dunces or hoodlums? Ex-marines or racketeers from Harlem come to get themselves fleeced in who knows what den of thieves.

But how touching they were, cheek to cheek, intently watching the future young professional point a long finger toward the Rue de Bac.

Yebga did not linger over this scene; he mechanically turned the pages of his Bloc Notes, looked at his watch. When he looked up again, the men had disappeared.

Yebga combed the boulevard once more with his eyes for the sake of his conscience, then went home, worried, feeling morose for no real reason.

The first thing he did was to listen to Maktar Diop's message again.

No doubt. He had not mistaken the time or the meeting place. One thing was certain: this nigger's voice oozed with fear.

Chapter Four

As she set her book down onto the pulpit of her desk (a book her employers would have doubtless classified as a war novel), the receptionist gave a start. She stared at them, one after the other, incredulous. One sported a blue tie sprinkled with yellow designs. It stood out from a white shirt. His trousers, an abundant piece of clothing, were worn to an almost threadbare brightness and fell too far onto his enormous shoes. He smiled in a disquieting manner, like one of those guys who, not satisfied just to steal the cash, looks ready to work you over in the process. His white teeth shone like pearls. He removed his hat with the folded-down brim and articulated a few words. The bewildered woman decided to interpret these as a greeting. The other man was a giant of about the same size. He was swathed in clothing the subtlety of which was comparable to that of the statue of Louis Maine in the middle of the Rue du Départ. Imitating his companion, he raised his hand to his headgear.

"If you're making a delivery," the receptionist forced herself to speak, "use the other door. The one on the left as you exit."

What could these two be doing at Gallimard? They had probably never opened a book in their lives, except the Bible!

The two men were black.

Dubois spoke.

"We would like to meet Mr. Chester Himes," he announced, somewhat strained.

If the two men spoke English, it was because they were Americans. And if they were Americans, they couldn't be deliverymen. What were they then? From the corner of her eye, Marguerite tried to get a better look at them. Boxers maybe, with those faces, singers or retired killers for hire. She couldn't decide. She was only aware of a pressing need to get up and call someone. Taking advantage of the fact that she barely spoke English, Marguerite rose.

"Moment, please. I don't speak English. Somebody come. Wait."

She had a Belleville accent, but Dubois understood. They watched her walk toward an office that was separated from the reception area by a glass partition. Ed Smith ogled her buttocks as she fled.

"What an ass, man. I wouldn't say no to that."

Jones Dubois gave him a reprimanding look.

"Just kidding, partner. But don't you think she's well put together for a white chick?"

The receptionist returned shortly with one of her superiors. She was an older woman, who appeared incapable of lust.

"These two gentlemen must have an appointment with an editor. I think it's for their memoirs," said the young woman. "They're boxers or something like that."

"Hello, sirs," said the woman with a good university accent. "What can I do for you?"

"We want to see Chester Himes," answered Jones Dubois.

"Chester Himes?"

"Yes. The writer. Are you his editor?"

The woman looked embarrassed. She looked at them strangely, stammered and said, "Wait a minute, please."

She picked up the telephone from the receptionist's desk and dialed a number. The receptionist looked on from behind a glass partition. Smith and Dubois heard her speaking in French. So as not to appear as if they were eavesdropping, they looked away, inspecting their surroundings. To their left was a long corridor dotted with a series of numbered doors. Their eyes met those of a man of about fifty. He was wearing a coal-gray suit; a white turtleneck sweater stood out from under his jacket. The man wore glasses with thin gold frames. His austerity reminded the two associates of certain white pastors they had had the opportunity to meet back in the United States. He was engaged in intense discussion with a little bald man. This one had quick eyes and was shabbily dressed. His manner reminded them of a rapist or a devotee of morbid tales. In the lobby, next to the entryway, a glass case housed books and photographs. Among those exhibited, Dubois and Smith recognized a guy with a vicious smile and graying temples smoking a pipe and a blond wearing an overcoat reminiscent of turn-of-the-century sailors. The two men had just stepped back into the office as the woman cupped the receiver.

"What are your names, please?"

"Edward Smith and W. Jones Dubois."

The woman relayed this and hung up.

"Please be seated," she said, motioning to some maroon armchairs behind the two men. "Robert Warin will be right down. He will be able to help you."

The two associates complied. The young receptionist, now reassured, furtively tossed them ambiguous glances in which the two former cops would have been able to read a curious mixture of fear and interest if they had raised their own glance above the waist of their hostess. The legend of the black male lives on!

Dubois and Smith didn't have time to wonder how a guy like Chester Himes, writing the books he wrote, could survive in an ambience of whispers, kiss-ass smiles and boudoir shadows, a thousand leagues from the lures of the "Big Apple." Presently a man came down the stairs into the receptionist's office. He exchanged a few words with her before approaching the two men. He was about fifty. Dubois and Jones admired his elegance.

"Gentlemen."

He held out a carefully manicured hand. A shadow briefly crossed his face. Then he resumed an attitude of calm self-confidence.

"Are you Ed Smith and Jones Dubois?" Warin spoke impeccable English.

"Yeah," answered Dubois.

"This is incredible," muttered the man, noticing Dubois's face. "You correspond exactly to the image that I had of Himes's characters. Coffin Ed and Grave Digger Jones were however created by Chester Himes. Do you know them?"

The two partners eyed him suspiciously, then looked at each other. They had to maneuver quickly. Smith made a slight sign, and Dubois knew instantly that they had to lie.

"Excuse me," the editor began again, "but it's so crazy. . . . How did that happen to you?" he asked Dubois, pointing to the red mark on his face.

"Vitriol. Harlem niggers aren't choirboys."

"And you are inspectors in Harlem?" continued Warin, ready to hear it all now.

"We were," said Smith bitterly. "We finished up as sergeants."

"Now we're good for pulp," added Jones Dubois.

Warin sat down in an armchair next to them. The look they gave him was like that of a starving child standing in front of the window of a delicatessen.

"And why do you want to see Himes?" the editor asked suddenly.

"To speak to him about his latest book. We don't much care for the blow he's given us," answered Smith.

"Blow. What blow?"

"We made an agreement at the beginning of this whole thing," said Smith. "We give him our characters, we tell him about our adventures, but he has to consult us before he publishes them. In the last book, he finishes us off. And we don't agree, if you know—"

"Are you saying that you're Coffin Ed and Grave Digger Jones?"

"Well, we are and we aren't, but it's a long story." Dubois swaggered.

There was a moment of silence while the two ex-cops heard the pounding blood rush to their temples. If Warin knew the truth, their cover would be blown. The editor attempted to organize his thoughts. His eyes continued to shift from one to the other.

"Too bad Duhamel isn't here anymore to see this," he muttered to himself. Then to the two cops, "If I understand correctly, Himes used you to model his characters after, and he didn't consult you before publishing the book where you both die. That's why you want to see him."

"You got it," confirmed Smith.

"Alas, he isn't with us anymore! I know he's living in Spain now, near Alicante. But I can't tell you much more. I'm replacing Marcel Duhamel. He knew Himes well. But I can call his new publisher if that would help you."

The telephone conversation lasted a fairly long time. From time to time, Warin looked suspiciously in the direction of the two giants. Finally he hung up and removed a card from his inside jacket pocket. He asked the switchboard operator for a pen and scribbled a few lines on it. Smith and Dubois stood up. They were holding their worn-out hats in their hands.

"Here," said Warin, handing them the card. Everything is here. It seems he's seriously ill."

"Don't worry," said Dubois, putting on his hat. "We'll take care of him."

The two men shuffled toward the exit. Warin looked at the door for a long time after they had disappeared. He realized only then that if the two giants had really been close friends of Himes's, they would have known both his address and the state of his health. On the other hand, Warin wasn't a cop. To each his own! He shrugged his shoulders and went back up to his office like a sleepwalker.

Eleanor Taylor Bland

The Man Who Said I'm Not

ELEANOR TAYLOR BLAND (1944–   ), the most prolific African American woman writer of mystery fiction, is the author of four novels featuring homicide detective Marti MacAlister— *Dead Time, Slow Burn, Gone Quiet,* and *Done Wrong.*

Bland describes Marti as a police officer who is committed to not abuse power, but who does not want to be excluded from exercising it in her life and work. "Marti is a survivor, and has had to come to terms with large doses of reality. Like so many women I know, she is strong, even in the weak places. She is compassionate. She wants to help make this a better, safer world." Bland says of her creative process, "How do I create characters who interest me and engage my attention? By intently observing the people around me. By seeking out and enjoying and being enriched by people who are different, unusual. By asking questions and learning about other cultures, other places, other people in relationship to place. By enjoying and being enthusiastic about the wealth of diversity all around me."

An accountant by profession, Bland is active in the community of mystery writers. She is a member of the Midwest chapter of Mystery Writers of America and national co-chair for Sisters in Crime's Outreach to Women of Color. She especially wishes to acknowledge Raymond I. Olsen, principal trombone, Waukegan Symphony Orchestra, for his assistance in

helping her "kill off" a classical musician in this, her first published short story.

AS DETECTIVE MARTI MACALISTER hurried down the aisle of
the crowded high school auditorium, there was a loud crash, then a
clattering sound. Marti glanced at her watch. It was ten minutes to
eight. She was just in time for the Lincoln Prairie Symphony Orchestra's Fall Frolic for the Family.

Her son Theo stood up, looked about, and waved when he saw her.
The planes and angles of his brown face were so much like her deceased
husband's that there were times like tonight when Marti almost caught
her breath, and other times when she ached, remembering.

Theo was sitting in the center of the fifth row. "Ma, you made it!"
Marti gave him a hug. "Would I miss this?"

Her daughter Joanna was standing near the steps that led to the stage.
Instead of the usual sweats or jeans, Joanna was wearing a green pantsuit
that complimented her eyes.

Joanna turned, saw Marti, and came over. "Hey, Ma! You're not
late! Way to go!"

Marti touched an auburn curl and smiled. Thanks to her children,
Marti was tonight's guest conductor. At the orchestra's annual auction,
Theo and Joanna had bid a month's allowance to win this once-in-a-
lifetime opportunity to lead the National Anthem.

"You look great, Ma!" Joanna adjusted Marti's bow tie. She had
rented a tuxedo.

It was crowded backstage. The orchestra was sixty-three members
strong. The conductor was waiting. He gave her a big smile. "Ready?
Don't worry. They can play the National Anthem in their sleep."

Marti felt a sudden flutter in the pit of her stomach. She had one
lesson last week. She was not ready. She took a deep breath and tried to
focus on the musicians instead of thinking about the crowded auditorium.

Marti's partner, Vik—Matthew Jessenovik—joined her. They
worked homicide and had just wrapped up a case.

"Geez, Marti, Theo's sitting right up front. Everyone will notice if
we have to leave."

Vik was tall and thin. His graying hair always looked unkempt. His beaked nose, slightly skewed, gave his craggy face a certain intensity. People always noticed him.

At a signal from the conductor the musicians went onstage and began warming up.

"See," Vik said. "This is what you get when you let bankers, teachers, lawyers, and housewives call themselves an orchestra and give them an audience—a bunch of amateurs."

"Isn't one of your relatives a member?"

"My cousin, Liz. Plays the cello. She's the old, short, fat bottle blonde with hair sprouting on her chin." He frowned. "They're not even in tune."

"The concertmaster will take care of that. See, he just signaled the oboe player to give everyone an 'A.' "

"Theo told you that, didn't he?"

Marti laughed. With typical enthusiasm, Theo had read a beginner's guide to the orchestra, then announced he was ready for violin lessons.

The conductor welcomed the audience, then introduced Marti. Vik gave her a push and she walked onstage. Marti took her bow, gave her kids a quick smile, turned to the orchestra, and raised the baton. The audience stood and joined in. When they came to "Oh, say does that star-spangled banner yet wave," there was a crescendo of cymbals and drums. The baton got caught in the conductor's stand and went sailing over the string section. Undaunted, Marti brought the song to a rousing conclusion.

"Throwing the baton like that was great," Vik said as they went to their seats. "Three inches closer and you would have harpooned the harpist. Wait until I tell the guys."

"Awesome," Theo whispered as Marti sat down.

Joanna gave her a thumbs-up. "Did you get a chance to meet the black guy playing the flute? He's gorgeous!"

The second flute was attractive—slender, skin the color of coffee with cream, straight hair, not kinky—and over thirty. "A gorgeous man," Marti said.

"I know. Mature."

"Well, when I went backstage he seemed to be paying a lot of attention to that mature red-haired woman playing the French horn."

Joanna sighed. "Why doesn't that surprise me?"

The Young Person's Guide to the Orchestra was next and they were invited to join the musicians onstage. Theo stood near the violinists and Joanna got so close to the second flute that he poked her once with his elbow. Back in her seat, Joanna said, "That man is awesome in profile. And you should smell his cologne."

When the lights came on for the intermission, Vik said, "Can we leave now? This is almost as bad as the ballet."

"Ballet?" Marti said. "Oh. So you've been to the ballet. Let's tell the guys that, too."

Vik scowled.

A few minutes later the conductor came to the microphone. "I've been advised that one of our musicians is ill. If there's a doctor in the house we'd appreciate it if you would go to the nearest usher. Thank you all for your patience. We'll begin in just a few minutes."

"Come on," Vik said. "Let's see what's going on. A corpse would be better than this."

"Are you doctors?" the usher asked.

"No, we're just cops," Vik said. "But we are CPR-certified."

"Well, there's something wrong with Laurence Davis, the second flute. Jim Weston is trying to help him. They're in the staff bathroom. Right down this corridor."

When they reached the bathroom Marti assumed that the man kneeling beside Laurence Davis was Jim Weston. She recognized him as one of three men who played the bass fiddle. Marti hurried over. "Mr. Weston?"

"Yes."

"Police."

"Help him. Please. Get a doctor. He was like this when I came in."

Marti felt for a pulse. The second flute was no longer handsome in profile. He had bled profusely from nose and mouth. His eyes were fixed in a wide stare. Looking up, Marti blinked twice, signaling Vik that Davis was dead. Vik nodded toward a blood-splattered flute under the sink and raised his eyebrows. Why would anyone bring a flute in here?

Marti looked at Weston. Sweat glistened on his pale face and damp hair clung to his forehead. There was blood on his hands and blood had soaked into the cuffs of his shirt. He stared at a place above her head and did not look down. A prominent Adam's apple bobbed several times. What was he doing here? Best to isolate him now and question him later, when they had more information.

"Mr. Weston," Vik said, as he helped him to his feet. "We'll take over now."

Weston gestured toward the body without looking down. "He was just laying there. I didn't know what to do."

"Just come with me, sir."

When Vik returned a few minutes later, he said, "A couple of uniforms are here, and I've got a call in for the coroner and crime scene techs. As far as I can tell, everything was more or less contained, musicians backstage, audience out front. The usher was very careful to keep the public away from here. We've got the exits secured. The audience will go out through the east exit and we'll check IDs and take names. Members of the orchestra will stay. Weston's with an off-duty cop working security." He rubbed his hands together. "This guy timed it just right. Now we don't have to listen to that." He jerked his head in the direction they had come from. They couldn't hear the music.

II

Marti had a security guard open up the school's administrative offices for interviews. There were desks on the other side of a long counter and offices for the deans and the principal. She brought in two more teams of detectives and assigned the musicians by section. While Vik questioned the ushers, Marti spoke with the conductor first. He was thirtyish. Wavy dark hair curled at his neck.

"Laurence did not throw his instrument case tonight and he and Jessica weren't really arguing," the conductor explained. "Jitters maybe. Rumor has it they were about to become engaged."

"Is Jessica a member of the orchestra?"

"French horn."

"The redhead?"

"Yes."

Marti referred to her list of musicians. "Who else did Davis socialize with?"

"Jessica Sachs, her brother Richard, Liz Zablonski, Stan Rosen."

Marti put a check mark beside their names, glad to see that Vik's cousin was included.

"Jim Weston?" she asked.

"Not that I know of."

"How long had Laurence and Jessica been dating?"

"Maybe a year."

Marti wondered how their families felt about an interracial relationship.

"Did Davis seem to get along with everyone?"

"Laurence was a rather private person, quiet, reserved. But friendly, and an excellent musician."

Jessica seemed reserved too. No tears, just a wad of dry Kleenex that she kept squeezing. She was not as young as she seemed from a distance. Thirty at least, with dark brown eyes. Thin, and tall.

"Who should we notify?" Marti asked.

"I have no idea. Nobody else knows this, but Laurence hadn't had any contact with his family since he went away to college. His mother's dead. He never knew his father. There might be a brother and sister in Chicago somewhere. They lived in one of those projects."

"Names?"

"Laurence changed his name legally. It was Hakeem . . ." She thought for a minute. "I'm sorry, I don't remember. He hated it and it wasn't important until now."

Hakeem . . . Laurence. Marti knew people who chose African names to reflect their ancestry, but until now, not the reverse. Laurence, not Larry. Distance. No familiarity.

"How did you meet?" Marti asked.

"Here. At rehearsal."

"And you were planning to marry."

"Yes, perhaps next fall."

Jessica seemed so detached that Marti wondered what the attraction was.

"Why?"

"You mean did I love him?"

"Yes."

"Of course. We loved each other very much, and there was much more substance to our relationship than mere physical attraction. Laurence was cultured, intellectual. He worked very hard to become who he was, achieve what he did. My family would have preferred someone else, but Laurence and I have . . ." Her voice faltered. She squeezed the wad of Kleenex until her knuckles turned white. "We had everything important in common. We were going to start our own business."

"Why were you arguing tonight?"

"Laurence? Arguing? With me or with Richard? Laurence did get a little upset when I asked him about something. It wasn't like him at all. My timing was poor. He's always keyed up before a performance."

"What did you ask him about?"

"We were going to our investment adviser tomorrow. There was something Laurence wanted to invest in, but he still didn't have the brochures."

"So he got upset and threw his instrument case."

"No. Laurence did not throw his case at Richard. He dropped it."

Stan Rosen was a balding, fussy little man who sat on the edge of the chair and kept wringing his hands. "This is such a terrible thing. I recommended Laurence to sit second flute. Do they know what happened? Hypertension, I bet. Exercise, diet, nothing worked. Even with medication it was hard to control. Genetic predisposition." Rosen shook his head. "Damned shame."

"How did you meet him?"

"Work. Tri-Cam Chemical. I'm a vice president. I recognized Laurence's ability as a chemist right away. Unfortunately, in the corporate environment it's still difficult for minorities to advance. I took it upon myself to do everything possible for Laurence. He was head of a venture team, very prestigious position. He was developing a very significant process. In another year . . . such a shame."

The real shame was that Davis would not have been able to advance without Rosen. Marti wondered if Davis resented that, if he intended to take his process with him when he and Jessica formed their own company. Did Rosen know of their plans?

Marti spoke with Jessica's brother next. Richard Sachs was younger than his sister, with the same red hair and dark eyes.

"Did you approve of your sister's relationship with Laurence Davis?"

"No."

"Why not?"

"Not because he was black."

"Then why?"

Richard examined the back of his hand, then looked Marti in the eye. "He just didn't fit. Know what I mean? He didn't belong. He worked hard at it, I've got to give him that. But you are what you are and nothing can change that, not the right school, not the elocution lessons, not the impeccable manners or the right address."

"And Laurence was . . ."

"Black."

The reality that a black male could be his equal would never disturb Richard's sense of superiority. That was more disturbing to Marti than dealing with those who acknowledged, then often tried to justify, their prejudices.

"I'm sure you understand what I mean."

Marti didn't react. There was no need to.

"Were those your only objections?"

"No. I didn't like him. Hell, I didn't know him. I don't think Jessica knew him. No way did Laurence grow up listening to Verdi and playing tennis. And despite what he told us about his middle-class background, he grew up poor, I'm sure of it."

"What makes you so sure?"

"Being rich."

New money, Marti decided. No class. "Why were you arguing with him tonight?"

"I wasn't. He was arguing with my sister. I just told him to keep his hands off of her."

"Why? Had he put his hands on her before?"

"No. But don't they all, sooner or later?"

This time, Marti choked back a response. "And if they married?"

"Jessica wasn't that stupid. She wanted what was inside his head, what he was working on at that chemical company. She wouldn't have married him unless that was the only way to get it."

Marti was inclined to agree.

"Well, if that's all, I'm going to take Jessica home now."

"No," Marti said. "You're going to go backstage and wait until I say you can leave."

Richard gave her an appraising look, but said nothing.

Vik's cousin was next. Liz Zablonski bustled in and gave Marti a hearty handshake and a big smile. "So, you're Matthew's partner." She settled herself in the chair. "I'm afraid I can't be of much help. I feel bad about Laurence's death, but I didn't know him very well. Last year when I asked him to help with our Thanksgiving food drive, he provided a turkey, ham, and fresh fruit and vegetables for every family. At Christmas he was just as generous with toys and warm clothing. But he wouldn't go with us to distribute any of it." The chair creaked as she leaned forward. "Does this mean it wasn't natural causes?"

"We won't know that . . ."

"I know. Until the inquest."

"Did you observe anything unusual tonight?"

"Well. Laurence has been friendlier. First he had words with Jim."

"Jim Weston?"

"Yes."

"Did you hear what they said?"

"Laurence said 'Now' twice. He did seem upset. Then, a few minutes later, he just about threw his case at Jessica. Or Richard. Hard to tell."

Richard must have said enough to provoke him. Did they continue it in the bathroom? And Weston. What was that all about?

Marti glanced at the names with check marks. Such a meager list, and everyone more an associate than a friend, even Jessica. She put a question mark beside Weston's name.

When Jim Weston came in, his face looked haggard. He seemed to have aged since Marti found him kneeling in the bathroom. Weston had not washed the blood from his hands and blood had dried in rust-colored stains on his shirt cuffs.

"I couldn't help him," he said.

"Tell me what happened."

"I don't know. I went to the rest room. He was there."

"Did you see anyone else?"

"No."

"Did you hear anything?"

"A door closing."

"Were you and Davis friends?"

"No!"

She decided to see if she could verify what Liz told her before asking him anything else.

III

Vik was scowling when he came in. "Well, Marti, over sixty people backstage and I still don't know when Davis or Weston left, or who else did, or when. Half of them weren't even aware of an argument. And, we can't find Davis's car—gray Lexus LS400. Girlfriend says he probably parked it on a side street nearby, worried about scratches."

"Anyone mention seeing Davis talking with Weston?"

Vik flipped through his notes. "Davis went to Weston when Weston came in. Weston walked away. Jessica came over, then Richard. They argued. That's it."

"Coroner tell us anything?"

"Off the record. Lewis probably took a hard whack in the wrong spot with that flute. Soft cartilage and bone fragments from his nose were pushed into his brain and bingo—goodbye world."

"Sounds more impulsive than premeditated."

"Maybe." Vik gave her a small, gray leather notebook. "We found this in a jacket pocket."

Marti checked a sparsely filled calendar. There was no indication of a meeting with anyone tonight. The ledger section detailed every dollar Laurence Davis had received or spent since January. "In the last two months Davis gave ninety thousand dollars to Ventures, Incorporated."

"I've got someone checking them out," Vik said.

"According to his girlfriend he wanted to invest in something and they planned to start a business. This could be related to either."

Vik held up a plastic bag. "Wallet contents. Driver's license, professional memberships, insurance card. There was ten grand in thousands in his pants pocket. We'll have to check the Federal Reserve Bank in Chicago tomorrow. That's the only place I know of where you can get cash in that denomination. They must keep a record of those transactions."

Marti checked the ledger. "Nothing. He must not have had time to put the money in his wallet or record it."

"If Davis's only reason for going to the bathroom was to get the money, maybe that's why he brought his flute. With so many people backstage that would have made more sense than leaving it there."

"Weston says he heard a door close while he was in there."

"No way. I went to school here, MacAlister. There isn't a door that close and no outside access to that corridor."

Marti filled him in on her interviews. "Richard Sachs and Jim Weston look like our best suspects, but we can't rule out Rosen. We need a motive. In a moment of fear, or anger, anyone could have picked up that flute."

A uniform came in.

"What is it?" Vik asked.

"We found the car, sir, four blocks north."

The uniform put a briefcase on the desk and Vik began toying with the combination lock.

"Contents of the glove compartment," the uniform said. He held up a plastic bag.

Marti reached for that. A car manual, several maps, and half a dozen glossy, full-color brochures.

"Well, take a look. Ventures, Incorporated." She handed one of the pamphlets to Vik. "Looks like it's got something to do with real estate. And check this, Jim Weston, President, and Laurence Davis, Vice President."

When Weston came in he stared at the brochures spread out on the desk, then collapsed in the chair and buried his face in his hands.

"He's dead," Weston said. "But I don't know how it happened. We were going to buy a hotel, rehab it, sell the units as condos. A sure thing, but he wanted out. Too risky. Interest rates went up again and he panicked. I didn't have the ninety thousand. I brought ten. He laughed, then got angry. He said he was going to tell everyone that I defrauded him. I don't know what happened. I just wanted him to stop yelling, to be reasonable, to listen."

Weston took a deep breath and shuddered. "He came toward me. He was furious. I picked up the flute." He had a dazed expression. "I just don't understand. I hit him with a flute. How could hitting him with a flute kill him? It's just a lightweight piece of metal. It's not heavy enough to kill anyone."

As they walked toward the east exit, Marti thought of Davis's Lexus. How long had he driven around looking for a safe place? How long had he been seeking a safe investment? Real estate. Solid. A sure thing, Weston said, but the variables weren't as important to Weston. Davis had to plan every move.

Vik said, "Damned shame."

"Davis and Weston?"

"No. Barber and Dvorak. We missed Samuel Barber's 'School for Scandal' Overture and Dvorak's Symphony Number 8 in G major. Too bad we couldn't have missed out on *The Magic Flute*, too."

Marti gave him an elbow in the ribs.

Theo and Joanna were waiting just inside the doors. As they came toward her, Marti held out her arms.

BarbaraNeely

Spilled Salt

BARBARANEELY (1941–   ) is best known for her mystery novels *Blanche on the Lam* and *Blanche Among the Talented Tenth,* both of which feature the strong, witty, no-nonsense Blanche White, a proud, dark-skinned domestic worker who maintains a strong belief in her value system, her community, and her spirituality.

BarbaraNeely says of her goals in writing the Blanche White novels, "I wanted to write about social issues in a way that was accessible and entertaining. I also wanted to pay homage to working women because they are the bridge that got *us* over. [My work] is about the people who are assumed not to have a worldview." Blanche and other characters in BarbaraNeely's fiction embody those principles and have earned the author critical praise as well as Agatha, Macavity, and Anthony awards for best first mystery and the Go On Girl! Award for Best Debut Novel for *Blanche on the Lam.*

The themes of BarbaraNeely's short stories are also consistent with her goals. Her stories have appeared in numerous magazines, literary journals, and anthologies. "Spilled Salt," which first appeared in Terry McMillan's *Breaking Ice: An Anthology of Contemporary African American Fiction,* has been described as a classic of the women's movement. It is as topical now as when it appeared in 1990.

BarbaraNeely is currently at work on the third title in the

> Blanche White series and a novel of magical realism set in
> slavery and a contemporary black neighborhood.

"I'M HOME, MA."

Myrna pressed down hard on the doorknob and stared blankly up
into Kenny's large brown eyes and freckled face so much like her own
he was nearly her twin. But he was taller than she remembered. Denser.

He'd written to say he was getting out. She hadn't answered his
letter, hoping her lack of response would keep him away.

"You're here." She stepped back from the door, pretending not to
see him reach out and try to touch her.

But a part of her had leaped to life at the sight of him. No matter
what, she was glad he hadn't been maimed or murdered in prison. He
at least looked whole and healthy of body. She hoped it was a sign that
he was all right inside, too.

She tried to think of something to say as they stood staring at each
other in the middle of the living room. A fly buzzed against the window screen in a desperate attempt to get out.

"Well, Ma, how've you—"

"I'll fix you something to eat," Myrna interrupted. "I know you
must be starved for decent cooking." She rushed from the room as
though a meal were already in the process of burning.

For a moment she was lost in her own kitchen. The table, with its
dented metal legs, the green-and-white cotton curtains, and the badly
battered coffeepot were all familiar-looking strangers. She took a deep
breath and leaned against the back of a chair.

In the beginning she'd flinched from the very word. She couldn't
even think it, let alone say it. Assault, attack, molest, anything but rape.
Anyone but her son, her bright and funny boy, her high school graduate.

At the time, she'd been sure it was a frame-up on the part of the
police. They did things like that. It was in the newspapers every day.
Or the girl was trying to get revenge because he hadn't shown any
interest in her. Kenny's confession put paid to all those speculations.

She'd have liked to believe that remorse had made him confess. But
she knew better. He'd simply told the wrong lie. If he'd said he'd been
with the girl but it hadn't been rape, he might have built a case that
someone would have believed—although she didn't know how he

could have explained away the wound on her neck where he'd held his knife against her throat to keep her docile. Instead, he'd claimed not to have offered her a ride home from the bar where she worked, never to have had her in his car. He'd convinced Myrna. So thoroughly convinced her that she'd fainted dead away when confronted with the semen, fiber, and hair evidence the police quickly collected from his car, and the word of the woman who reluctantly came forth to say she'd seen Kenny ushering Crystal Roberts into his car on the night Crystal was raped.

Only then had Kenny confessed. He'd said he'd been doing the girl a favor by offering her a ride home. In return, she'd teased and then refused him, he'd said. "I lost my head," he'd said.

"I can't sleep. I'm afraid to sleep." The girl had spoken in barely a whisper. The whole courtroom had seemed to tilt as everyone leaned toward her. "Every night he's there in my mind, making me go through it all over again, and again, and again."

Was she free now that Kenny had done his time? Or was she flinching from hands with short, square fingers, and crying when the first of September came near? Myrna moved around the kitchen like an old, old woman with bad feet.

After Kenny had confessed, Myrna spent days that ran into weeks rifling through memories of the past she shared with him, searching for some incident, some trait or series of events that would explain why he'd done such a thing. She'd tried to rationalize his actions with circumstances: Kenny had seen his father beat her. They'd been poorer than dirt. And when Kenny had just turned six, she'd finally found the courage to leave Buddy to raise their son alone. What had she really known about raising a child? What harm might she have done out of ignorance, out of impatience and concentration on warding off the pains of her own life?

Still, she kept stumbling over the knowledge of other boys, from far worse circumstances, with mothers too tired and worried to do more than strike out at them. Yet those boys had managed to grow up and not do the kind of harm Kenny had done. The phrases "I lost my head" and "doing the girl a favor" reverberated through her brain, mocking her, making her groan out loud and startle people around her.

Myrna dragged herself around the room, turning eggs, bacon, milk, and margarine into a meal. In the beginning the why of Kenny's crime was like a tapeworm in her belly, consuming all her strength and sustenance, all her attention. In the first few months of his imprisonment she'd religiously paid a neighbor to drive her the long distance to the prison each visiting day. The visits were as much for her benefit as for his.

"But why?" she'd kept asking him, just as she'd asked him practically every day since he'd confessed.

He would only say that he knew he'd done wrong. As the weeks passed, silence became his only response—a silence that had remained intact despite questions like: "Would you have left that girl alone if I'd bought a shotgun and blown your daddy's brains out after the first time he hit me in front of you?" and "Is there a special thrill you feel when you make a woman ashamed of her sex?" and "Was this the first time? The second? The last?"

Perhaps silence was best, now, after so long. Anything could happen if she let those five-year-old questions come rolling out of her mouth. Kenny might begin to question her, might ask her what there was about her mothering that made him want to treat a woman like a piece of toilet paper. And what would she say to that?

It was illness that had finally put an end to her visits with him. She'd written the first letter—a note really—to say she was laid up with the flu. A hacking cough had lingered. She hadn't gotten her strength back for nearly two months. By that time their correspondence was established. Letters full of: How are you? I'm fine. . . . The weather is . . . The print shop is . . . The dress I made for Mrs. Rothstein was . . . were so much more manageable than those silence-laden visits. And she didn't have to worry about making eye contact with Kenny in a letter.

Now Myrna stood staring out the kitchen window while Kenny ate his bacon and eggs. The crisp everydayness of clothes flapping on the line surprised her. A leaf floated into her small cemented yard and landed on a potted pansy. Outside, nothing had changed; the world was still in spring.

"I can't go through this again," she mouthed soundlessly to the breeze.

"Come talk to me, Ma," her son called softly around a mouthful of food.

Myrna turned to look at him. He smiled an egg-flecked smile she couldn't return. She wanted to ask him what he would do now, whether he had a job lined up, whether he planned to stay long. But she was afraid of his answers, afraid of how she might respond if he said he had no job, no plans, no place to stay except with her and that he hadn't changed in any important way.

"I'm always gonna live with you, Mommy," he'd told her when he was a child, "Always." At the time, she'd wished it was true, that they could always be together, she and her sweet, chubby boy. Now the thought frightened her.

"Be right back," she mumbled, and scurried down the hall to the bathroom. She eased the lock over so that it made barely a sound.

"He's my son!" she hissed at the drawn woman in the mirror. Perspiration dotted her upper lip and glistened around her hairline.

"My son!" she repeated pleadingly. But the words were not as powerful as the memory of Crystal Roberts sitting in the courtroom, her shoulders hunched and her head hung down, as though she were the one who ought to be ashamed. Myrna wished him never born, before she flushed the toilet and unlocked the door.

In the kitchen Kenny had moved to take her place by the window. His dishes littered the table. He'd spilled the salt, and there were crumbs on the floor.

"It sure is good to look out the window and see something besides guard towers and cons." Kenny stretched, rubbed his belly, and turned to face her.

"It's good to see you, Ma." His eyes were soft and shiny.

Oh, Lord! Myrna moaned to herself. She turned her back to him and began carrying his dirty dishes to the sink: first the plate, then the cup, the knife, fork, and spoon, drawing out the chore.

"This place ain't got as much room as the old place," she told him while she made dishwater in the sink.

"It's fine, Ma, just fine."

Oh, Lord, Myrna prayed.

Kenny came to lean against the stove to her right. She dropped a knife and made the dishwater too cold.

"Seen Dad?"

"Where and why would I see *him?*" She tried to put ice in her voice. It trembled.

"Just thought you might know where he is." Kenny moved back to the window.

Myrna remembered the crippling shock of Buddy's fist in her groin and scoured Kenny's plate and cup with a piece of steel wool before rinsing them in scalding water.

"Maybe I'll hop a bus over to the old neighborhood. See some of the guys, how things have changed."

He paced the floor behind her. Myrna sensed his uneasiness and was startled by a wave of pleasure at his discomfort.

After he'd gone, she fixed herself a large gin and orange juice and carried it into the living room. She flicked on the TV and sat down to stare at it. After two minutes of frenetic, overbright commercials, she got up and turned it off again. Outside, children screamed each other to the finish line of a footrace. She remembered that Kenny had always liked to run. So had she. But he'd had more childhood than she'd had. She'd been hired out as a mother's helper by the time she was twelve, and pregnant and married at sixteen. She didn't begrudge him his childhood fun. It just seemed so wasted now.

Tears slid down her face and salted her drink. Tears for the young Myrna who hadn't understood that she was raising a boy who needed special handling to keep him from becoming a man she didn't care to know. Tears for Kenny who was so twisted around inside that he could rape a woman. Myrna drained her gin, left Kenny a note reminding him to leave her door key on the kitchen table, and went to bed.

Of course, she was still awake when he came in. He bumped into the coffee table, ran water in the bathroom sink for a long time, then quiet. Myrna lay awake in the dark blue-gray night listening to the groan of the refrigerator, the hiss of the hot-water heater, and the rumble of large trucks on a distant street. *He* made no sound where he lay on the opened-out sofa, surrounded by her sewing machine, dress dummy, marking tape, and pins.

When sleep finally came, it brought dreams of walking down brilliantly lit streets, hand in hand with a boy about twelve who looked, acted, and talked like Kenny but who she knew with certainty was not her son, at the same time she also knew he could be no one else.

She woke to a cacophony of church bells. It was late. Too late to make it to church service. She turned her head to look at the crucifix hanging by her bed and tried to pray, to summon up that feeling of near weightlessness that came over her in those moments when she was able to free her mind of all else and give herself over to prayer. Now nothing came but a dull ache in the back of her throat.

She had begun attending church regularly after she stopped visiting Kenny. His refusal to respond to her questions made it clear she'd have to seek answers elsewhere. She'd decided to talk to Father Giles. He'd been at St. Mark's, in their old neighborhood, before she and Kenny had moved there. He'd seen Kenny growing up. Perhaps he'd noticed something, understood something about the boy, about her, that would explain what she could not understand.

"It's God's will, my child—put it in His hands," he'd urged, awkwardly patting her arm and averting his eyes.

Myrna took his advice wholeheartedly. She became quite adept at quieting the questions boiling in her belly with "His will" or "My cross to bear." Many nights she'd "Our Fathered" herself to sleep. Acceptance of Kenny's inexplicable act became a test God had given her. One she passed by visiting the sick, along with other women from the church; working on the neighborhood cleanup committee; avoiding all social contact with men. With sex. She put "widowed" on job applications and never mentioned a son to new people she met. Once she'd moved away from the silent accusation of their old apartment, prayer and good works became a protective shield separating her from the past.

Kenny's tap on her door startled her back to the present. She cleared her throat and straightened the covers before calling to him to come in.

A rich, aromatic steam rose from the coffee he'd brought her. The toast was just the right shade of brown, and she was sure that when she cracked the poached egg it would be cooked exactly to her liking. Not only was everything perfectly prepared, it was the first time she'd had breakfast in bed since he'd been arrested. Myrna couldn't hold back the tears or the flood of memories of many mornings, just so: him bending over her with a breakfast tray.

"You wait on people in the restaurant all day and sit up all night making other people's clothes. You need some waiting on, too."

Had he actually said that, this man as a boy? Could this man have been such a boy? Myrna nearly tilted the tray in her confusion.

"I need to brush my teeth." She averted her face and reached for her bathrobe.

But she couldn't avoid her eyes in the medicine cabinet mirror, eyes that reminded her that despite what Kenny had done, she hadn't stopped loving him. But her love didn't need his company. It thrived only on memories of him that were more than four years old. It was as much a love remembered as a living thing. But it was love, nonetheless. Myrna pressed her clenched fist against her lips and wondered if love was enough. She stayed in the bathroom until she heard him leave her bedroom and turn on the TV in the living room.

When he came back for the tray, she told him she had a sick headache and had decided to stay in bed. He was immediately sympathetic, fetching aspirin and a cool compress for her forehead, offering to massage her neck and temples, to lower the blinds and block out the bright morning sun. Myrna told him she wanted only to rest.

All afternoon she lay on her unmade bed, her eyes on the ceiling or idly roaming the room, her mind moving across the surface of her life, poking at old wounds, so amazingly raw after all these years. First there'd been Buddy. He'd laughed at her country ways and punched her around until he'd driven her and their child into the streets. But at least she was rid of him. Then there was his son. Her baby. He'd tricked a young woman into getting into his car where he proceeded to ruin a great portion of her life. Now he'd come back to spill salt in her kitchen.

I'm home, Ma, homema, homema. His words echoed in her inner ear and made her heart flutter. Her neighbors would want to know where he'd been all this time and why. Fear and disgust would creep into their faces and voices. Her nights would be full of listening. Waiting.

And she would have to live with the unblanketed reality that whatever anger and meanness her son held toward the world, he had chosen a woman to take it out on.

A woman.

Someone like me, she thought, like Great Aunt Faye, or Valerie, her eight-year-old niece; like Lucille, her oldest friend, or Dr. Ramsey, her dentist. A woman like all the women who'd helped feed, clothe, and care for Kenny; who'd tried their damnedest to protect him from as much of the ugly and awful in life as they could; who'd taught him to ride a bike and cross the street. All women. From the day she'd left Buddy, not one man had done a damned thing for Kenny. Not one.

And he might do it again, she thought. The idea sent Myrna rolling back and forth across the bed as though she could actually escape her thoughts. She'd allowed herself to believe she was done with such thoughts. Once she accepted Kenny's crime as the will of God, she immediately saw that it wouldn't have made any difference how she'd raised him if this was God's unfathomable plan for him. It was a comforting idea, one that answered her question of why and how her much-loved son could be a rapist. One that answered the question of the degree of her responsibility for Kenny's crime by clearing her of all possible blame. One that allowed her to forgive him. Or so she'd thought.

Now she realized all her prayers, all her studied efforts to accept and forgive were like blankets thrown on a forest fire. All it took was the small breeze created by her opening the door to her only child to burn those blankets to cinders and release her rage—as wild and fierce as the day he'd confessed.

She closed her eyes and saw her outraged self dash wildly into the living room to scream imprecations in his face until her voice failed. Specks of froth gathered at the corners of her mouth. Her flying spit peppered his face. He cringed before her, his eyes full of shame as he tore at his own face and chest in self-loathing.

Yet, even as she fantasized, she knew Kenny could no more be screamed into contrition than Crystal or any woman could be bullied into willing sex. And what, in fact, was there for him to say or do that would satisfy her? The response she really wanted from him was not available: there was no way he could become the boy he'd been before that night four years ago.

No more than I can treat him as if he were that boy, she thought.

And the thought stilled her. She lay motionless, considering.

When she rose from her bed, she dragged her old green Samsonite suitcase out from the back of the closet. She moved with the easy, effortless grace of someone who knows what she is doing and feels good about it. Without even wiping off the dust, she plopped the suitcase on the bed. When she lifted the lid, the smell of leaving and good-bye flooded the room and quickened her pulse. For the first time in two days, her mouth moved in the direction of a smile.

She hurried from dresser drawer to closet, choosing her favorites: the black two-piece silk knit dress she'd bought on sale, her comfortable gray shoes, the lavender sweater she'd knitted as a birthday present to herself but had never worn, both her blue and her black slacks, the red crepe blouse she'd made to go with them, and the best of her under-wear. She packed in a rush, as though her bus or train were even now pulling out of the station.

When she'd packed her clothes, Myrna looked around the room for other necessary items. She gathered up her comb and brush and the picture of her mother from the top of her bureau, then walked to the wall on the left side of her bed and lifted down the shiny metal and wooden crucifix that hung there. She ran her finger down the slim, muscular body. The Aryan plaster of Paris Christ seemed to writhe in bittersweet agony. Myrna stared at the crucifix for a few moments, then gently hung it back on the wall.

When she'd finished dressing, she sat down in the hard, straight-backed chair near the window to think through her plan. Kenny tapped at her door a number of times until she was able to convince him that she was best left alone and would be fine in the morning. When dark came, she waited for the silence of sleep, then quietly left her room. She set her suitcase by the front door, tiptoed by Kenny, where he slept on the sofa, and went into the kitchen. By the glow from the back alley streetlight, she wrote him a note and propped it against the sugar bowl:

Dear Kenny,

I'm sorry. I just can't be your mother right now. I will be back in one week. Please be gone. Much love, Myrna.

Kenny flinched and frowned in his sleep as the front door clicked shut.

Charlotte Watson Sherman

Killing Color

CHARLOTTE WATSON SHERMAN is the author of the short story collection *Killing Color* (winner of the Washington State Governor's Writers Award) and the novel *One Dark Body*, as well as editor of the anthology *Sisterfire: Black Womanist Fiction and Poetry*. Her work has been published in such magazines as *Essence, Ms.,* and *Parenting* and included in several anthologies, most recently *In Search of Color Everywhere* and *I Know What the Red Clay Looks Like: Interviews with Black Women Writers*.

Ms. Sherman says that her motivation for the story *Killing Color* came from a visit to her mother's home in Louisville, Mississippi, in 1988. "The lush, verdant landscape, the friendliness of strangers, and the food cooked only the way a Mississippian could flavor it, all combined into a heady mix for a native Seattlite. I could hear the crowd surrounding a black body hanging from a bare tree. I could see the river swirling around the ankles of a runaway slave. I could smell the blood flowing deep in the rich earth, the sweat on the backs of longing sharecroppers.

"Mississippi is a powerful, all encompassing state of mind. Freedom, justice, hatred, retribution, forgiveness, God, all became more than abstract concepts to me. I wanted to create a character and a story that would capture all of that energy. The rage at first was red, then softened to yellow. But its heat was just as bright. Who was this woman Beulah Mae Donald? What was alight inside her that made her take on the Klan? I feel there are many hungry black spirits wandering the roads of all the Mississippis in this land, searching for something—revenge, retribution, peace."

Her new novel, *touch*, was published in 1995.

For Beulah Mae Donald, a Black woman who won a $7 million judgment against the Ku Klux Klan for the murder of her son Michael, who in March 1981, at the age of nineteen was strangled, fatally beaten, then had his body hung from a tree. Mrs. Donald was awarded the United Klans of America, Inc., headquarters property in Tuscaloosa, Alabama. She died September 17, 1988.

THEY SAY they got trees over seven hundred years old down in that yella swamp where even the water is murky gold. Bet them trees hold all kind of stories, but ain't none of em like the one I'm gonna tell bout Mavis.

Now, I'm not sayin Mavis is her real name. That's just what I took to callin her after seein them eyes and that fancy dress. Mavis had so much yella in her eyes it was like lookin in the sun when you looked right in em, but a funny deep kind of sun, more like a ocean of yella fire. You was lookin on some other world when you looked in Mavis's eyes, some other world sides this one.

I first saw Mavis leanin up against that old alabaster statue of some man my Aunt Myrtice call George Washington, but I don't think so cause it's got this plaque at the bottom bout the Spanish-American War and George Washington didn't have nothin to do with no Spanish-American War.

Anyway, I don't like talkin bout that statue too much cause it just gets Aunt Myrtice to fussin and I was always told it ain't right to talk back to old folks, so I don't. I just let her think she right bout things even though I know better. Still, that statue's where I first seen Mavis, and seem like don't nobody know where she come from. We just look up one day and there she was, leanin against that alabaster statue of not-George Washington.

I ain't no fancy woman or what some might call a hellraiser, but I know a woman full of fire when I see one, and if somebody hadda struck a match to Mavis, she'da gone up in a puff of smoke.

Mavis got honey-colored skin look like ain't never had nothin rough brush up against her. She had on some kinda blood-red high heel shoes. She the kind wear genuine silk stockins with fancy garters to hold em up, nothin like them old cotton ones I keep up on my leg with a little piece of string tied round my thigh.

Now she was wearin all this right here in Brownville, in the middle of town, in the noonday sun when all you could smell was the heat risin. So naturally I stopped and got me a good look at this woman leanin up against that statue with her eyes lookin straight out at that old magnolia tree front of the courthouse.

Most of us folks in Brownville try our best to look the other way when we walk by that big old barn of a courthouse. In fact, old Thaddeous Fulton, who I likes to call myself keepin company with, won't even walk on the same side of the street as the courthouse, cause most of us know if you brush against the law down here, you sho'nuff gonna get bad luck.

But Mavis was lookin at that old courthouse buildin full on with them yella eyes of hers never even blinkin, and she did it with her back straight like her spine was made outta some long steel pole.

When Tad come round that evenin, I tried tellin him bout Mavis standin up lookin at the courthouse, but he just shook his head and said, "Sounds like trouble to me." He wouldn't talk bout it no more, which got me kinda mad cause I like to share most of my troubles and all of my joys with this man, and I don't like seein his face closin up on me like he's comin outta some bad story in a book. But that's just what he did when I tried tellin him bout Mavis.

That man had somethin else on his mind for that evenin. I could tell by the way his eyebrows was archin clear up in his forehead.

Tad's slew-footed as they come and was born with only half his head covered with hair, so the front of his head's always shinin like a Milk Dud. But can't nobody in all of Brownville match that man for kissin.

Seem like he tries gobblin up most of my soul when he puts them sweet lips of his on mine and sneaks his tongue in my mouth. I nearly fell straight on the porch floor the first time he give me one of them kisses, and it wasn't long fore we got started on one of our favorite pastimes—debatin bout fornication. We always waited till Aunt Myrtice dozed off in her settin chair fore we slipped out to the porch and started up our discussion.

"Now, Lady (he likes to call me Lady even though it ain't my given name). Lady, I done lived a good part of my life as a travelin man, and you know I lived in Chicago a good while fore I come back home. And things everywhere else ain't like they is in Brownville. People be different. I knowed quite a few women that was good women. Good, decent women. But we wasn't married or nothin. We was just two good people tryin to keep they bodies warm in this cold, cold world. Now what's wrong with that?"

"Well, the Good Book say that them livin in the lusts of the flesh is by nature the children of wrath."

"I done seen more of life and people than ever could be put in a book. And I ain't never met nobody that died from lustin with they flesh. What I did see was folks full of wrath cause they wasn't gettin no sin."

"Well the Good Book say . . ."

"Lady, I don't b'lieve in no such thing as the Good Book cause I know there's lots of ways of lookin at things and you can't put em all in one book and say this be the Good Book."

"Watch out now, Thaddeous Fulton. You can't come round my house blasphemin."

"I still don't b'lieve in no such book. But I do b'lieve in a good life full of love. Now come on over here and give me a kiss."

Right away I started gigglin and actin silly even though I left my girlhood behind fifty years ago. It seems like I never had a chance to be a girl like this and then Tad start up to ticklin me and nobody passin on the road woulda guessed that the muffled snortin lovin sounds was comin from two folks with all kinds of wrinkles all over they bodies.

Tad always ask, "Well, if it's really the Good Book, then shouldn't everything that feel good be in it as a good thing to be doin?"

"That depends on what the good thing is cause everything that feels good ain't good for you," I always say.

"But, Lady, look at all the bad that's out there in the world. Folks gotta have some things that make em feel good. Things gotta balance some kinda way, don't they?"

And I always agree there needs to be some kinda balance to what's good and what's bad. Then Tad always starts talkin bout how good he feels just lookin at me and listenin to me talk bout the world.

"I try to show you how much I preciate you with my lips," he say and give me one of them devilish kisses. "Don't that feel good?" he ask and then keep on till we whisperin and kissin and doin pretty near what the Bible calls fornicatin out on the porch.

The next day I went to town and there Mavis was standin in the same spot by that statue, lookin at the courthouse.

Folks was walkin by lookin at her and tryin not to let her see em lookin, but Mavis wasn't payin nobody no mind cause she wasn't studyin nothin but that courthouse and that magnolia tree.

By Sunday, everybody was talkin bout her and wonderin why she kept on standin in the middle of town lookin at the courthouse. Then Reverend Darden started preachin gainst worryin bout other folk's business and not takin care of your own, so I started feelin shamed. But deep inside I was still wonderin bout Mavis. I decided I was gonna walk up to Mavis and find out what she was up to.

Next day, I got up early, went to town, and walked right up and waited for her to say somethin. But she acted like she didn't even know I was there. So I started talkin bout the weather, bout how that old sun was beatin down on us today, and wasn't it somethin how the grass stayed green in all this heat? Then I commenced to fannin myself, but Mavis still didn't say a word.

I was standin there fannin for bout five minutes when Mavis turned them yella eyes on me. Now, I heard stories bout people talkin with they eyes and never even openin they mouths, but I never met nobody like that before.

Mavis had them kinda eyes and she put em on me and told me with them eyes that she come for somethin she lost, then she turned her head back round and fixed her eyes on that courthouse again. Well, it was plain to me she wasn't gonna say no more, and I was ready to go home and sit in some shade anyway, so I did.

That evenin when Tad come by for a visit, he was all in a uproar.

"Why you messin round with that woman?" he ask after I told him I'd stood up at the statue with Mavis for a while. "I told you that woman sound like trouble. Folks say she rode off with that old Ned Crowell yesterday evenin and he ain't been heard from since."

"Where she at?" I asked. For some strange reason I was scared for her.

"She still standin up there like she always do. Layin back on that old statue. Somethin wrong with that woman. I told you the first time you told me bout her. Somethin wrong. You best stay away from her fore you get tangled up in some mess you be sorry bout. You know how them folks be."

"Don't go and get so upset your blood goes up, Tad. Ain't nothin gonna happen round here."

I tried to make Tad loosen up and grin a little, but he was too worked up and decided he was goin home to rest. I wasn't gonna tell him bout Mavis and her talkin eyes cause he'da probably thought I was losin my mind.

I let three days pass fore I went to town to see if Mavis was still standin at that statue, and sure enough, there she was.

I went and stood next to her and started talkin bout nothin in particular. I fixed my eyes on the courthouse but couldn't see nothin that hadn't been there for at least fifty years.

"You know they keep that buildin pretty clean and old Wonzell Fitch picks up round the yard every evenin. You might wanna check with him bout findin somethin you lost," I whispered.

She turned her head and told me with them yella eyes she was lookin for somethin that b'longed to her. She didn't even hear what I said. I didn't say nothin else, just stood with her for a while, then went on home.

Tad came by later on with his face all wrinkled up like a prune, but I didn't make fun of him cause I could see he was troubled.

"Seem like three more of them Crowells and one of them Fitzhughs is gone."

"Don't nobody know what happened to em?" I asked. "Don't seem possible four grown men could disappear without a trace. What do folks think is happenin?"

"Don't know for sure, but some folks say they saw least two of them Crowells and old Billy Fitzhugh go off with that crazy woman late in the evenin."

"Do the sheriff know bout that?" I asked.

"Naw, and ain't nobody gonna tell him neither. If they do they likely to get locked up."

"Well, sure is mighty strange. Didn't think she even left that spot at the statue to go relieve herself. She just stand there starin, don't ever see her drink no water or nothin, just standin in all that heat."

"Well, look like come evenin she find herself one of them old white men and go off with em and don't nobody see that man no more. You ain't goin round her, is you? I sure hate to see what happen when the sheriff find out bout her bein the last one seen with them missin men, cause you know well as I do what that mean."

Me and Tad just sat together real quiet and still on the porch holdin hands like old folks is supposed to do.

Next day I had to take Aunt Myrtice to evenin prayer service so I decided I was gonna sit outside and watch the statue from the front steps of the church.

"You bout to miss service and then have the nerve to sit on the front steps of Reverend Darden's church?" she fussed.

"I'm gonna do just that and ain't nobody gonna stop me, neither."

"You gonna sit outside when you need to be inside?"

"Yep," I replied. Then I just stopped listenin. I already made up my mind bout what I was gonna do, and even Aunt Myrtice's fussin wasn't gonna change that.

So after all the folks had gone inside, I sat on the porch and watched the sun go down and watched Mavis standin at the statue lookin at that same buildin she'd been lookin at for almost a month now.

When the shadows had stretched and twisted into night, I saw the lights from some kinda car stop in front of the statue. Mavis jumped in the car with what sounded to me like a laugh, and the car eased on down the street.

"No tellin where they goin," I thought out loud as the car moved slowly past the church. I could see the pale face of old Doc Adams at the wheel. Mavis never even turned her head in my direction or anyone else's. Her yella eyes was lookin straight ahead.

"Nuther man gone," Tad mumbled when he stopped by the next day.

"Was it old Doc Adams?" I asked, scared to hear the answer.

"How'd you know? I done told you you better stay way from that woman. God knows what she's up to and I sure don't want no parts of it. You askin for trouble, Lady, foolin round that woman. Best go on in the house and read some of that Good Book you always talkin bout. I know it don't say nothin good bout killin folks!"

"Now how you know anybody been killed, Tad? How you know that? Some folks is just missin, right? Don't nobody know where they at, right?"

"You don't have to be no schoolteacher to see what's happenin! Them men be dead. Just as sure as we sittin here, they dead! Now you better stick round home with Miss Myrtice cause this town gonna turn upside down when they go after that woman!"

That night I turned over in my mind what Tad had said. Could

Mavis have killed all them men? How could she do it? She ain't even a big woman. How could she kill even one grown man, even if he was old? And why wasn't the sheriff doin somethin bout it? Couldn't he see Mavis standin right in the middle of town leanin on that statue, like we see her every day?

I could feel pressure buildin up in my stomach, a kinda tight boilin feelin I always got when somethin big was bout to happen. So I decided I best go up to town and tell Mavis to be careful cause folks was sayin and thinkin some pretty nasty things bout her. Not cause of the way she was dressed, but cause of her bein seen ridin off with all them white men and ain't nobody seen em since.

Well, there she was standin in her usual spot with her eyes burnin holes in the courthouse. I didn't have time to mince words, so I didn't.

"Folks is talkin, Mavis. Talkin real bad bout you. Sayin crazy things like you tied up with the missin of some men round here and how you up to no good here in Brownville."

Mavis didn't say a word, just kept on lookin.

"This town'll surprise you. You might be thinkin we ain't nothin but backwoods, country-talkin folks, but we got as much sense as anybody else walkin round on two legs. And don't too many people sit up and talk this bad bout somebody they'd never even laid eyes on a month ago without some kinda reason and some pretty strong thinkin on it. Now I don't wanna meddle in your business none, but I think you got a right to know folks is callin you a murderer."

Mavis turned them yella eyes on me for so long I thought I might start smokin and catch afire. I mean, she burned me with them eyes: "I come for what is mine, somethin that belong to me, and don't none of y'all got a right to get in my way."

I stepped back from her cause she was lookin pretty fierce with them eyes of hers alight, but I still reached out to touch her arm.

"I just hate to see bad things happen to folks is all. I don't mean no harm."

And I turned to walk away. But it felt like a steel band grabbed my arm and turned me back round to look at them yella eyes: "Now you listen, listen real good cause I want all of y'all to know why I was here after I'm gone and I'm not leavin till my work is done.

"Way back when, I lived on what was called Old Robinson Road. Wasn't much to look at, but we had us a little place, a little land, some chickens and hogs. We growed most of our own food right there on

our land and didn't hafta go off sellin ourselves to nobody. Not nobody, you hear me? We was free people: livin our lives, not botherin
nobody, not messin in nobody's business, didn't even leave the place to
go to church. We just lived on our land and was happy.

"Now some folks right here in this town got the notion in they
heads that colored folk don't need to be livin on they own land, specially if it was land any white man wanted.

"Old Andy Crowell, who looks like the devil musta spit him out, got
it in his head he was gonna take our land. Well, I don't know if they
still makin men like they made mine, but my man knew and I knew
wasn't nobody gonna get this land, not while we was standin and
drawin breath.

"So we took to sleepin with a shotgun next to the bed and one by
the front door, and my man even carried a little gun in his belt when he
was out in the fields. I kept one strapped to my leg up under my dress.

"We went into the courthouse right here, and tried to find out bout
the law, cause we knew had to be a law to protect us, one for the
protection of colored folks seein as how slavery had been over and
wasn't no more slaves we knew bout.

"We went up to that buildin and s'plained to a man what call hisself a
clerk that we had a paper tellin us to clear off our land. My man had the
deed to that land cause he got it from his daddy who got it some kinda
way durin slavery time, and nobody bothered him bout it cause he
didn't let nobody know he had it.

"But it was his and we had the paper to show it, and that rat-faced
gopher callin hisself a clerk looked at the deed to our land—our land
I'm tellin you—and that clerk took the deed to our land and crumbled
it up and threw it on the floor and told us to get outta his office.

"My man was just lookin right in that clerk's face. Wasn't flinchin.
Wasn't blinkin. Just lookin. But his eyes, oh his eyes was tellin that man
a story, a story that old fool didn't even know he knew. And my man
told that clerk all about it, and I picked up the deed to our land and we
left.

"Well, it wasn't long after we'd gone to the courthouse fore they
come for him.

"You know how they do.

"Sit up and drink a buncha liquor to give em guts they don't have,
then they posse up and come ridin for you soon as the sun go down.

"You know who it is when you hear all them horses on the road.

Then you look through the window and see them little flickers of light comin closer and closer, growin bigger and bigger till it looks like the sun's come gallopin down the road. Then they all in your yard holdin up they torches till the yard's lit up like daylight, but you know it's the devil's own night. You can smell him out in the yard all tangled up with flint and sweat and liquor. I know the stink of evil anywhere. Then my man picks up his gun and steps out into that red night and tells em to get off his land or he'll shoot. I could see the claws of the devil pullin on my man and I tried to pull him back to the house, but he pushed me back inside and his eyes told me how he loved me like he did his own life. Then the devil's fingers snatched him and his tongue wrapped round my man's arms and drug him out into the middle of Satan's circle, where they all had white handkerchiefs knotted round they faces from they red eyes to they pointed chins. Then they knocked my man down with his own shotgun and they kicked him, each one takin a turn. I picked up the shotgun standin near our bed and ran out the house screamin and fired a shot. Two of em fell to the ground, but some of em grabbed me from behind and beat me in the head. By the time I opened my eyes, my man was gone. It was Edith Rattray who come round and found me lyin in the yard and cleaned me up and nursed me. I musta laid in bed for over a month fore I could get up and go to town and find out what happened to my man.

"And what I found out was this: Evil can grow up outta the ground just like a tree filled with bad sap and turn every livin thing to somethin rottin in the sun like an old carcass.

"Now, you tell them folks what's wonderin why I'm here and what I'm doin and what I'm up to, you tell em that I'm cleanin that tree right down to the root."

Sayin that seemed to make that cold steel band slip from my arm. Mavis turned her eyes back on the courthouse.

I sat on the porch even though it was in the middle of the noonday sun and thought about what Mavis's eyes had told me.

"I must be losin my mind," I said to the listenin trees.

How in the world could a woman tell me any kinda story with no sound comin outta her mouth? What kinda woman was she? And what kinda woman am I? And what would God say bout all of this? I went inside the house and reached for my Bible. Surely some kind of answer could be found there.

After readin a while, I still hadn't found the answer I was lookin for, so I went into the kitchen and started cookin instead.

"What's for supper, daughter?" Aunt Myrtice asked.

"Oh, I'm fixin some squash, some fried catfish, some salt pork, a pot of blackeye peas, a pan of cornbread, and some peach cobbler for dessert."

"Um um. Tad must be comin by. I know you ain't fixin all that food for just me and you."

"Yeah, Tad did say he was comin round here later this evenin. Maybe I'll take you up to prayer meetin fore he gets here."

"Umhum. Y'all gonna get me outta the way so you can sit in this house kissin while I'm gone. You oughtta be shamed of yourself, old as you is."

"I might be gettin on in years, Aunt Myrtice, but I ain't dead yet." I kept on cookin.

I decided I was gonna get Tad to help me watch and see what Mavis was up to that evenin after we dropped Aunt Myrtice off at the church.

"You want me to do what?" Tad shouted after I told him what I wanted. "I ain't goin nowhere near that woman and you ain't either. You wanna get us both killed?"

I patted his arm and talked to him soft as I could to try to calm him down. No sense in his blood goin up over this foolishness.

"Tad, I just wanna prove to you and everybody else that Mavis ain't killed nobody and she ain't done none of us no harm by standin up by that statue. She can't even talk, how she gonna kill a big, old man?"

Tad gave in even though I could see he didn't wanna. He parked the car bout a block away from the statue. We didn't worry bout whether or not Mavis could see us cause she wasn't lookin at nothin else but that tree in front of the courthouse.

"Now look at her. You know somethin wrong," Tad said.

"Don't go and start workin yourself up. We ain't gonna be here long cause it's already startin to get dark and you said she usually leaves bout this time, didn't you?"

"I don't know when she leaves, cause I ain't been round here to see it. Folks just been sayin she leaves bout this time."

"Well, we'll wait a little while and see."

Sure enough, fore too long, an old red pickup pulled up next to Mavis and she ran around the front of the truck and jumped inside.

Even from where we was parked we could hear the sound she made when she got in the car. It wasn't no laugh, like Tad said, it was more like a high–pitched cryin sound mixed up with a whoop and a holler. It made the hair on the back of my neck stand straight up, and Tad said it made his flesh crawl.

Anyway, the truck pulled off and we followed a ways behind it. Couldn't see who was drivin on accounta that big old rebel flag hangin up in the back window.

We followed em anyway: out past the old poorhouse, past the pea and okra shed, past the old Lee plantation, out past Old Robinson Road.

Tad started gettin mad again cause he wanted to turn round and go back home. "You know we goin too far from home. Ain't no tellin where that crazy woman goin."

"Hush, and keep drivin. We gonna prove somethin once and for all tonight. Put a end to all this talk bout murder."

So we kept on drivin, but it was so dark now, we couldn't really make out what we was passin.

After a while, Tad said, "I don't think we in Brownville no more. You can tell by the shape things make in the dark."

I didn't say nothin. Just kept my eyes on the truck's red lights in front of us. A few minutes later, the truck pulled off the road and went into the trees. When we reached the spot where they turned off, we couldn't see no road, no lights, no nothin. Just trees.

"Well, I guess this is far as we go. Ain't nowhere to go now but back home," Tad said. "They probably went back up in them woods to do they dirty business."

"What dirty business, Tad? What dirty business? First you callin her a murderer, now what you callin her?"

"What kinda woman drive off with men in trucks in the evenin? What you think I'm callin her?"

"Let's just walk a ways in there to see if we can hear somethin."

"I'm not walkin back up in them woods. Now you go on and walk up in there if you want to, I ain't goin nowhere but back home."

While we was fussin, a car pulled off the road next to Tad's car. A skinny-faced man leaned out the window.

"You folks havin trouble?" he asked.

"I musta made a wrong turn somewhere back down the road and we just tryin to figure out the best way to get back home," Tad replied.

"You sure musta made a wrong turn cause ain't nothin out this way but trees and swamp."

"Is that right?" Tad asked.

"Yep, that's right. That big old yella swamp is bout two miles in them trees and it ain't nowhere no human man or woman needs to go. Ain't nothin livin that went in that swamp ever come back out that way. Nothin but the shadows of death back up in there. You step through them trees and it's like you stepped down into a tunnel goin way down into the ground. Down there them old snakes hangin down from them trees like moss is yella. Mosquito bites turn a man's blood yella. Yella flies crawl on the ground where worms come up out the yella mud and twist like broken fingers from a hand. Shadows come up and wrap they arms round you, pullin you down into yella mud where sounds don't come from this world. Nothin down there but yella."

Me and Tad thanked the man and turned the car around and went back home. The skinny-faced man's words burned our ears.

"Now don't you try to get me to run round on no wild goose chase behind that woman no more. I don't care what she's up to, I don't want nothin else to do with her."

Next day first thing, I went to town to talk to Mavis. Sure enough, there she was standin next to that statue.

"I been thinkin bout what you told me bout the evil way back when, and it seems it might be better just to let things lay and forgive the ones that did it like Jesus would."

Well, what did I go and say that for? Mavis whipped her head round and shook me with them eyes.

"Who you to forgive all that blood? Who YOU? Put your head to the ground and listen. Down there's an underground river runnin straight through this town, an underground river of blood runnin straight through. Just listen."

Then her eyes let me go and she turned back round. When I turned to walk back home, I saw some old dried-up mud caked round the bottom of that red dress she was wearin, mud that was yella as mustard, but dried up like old blood.

Not long after Mavis shook me up with them yella eyes of hers, I got sick and Aunt Myrtice, poor thing, had to tend me best she could, bless her heart.

Tad came by and helped when he could, but I'm the type of person don't like folks to see me hurtin and I sure didn't want Tad to keep seein me with my teeth out and my hair all over my head, though he claims I still look good to him.

Aunt Myrtice act like she don't hear him, but I could see her eyes light up.

Once I got to feelin better and was almost back on my feet, Tad started hunchin up his eyebrows, so I knew pretty soon we was gonna go out on the porch and get to arguin bout fornicatin, which to tell the truth, I'd rather be fussin over than that foolishness bout Mavis.

But Tad told me Mavis wasn't standin up at the statue of not-George Washington no more and nobody knows where she went off to. She just disappeared easy as she come.

The sheriff never did find out bout her. It turned out all them old missin men had been tangled up with the Ku Klux years back and had spilt plenty blood in the yard of that courthouse, hangin folks from that magnolia tree.

Sometimes, now, I think bout what Mavis told me how evil grow up outta the ground and how that old underground river flows with blood, and I think about puttin my head to the ground just so's I can listen. But I just go and stand by that statue and look up at that court-house, feelin Mavis in my eyes.

Aya de León

Tell Me Moore

AYA DE LEÓN is an Afro-Latina writer of mystery fiction and
other prose. A graduate of Harvard College, she is a cofounder
of the Mothertongue Fiction Academy, a writing program for
African American women.

Her critique of John Ball's Virgil Tibbs and Ernest
Tidymann's John Shaft, "The Black Detective in the White
Mind," appeared in the Fall 1993 issue of *The Armchair Detective*. In it, de León, analyzes the detectives' self-perception,
their relationship to the African American community and to
black women, and concludes, "Creating a man and coloring
him brown does not make him a Black man; putting a badge or
a private detective's license into his hand does not make him a
hero."

Madeline Moore, a young Oakland, California, detective
immersed in her culture and community, is the antithesis of
Tibbs and Shaft. Like her detective, de León lives in Oakland,
where she is working on the first novel in the Madeline Moore
mystery series.

For Denise, John, and Kamau

"SO HOW WAS your first week of self-employment?" Liz asked.

"I bought a gun," I said.

"What?!" Liz asked, putting down the deck of cards she had been shuffling. Liz could do those crazy tricks where you stream the cards from one hand into the other from about a foot apart.

"I'm really not happy about this," Yamile said. On the one hand, it was none of her business, but on the other hand, it was. She was my best friend and we lived under the same roof, but in separate apartments.

"Wait a minute," Liz said, "is this the same Madeline Moore who refused to let me *give* her a gun for the two years she worked for me? 'I don't need one,' " she mimicked me in a high voice that sounded nothing like me, " 'I just don't feel comfortable with guns.' "

"And you shouldn't feel comfortable with guns," Yamile said. "It just lulls you into a false sense of security, and you're more likely to get hurt yourself than deter an attack with it."

"Yeah, well," I said, "I got into some potentially life-threatening drama."

"Domestic case?" Liz asked, dealing the cards.

"How did you know?" I asked.

"Just a feeling. Wait 'til you've been in the investigation business twenty years. Sometimes you just know."

After my experience that week, I didn't know if I wanted to be in the investigation business twenty years. But I certainly hadn't found anything I liked better. Then again, in my six years out of college, the only other things I had been were a research assistant and a paralegal.

Liz dealt smoothly and with lightning speed. "Come on now," she said as she dealt. "Baby needs a new pair of shoes!"

"Liz," Yamile pointed out, "we're not playing for money."

"Doesn't matter," Liz said, "I say it for luck."

I had a hunch that before she was in the investigation business, Liz was into some gambling racket, but she didn't talk about it, and I didn't ask.

"Black is back," Liz gloated as she arranged her hand. The game was spades, and it was time to bid.

"I got four," I said.

"I got seven," Liz said.

"I got . . ." Yamile began.

"Watch old sandbag Sally over there underbid again," Liz said to me.

"I am not gonna underbid," Yamile said defensively.

"Whenever I'm her partner, I always jack up my bid," Liz said to me.

"I can't believe it!" Yamile said, indignant.

"And don't we win?" Liz asked.

"Sometimes," Yamile said, "and other times, we go down in flames because we can't make our bids. Then Liz tries to talk me into those crazy blind sevens."

"And doesn't it work?" Liz asked.

"One time. It worked *one* time. And we probably would have won anyway," Yamile said.

"Liz," I said, "would you stop harassing the girl so she can bid."

"Sorry," Liz said, taking a sip of her wine.

"I got . . . five," Yamile said defiantly, and took a swig of her mango juice.

There were only three of us—Liz, Yamile, and me, so we were playing spades. Usually, we played bid whist or spades with partners, but Liz's girlfriend, Ronetta, was out of town.

"You miss your honey?" Yamile asked Liz.

"Girl, I miss that fine brown woman every day when I have to go to work," Liz said with a grin.

"I heard that," said Yamile.

Ronetta was at Princeton for the graduation of her son, Gus Junior.

"When is she coming back?" I asked.

"Next week," Liz said with a sigh.

Liz and Ronetta had been together over ten years. They were still madly in love, but it was an open kind of love. Not the kind where the lovers lock themselves away and hoard it only for themselves. They played cards with Yamile and me every other week and went out with friends.

But don't think for a minute that Liz and Ronetta weren't tuned into each other. They had that serious lovers' telepathy, and we had to break them up when we played cards. Yamile and I had only been neighbors and best friends for a year and a half, and we were no match for those two. To keep it even, we switched off when we played partners. One week it would be me and Liz versus Yamile and Ronetta. The next week, it would be me and Ronetta against Yamile and Liz.

We also switched locations; that day the game was at Liz's apartment in Oakland. Her dining room looked out onto Lake Merritt, which was beautiful at night. It was too dark to see all the pollution, and the perimeter was surrounded by a string of yellow lights.

I took a sip of my root beer, and looked at the Tobe Correal original sculpture across from me. It was the bodice of a nude, glazed in glossy black with flecks of copper. Her breasts seemed to disagree, one pointing directly forward, and the other upward, as if one of her invisible arms was raised. Her full buttocks jutted out behind her in counterpoint to her round stomach. The sculpture sat on top of a 1940s-style radio with a front panel that swung open to reveal a Denon stereo. From the speaker within a speaker came the sounds of Billie's voice, telling us that we didn't know what love was.

"So what happened with this dramatic case," Yamile said as she started the game with the ace of hearts.

"I thought you'd never ask," I said. "I put this ad in the *Tribune* . . ."

"That rag," Liz said.

"It's better than the *Chronicle*," Yamile said.

"Please," Liz shot back, "those fools took the Oakland out of the *Oakland Tribune*."

"Yeah," Yamile said defensively, "but at least we got Brenda Payton. Name one Black female perspective you get in the *Chronicle*—"

"Enough of the battle of the newspapers," I said. *"I'm* telling this story." It had all just ended the day before, and I needed to get it off my chest. "So my ad came out on Monday. 'M. Moore Investigations,'" I quoted, " 'affordable, effective.' " It had also included my private investigator's license number and phone number. "Those three lines cost me $41.10 for two days," I said. "I sat around on Monday and Tuesday thinking I had wasted my money. Finally, on Wednesday, I got a call."

"Oh, damn," Liz said as she watched Yamile cut her queen of clubs with a three of spades.

"Anyway," I said, "this woman calls and says she wants me to follow her husband, she suspects him of having an affair."

"And what did you tell her?" Liz asked.

"I said I would shadow him, I would be willing to photograph him in public places or on the street, but not inside any private buildings, and no video."

"That's right, honey, 'cause you don't need no photo or video of nobody doing the do, to know somebody's doing the do. And you don't need no B and E rap to get 'em," Liz said.

"What's B and E?" Yamile asked.

"Breaking and entering," Liz said, reaching for a buffalo wing. She had made them, and they were good and spicy.

"Will you give me some of those wings?" I asked Liz and passed my plate to her. "Oh, and give me some of that sweet potato pudding while you're at it," I added.

"Oh, you like that, huh?" Yamile asked.

"It's not bad," I said, "considering it's probably good for me."

"Well," Yamile said, "it has no sugar, no flour, no butter, and no milk, but I'd be glad to give you the recipe."

"No thank you," I said, "telling me all the healthy soybean ingredients will just spoil it for me. Besides, what am I gonna do with a recipe? I'm no chef." For our card parties, I always brought the soda, juice, and wine.

"One of these days we gonna make you cook something," Liz said.

"And you'll be sorry," I told her.

"I'm a witness," Yamile said, tossing out the ace of diamonds.

"So this woman comes down to my office," I began again.

"How did she look?" Yamile asked.

"Well, she was about your color," I said. Yamile's skin was the color of butterscotch, midway between her Black father and her Puerto Rican mother. Her dark hair was twisted into little ropes and pulled back in a ponytail. Her oval face rested on the knuckles of her fist and her forearm was covered in brightly colored beaded bracelets. Yamile is a tall, kinda pear-shaped woman.

"But the similarity ended there," I continued. "You're kind of the young, earthy, artistic type. This woman was a Jack and Jill type, with real long sandy-colored hair, and she was petite and slight. She had on this black and white tuxedo coatdress, high heels, expert makeup—you know, not a hair or a thread out of place. The girl looked like she had walked out of an *Essence* magazine 'fierce looks for winter' layout."

"Like something I would wear?" Liz asked. At that moment Liz was wearing a pair of red denim jeans and a plain white button-down shirt. This was very unusual for Liz, who had most of her clothes custom made for her voluptuous figure. At work she wore form-fitting suits and high heels. Liz took seriously all those studies about "power colors," and wore a lot of red. Liz was a milk-chocolate brown, and conservative folks might say she shouldn't wear red, but any fool could see that it worked on her. Besides, I'm a shade darker than Liz, and I wear any color I feel like.

"No, this woman wasn't like you at all," I said to Liz. "I think of you as a sort of urban diva. She acted like she wanted to pull the white silk handkerchief out of the pocket of her coatdress and wipe the chair off before she sat in it."

"It was like that, huh?" Liz asked as she cut Yamile's jack of diamonds with a spade.

"Yeah," I said, "and I told you I scrubbed that office from floor to ceiling."

"I don't understand why you're paying alla that rent when you know you can see clients at Front Rowe," Liz said.

I had worked for her at Front Rowe Investigations for two years. Liz Rowe was somewhere in her early forties and was basically my mentor. I had thought that seeing a client there would be like spending a night with a man at my mother's house. Even if I had permission, I would still feel inhibited; it wouldn't be *my* house. But with the rent they had me paying at that run-down office building, and the drama of this case, I was reconsidering.

"Miss Essence must have raised a sandy eyebrow at your short afro," Yamile said.

"That's right," Liz said, "and I'll bet you were dressed in . . . let's see, was it sweats or blue jeans?"

"Jeans," I said defensively, "with a new burgundy turtleneck, thank you." Liz and Yamile were always trying to get me to *diversify* my wardrobe. Shoot, no one told Coffin Ed and Grave Digger Jones to stop wearing those rumpled suits.

"So was she impressed with your outfit?" Yamile asked.

"No," I said, "but she handed me a photo of her man and told me where to find him. And she wrote me a rather large check for a retainer, which didn't bounce."

"Good sign," Liz said.

"I wish it had been," I said.

"Hey, wait a minute," Liz said to me. "I thought you was cuttin' clubs."

"No," I said, "Yamile's cutting clubs. I threw the club."

"Dang, just set her up, why don't you," Liz said and tossed out a four of clubs, only to be cut by Yamile's six of spades. "Go on back to your story," grumbled Liz.

"Well, it was about three o'clock in the afternoon when the wife left, so I drove out to the husband's business. Ken's Men's Emporium on East Fourteenth street—they sell suits and stuff."

"Let me clarify here," Liz said, "you mean real suits, or the kind of low quality, buy on credit, wear it to the nightclub to impress the ladies type suits they sell in the 'hood."

"Well, I didn't go in," I said, "but I think it was pretty mediocre stuff. When I drove by, I could see him through the plate-glass window of the store handling a transaction. I parked my car in the supermarket lot across the street and watched him through my binoculars.

"Now, I must say," I went on, "the photo she gave me didn't do the man justice."

"Was he foyne?" Yamile asked in her best New York Puerto Rican girl imitation.

"He was a very good-looking man," I said. "Not my type at all, mind you. Tall, broad-shouldered, nice build, but he had that kind of light-skinned slick look. First of all, you could tell he didn't buy his suits at his own store."

"I know that's a fact," Liz said.

"And he looked like he was right out of an ad for Dax," I went on. "My man's head was waved *up.*"

"I'm surprised you couldn't see the mark on his head from the do-rag," Liz said.

"No," I said, "this guy was definitely not the do-rag type. He was more upscale, like his wife. I could imagine her saying something like 'Kenneth and I frown upon that kind of ghetto mentality,' in her prim voice."

"Hold up," Liz said. "What did you just throw out?" she asked me.

"The five of hearts," I said.

"Hearts led, and you threw the diamond?" Liz asked Yamile.

"I'm afraid so," Yamile said.

"Aw, sookie sookie," Liz said, grinning, and took the book with a four of spades.

"But anyway," I went on, "the brother is easy on the eyes, which is good, because I'm watching him all afternoon. Folks going in and out, buying mostly on layaway, but nothing to suggest any fooling around on his part. Then, at seven o'clock, he closes down, pulls the metal gate over the front of the store, and leaves. I follow him to their two-story white house. She had given me the address as being in Piedmont, but really it's on the Oakland side of the Oakland/Piedmont border."

"Who does she think she's fooling?" Liz asked.

"I hate that," Yamile said. "Let a city get too many colored folks, and everyone starts trying to disassociate themselves, even the colored folks."

"Look," Liz said, "if colored folks wanna do the upscale thing, do it. But if you can't really afford it, don't perpetrate."

"Well, I don't understand why Black folks can't just stay in the community," Yamile said. "Like this is a great apartment. There are plenty of really nice places to live, right here in Oakland."

"Hey, you two," I broke in, "I'm trying to tell this story, so will you stop interrupting me?"

"Well," Liz said, "it's okay with me, if it's okay with Miss Power-to-the-people over here."

"Don't start with me, Shelby Steele," Yamile said. "Go ahead, Madeline."

"Well anyway," I said, "I go home and check my messages. She's on my work machine, asking me to call. When I call the house, he answers, and, girls, I must say the man is really Barry White in disguise." I said "hello," in my deepest, suavest voice, just to give them the idea.

"Oh," Yamile said, "I love a man with a nice voice." She fanned herself facetiously, and took a long swallow of her mango juice.

"Yes, he had a *very* nice voice," I continued. "So then she gets on the phone, and I tell her who it is. So she says, 'Oh, hello, how did the meeting go?' and I say, 'There wasn't any meeting, but I'll be back tomorrow.' And she says, 'Okay, ciao!' "

"She didn't say 'ciao'!" Yamile said.

"Right on the Oakland/Piedmont border," I said. "So the next day, I'm down at the spot bright and early. I see him open up at nine o'clock. Same deal, I wait in the parking lot; folks buy suits on layaway. Then, at twelve-thirty, the man strolls out of the store, leaving his trusty assistant in charge. The assistant is a slightly younger and browner version of himself, maybe his brother or his cousin. Then he rolls out in his late-model BMW convertible—"

"He drove a convertible BMW?" Liz asked.

"A red one," I said. "I didn't tell you that?" They shook their heads. "Oh, well, while I was following him, I felt like *Ebony* was gonna have to feature the husband and wife team at any moment."

"I can see it now," Yamile said, " 'Raveen Relaxer woman meets the S-Curl man; love at first sight.' "

"Yeah," I said, "either that or 'Young Black entrepreneur and lovely wife lead dream life in Piedmont, California.' Then there's a photo of them in front of the car parked by the house, and another photo of him in front of his business."

"Or there's the other angle," Liz said. " 'All the good men are married, gay, or in jail: one woman's struggle to keep her marriage together and to keep her good Black man from going astray.' "

"Hold that thought; it gets deeper," I said. "I follow him for a while, and it becomes apparent that he's not just going to the local deli for lunch. Instead, he drives out to San Leandro and goes by this apartment building. He rings the bell and I get a photo of him in the foyer. He gets back in his car and out comes this woman."

"Hold up," Liz said. "What did you just throw out?" She pointed to Yamile with the cards in her hand facedown.

"The two of spades," Yamile said.

"You threw out the highest spade in the deck to take a four and eight of hearts?" Liz asked.

"Oh, oops," Yamile said, "I forgot that the two was high."

"We said we were playing Madeline's crazy Back East way," Liz reminded her.

"Well I got distracted by Madeline's story," Yamile said. "Can I take it back?"

"Take it back? Girl, you must be from Berkeley," Liz said. "I been to card games where folks'll pull a knife just for *asking* to take something back."

"Yeah, but we're all unarmed here," Yamile said. "At least I hope so." She glanced at me disapprovingly. "So can I take the card back or what?" she asked Liz.

"What do you think?" Liz asked me.

"Well, I do tell a good story if I say so myself," I said, grinning. "I think she has a good excuse."

Liz rolled her eyes. "Go ahead, Yamile."

Yamile eagerly snatched up the two and took the book with a ten of spades.

"I think this California living is making me soft. Folks back home in Texas would be scandalized that I let that go by, just scandalized," Liz said. "So, Master Storyteller, go back to your tale of woe."

"Where was I?" I asked.

"The woman was coming out of the building," Yamile prompted, reaching for a buffalo wing.

"Yeah, right. So the woman was coming out of the building. I photograph her coming out and getting into his car. Now she's another *Essence* model type."

"Like me?" Liz asked.

"Yeah, this sister was a little more like you," I said. "A little darker than you, with a thicker build. Her hair was cut real short in the back, but was full on top, and pressed super-ultra straight like yours. Makeup for days, killer nails like yours. She had on this cream-colored pantsuit with flared legs, and a pair of brown patent leather pumps, with a matching brown patent leather bag. And I must say, the girl was *wearing* the pantsuit."

"Was she wearing it?" Liz asked.

"Yeah," I said, "she was just strutting to the car."

"Large and in charge," Liz said. "You gotta love that."

"Well, I don't know about in charge," Yamile said. "She is involved with a married man."

"Good point," Liz conceded, taking a sip of her wine.

Yamile was a counselor, and had heard every crazy story from "he's been gonna leave her any day now for years" to "I know he has another woman but he loves me more." "I mean, even if he lied," Yamile said, "she'd have to be blind not to know. With a wife like he's got, Ms. San Leandro can't be calling the house or coming by the job. If she doesn't know he's married, it's like the way white folks don't know Egypt is in Africa. 'Cause it's all about de Nile!" She laughed at her own joke. Liz chuckled.

These girls were not gonna let me tell this story. "Anyway," I said when their laughter subsided, "they drive out to a motel in San Lorenzo, and I photograph them going in, and then I wait. And it was weird, sitting there. I mean, I know at some level that even as we're here playing cards, someone is sleeping with someone else's man or woman. But to be in the parking lot while they're at it. That was another thing entirely. I felt a little cheap and tawdry, I must admit. But mostly, I felt like a voyeur."

"Honey," Liz said, "this business is about voyeurism. You investigate people's dirty laundry."

"Yeah, but the sexual part was just too personal for me," I said. "I didn't like it. So I just sat there feeling uncomfortable until they came out an hour later—"

"Only an hour?" Liz asked.

"Hey," Yamile said, "if he's gonna make it into *Ebony,* he can't afford to waste too much time."

"Yeah," I said, "but the wildest thing was, when they came out an hour later they were both immaculate, like nothing had happened. Not a wave or a curl out of place."

"Maybe they didn't have sex," Yamile suggested.

"Are you kidding me?" Liz asked. "There are a million ways to do the do without messing up your do. And you can also best believe that her matching brown patent leather bag had every styling implement and makeup accoutrement known to womankind," Liz said, laying down the little joker.

"Damn," said Yamile, grudgingly tossing out the king of spades. "You know that means she has the big joker." I nodded my agreement.

"Not necessarily," Liz said, scooping up the book.

"Watch," Yamile said.

"Go on with your story," Liz said and threw out the big joker.

"See!" Yamile said, and threw out the two in disgust.

I had no more spades anyway; my hand had been mostly clubs. I tossed out the five of clubs and went on with my story.

"I photographed them getting back into the car, him dropping her off at her apartment, and him back at work by two-thirty. I wait until four o'clock, but it's all quiet. So I go to a one-hour photo place to get the film developed.

"While I'm waiting, I go get a burger, then I come back and the film is out. I'm no brilliant artist, here, but I've got good, clear photos. I love that zoom lens; you can see him, you can see her, you can see them in the car, going into the motel, his arm around her waist. You can even see them kiss in one shot."

"Like I told you," Liz said, "you don't need to be in the room to know what went on."

"Yeah," I said, "that was my problem. I realized a little too late that I didn't want to know. But it was my job, so I was gonna finish it.

"I get home around six o'clock," I went on. "I pick up my work messages. She wants me to call her at home. This time I don't get Barry White; I get her. I tell her I got the photos. She's quiet for a minute, then she says she's on her way to my office, will I meet her there. I say yeah.

"My office is locked after six o'clock, so I stand around in the lobby waiting for her. She shows up a little after seven, this time in a geometric print dress, and she's smoking. We take the elevator up to the third floor, and I tell her not to smoke in my office. She mumbles how she's sorry, how she doesn't usually smoke, and she puts the cigarette out in the ashtray in the hall.

"I present her with the bill and ask for the final check before I release the photos."

"I taught you well," Liz said.

"Yeah," I continued, "and she says, 'Sure, whatever.' When she signs the check, there's a little tremor in her hand. I turn over the photos, prints and negatives, like I promised in the contract.

"I don't think I knew what to expect," I said, taking a sip of my root beer. "I mean, I had never done domestic investigation before. Maybe she would break down and cry, or get angry and run out, but never in my wildest dreams could I have imagined what she did."

"So what did she do?" Liz asked impatiently.

"I'm trying to tell you," I said. "She picks them up and looks at the photo of him in the foyer of the apartment building in San Leandro. Then she looks at a shot of him with his arm around the woman, taken from behind. Then she looks at a shot of them kissing, and in that photo you can see the woman's face much more clearly. Then the wife's eyes get all wide and crazy. I'm thinking fire is gonna come shooting out of them at any time. She just sits there for a minute, shaking. Then she says, 'Mother . . . fucking . . . Black . . . BITCHES! Black bitches! Black bitches!' I mean, the woman is screaming. She just goes *off*. 'I'll kill you, motherfucking Black bitches! All you Black bitches trying to take my man.' " I looked at Yamile and Liz; both of their mouths were hanging open.

"Whaaat?!" Yamile asked.

"Yes! I mean she just loses it," I said. "I tell her, 'I think you'd better—' but before I can even say 'leave now,' she reaches for her pocketbook. Now I don't know what she's carrying, and my heart is already jumping from her initial outburst, and now I'm really scared, so I go for the door.

"By the time I yank it open, I look over my shoulder, because I am aware that I will be leaving a crazy woman alone in *my* office. Do you know she has pulled out a *huge meat cleaver?*" I gestured for them, with my hands about a foot and a half apart. "Mind you, all the time this woman is screaming about *you* Black bitches who want to take her man, meaning me, I guess, 'cause I was the nearest Black woman, and in reality I'm the only person anywhere nearby, and I am terrified.

"So by now, I'm out the door, but this woman is stepping on my shadow, screaming at the top of her lungs, waving this huge knife, and calling me everything but a child of God.

"I take off, with her right on me! It's seven o'clock, and there's no one left in the building. I'm screaming, 'Help! Help!' She's screaming, 'I'm a kill you bitch! I'm a kill you, hoe!' I'm running for the stairs, praying she doesn't throw the knife at me. I hit the stairwell, close the door behind me, and lean on it. Now I know I'm skinny, but I'm six feet tall, and she's a thin five feet two. There's no way she can force the door open, so I figure I've bought a little time, maybe she'll even calm down or wear herself out.

"She's banging on the door screaming at me to open it up so she can kill me, screaming, screaming, 'You ugly nasty nappy head bitches need to keep your dirty black hands off my man!' I swear the woman did not take a breath. Meanwhile, I'm trying to figure out which floors I can get out onto.

"The super had told me something about the stairwell doors getting locked at such and such a time, and I wasn't paying all that much attention when he said it, but with this crazy woman on the other side of the door, it suddenly seems very important, and I'm trying to figure it out. So I think I've got things somewhat under control, when all of a sudden glass shatters right by my ear, and the square top of the huge knife comes through the window."

"*¡Ay Dios!*" Yamile said.

"You got that right," I said. "I jump away from the door, scared out of my mind. It takes her half a second to get the door open. By now, I'm halfway down the stairs and *praying* the first-floor door is open. If I'm trapped in the stairwell with this woman, she's gonna hack me to death.

"I tear down the stairs and reach for the doorknob. *Please, please, please, don't be locked.* Praise God it opens! Now you all know I practically made the Olympic team, so I figure I can get away from this psychopath if I can just get outside.

"So I come flying out of the building, and she comes flying out of the building right behind me. I'm screaming, 'Help, help, call the police!' She's screaming she's gonna kill me. She has the knife in one hand, and her purse in the other hand. We musta looked so crazy, but there's no one around to see it. No one. I told you my office is on Third Street in that sort of warehouse district near Jack London Square. Well it's dead at seven o'clock. I mean *dead.* So she chases me for four blocks. But because she's got the heels, the knife, the purse, and the dress, she's no match for me.

"When I come around a corner onto Second Street, I've got about a half-block lead on her. I see that we're headed toward that club, Cherie's, at Second and Broadway right? Well, there are a whole bunch of Black people standing outside, and they've all turned to look and see what the noise is about.

"Do you know that when the woman came around the corner and saw those people, she lowered her weapon and slowed down to a walk? A casual *walk?*" I gestured for them, my hand with a buffalo wing in it, raised over my head. Then slowly, I lowered my arm down and dropped the wing on my plate. "Yes she did, and she put that meat cleaver back in her purse so nonchalant, like it was just a big old lipstick."

"No," Liz said, finding her voice for the first time. "No, she didn't!"

"I am not lying," I said. "I was backing away from her, my eyes wide, panting, all out of breath, and she was just strolling, cool as you please, down the street. That woman ran her fingers through her sandy hair, smoothed down her dress, pulled out her handkerchief, and wiped her brow. Then she walked the remaining twenty yards to Broadway at a leisurely pace." Liz and Yamile were shaking their heads in disbelief. "The girl was just strolling along like it was a spring day.

"Now, I crossed the street and kept a good distance between us, in case she went off again. Do you know that woman hailed a taxi and got in it? She drove off, and there I was, standing on the street, with all these suited up Black people in front of this club staring at *me!* Do you hear me?

"Well, at first I was almost embarrassed, but then I realized that I was alive—that a crazy woman had tried to kill me, but I was alive. And I started laughing. Somehow, it was just so funny to me. She was acting like she was sane, because she didn't want those people to think she was crazy, and I didn't care if they thought I was crazy, just as long as I was *alive.* I've never felt so . . . elated. I just walked down the street, laughing hysterically."

"And called the police, I hope," Yamile said.

"Damn skippy," I said. "I dialed 911 at the first phone booth I saw. That woman was out of her Black mind. I believe she really would have killed me, and was liable to kill someone else.

"When they picked her up," I went on, "she acted all surprised and calm. She said she didn't know what they were talking about. But when they took her down to the station, there was this Black woman cop there, and the woman went off on *her.*"

"On the cop?" Liz asked.

"Yes, ma'am," I said. "That's what the other cop told me."

"That is such epic drama," Yamile said.

"Oh, it was *drama,*" I said.

"All this happened yesterday?" Yamile asked.

"Yesterday," I said.

We were quiet for a moment. The cards lay in undisturbed piles in front of us where Liz had dealt them. The game had stopped long ago. I took a sip of my root beer. In the silence, Billie took to telling us how she was crazy in love.

"Well damn," Liz said. "That's quite a story."

"Yeah," I said, "I'm just glad I lived to tell it."

"I'm glad, too," Yamile said.

"Folks are to' up," Liz said.

Yamile scooted her chair next to mine. "Are you okay, sweetie?" she asked, putting her arm around me.

"Yeah," I said hastily, "I'm fine."

"Are you sure?" she asked me pointedly. "That was really traumatic."

"Well," I admitted grudgingly, "I kind of broke down and cried for a little while at the police station." I had thanked God that it was a Black cop, because I hate to cry in front of white folks. And he was really nice about it.

"So you bought a gun?" Liz asked.

"Yeah, and, uh, I'm even thinking of taking you up on your offer to use office space at Front Rowe," I said. "I'd do most of my work at home, but only use Front Rowe when I needed to see a client. That is, if the offer still stands."

"Of course it does," Liz said, "I know it's a drag paying that high rent."

"It's not so much the rent," I said. "It's more that a client could go off on me and no one would have my back."

"I got your back," Liz said.

"Me, too," said Yamile.

"I know," I said. "Both of you always have."

"That poor woman," Yamile said. "Imagine how much pain she must be in to act like that. I hope she gets some help."

Liz just shook her head.

I was kind of mad at Yamile for sympathizing with the woman. I guess it's hard to sympathize with someone who tries to kill you.

Did I hope she would get help? I guessed so. It was hard for me to see her as someone who needed help. Mostly I thought of her as crazy and dangerous. But I guessed people weren't just born crazy. It's not like as a kid she said, "I want to grow up to be out of my mind." Maybe I could sympathize with her, just so long as she stayed the hell away from me.

Now that I'd finally gotten the whole story out, I didn't want to think about it anymore. I changed the subject. "Now excuse me, but weren't we playing cards?" I asked.

Yamile scooted her chair back, but gave me that best friend we'll-talk-later-when-we're-alone look.

"Well, come on then," Liz said, picking up her hand, "baby needs a new pair of shoes."

I picked up my cards. "Aw, sookie," I said, arranging them. "Black is back."

Penny Mickelbury

From Night Songs

PENNY MICKELBURY worked as a Washington, D.C., newspaper, radio, and television reporter before turning her attention to teaching and writing. She is the author of *Keeping Secrets,* the first Gianna Maglione mystery, and *Night Songs,* the second in the series, published in 1995 by Naiad Press and excerpted here.

Booklist said of *Night Songs,* "The book's fictional insider's look at the nation's capital uses the ritualistic slayings of street prostitutes as a vehicle for exploring the shifting priorities of police work, in which, all too often, victims are seen as worthless throwaways."

Concerned with issues of importance to the underclass, minorities, and gays, Mickelbury is currently at work on a historical novel and a collection of short stories.

HIGH HEELS click-clacked on the cracked pavement—stiletto, spike, the highest-of-the-high heels—extensions of long shapely legs made longer by the abbreviated and skintight black spandex dress. The woman was what she appeared to be: hooker, whore, prostitute, trick baby, shady lady, bitch. She'd been called all of those names applied to women who exchanged sex for money. She'd been called most of them within the last hour by a pitiful excuse for a man who blamed her because no matter how hard they both tried, he remained limp. And then he'd called her the names, loudly and violently and with a deep hatred, as if people like her didn't have feelings that could be hurt. Then, finally, expectedly, he'd called her "stupid nigger cunt."

"If I'm such a piece of shit, and you're here with me, what does that make you?" she'd finally snarled. And he'd hauled off and hit her, punched her right in the stomach. And she'd kicked him in his flaccid balls, then delivered a perfectly placed right hook to his weak chin, laying him out on the dusty floor. "You got a lot of nerve calling me names, you pitiful piece of poor white trash!" And with that she'd grabbed his pants, her shoes, jacket, and purse, and run like hell, out of the seedy New York Avenue motel and into the chilly, early spring night, wishing as she always did that if white men couldn't stay at home, they could at least leave their venom there. She was so weary of the self-hatred they inevitably visited upon her, and women like her, as if punishing them would somehow absolve the men of the misery that was their lives. And at these times she was always ambivalent in her feelings about their wives, vacillating between pity that they must put up with such jerks, and believing that anybody stupid enough to marry one of these fools deserved whatever she got.

In an alley two and a half blocks and a world away from the motel, between a twenty-four-hour gas station and a twenty-four-hour carry-out, she quickly put on her fuzzy mohair jacket, shoes and stockings, rearranged the cinnamon-brown real-hair wig, and counted the money in the creep's wallet. She whispered a silent prayer of thanks for the three hundred dollars that would allow her to go home and get a decent night's sleep for a change. She'd even be able to wake up early enough to feed and dress her daughter and send her off to second grade with a hug and a kiss, like all good mothers do. As a gesture of the gratitude she felt, which was part of her emerging new spiritual awareness, after she'd wiped the creep's wallet and its contents clean of her fingerprints (for like many in her profession she was not unknown to the police department) she tossed it—credit cards and all—into the garbage Dumpster, instead of selling the cards to her pal, Bo, as she'd once have done. American Express and Visa Gold—those cards were worth extra. But what the hell . . .

Now, here she was, safe and free and walking aimlessly on a tree-lined residential street, comforted by the silent, dark houses in which normal people were doing normal things, like drinking beer and eating chips and watching television and falling asleep. This was not a neighborhood of the wealthy: the houses were small and the vehicles in the driveways utilitarian. But all was neat and clean and so very well cared for: perfectly clipped grass and hedges; doors and windows symmetrically aligned and adorned; the presence of children's games and toys at virtually every house indicative of proper nurturing; several of the yards bearing evidence of early spring fertilizing and planting. Her own mother had just the previous weekend deemed the soil soft enough for tilling and liming. She felt almost like she could be one of them in that moment, unfettered by the need to attract paying customers, overcome by the normality of it all.

Enveloped by the night, the clickety-clack of the stiletto heels was the only real proof that she strolled there, inside the shadows. Since she wore all black, including her skin, the deep darkness of the still night became part of her wardrobe. Somewhere in her consciousness was the understanding that she'd have to return to the bright lights and action of New York Avenue to find a taxi. But most of her mind, when she let go of the anger and pain of the creep's words, was on the decision taking shape and form there. Actually, she'd made the decision earlier in the day; but since night was her strong time, the time when she thought most clearly, when she could take action, she strolled, releasing the tension and finding comfort in the increasing chill of the night. She walked herself through the mental exercises and reaffirmed her decision. She checked her watch: just past midnight by the luminous digital readout. Not too late to call, she decided.

She turned a corner, angling toward the main drag and a taxi, and spied a lighted phone booth. She crossed New York Avenue against the light and had to scamper the last few steps to avoid being nailed by a pizza delivery truck. She shot the driver a "fuck you" with one hand while the other burrowed deep inside the huge, black leather bag in search of a small notepad. She was rehearsing what she'd say, how she would tell part of the story but withhold some of the juicy details in hopes of making a few dollars, even though the woman already said flat out she didn't pay money for information.

How to make money without selling her body was the new thought that filled her mind so that she did not hear the car that drew up to her from behind—a shiny, new black Jeep Wrangler with the top off a full month too early; did not feel it ease past her and slow to a crawl; did not see the man in the passenger seat turn and nod to the one who sat behind him; did not see, until it was too late, the shiny object spinning end over end toward her. And in truth, had she seen it in time, she would not have recognized it nor could she have prevented it from finding its designated home. The expertly hurled hunting knife lodged in her chest, just below the clavicle, and penetrated her heart. The look of confused surprise that spread across her face died with her, but not before the sound that was in her throat struggled to live: "I know about you!" she cried out. But the men didn't hear. They turned up the music as the Jeep was shifted into high gear and disappeared into the night. The song was one of death.

Way down and all the way across town from the northeast end of New York Avenue, across the Anacostia River, deep within Southeast Washington, inside a tiny brick row house, a second-grader cried out in her sleep, flinging her arms wildly, waking her grandmother who grabbed the child to her bosom and uttered her own, quieter cry, one born of a fear not defined but all too well understood.

Closer to the stilled stilettoes, but yet far enough away to make a huge difference in rent, in another darkened bedroom, Gianna Maglione also cried out, but not from inside the distress of a bad dream. She was powerless to control her responses to the mouth and touch of her lover, Mimi Patterson, and Mimi's mouth was, at the moment, lodged hungrily between Gianna's legs and she could only cry out in the joy of release. She could hear her own heartbeat, feel it pushing and pounding within her chest even as her body relaxed, tension ebbing. She felt Mimi wipe her mouth on the sheet, then felt her crawl up the bed and lie close beside, her head on Gianna's breast listening to her heart. Gianna plunged her hands into the wild, curly mass of Mimi's hair and whispered in her ear. Mimi shivered and sighed. A gust of chilly night air rushed into the slightly opened window, rattling the tiny-slatted blinds, bringing with it snatches of Sarah Vaughan from the neighbors' stereo.

The moon hung high and luminous in the inky sky. Gunshots vibrated, dogs howled, sirens split the air. Life and death, love and hate, beauty and evil—all danced to the songs of the night as another April night in the nation's capital ticked its way into memory.

Herman Bashinski was sweating bullets. It was not a phrase the computer salesman would have used to describe his current predicament; rather, it was how the homicide detective would have described the scene before him, had he been asked, as he watched Herman try, for the fourth time, to explain that no, he did not know a woman named Shelley Kelley, nor did he know a man named George Thomas, and he most certainly had been at home with his family on Friday night past. If the police didn't believe him they could ask his wife. And Herman, for the fifth time, wiped his high-domed, freckled forehead with his now-damp handkerchief and tried to act belligerent, the way upstanding citizens do when their most sacred, God-given rights are being trampled upon.

The door to the interview room opened and a uniformed officer ushered in a small, tidy, mocha-colored man who took several appropriately small and tidy steps into the room and stood before Herman. George Thomas looked from Herman to the detective and back to Herman.

"That's him, Detective. Elijah, the night porter, had to lend him a pair of pants, and then help him break into his car. Green 1992 Chrysler LeBaron, Maryland license 2009 ZQ. And of course, there was no tip for Elijah because the gentleman had no wallet."

And with those words, George Thomas stepped carefully and distastefully away from Herman and the detective, folded his arms across his chest, and waited, either to be allowed to leave, or for questions. He had no pity for Herman and no liking for the police. He knew they thought him little better than the hookers and pimps and johns that frequented his motel and paid for the barren, musty rooms by the hour. He knew that despite the elegant perfection of his hand-tailored silk and wool navy blue suit, cream-colored linen shirt, cordovan calf slip-ons, the police and the Hermans of the world saw only a Black man who catered to low-lifes. But George Thomas had the memory of truth to fuel his existence.

He remembered the day forty-three years ago when he and his dearly departed Rachel bought the motel on New York Avenue, right on the major route from New York City to points South, to the original homes of most of the Blacks who now lived in the Northeast. It was a time when Black families en route to or from visiting kin in New York or in Georgia kept his rooms full year round because they could not, in those days, book rooms in Holiday Inns and Howard Johnsons. They kept the rooms full and the restaurant busy day and night, winter and summer, and made him a wealthy man. But times changed, and so did New York Avenue, and so did the people who needed his rooms. And his Rachel, God rest her, was gone. So he had drained the pool and closed the restaurant and removed the televisions and the oil paintings from the rooms and accommodated his paying customers: What they wanted was a bed and a toilet, not a home away from home. But George Thomas still ran a clean establishment, just like in the old days, and he paid close attention to who came and went and he had a nose for trouble. So when Shelley Kelley came barreling down the hallway barefoot, orange wig sideways on her head, her shoes and some clothes in one hand, and dragging behind her the monstrous black purse that women of her profession seemed to prefer, George quickly grabbed the .357 Magnum—for which he had a license—from his desk drawer and waited. And finally, after almost half an hour, Herman Bashinski crept down the hall and around the corner and motioned to George.

"Psst. Hey, buddy. C'mere a minute, would ya?"

"What do you want?" asked George coldly, not moving.

"I just need to talk to you for a minute, that's all."

"About what?" George fingered the trigger of the heavy gun.

"I need your help!" Herman whined piteously and stepped cautiously around the corner, pudgy pink legs tightly together, dingy yellow boxer shorts chafing. That's when George realized what Shelley Kelley had carried in her other hand along with her shoes. She'd been moving too fast for him to see clearly.

"What do you want?" asked George again.

"Some pants. And some help getting my car started. My keys are in my pants and my pants are . . ." Herman abandoned the explanation, sweat popping out on his head.

George Thomas was five feet four inches tall; but even if he shared Herman's lofty six feet he'd not have given him a pair of his pants. Showing no movement detectable by Herman, George used his foot to press a button under the counter and in less than half a minute, a tall, well-built, but elderly man appeared behind Herman and when he spoke, Herman jumped.

"Yessir, Mr. Thomas?" Elijah said softly.

"Help him if you can and if you wish." And George said no more; indeed, paid no more attention to Herman and his problems.

George Thomas did not like this man nor those like him, suburban white people who came into D.C. specifically to break the law—to buy drugs or women or weapons—and then to return to their safe, clean communities and point accusingly at the Sodom that was the nation's capital. George Thomas did, however, like Shelley Kelley. He was an observant man, and an excellent judge of character. He was always correct when he assessed a young woman as being "wrong" for the work of the prostitute. He had advised Shelley to make a better life for herself, and was as proud as any father when he learned that she'd attached herself to some group that taught her how to do yoga and meditation and be a vegetarian. George didn't understand exactly what it was all about and he didn't need to; what mattered was that this bright, vivacious young girl was getting out of the street life. So when he heard that Shelley Kelley's body had been found eight blocks away with a hunting knife in her chest, he called the police and gave them Herman Bashinski's description and the license number of his car.

"So, Herman," drawled the detective. "You wanna tell us about this here Shelley Kelley?" He leaned back and balanced himself on the chair's two rear legs and watched Herman's face work.

"I . . . I already told you. I don't know anybody by that name."

Irritated, the detective let the chair fall on its front legs with a thud and in a single motion reached to the folder on the table before him, snapped it open, and whipped out a glossy black and white photograph which he shoved toward Herman. "You tellin' me you don't know her, Herman?"

"No. I mean yes. I mean, I never knew her name. Not really. You know, you don't exactly get acquainted . . ." Herman's voice trailed off and he wiped the sweat from his face again and told the detective the whole story, from the beginning, including how he was unable to have an erection and how he'd punched the whore and how she'd kicked him and then run off with his pants.

And because the police had already found Herman's pants and wallet in the Dumpster, the detective believed his story, told him to keep his sorry, limp dick at home, told him and George to beat it. And that left the weary homicide detective without a single lead in his investigation of the murder of one Shelley Kelley because if Herman Bashinski didn't kill her the detective didn't know who did and he really didn't have the energy to care. This was his ninth murder this week, the thirteenth in his open and active case file. And she was just a hooker.

Carolyn King stood stonily dry-eyed watching the two policewomen search her daughter's bedroom. *They're just about Sandra's age,* she thought, as they calmly stripped away every vestige of her daughter's privacy. Carolyn had never interfered with or searched Sandra's things and it was uncomfortable for her to watch two total strangers do what she'd never done.

"Did your daughter have an address book or a diary, Mrs. King?"

asked one of the officers as she emptied the contents of the desk drawers onto the desktop.

"That kind of thing she kept with her. In that big, black purse she carried with her everywhere," said Carolyn King dully, looking at the stacks of envelopes and piles of papers held by rubber bands and paper clips, and remembering how neat and orderly Sandra was, even as a girl.

"Who were Shelley's friends, Mrs. King?" The second officer piled a stack of clothes from the closet on the bed and began sifting through them, checking the pockets. These were the normal clothes, the jeans and slacks and shirts and dresses that Sandra wore around the house, to the store, and, on occasion, to church.

Carolyn looked blankly at the officer, her face saying what her mouth could not: *Why are you asking me about this Shelley?*

"Who did she hang out with, Mrs. King? Where? Did she hang with old high school friends? Who?" The officer struggled not to sound bored, not to show the irritation she was feeling with the woman whose blank, dry eyes stared at her.

"You mean Sandra?" asked her mother.

"She used the name Shelley Kelley on the street."

And that's when Carolyn King broke. "My daughter's name is Sandra Ann King! That's what I named her! That's what it says on her birth certificate! I don't know nothin' about no Shelley Kelley!" And Carolyn King rushed from her dead daughter's bedroom into the small, neat living room and sank into the new sofa that Sandra had recently bought for her and cried for every one of the twenty-two years her only daughter had wasted.

Lt. Gianna Maglione stood up from her desk and stretched every inch of her lithe, five-foot-eight-inch frame, arms high above her head, back arched almost in half. That she was in the tenth hour of what would likely be a fourteen-hour day had no negative effect on the starched crispness of her white shirt and the sharpness of the crease in her black slacks. Her tie was still perfectly in place, as was her wild mane of heavy, mahogany hair: twisted into thick ropes on either side of her head and held firmly in place with ivory barrettes that once belonged to her great-grandmother. She rubbed her clear, hazel eyes, tired from the hours of staring at the computer screen; rotated her neck; did a set of deep knee bends; and breathed deeply in and out for sixty seconds. None of it could remove all of the tension stored in her body, nor could it compensate for the lack of sleep; but she revived enough to continue work on the monthly crime report and analysis due on her boss's desk at 8 A.M. sharp—which was in about eleven hours. She knew with absolute certainty that Inspector Eddie Davis, head of the Intelligence Division of the Washington, D.C. Police Department and her immediate boss, would not tolerate her being even one minute late. Not because he was an unreasonable or unkind man, but because he had warned her time and again about participating in her investigations instead of directing them, and when she'd persisted he'd issued a direct order: behave in a manner befitting a lieutenant or else. The "or else" was looking better and better. The only benefit to being a lieutenant as far as she was concerned was being the boss: She was head of the three-year-old Hate Crimes Unit.

Seven of Washington's finest—including herself—bore the responsibility of bringing to justice those who would violate the legal and civil rights of persons based on race, religion, or sexual orientation. But hate was big business in D.C., as well as in most of America, much too big for six dedicated but grossly overworked cops to contain. So, bucking the established order and incurring its wrath, she frequently joined her team in the street investigating crimes of hatred. And because she did, she usually was late submitting the paperwork required of those who held the rank of lieutenant and above, of those elevated to the level of "white shirt," which separated the high-ranking cops from the rank and file who wore blue shirts. Not that she often wore the shirt or the uniform. She had it on today because she'd been summoned to testify before a committee of the City Council. She put a stopper in the feelings of anger and frustration that such appearances always generated and returned to her seat behind the desk and the crime report on the computer screen.

She looked up at the sound of a knock at her door. Familiar with the modus operandi of the chief and of her boss, she waited for the door to open and for one of them to stick his head in. When instead there came a second knock, she frowned and called out, "Come on in." The door opened to admit an attractive woman of about thirty-five wearing a well-cut, form-fitting cranberry knit dress and, pinned to the collar, the ID badge of the civilian employee of the Police Department.

"Sorry to disturb you, Lieutenant, but I knew you were still here and I need to talk to you."

"Have a seat." Gianna gestured to the leather armchair at the corner of her desk and watched the woman approach, watched her make up her mind even as she sat down that she would, in fact, say what she'd come to say.

"I'm sorry I don't know how to pronounce your name. I've heard it said but I just don't remember."

Gianna laughed easily, putting the woman immediately at ease.

"Don't worry. The chief can't pronounce it either and I've known him for twenty years. What can I do for you?"

"My name is Gwen Thomas and I work in records, which doesn't have anything to do with why I'm here . . ." She stopped, stared down at her perfectly manicured nails which were the same color as her dress, took a deep breath, and continued. "I've read about you, about your cases, and I hear people in the building talk about you. They say you're one of the real people."

Gianna didn't speak but held the woman's dark, sad eyes with her own calm, clear, hazel ones and waited.

"My sister got killed two months ago. She was a hooker and a drug addict. Not one of your upstanding citizens, I know, but she was my sister and she was murdered and she didn't deserve to die. Not like she did." Overcome now by emotion and struggling to control the tears that formed and dripped, she stopped again, staring again at the hands folded tightly in her lap.

"Did you come to me because you don't think the police are handling the investigation properly?" In D.C., as in other big cities, poor people, and especially poor people of color, believed they got short shrift from an overburdened justice system, and they quite often were correct. Perhaps Gwen Thomas thought that her proximity to the department might get better results.

"Didn't you say once that crimes against women were hate crimes, too, just like crimes against Jews or Black people or gay people?" She was in control now, pain replaced by anger, and Gianna knew this was no bullshit visit by a disgruntled citizen.

"Yes, I said that." She leaned across the desk, closing the distance to Gwen Thomas.

"My sister was killed because she was a woman. Because she was a hooker. Three more were killed, just like she was—"

"What do you mean, just like she was?" Gianna asked, and she knew deep within herself that the answer would spell trouble.

"Somebody threw a knife at her. A big hunting knife, not a kitchen knife. Threw it in her chest."

Gianna's heart raced, her stomach dropped, and her brain buzzed as she visualized the scene.

"You're telling me that four women—all prostitutes—have been killed by hunting knives thrown into them?" Gianna wasn't easily or often surprised so she didn't cover it well, or recover from it quickly, and Gwen Thomas misunderstood.

"That's exactly what I'm telling you and if you don't believe me you can ask those stupid motherfuckers in Homicide!"

"I believe you, Miss Thomas." And, Gianna thought, I also know which stupid motherfuckers in Homicide you mean. "And I fully understand your anger. But I need for you to very calmly tell me everything you know, beginning with your sister's murder."

The murdered Andrea Thomas had begun life as a good girl, graduated from high school and secretarial school, got married, got a job, had a baby. Smoked crack. Once. To experiment. A year later, at the age of twenty-five, she was out on the street selling her body to support her habit. In rare moments of lucidity she professed her love for her husband and child and family and pledged to restore her life. But Gwen Thomas didn't know of anyone who had successfully kicked crack and she didn't expect her baby sister to be the exception to the rule.

"I wasn't holding my breath waiting for her to change. I used to drive by places where I knew she hung out, just to make sure she had clothes and food. I didn't like her life but it wasn't my place to judge her. She was my baby sister and I loved her."

About a month ago, Gwen Thomas said, she began searching for her sister in all her known haunts. Nobody had seen Andrea. Nobody knew anything. Three or four nights a week she searched, becoming more and more worried and frightened. Finally, standing at the mouth of an alley under a high intensity streetlight designed to deter crime, she held up a twenty-dollar bill and promised it to the first person who told her where to find Andrea. An hour later she was on the grounds of D.C. General Hospital, in the shadow of the city jail, at the morgue, identifying Jane Doe 23-1993 as Andrea Thomas Willoughby, who'd been there for three weeks, waiting to be identified and claimed.

"I thought she ODed, but when this morgue person told me, almost by accident, that she was found with this big knife sticking out of her chest, I damn near peed on myself. Last time Andrea was rational enough to have a normal conversation, which was back in April, she told me that her good friend Sandra King had just gotten killed that same way. And then at the funeral last week—at Andrea's funeral—

another girl told me the same thing happened to two other girls."
Gwen Thomas seemed to be reliving the moment that she realized her
sister's death was but one thread in a larger fabric.

"My sister did some wrong things in her life, Lieutenant, but if the
people she hurt the most still loved her, no damn body had the right to
kill her."

And with that, Gwen Thomas shook hands with the woman she
believed would avenge her sister's murder, and returned to the computer terminal where she searched out citizens with overdue parking
tickets and sent them notices explaining that the original fine had now
doubled or tripled, leaving Lt. Maglione staring at her own computer
terminal but seeing large knives protruding from the bodies of women
hated because they used their bodies to bring pleasure to those who
hated them.

Permissions

Appendix:
Mystery Chronology

WHAT FOLLOWS is the beginning of a more inclusive chronology of mystery fiction one that includes some of the more significant black contributors (in boldface). For the sake of brevity, a representative rather than exhaustive array of contributors and events is included. The editor hopes future literary criticism and scholarly works on the history of mystery fiction will include these notable black contributors to the genre.

1809   Edgar Allan Poe born. Creator of the American detective story.

1820   **Congregational minister and Revolutionary War hero Lemuel Haynes publishes the first true crime narrative by an African American, *Mystery Developed*, the account of the disappearance of Russell Colvin of Manchester, Vermont, the trial of his brothers-in-law for murder, and their subsequent exoneration.**

1832   Emile Gaboriau born. Creator of Lecoq, first modern fictional police detective in several serials and novels, most notably *Monsieur Lecoq* (1869, in English 1888).

1841   "The Murders in the Rue Morgue" by Edgar Allan Poe is published, featuring C. Auguste Dupin, the first successful amateur detective and the "locked-room" mystery device.

1842   "The Mystery of Marie Roget" by Edgar Allan Poe is published. Features the technique of abstract deduction from reported facts.

1843   "The Gold Bug" by Edgar Allan Poe is published. The story features the scientific method of deciphering encoded messages.

1844   "Thou Art the Man" by Edgar Allan Poe is published. Features the least likely character as the murderer, the planting of false clues, and the use of ballistic evidence.

1845   "The Purloined Letter" by Edgar Allan Poe is published. The story features the art of concealment by display.

1852–53 *Bleak House* by Charles Dickens is serialized and introduces Inspector Bucket, the first police detective in English fiction.

1856   **Pauline E. Hopkins born. Writer of the first African American mystery stories.**

1859   Arthur Conan Doyle born. Creator of Sherlock Holmes, first and arguably the greatest detective.

1867   *The Dead Letter* by Seely Regester is published, often credited as the first mystery novel written by a woman.

1868   *The Moonstone* by Wilkie Collins is published. It is the first English detective novel.

1874   G. K. Chesterton born. Author of the Father Brown mysteries.

1875   **George S. Schuyler born. Harlem Renaissance journalist, novelist, and critic. Author of the satirical novel *Black No More* as well as over a dozen mystery and thriller stories serialized in the *Pittsburgh Courier* in the 1930s, including "Black Internationale," "Black Empire," and "The Ethiopian Murder Mystery."**

1878   Anna K. Green's *The Leavenworth Case: A Lawyer's Story* is published, the first million-copy-selling mystery by an American woman.

1884   Earl Derr Biggers born. Creator of Charlie Chan, Chinese detective of the Honolulu Police Department who first appeared in *The House Without a Key* (1925) and five other novels.

1886   Rex Stout born. Creator of Nero Wolfe, the obese food- and orchid-loving detective who first appeared in *Fer-de-Lance* (1934).

1887   *A Study in Scarlet,* Arthur Conan Doyle's first Sherlock Holmes mystery, is published.

1888   Raymond Chandler born. Famous for his creation of Philip Marlowe, the detective who appeared in *The Big Sleep* (1939) and six other novels.

        S. S. Van Dine (pseudonym of Willard Huntington Wright) is born. Creator of the amateur detective Philo Vance.

1889   Erle Stanley Gardner born. Creator of attorney/sleuth Perry Mason, hero of over eighty novels.

1890   Agatha Christie born. Her most famous detective creations were Hercule Poirot, who first appeared in *The Mysterious Affair at Styles* (1920), and Miss Jane Marple, who first appeared in *The Murder at the Vicarage* (1930).

1893   Dorothy Sayers born. Creator of Lord Peter Wimsey, hero of eleven novels, most notably *Strong Poison* (1930) and *Murder Must Advertise* (1933).

1894   Dashiell Hammett born. Author and one of the greatest proponents of the hard-boiled detective story, including the Continental Op stories and the novels *The Red Harvest* (1929), *The Maltese Falcon* (1930), and *The Glass Key* (1931).

1897   **Rudolph Fisher born. Member of the Harlem Renaissance cir-**

              cle of writers and artists. First African American to write a mystery novel set in the black community, *The Conjure-Man Dies* (1932).

1899   Ngaio Marsh born. Creator of Chief Inspector (later Superintendent) Roderick Alleyn.

1900   **Pauline E. Hopkins publishes two short stories with mystery themes: "The Mystery Within Us," a tale of magical realism and spirituality, and "Talma Gordon," a locked-room mystery with themes covering miscegenation and the "tragic mulatto."**

1904   Margery Allingham born. Creator of Albert Campion, amateur sleuth and hero of numerous novels, including *The Black Dudley Murder* (1929) and *The Tiger in the Smoke* (1952).

1907–08   **"The Black Sleuth" by John Edward Bruce is serialized in *McGirt's Reader*. An early detective story featuring a black protagonist.**

1908   **Hughes Allison born. Wrote two significant mystery works, the 1937 play *The Trial of Dr. Beck* and the 1948 short story "Corollary."**

              Richard Wright born. Author of novels that address racism, crime, and their consequences, including *Native Son* (1940), *Savage Holiday* (1954), *The Long Dream* (1958), and several short stories on related themes, such as "The Man Who Lived Underground" and "The Man Who Killed a Shadow."

1909   **Chester Himes born. Creator of the famous black detective novels, the "Harlem domestic series," featuring Coffin Ed Johnson and Grave Digger Jones, who first appeared in *For Love of Imabelle* (later *A Rage in Harlem,* 1957) and nine other novels.**

1911   John Ball born. Although not an African American, he created the black detective character Virgil Tibbs, who first appeared in *In the Heat of the Night* (1965).

1915   Ross MacDonald born. Famous for Lew Archer *(The Moving Target,* 1949) and Travis McGee *(Free Fall in Crimson,* 1981) detective series.

1917   **Beginning of the Harlem Renaissance, also called the New Negro Arts Movement. Prominent literary members included Langston Hughes, Countee Cullen, Jean Toomer, Zora Neale Hurston, James Weldon Johnson, Rudolph Fisher, W. E. B. Du Bois, among others. The era lasts until 1935.**

1918   Mickey Spillane born. Creator of hard-boiled detective Mike Hammer, who first appeared in *I, the Jury* (1947).

1920   P. D. James born. Famous for a series of mystery novels, including *Cover Her Face* (1962), featuring police detective/poet Inspector

Adam Dalgleish, and *An Unsuitable Job for a Woman* (1972), notable for its realistic female detective.

Lawrence Sanders, author of such novels as *The Anderson Tapes* (1970) and *The Seventh Commandment* (1991), is born.

Dick Francis, author of a series of horse racing-influenced mysteries (*Twice Shy,* 1981, and *Longshot,* 1990), is born.

Black Mask magazine founded by H. L. Mencken and George Jean Nathan. Noted for its popularization of the hard-boiled crime story and the emergence of such authors as Dashiell Hammett and Carroll John Daly.

1922   "The False Burton Combs" by Carroll John Daly is published in *Black Mask* magazine. Considered the first hard-boiled detective story.

Agatha Christie's *The Secret Adversary* is published, featuring the first husband-and-wife detective team, Tommy and Tuppence Beresford.

1923   Dashiell Hammett's short story "Arson Plus" is published. The story's unnamed detective, nicknamed the Continental Op, is the first professional private eye.

George Baxt born. Author of a series of mystery novels featuring homosexual black detective Pharoah Love, beginning with *A Queer Kind of Death* (1966).

1925   **John A. Williams born. Author of nineteen books, including the thrillers *The Man Who Cried I Am* (1967), *Sons of Darkness, Sons of Light* (1969), *Captain Blackman* (1972), and *Jacob's Ladder* (1987).**

Tony Hillerman born. Author of two detective series featuring Navajo detectives Joe Leaphorn and Jim Chee in such novels as *Dance Hall of the Dead* (1973), *Coyote Waits* (1990), and *Sacred Clowns* (1993).

Elmore Leonard born. Author of best-selling crime stories including *Fifty-Two Pickup* (1974), *La Brava* (1983), and *Rum Punch* (1992).

1926   S. S. Van Dine's *The Benson Murder Case* is published. Most scholars note this date as the beginning of "The Golden Age of Mystery Fiction," a period that would last until the 1930s and see such classic mystery writers as Agatha Christie, Dorothy L. Sayers, and others come to prominence.

***The Haunting Hand* is published by Jamaican-born W. Adolphe Roberts. The first mystery by a black writer, although it does not feature black characters.**

Ed McBain born. Author of the 87th Precinct police procedurals and novels under the pseudonym Evan Hunter.

1927   Robert Ludlum born. Best-selling spy novelist of the 1970s and 1980s (*The Bourne Identity,* 1980).

1928   Ernest Tidyman born. Although not African American, he is the author of seven John Shaft novels, including *Shaft* (1970) and *Shaft's Big Score* (1972).

1929   *The Roman Hat Mystery* is published. Authored by cousins Frederic Dannay (1905–82) and Manfred B. Lee (1905–71) under the pseudonym Ellery Queen.

1930   Colin Dexter born. Creator of Chief Inspector Morse novels including *The Riddle of the Third Mile* (1983).

Ruth Rendell born. Author of the Chief Inspector Reginald Wexford series and psychological crime stories under her own name and as Barbara Vine.

The Maltese Falcon by Dashiell Hammett is published, which introduces detective Sam Spade.

1930   **Sam Greenlee born. Author of two political thrillers, *The Spook Who Sat by the Door* (1969) and *Baghdad Blues* (1986).**

1931   Georges Simeon publishes his first Maigret detective novel, *The Death of Monsieur Gallet.*

1932   ***The Conjure-Man Dies* by Rudolph Fisher is published, the first mystery novel by an African American to feature black characters. Introduces the detective team of Dr. John Archer, a Harlem physician and amateur sleuth, and Perry Dart, NYPD police detective.**

The Thin Man by Dashiell Hammett is published. Features the urbane detective husband-and-wife team Nick and Nora Charles.

Robert B. Parker born. Creator of Spenser, a Boston private eye and his African American sidekick, Hawk, who made his debut in *Promised Land* (1976).

1933   **While serving a prison term for armed robbery, Chester Himes publishes his first crime stories, including "His Last Day," "The Meanest Cop in the World," and "Prison Mass."**

1936   James Lee Burke born. Creator of Dave Robichaux, Cajun ex-cop and protagonist of several novels *(Dixie City Jam,* 1994).

Carolyn Hart born. Creator of Annie Laurance/Max Darling mystery series *(Death on Demand,* 1987) and nonseries mystery novels *(Skullduggery,* 1983).

1937   Joseph Wambaugh born. A former policeman, his crime novels set in Los Angeles include *The Choirboys.*

The Trial of Dr. Beck, a play by Hughes Allison, opens on Broadway. Story of a physician on trial for the murder of his wife, the founder of a hair care empire.

1938   Anne Perry born. Author of numerous mysteries set in Victorian England, including *The Cater Street Hangman* (1979) and *A Sudden, Fearful Death* (1993).

Lawrence Block born. Creator of three series characters, most notably recovering alcoholic Matt Scudder *(Eight Million Ways to Die,* 1983, and *A Dance at the Slaughterhouse,* 1991).

Barbara D'Amato born. Writer of Cat Marsala series of mysteries *(Hard Case,* 1994).

1938   **Ishmael Reed born. Author of seven nongenre novels plus *Mumbo Jumbo* (1972) and *The Last Days of Louisiana Red* (1974), which features the hoo-doo priest and reluctant detective PaPa LaBas.**

1939   *The Big Sleep* by Raymond Chandler published. Classic example of the hard-boiled detective novel.

1940   **Richard Wright's *Native Son* published. A Book-of-the-Month Club selection, it sells 215,000 copies in three weeks.**

Percy Spurlark Parker born. Author of the Bull Benson novel *Good Girls Don't Get Murdered* (1974) as well as a series of short stories featuring the same amateur detective that appeared in *Alfred Hitchcock's Mystery Magazine.*

Sue Grafton born. Creator of Kinsey Milhone of *A is for Alibi* (1982) and other alphabet-themed mystery titles.

1941   **BarbaraNeely born. Creator of feminist domestic worker Blanche White *(Blanche on the Lam,* 1992, *Blanche Among the Talented Tenth,* 1994).**

1942   Andrew Vachss born. Creator of the ex-cop detective Burke of the novels *Sacrifice* (1992), among others.

Otto Penzler born. Mystery historian, bookseller, founder of the Mysterious Press, Otto Penzler Books, and one-time publisher of the mystery magazine *The Armchair Detective.*

1943   ***Flour Is Dusty* by Curtis Lucas is published. The crime novel focuses on drugs and crime in Atlantic City's black community.**

Bill Pronzini born. Creator of the Nameless Detective mysteries as well as author of historical mysteries and editor of several anthologies.

1944   Francis Nevins, Jr., born. Mystery novelist *(The Ninety Million Dollar Mouse,* 1987), anthologist, editor, and historian *(Cornell Woolrich: First You Dream, Then You Die,* 1988).

Marcia Muller born. Creator of one of the first hard-boiled female detectives, Sharon McCone, as well as editor of several anthologies.

Eleanor Taylor Bland born. Her Marti MacAlister novels include *Dead Time* (1992), *Slow Burn* (1993), *Gone Quiet* (1994), and *Done Wrong* (1995).

1945   Nancy Pickard born. Author of Jenny Cain mysteries and the food-oriented mysteries starting with *The 27-Ingredient Chili Con Carne Murders* (1992).

1946   *The Street* by Ann Petry is published. It will be the first best-seller by an African American woman.

Hugh Holton born. A commander on the Chicago police force and creator of Commander Larry Cole, protagonist of novels *Presumed Dead* (1994) and *Windy City* (1995).

Mike Phillips born. Creator of West Indian journalist/sleuth Sam Dean who first appeared in the novel *Blood Rights* (1988).

1947   Sarah Paretsky born. Creator of hard-boiled female detective V. I. Warshawski in *Indemnity Only* (1982) and several other novels.

Valerie Wilson (later Wesley) born. Creator of Tamara Hayle, a Newark, New Jersey, detective of the novels *When Death Comes Stealing* (1994) and *Devil's Gonna Get Him* (1995).

1948   "Corollary" by Hughes Allison is published in the July issue of *Ellery Queen's Mystery Magazine*. It is the first short story published by an African American in the magazine.

James Ellroy born. Author of the novels *The Black Dahlia* (1987), *L.A. Confidential* (1990), and *White Jazz* (1992), among others.

1949   Jonathan Kellerman born. Author of several psychological mysteries, including *When the Bough Breaks* (1985).

1952   Walter Mosley born. Creator of the reluctant detective Easy Rawlins, who first appeared in *Devil in a Blue Dress* (1990).

1954   Gar Anthony Haywood born. Author of two detective series featuring Aaron Gunner *(Fear of the Dark,* 1988) and Joe and Dottie Loudermilk *(Going Nowhere Fast,* 1994).

1955   Gary Phillips is born. Author of *Violent Spring* (1994), first entry in the Ivan Monk mystery series.

1958   Chester Himes's *La Reine des pommes* (also called *For Love of Imabelle* and *A Rage in Harlem*) wins the Grand Prix de la Littérature Policière in France.

Patricia Cornwell born. Her novels feature medical examiner Dr. Kay Scarpetta *(Post Mortem,* 1990; *The Body Farm,* 1994).

1962   *Cover Her Face* by P. D. James is published. Marks the debut of Inspector Adam Dalgliesh.

1967   *The Man Who Cried I Am* by John A. Williams is published. Most notable novel in the African American political thriller genre.

1969   *The Spook Who Sat by the Door* by Sam Greenlee is published.

1981   *A Soldier's Story* by Charles Fuller opens on Broadway. The play, in part a murder mystery, wins the Pulitzer Prize for drama in 1982.

1985   *The Case of Ashanti Gold* by Clifford Mason is published, featuring Joe Cinquez, a fifty-year-old black detective.

1987   *Coffin & Co.* by Njami Simon is published in the U.S. It features

Coffin Ed Johnson and Grave Digger Jones, the detective duo made famous by Chester Himes.

1988   Black private investigator Clio Browne makes her debut in Dolores Komo's *Clio Browne: Private Investigator*.

1991   English writer Mike Phillips's novel *The Late Candidate* wins the Silver Dagger Award presented by the British Crime Writers Association.

1993   *Blanche on the Lam* by BarbaraNeely wins the Anthony Award for best debut novel. It is one of three major awards the book wins.

1994   *Keeping Secrets* by Penny Mickelbury is published. Novel features detective duo and lovers Gianna Maglione and Mimi Patterson.

1995   Walter Mosley begins his term as President of the Mystery Writers of America, the first African American to hold the position.